# "Overland"

## A Period Science Fiction Novel

by,

Robert A. Boyd

## "Prologue"

### Sisters Of Mercy Hospital
### San Francisco, California
December, 1876

I vaguely remember them bringing me here, even though the whole chain of events that led me here was just a blur. The doctor in Reno doped me up with Laudanum for the pain, so I was pretty well out of it when they shipped me down to Sacramento. Sacramento did what they could for me, but my injuries were too severe, plus gangrene was setting in, so they loaded me on a ferry with a doctor to watch over me, and shipped me down to Frisco.

That was only the beginning of my woes. The Sisters Of Mercy is one of the best hospitals in the state, but I was pretty far gone when they got me. Over the next several weeks, they amputated three toes, three fingers on my left hand, and two on my right. They had to stop there to give me time to recover before continuing to hack away frost-bitten parts of me. My weight dropped sharply, and the fevers racked me to where they thought I would die. I almost did. As well as frostbite, they said my lungs were scorched by the bone chilling cold, and my body was so depleted by starvation that they wouldn't believe I was only out there for a night and a day. The one thing that kept me alive was my first rate physical condition...and the faint memories of what happened...the memories of *her*.

I became a local celebrity after the story got round, and my injuries were enough that the doctors wanted to keep a close eye on me, so I wound up in a single room under the tender loving care of Sister Grace. This place is first rate, as hospitals go. The walls are painted a restful tan, and there is a gas light and a small fireplace which the boy keeps stocked with coal. My bed has a firm horse hair mattress and a warm wool blanket, and the window next to my bed gives me a view of the bay. When I'm awake, I lay there listening to the Yuletide carolers and the fog horns in the distance and feeling sorry for myself. At times, when the wind is right, I can hear the faint whistles from the factories along the bay. They sound like train whistles: they bring back the memories, and when that happens, I cower under my cover trying not to relive *it* again.

I didn't remember much at first: disjointed bits and pieces which made just enough sense to scare the hell out of me. But the pain brought blessed, merciful Laudanum, and the Laudanum brought the memories back bit by bit. They would dope me up until the pain faded and I sank into a numb semi-sleep, and the memories would come, one tiny fragment after another. There were a lot of gaps between moments of sheer terror and hot passion, and I couldn't tell what was what for the longest time. It went on like that for weeks. Why I kept going, I can't understand, but I knew I had to. They kept filling me with hot soup and Laudanum while they worked on me and I recovered in turn, and the memories added up one by one.

And as the memories began to stitch themselves together, an incredible story emerged. I couldn't believe it at first, and then I was afraid to believe it, but it must have happened: it explained too much. I thought about it endlessly, trying to make sense of it, and trying to decide if I wanted to tell the doctors about it. The railroad police hounded me for a while at first, and after they quit coming around, the doctors kept after me. They couldn't understand why I was so gaunt and thin, like I had starved for weeks. But in plain fact I was only missing off the 'Overland' for twenty-four hours before I stumbled half frozen into a trackside telegraph shanty the next evening. I should have frozen to death long before. Not that it mattered as far as my treatment, really, but

4

there were too many things that just didn't add up. So even after they quit, I continued to agonize over it.

I wanted to tell them at first while the story was no more than incoherent fragments, but the more sense it made, the more afraid I was that they wouldn't believe me. Hell, I didn't believe it either. And as time went by, I worried more and more that they would put me in a mad-house if they knew. They would be tempted: a sanatorium might be more merciful than turning what was left of me loose to fend for myself. So I kept the truth hidden, and tried to shrug off their curiosity.

§

My fight promoter, Howard, came to see me at one point. He was all concern and forced cheer, of course, but I knew he was there to say goodbye. He said the fight was cancelled and the prize awarded to Wild Man McGurk when I didn't show, and he hoped I would recover soon so that maybe he could arrange a rematch. We both knew better. Even if I survived, my career as a heavyweight boxer was over. I could hardly sit up just then, and I would never be in shape to go back into the ring. He left after doing his duty, promising he would visit me often. I never saw him again.

§

I was more or less coherent when Christmas week came, although it was still all I could do to sit up in bed.

"My, but you're looking better every day," Sister Grace would say as she changed my bandages. "We'll have you back on your feet in no time, and then you can look to doing *honest* work."

She's a good-hearted soul, and as attentive as could be, for all that she can bark like a drill sergeant. Don't let her ruddy cheeks and silver hair fool you: she can be a holy terror. She didn't approve of prize fighting, and didn't hesitate to make her feelings plain.

"This is the Lord's will, you know," she said primly as she bound my left hand. "This is your calling to turn away from violence, and become a man of peace."

"I don't have much of a choice, do I?" I flexed the two fingers I had left once she was finished. "But what can I do? I've got no schooling, and I ain't fit for labor no more."

5

She paused, and gave me a smile of reassurance. "Don't you doubt the Lord's purpose, Nate Poole. He has turned you to a new path, and called you to serve humanity in His name. You'll find a way."

I had to wonder if she was right. Lord knows there has been enough violence in this world, in my life. That brought to mind the memories of what happened up there in Donner Pass: she didn't know it, but my life as it was would have lead to unspeakable horror. Perhaps this was the Lord calling me to a new path.

My non-existent fingers hurt. "Well He didn't need to beat me over the head with it," I grumbled.

Under her relentless care, I regained my strength a little at a time. My ordeal continued with another toe and more skin lost, followed by another bout of infection. But despite the fevers and the amputations, I began to slowly recover. Christmas day brought me my first solid food in two months. My weight loss stopped when I hovered at Death's door, then began climbing again. They hailed me as a medical miracle, which I guess I was, and it brought a new bout of curiosity about what happened up there. A reporter from the local paper did a follow-up interview, but I didn't tell him much despite his badgering. The world in general largely forgot me, and when the doctors thought to quiz me about my experiences, I kept my mouth shut, and tried not to think about it.

§

They finally finished cutting, and started to wean me off the Laudanum, which was an ordeal in itself. They would give me just a bit when the shakes and cramps got to be too much, enough to ease the pain, and I would drift off in a semi-sleep for a few hours before emerging once again to face the world. And during those drugged sleep times, the memories continued to surface one by one. I had a pretty fair picture of what happened by then, and it made me wonder if I should have stayed out there and died. That would have been the simple, fool-proof way. For the life of me, I couldn't see how I could serve humanity better than by dying. Maybe the Lord did have a purpose for me; but I was darned if I could see it.

§

6

It was shortly before the New Year that I received an unexpected visitor. "He's right in here," Sister Grace's voice came through my Laudanum haze. I came out of a stupor to find someone sitting at my bedside with Sister Grace hovering over him. "Now you mind that he's been through a lot," she lectured him. "Don't you excite him or over-strain him, and if he has any trouble, you call me at once."

"Of course, Sister." She gave him a stern look, and left.

I stared at him dully for a bit. He seemed familiar, but in my state I couldn't put a name to him. He was a bit taller than me, average built, about my age, dressed in a respectable suit; and he studied my face with obvious concern.

"Hello, Nate," he said, softly.

I finally connected with the voice. "Wha? Well...hello, cap'n." This was someone I never expected to see again. Tom Clark was an old friend from Southern Illinois. We enlisted together in '62, and since he had some schooling, he got a field commission, and rose to command what was left of our company of the 27th Illinois. I struggled to sit up, which took some effort. "Ain't seen you since we mustered out in '65. How you been?"

"Managing, I suppose. Doing better than you, it seems."

My strength gave out, and I sagged on the bed again. "You got that right. So what you doing here in 'Frisco?"

"I came out here after the war to make my fortune in the gold fields." He shook his head and gave me a wry smile. "Idealistic youth, eh? I run a dry goods emporium now, doin' all right. I heard you were going to be in town for that big prize fight, so I was planning to look you up, but then you went missing. I saw a story about you in the paper the other day, so I came to see how you're doing." He paused and looked me over with a worried frown. "Lord Almighty, Nate, you look terrible."

"You don't know the half of it, Tom."

He gave me a forced smile. "But don't you worry; you'll get better. You always were the scrapper, and I've never seen you back down from a fight."

I sighed, and raised my left hand to show him the bandaged stumps. "There are some fights a man can't win, Tom."

7

He eyed my bandaged hand uneasily, no doubt remembering the horrors we both witnessed during the Civil War. "If...you need work after you get out, look me up. I'll find something for you, something to give you a new start, anyway."

I was touched by that. "Thank you, Tom."

There was a painful silence as we regarded each other. "What happened, Nate?" he asked at last.

"It's...kind of hard to explain."

"The doctor said you fell off the train, and must have wandered around up there in Donner Pass for a month, you were so starved. But that can't be: nobody'd last an hour in those blizzards in nothing but street clothes, and you weren't up there for a month, anyway."

"I...don't know for sure what happened, Tom." I hesitated for a time, wondering if I should tell him—if I should tell anyone what I *think* went on up there in the High Sierras. The thought of winding up in a sanatorium haunted me almost as much as the thought that a sanatorium might be where I belonged. But if I couldn't trust my old friend and comrade in arms to believe, or at least to keep it to himself, who could I trust? And I *had* to know. "Tom," I said at last. "I'll tell you what I remember, but you got to do me a favor in turn."

"What's that, Nate?"

"I want you to listen to what I have to say, no matter what, then I want you to tell me honestly if I've gone mad."

He considered that, then nodded solemnly. "All right, Nate."

I settled on the bed and stared at the ceiling for a bit, trying to marshal my thoughts. The cold was what I remembered the clearest; I pulled the heavy woolen cover up to ward off *that* memory. "It...started in Omaha..."

\*\*\*\*\*

## "The First Day: Mid Morning"

...Omaha...mid-October, 1876...

It amazed me to think that *this* raw frontier boom town was the Capitol of the brand new State of Nebraska. It didn't need the endless chill rain to be a dismal place. The streets were bottomless mud, and in weather like this, the only way to move around town was by the boardwalks and occasional planks the locals might decide to lay across at street corners. We were stranded at the train station as surely as if we were all on a South Sea island. There were a few brick buildings here and there, all belonging to the railroad, but most were crude wooden false-fronts, with a solid two story hotel on the corner. I spent the last night there, and wouldn't miss it. In fact, I wouldn't miss the whole damned town.

The rain was tapering off again, which gave me precious little comfort as I stood on the station's boardwalk and watched that ugly sky. This late in the year, a trip across the Wild West to San Francisco, even on a modern steam train like the 'Overland', was not something done lightly. That sky said the trip looked doubtful.

"It's my own damned fault," I muttered as I hunched up my overcoat against the brisk wind, and eyed the scene around me with no favor.

9

The grandly titled 'Omaha Union Station' was a wooden shed: more ornate than some, but already outdated and outgrown. The dim light of the store windows across the street faded into the gloom within a few blocks, with the unfinished capitol dome faintly visible in the background. The fog of wood smoke from nearby chimneys and the railroad's shops in the distance added to the gloom. There were no street lamps.

Omaha soon lost my interest, and I watched idly as the train crew fussed around their locomotive, oiling here and poking there as they made ready to leave. I envied them, as hard as their lot was. I used to be a railroad man before I took up fisticuffs; it's the one thing in life that stirs me even a little. The locomotive was a large modern machine, over-decorated with red paint and gold leaf trim in the fashion of the day. Steam oozed and hot water dripped, there was a steady *hiss-clunk, hiss-clunk* of its air compressor, and the rumble of its fire. The sweet, pungent smell of hot oil and wood smoke drifted to me on the breeze. I inhaled the fragrance deeply; it brought back memories of my years on the high iron when life was simple, and I still thought I controlled my destiny.

"Maybe I should go back to railroading," I grumbled. That was a foolish notion; folk like me rated no better than laborers, and I had no skills that might earn me a slot in the roundhouse. The best I could hope for was to become a yard bull, and I had enough of a sense of shame not to stoop to that. It was an old debate I had with myself in moments like this; not that I ever found an answer. The locomotive's safety valve lifted, shooting a jet of steam high in the air. That machine wanted out of here as much as I did.

I dug out my pocket watch and checked the time again. We were three hours late for departure, with no sign of leaving any time soon. Our train was sitting right there by the station ready to go; why didn't they let us board so we could at least be out of the weather? Some self-important bastard was throwing his weight around, no doubt. I fumed with impatience; what was holdup this time? It was probably an eastbound train running late. The Union Pacific, 'backbone of America', vital link to California, was a single rough track that ran fifteen hundred miles with no more than occasional crude settlements along the way. They improved it since it was built, but it was still a poor cousin to the established roads in the east. It was all too easy for traffic to get bottled up. Between derailments, breakdowns, weather, and the occasional train robbers or indian raids, trains could be hours—even days— late. The nearest siding where trains could pass each other was likely twenty miles away. A lot can happen in twenty miles.

The wind kicked up, bringing with it a renewed shower. "Why the hell am I doing this?" I grumbled as I wiped the chill spatter off my face, and wondered why I didn't turn around and catch the next steamboat back across the river.

My thoughts drifted to San Francisco and the reason I was here. It wasn't like I needed the money. I was in this Godforsaken hole because I couldn't turn down a challenge from the reigning heavyweight champion of the west coast. Wild Man McGurk and me were booked for what promised to be an epic prize fight in San Francisco in ten days' time, assuming I got there safely. I wasn't looking forward to that fight, which contributed to my foul mood. I guess, now that I think of it, that in the back of my mind I was afraid of not stepping up to the challenge. A bare-knuckle pugilist has to be abso-*damn*-lutely self confident, and I was starting to feel the years and the miles.

The wind picked up a bit more, and the renewed sprinkle grew stronger. I pulled my coat tight with a muttered curse, and dug my hands into my pickets. Sometimes, when I'd been drinking, I wondered if I was really in control of my fate...

"Excuse me, sir." It was one of the yard bulls assigned to keep order in the crowd of immigrants on the boardwalk. He was a big, surly brute with cold eyes; your typical copper. "You'd best be mindful of those bags." He gestured at the two carpet bags at my feet. "They're likely to disappear with all this foreign trash around if you get careless."

"I will, thanks." He nodded and went on his way. I ignored the noisy crowd, and went back to staring at the sky. San Francisco: as much as the trip ahead, I hated the thought of what I'd find there. No sense in fretting over it. I tried to lose myself in the low, scudding clouds and the occasional rain showers, and wished that life might have been different somehow.

"Hey, Germans!" My brooding was interrupted by a rough fellow in a cheap suit, who waved a sheaf of papers to get the attention of the mob on the station's boardwalk. "*Deutsche Immigranten! Come on* you *Deutsche,* over here!"

"*Immigrés! Ici!* Utah and Nevada, right here!" another was yelling in atrocious French.

Land speculators, trolling for warm bodies. I've seen my share of bottom feeders in this life, and these two and their kind were right down there in the muck. The station's boardwalk was packed with foreign refuse seeking a better life in the New World. The land agents were drumming a brisk trade, trying to corral as many as possible and jam them into the crude coaches of an immigrant train standing right behind the 'Overland'. I eyed the string of dilapidated, over-aged coaches with no favor, remembering them from when I served with the Army of the Tennessee. They were dirty and faded, and some of the windows were boarded up. Those cars were hazardous enough when new and well kept, which these weren't. The thought of a week or more on those hard wooden benches as they trudged across the barren Midwest made me shudder. The only virtue separating them from cattle cars was that they had wood-burning stoves.

The air was filled with the jabber of a half dozen European languages, with the occasional English from a traveling salesman or one of the locals sprinkled here and there. Huddled masses: most fleeing persecution or unrest in their countries. The only virtue separating them from cattle was that they were considered more valuable alive than not, which brought them no favor from the Land Agents. I watched them sourly for a bit, then turned with a weary sigh, edged through the crowd to the far corner of the boardwalk, and gazed idly up the street. Not that it did me any good: this platform was too crowded for me to find much solitude.

"*When* are we going to leave?" I grumbled to myself.

An angry voice—English, for once—caught my ear. "You watch. Th' Army'll catch up to them savages, an' give 'em what they got comin'."

"Yeah? Well Gen'l Custer was all set to give 'em what, an' look how that turned out."

Four roughnecks were standing by the station door. From their looks, they were probably cowpokes—lean, rangy, and wind-burnt. Along with their holstered revolvers, the tall one carried a Winchester repeater tucked under his arm. They had a snoot load of cheap whisky on board even at this hour, and it made all four loud and combative.

The tall one snorted in contempt. "Custer? Damn fool show off. If he'd come down to Texas, we'd-a showed him a thing or two."

"Well now, Jim, he did okay for himself during the war, for Yankee cavalry," one of the others said.

Jim was not impressed. "Sure he did, Ed. Anyone can look good when he outnumbers us ten to one. Them Sioux gave him a taste of his own medicine!"

That brought a round of unfriendly laughs and coarse remarks at the late General's expense. The locomotive's safety valve opened again, thankfully drowning their chatter with the hiss of escaping steam. That distracted me, and I drifted over by the track and idly watched as they made ready.

Behind the locomotive was the Union Pacific Railroad's 'Overland', the premiere train to San Francisco, and it was a far cry from the immigrant train that would run as a second section behind us. The first car was a combined baggage and crew dormitory, followed by two sleepers, then the diner, then two more sleepers, with a lounge car in the rear. The whole was painted bright maroon and yellow, and buried in ornate gold leaf scrollwork. It was a fancy train even by by the standards of the times.

The rain tapered off a bit. The track edge of the boardwalk was dotted with baggage carts and tool caddies, and a horde of workmen were busy at last minute preparations. A baggage cart full of cordwood was parked next to the locomotive while some laborers replenished the fuel supply used up by our late departure. Mid-train, two men were loading more food supplies into the diner. Further forward, another man handed a late shipment of heavy leather mail sacks into the baggage car while a cold-eyed Pinkerton man hovered nearby to keep the herd at bay. The car toads from the local roundhouse were adding oil to the axle journals and inspecting the couplings. I hardly noticed the busy scene around me. Those cowpokes brought back memories better left buried and forgotten.

That shallow groove in my left temple is a souvenir of a minnie ball that came as close as it could and still leave me to shudder at the memory. That was Chattanooga, and far too many good friends weren't as lucky. The Civil War burned the innocent youth out of me, leaving me world-weary and bitter. At that I beat the odds: there were only one hundred and thirty-five men in the regiment when we mustered out. Those years still haunted me.

*"Mesdames and messieurs, montent àbord de train, ici!"* And those damned speculators were still at it, although for once their distraction was welcome.

*"¡Esta manera! ¡Esta manera* your train! *¡Consiga* aboard!"

"Come on, you Dutchmen! Get in line!" One burly fellow was shoving and poking the immigrants like cattle, which they endured stoically. From the bedraggled, numb look of most of them, they probably felt lucky to be here in the Land Of Golden Promise, callous handling and miserable weather notwithstanding.

*"¡Inmigrantes* for Nevada *aquí!"* a third one yelled to be heard over the crowd noise. From the wary looks they gave each other, they were probably from three competing land agencies, each trying to hustle unwitting foreigners into homesteading out there on the Godforsaken prairie. Each one tried to collect as many transit slips as possible from the uncomprehending souls, and cram them into their allotted cars at a dollar a head. The bribery and backstabbing they resorted to for extra car space was infamous.

I turned away, and went back to watching the locomotive. Life was no kinder for me, and in my late 30s, I had precious little to show for it. I was a bit short for a heavyweight bare-knuckle pugilist, but I made it up in my beefy frame and the muscles earned in years of hard labor. I suppose I was handsome in a rough sort of way when I was younger, but the years had marked me. I worked for the railroads for a while after the war, labored like a field hand laying rails in the sweltering western sun until I bulged with hard muscle. I got into plenty of scrapes in the dismal line camps, and eventually was good enough to catch the eye of a fight promoter from St. Louis. Prize fighting earned me a crooked nose, gnarled knuckles, battered brows, another scar on my right cheek, and a deep sense of hopelessness and futility. I was not the sociable sort, and not someone to annoy.

Sometimes, when I'd been drinking, I missed the innocence. I was sober then, but boredom and brooding brought that lost youth to mind. I wished there was something in this life worth fighting for, something worth believing in. But there was nothing: nothing but prize fights and laying rails and dirt farming in the Nebraska mud. This world is not kind to childhood innocence.

"Ought-a kill 'em all." Those four cowpokes were getting louder as tempers rose. "Bunch-a animals. Do 'em good, I say."

"You got that right, Jim," Bill said.

"Can't blame 'em for Custer's stupidity," Ed objected.

Jim turned on him. "Ed Fergus, you're a damn fool, an' you don' know beans about nothin'."

"Ain't neither! I'm just sayin' what ever-one knows! Custer walked into it, an' they handed him his ass!"

"Serves him right, damnyankee!" the fourth added.

"Now don't you start, Frank!"

The people around them were becoming nervous at how riled up they were, and their heated talk was drawing hostile glares from a number of Union veterans. An open area grew as the crowd drifted away from the four.

"Well I still say them Sioux ain't no good fer nuthin' but fertilizer!" Jim shouted. "An' if you was a real Texan, you'd agree!"

That got Ed riled, and he advanced on the larger man with his fists cocked. "I'll show you a real Texan!"

At that point one of the yard bulls came over to break it up. "All right, that will be enough from the lot of you!" The four turned on him angrily, but he was backed up by two Pinkerton detectives whose icy faces said that they meant business. There was a tense moment as they stared the four down, then the yard bull sent them on their way. They drifted over to the other end of the platform with dark looks and angry muttering, and went back to arguing. Life went back to normal for everyone else.

15

"*Aufenthalt* in *der Linie dort*, you bastards!" The land agents were getting frantic as departure time neared. "Come on, move it!"

I sighed in aggravation, and wished I could leave this mob behind altogether, not that there was anywhere else to go. The sprinkle picked up again; *just* what the moment needed.

"*Déplacement* your *subsistance*, you bastards!"

"*¡Mudanza de subsistencia!*"

"Come on! *Aufenthalt!*"

And as dismal as it was, this was the last outpost of civilization between here and Utah.

"...only good injun is a dead..."

I turned my collar up against the chill, and thought about going back inside, but the tiny waiting room was jam packed, which was why I was out here. The herd of foreigners milled dumbly about under the watchful eye of three railroad bulls, while their betters enjoyed the dubious comforts of the station. At least out here I could get some fresh air. A heavyset man in western garb and ten gallon hat passed nearby, and I noticed the tin star pinned to his lapel: the local Sheriff perhaps. Our eyes met, and the stranger regarded me for a moment, then nodded courteously and went about his business.

My thoughts drifted back to San Francisco and the big fight in ten day's time. McGurk was a brawler: vicious enough, and no one to take lightly, but not very scientifical in his fighting. It would take a lot to wear him down, but I knew I could handle that drunken Mick. Not that I would get any satisfaction from it. Looking back on it now, I guess this fight was about denying my own human frailty, denying that I might not step up to the challenge. That was the real reason for the tedious four day trip from Omaha—a week or more from New York City. I *was* feeling the years and the miles, and I had something to prove to myself. Too bad for McGurk.

The locomotive vented off more steam with a subdued roar. I dug my pocket watch out and checked the time again, wondering irritably what the delay was. "For cryin' out loud. Hell of a way to run a railroad." Three and a half hours late; this was ridiculous. It made me wonder what the rest of the trip would be like.

A shrill whistle caught my ear. "Ladies and gentlemen, your attention please!" The speaker was a short, slender man in a conductor's uniform who perched on one of the open car platforms and waved to get attention. "Those who are taking the 'Overland', please prepare to board."

"About damned well time," I grumbled as I tucked my watch away, hefted my carpet bags, and headed for the train.

The three railroad bulls forced the herd back to make a path across the boardwalk, and to keep them separated from their betters as the passengers came spilling out of the waiting room. Despite my head start, I wound up ninth in line, where I waited impatiently for the Conductor, a dapper, self-important little man in a cutaway waistcoat—one 'Beauregard W. Doggett' by the nameplate on his breast—to check his passengers off. The name fit.

"Ogden?-second-car-to-your-left-beyond-the-diner-the-porter-will-show-you-your-section-welcome-aboard-sir-next-please," he chanted in a high pitched sing-song as the first passenger surrendered his tickets. This must be a tedious routine to him, even if the rest of us were eagerly waiting to board. No sooner did he collect the first set of tickets then he turned to the next person. "San-Francisco?-first-car-to-your-left-beyond-the-diner-the-porter-will-show-you-your-section-welcome-aboard-sir-next-please."

At least things were finally moving, which did a lot to help my mood, and a whiff of wood smoke added the right touch to the occasion. The car toads slammed the last journal box lids down and retreated. The baggage car door slid shut, and the baggage cart was wheeled away.

"Reno?-second-car-to-your-left-beyond-the-diner-the-porter-will-show-you-your-section-welcome-aboard-sir-next-please."

There was a goodly crowd waiting to board. It's always like this late in the year; travelers anxious to get their journeys done before the winter came on. The train would be nearly full. I made a mental note to hit the dining car as soon as I was settled in. Luxury train or no, the trip would be a crowded one.

"Roseville?-first-car-to-your-left-beyond-the-diner-the-porter-will-show-you-your-section-welcome-aboard-sir-next-please."

The locomotive vented off more steam as the fireman built up his fire. A chill gust of wind tugged at my overcoat. The crowd was becoming more animated as departure time approached. I was thankful to be in a compartment where I would find a little privacy and avoid the aggravation of the herd. With my mood what it was (pushed into the background for now), the extra fare was money well spent.

"Sacramento?-second-car-to-your-right-second-compartment-welcome-aboard-sir-next-please."

A commotion behind us caught my attention, and I turned just as *she* came out of the station and overwhelmed the boardwalk. The crowd fell silent as they made way for her, and the sight of her took my breath away. She was as tall as me, and her honey-gold hair was piled high. Her face was oval, with high cheekbones, a small straight nose, full lips, and clear pale skin. Her figure was flawless, her head held high. I was stricken suddenly by a man's need...my mouth was dry, and my wind was up...I couldn't take my eyes off her. She was a mystery who regarded the world from some Olympian distance as she passed.

She was dressed in fashion, and wore a leather pouch on a belt instead of carrying a purse, with one hand tucked under the flap as if she was guarding something. She carried a single carpet bag which seemed much too large for her although she handled it easily. She moved through an awed silence, her stride as bold and firm as a soldier's, ignoring the murmurs around her as she strode to the head of the line.

Those four cowpokes were a half-dozen places back from me. Jim tipped his hat back and followed her with obvious interest. From the way he swayed, it seemed his breakfast was finally getting to him. "Hey, what's your name, little lady?" he called as she passed.

She paused and gave him a contemptuous glare. "I ney am interested, so my name ney concerns you." She had an odd accent, something I couldn't place, something vaguely German-sounding. From that and her haughty air, I figured she was likely some European noblewoman. I watched, fascinated, as she fearlessly confronted the roughneck.

18

Her rebuff brought on a chorus of catcalls from the other three. "You gonna take that, Jim?" one of them asked in a too-loud voice.

"Looks like he's losin' his touch," another one crowed.

"She don't know what she's missing," the third added. "Or maybe she does, eh?"

Jim evidently though he was a ladies man, and his friends' goading got to him. "Aw, come on, honey," he said with a hint of anger. "I'm just thinkin' a little companionship would be nice on our trip."

"I ney am a little companion." She dismissed him with a curt look, and continued to the head of the line as he watched her sullenly. No one spoke up to object as she did.

She glanced at me as she passed, then paused and gave me a quick once-over, followed by a faint smile which struck me like lightning. Her eyes...her eyes were cold, pale blue...like a stiff breeze that sends a chill down your spine...but there was something remote about them. I was stunned by her, and it took me a moment to realize that I was responding physically. Surprised and a bit shaken, I tipped my hat to her. Her gaze lingered for another moment, then she nodded in turn, then went on and handed the conductor her tickets.

"Um..." Doggett was shaken out of his complacent routine by her presence. "San Francisco?" he mumbled. "Ah, welcome aboard, miss." He studied her tickets again nervously. "Your compartment is the first one in this first car." He gestured to the car on his left.

"Thank you, sir," she said, with a condescending nod. Doggett jumped to take her bag, but faltered when he tried to lift it, and had to wrestle the thing up to the car's platform by main strength. She ascended the steps in one swift move, hefted her bag effortlessly, and disappeared into the car.

The sensation passed, and the murmur of conversation started to pick up again. The line moved forward steadily while I wondered about her. There was a lot more to her than her flawless beauty and willful air. She had an uncanny magnetism which drew every male in sight. Yet aside from her brief smile to me, she was hardly forward or inviting. What was her name, I wondered?

From the grumbling behind me, it seemed she made a big impression on those four cowpokes, too.

"Reno?" Doggett was back to his chanted routine. "Second-car-to-your-left-beyond-the-diner-the-porter-will-show-you-your-section-welcome-aboard-sir-next-please."

She was quality, and her odd accent struck me. Where did she come from? Why was she going to San Francisco? Try as I would, I couldn't figure why someone like her would make such a journey. Her mysterious aura set her apart from every other woman I ever knew, and that smile... There was a lot unspoken in that brief exchange. She seemed well disposed toward me for some reason; enough that we might share a table in the diner for conversation, at least. I didn't understand her interest, but that would make the trip a lot more pleasant.

"Sacramento?-second-car-to-your-right-the-porter-will-show-you-your-section-welcome-aboard-sir-next-please."

She was something new and mysterious in my jaded life, and the memory of that brief smile haunted me. Yeah, maybe this trip wouldn't be so boring after all. That thought, and the memory of those haunting eyes, pushed my brooding melancholy into the background. Learning about her could take up the entire journey, and more.

"Tickets, sir?"

My distracted haze was interrupted by Doggett, who held out his hand impatiently. I'd reached the head of the line without noticing, and felt a bit sheepish as I surrendered the two paperboard receipts, one for train fare, the other for my compartment.

"San-Francisco?-first-car-to-your-left-beyond-the-diner-first-compartment-welcome-aboard-sir-next-please," Doggett chirped as he turned to the next in line. I tossed my bags up on the platform as the rain picked up again, then hauled myself up on the steps, already forgotten.

*****

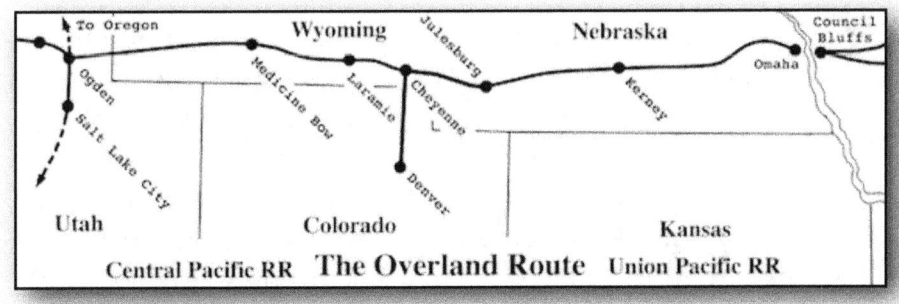

Central Pacific RR  The Overland Route  Union Pacific RR

## "The First Day: Afternoon, Evening"

This was one of the fancy sleeping cars which were being shifted westward to make way for even fancier cars back east. It was a bit overdone for my taste, with its polished woodwork and gold leaf trim, but I had to admit they were comfortable. There was a small washroom, and then a compartment at either end, all opening onto a narrow corridor along one side. Between them were ten open sections with red velvet plush cushions and fancy brasswork. The air was heavy with moist steam heat, and the gaslights in the ceiling drove back the gloom beyond the windows. The floor was carpeted, and there were polished brass spittoons along the aisle between each pair of seats. Those seats could fold down to make the lower berths, while the upper berths were hinged above the windows, and were tucked up out of the way for now. The whole could be closed off at night with heavy curtains, which offered privacy but wasn't exactly dignified. The aisle was crowded with passengers settling in and tucking their travel valises under the seats. Having ridden the cushions many times in recent years, and I was thankful that I could afford a compartment with its greater privacy.

The negro porter in black trousers and white short coat caught me at the door. "Welcome aboard, suh. Mah name is Samuel, and ah'm here fo' youah every need." He relieved me of my two carpet bags, maneuvered the narrow confines of the hallway to my compartment, placed the bags on the seat, and ushered me in with a flourish. "If they's anythin' you want, you call on ol' Samuel, and ah'll take proper care of you."

"Thank you," I mumbled. I tipped him two bits, sent him on his way, and slumped in one of the seats with a weary sigh.

My home for the next four days was a compact seven feet by six, with a pair of seats by the window, a fold down upper berth, and enough room between them and the door to turn around. The berth over my head was beautifully inlaid and polished until it shown like a mirror. The rest of the compartment was done in light wood paneling, and the floor was carpeted. There was a brass gaslight in the ceiling, and a tiny radiator right behind the door to provide heat from the locomotive's steam.

I shoved my carpet bags between the seats, put my feet up, and stared moodily out the window. It was pouring out there, and the street beyond the station was lost in a thin fog. The window was open a bit, which let the chill damp in. I'd had enough cold and wet for one day, so I pushed it shut, and sat watching the crowd on the boardwalk. At least I avoided getting soaked. The passengers waiting to board sheltered as best they could under their bags, umbrellas, and occasional newspapers as the line inched steadily forward. The herd waiting to board the immigrant train stood silently in the wet. Some children huddled under their mothers' coats, but for the most part, they simply endured. It reminded me of slogging down the bottomless mud roads during the war, so weary and beaten down that the wet chill no longer mattered. I almost sympathized with them, but they were here of their own choice, huddling in the downpour anyway.

A messenger boy came out of the station carrying a telegram form. He forced his way through the crowd and handed the form to Doggett before retreating post-haste. I watched gloomily, wondering if it was another last minute delay. Doggett glanced at the form, tucked it in his pocket, and went back to collecting his tickets. I relaxed. Watching that rainy damp was getting me down, so I headed out again. With everyone busy settling in, this would be a good time to visit the dining car.

§

The dining car was already filled with seasoned travelers excited to be on their way, or perhaps to be out of Omaha. The dining room filled two-thirds of the car, with the rest being the kitchen. The room was pleasantly warm and bright, and the air rich with cooking aromas. The car was beautifully done with polished wood, ornate rugs, and glowing gas lamps. The tables themselves—for four on one side of the aisle, for two opposite, were set with linen and fine tableware like one of those fancy New York City eateries. The colored waiters were jumping, and there was a steady clatter from the kitchen where the three-man staff were hard at work. It was a stark contrast to the boardwalk, and the good cheer in the room helped improve my temper.

The dining car steward was a dandy fellow in a cutaway waistcoat; one would think I was the President of the railroad, or perhaps of the United States by how he greeted me. "Welcome aboard, sir. Table for one? Right this way, if you please." He showed me to a single table at the end of the room, seated me with all the courtesy of a fine restaurant, and presented the embroidered menu like it was a college diploma.

"We have an excellent mock turtle soup today, and I can recommend the roast chicken, a specialty of our master chef." He hovered over me pointing out the menu's delights until he started to get on my nerves; then, tip in hand, turned his attention to the next arrivals. As soon as he left, the waiter was there for my order.

I was hungry after standing around in the wet all morning, and was going over the menu trying to decide between the buffalo steak and the roast chicken when the room quieted and someone muttered, "Will you look at that?" I looked up just as *she* entered the far end of the room near the kitchen. She was wearing one of those fine ladies gowns which made no secret of her figure, and her hand was still tucked under the flap of her pouch. Like on the boardwalk, she overwhelmed the crowd, and I felt my need stirring just from the sight of her. She was met with an awed hush, and the Steward came running to serve someone so obviously important.

Those four cowpokes were seated at a table in the middle of the car, and Jim noticed her. "Well, hello there, lil' lady," he called to her. She ignored him, so he rose from his seat and went over to where she stood talking with the steward. "I'm thinkin' it'd sure be nice to have your company for lunch. What's your name, honeylamb?"

She gave him an annoyed glare. "I ney repeat myself," she snapped. "And my name ney iss 'Honeylamb'."

Nobility or not, this cowpoke was not amused by her attitude. "I'm jus' tryin' to be friendly, little lady," he said, sullenly. "Ain't no call to get all uppity. You can't blame a feller for admiring a pretty woman, can you?"

"Well if you wish to admire me, you may do so from the other side of the room, in silence."

I watched uneasily as the tension rose between them. She was pushing her luck with that drunken rowdy, perhaps thinking her station would protect her despite how she provoked him. That wasn't surprising for a foreign noblewoman, but she must not realize just how far she was from the European courts. This was turning nasty from the look of things, and I wasn't happy about coming to her rescue. I could handle that drunken lout, but the four of them together could overwhelm me; not to mention they were all armed. Seeing how she treated him, I was tempted to mind my own business, not that I could.

Her last rebuff pushed him over the edge, and he grabbed her arm as she turned away. "Lookie here, little missy..."

Swift as a striking rattler, she grabbed his wrist and *squeezed*. He let out a startled howl to match the ugly crunching sound, then recovered and swung a crude roundhouse left at her head. She ducked, kneed him savagely in his groin, then grabbed his hair as he curled up, and slammed his face on the table hard enough to set the dishes bouncing. Then she grabbed his belt and the scruff of his neck, and sent him crashing headlong through the window to land in a heap on the boardwalk outside. I'd hardly had the chance to get out of my seat before it was over.

"My...God..." the steward gasped. Aside from that and the tinkle of falling glass, the car was dead silent. She wasn't even breathing hard as she stood looking out the window in annoyance, then turned and surveyed the car.

"Next?"

No answer. Not a peep. She gave his three friends a cold smile, and settled at the opposite table as if nothing happened. The stunned waiter handed her a menu more or less by habit.

She was going through the menu when the steward recovered his wits. "What have you done?" he cried. "Look at this mess! We can't run all the way to San Francisco with a broken window!"

Her annoyed look made him step back. "You should have thought of that before you let low-life on your train." Two tables over, the three surviving roughnecks stared in stunned disbelief, as did everyone else.

"We're leaving in five minutes! What are we going to do?" The poor fellow was distraught over the damage to his beautiful dining car.

"Well if you ney can handle such a simple matter, I suggest you get someone to board it up."

"But that will take at least a half-hour, and we're already late!"

She glanced at the menu briefly, then handed it to him. "Then you will have time to bring me one of everything."

§

Beauregard Doggett was next up, reinforced by the local sheriff who more than made up for his skimpy proportions. They fared no better against the lady than the steward did.

"This is *completely* unacceptable!" he huffed at her like an agitated chihuahua. "We cannot have such behavior on this train!"

"Oh?" She paused working on her buffalo steak and looked him over coldly, then in a loud voice, "So iss this railroad in the habit of allowing ladies to be assaulted on their trains?"

Doggett was scandalized. "I...well, no, of course not!"

"So, I *suppose* you would have thrown him off the train yourself, then?"

Doggett looked uncomfortable but didn't answer. Each of the four ranchers was larger than him, and he was not a man of action.

"No?" She eyed him contemptuously, then turned to look around the room. "Then I suppose the *gentlemen* in this car would have done so for you?" she demanded in a voice that carried. Her gaze paused on me as she spoke. "And I am sure any *real* man would have given him ass bad in the process." She scanned the silent crowd with a look of contempt, paused to consider me again, then turned her attention back to Doggett. "Evidently ney. So if a lady ney has someone to protect her, she has to protect herself."

"But...you might have killed him!"

She eyed him over her coffee cup. "Did he die?" She was obviously enjoying this.

"No, thankfully!"

"Good," she said loudly. "Because after that kick, he ney will molest any ladies again, ever." Doggett and the sheriff were flabbergasted by that bold remark, the subdued murmur of the onlookers rose sharply, and the three surviving cowpokes winced. "Ass for your window, consider that a small price to pay for letting riff-raff on board."

Doggett gaped in confusion, then turned to the sheriff. "Well? What will you do?"

The sheriff scratched his head doubtfully. "Looks t' me like the lady was defendin' herself. Can't fault her for that, even if she did go a mite overboard about it." He clearly didn't want to tangle with her, even though he was twice her weight.

"Surely someone can say otherwise?" Doggett turned to the crowd behind him. "You all saw what happened! Tell him!"

One of Jim's three friends almost spoke up, but she gave him a cold look, and he subsided.

"Nobody?" the sheriff muttered at last. "Then it ain't my business." He glanced at Doggett, then at her. "Unless you want t' press charges against that feller?"

"I think he has learned his lesson."

The sheriff wilted under her bold gaze. "I reckon he has." He tipped his hat and beat a dignified retreat, leaving Doggett standing there in dismay.

In fact, it was nearly an hour before the wreckage was cleared away, the window boarded up, and the 'Overland' got under way.

§

I finally settled on the roast chicken, which lived up to the steward's claim, then headed back to the lounge car at the end of the train, where I helped myself to a drink and a cigar, and sat brooding about life as the track slid away behind us. The lounge car is the social center of any better class of train, where the gentlemen whiled away the time with cigars, a well stocked bar, card games, and loud talk. The gossip was lively that afternoon, and all on one subject. Her exploits were already legend, and were debated with the earnest gravity usually reserved for vital topics of the day such as the Indian Wars.

I ignored them and sat in the last seat near the rear windows so I could watch the scenery and brood in peace. I didn't bother to follow the gossip, but I couldn't help thinking about her nonetheless. She was an eye full, a real standout, and her bold nature made her all the more noticeable, as if anyone could ignore her. And her amazing performance...the very idea of a woman slapping a grown man down like that fascinated me. There was so much about her that was strange, so much that didn't add up, that I couldn't keep her off my mind.

Conductor Doggett came in a short time later, and was met with an embarrassing silence and no few grins. By the latest tale going round, he tried to get the dispatcher throw her off the train before we left Omaha, and that worthy had no better luck than he did earlier. His business done, Doggett retreated in humiliation, followed by a renewed storm of gossip.

I sipped my beer, nursed my cigar, and pondered her as the track flowed away to the horizon. I was bemused by the sheer overwhelming power of her attack: I couldn't imagine how she picked that man up and tossed him through a window so easily. That was the most obvious mystery about her, but there was more. She didn't fight by the Marquess of Queensberry's rules: she was a street brawler, as vicious as they come. As a professional boxer, I saw her obvious skill, but it was completely out of character for a high-born lady, as was her amazing strength. I didn't know what to make of it.

I sighed in frustration. My stein was empty, so I waved to the bartender, another negro dressed in burgundy and black, who nodded, and brought me another beer. Like the rest of the train, the bar was compact and well equipped with a brass foot rail, draw handles for beer, and an array of bottles on the back wall. There was a small niche at the end of the bar near the newspaper rack where the rear brakeman sat and tried to keep out of the way. If the lounge car was the social center of the train, the bar was its center in turn, and the trade was lively.

I sat for a couple of hours, alone in the crowded room, alternately brooding about life and wondering about her. The gentle rocking of the car and the endless track sliding away to the horizon were hypnotic. My thoughts drifted...pale blue eyes...San Francisco...Marquess of Queensberry's rules...the Sierra Nevadas...that strange accent...my manly need stirred vaguely just from the thought of her...

A ruckus finally drew me out of my daydreaming. Those three ranch hands had invaded the scene, and were well into the liquor. "Yeah, well, she sure made a monkey out-a Jim, didn't she?" the shorter one said.

"She's a no-account whore, I reckon," the larger one said too loudly. He was nearly as large as the late Jim, with the wiry build of a horseman, rough windburned features, and more hooch in him than his two pals. "She got no call gettin' better than herself with any man!"

"She's quality, Frank," his partner insisted. "Jim's got a roving eye, we all know that, but he should-a kept his hands off her."

"Yeah?" Frank confronted him angrily. "Ed, there ain't no woman can go slap a man down like that!"

Ed glared right back at him. "She was in her rights. The sheriff said so."

"Can't let a woman get all high-handed, an' slap a man down like he was some nigger! She needs to learn a lesson!"

"And I suppose you're the one to teach her?" the third said. He wasn't far behind the other two in his drinking.

"Damned right I am!"

I smiled at the thought of how she would handle that drunken galoot. These three clean forgot that she *could* slap them down, with ease.

"Seems to me she don't need no lessons from the likes of Jim, *or* you!"

"Ed Fergus, you're a drunken fool!" Frank shouted.

Ed huffed at him in near rage. "Ain't neither! And if you was any kind-a man, you'd agree with me!"

Frank crowded up to him with his fists cocked and fire in his eye. "You wanna find out what kind-a man I am..."

"That will be enough!" A large, heavyset man, the lawman from the station earlier, stepped between them and pushed them apart. "I'll trouble you boys to hold your voices down a mite," he growled. The three of them turned on him, but the look in his eyes stopped them. "This ain't the way we do things down in Amarillo, no, sir." He gave each a hard look. "Now, what happened to your friend was unfortunate, but he shouldn't ought-a hassled the lady. You three need to keep that in mind, and not bother the good folks in this car."

The two hemmed and hawed uncertainly, while Frank only got angrier.

"Now, why don't you boys settle down and have another beer?" The man nodded to the bartender, who got busy.

"Yeah?" Frank was a redneck rowdy, drunk and spoiling for a fight. He didn't know when to quit. "So who are you, anyway?"

"The name's Parker." The big man brushed his jacket back, revealing his tin star and clearing the six-gun on his hip. "Ned Parker." He gave Frank a cold smile as the man paled. "I see you heard of me. So why don't you boys relax and enjoy the ride?"

Frank nodded hollowly, and they settled in their seats. Parker gave them a severe eye, then ambled back over to the bar. The conversation slowly picked up again. I chuckled to myself at those three rowdies meeting their match in one of the most notorious lawmen in the West.

Parker came back to the rear of the car some time later, settled in the seat opposite, and sat watching the horizon as he nursed his beer. He was burly and broad shouldered, with the rough, dignified features women are attracted to. His hair was steel gray, and his eyes dark and dangerous. After a bit, he turned and said, gravely, "I believe I know you, sir. Nate Poole, if I'm not mistaken."

"You are correct, sir," I said, warmly. "But I haven't had the pleasure."

"The name's Parker." He made a show of stoking up a cigar. "Ned Parker, Texas Rangers. And I'm pleased to meet you, Mister Poole."

"The pleasure is mine, sir."

29

"I saw you in Saint Louie, three years back. You took Big Mike Jorgensen in twenty-five rounds." He considered me closely. "I admire a man who knows how to use his fists. I admire a man who knows how to use his wits, too."

"That was a tough one." I smiled awkwardly at the memory: the battle went poorly until I spotted Jorgensen's pattern and used it against him. "I admired how you handled that little scene earlier."

Parker gave me a mirthless smile, and took a couple puffs on his cigar. "Learning how to get inside a man's head makes life a lot more *predictable*." This from someone who brought more than his share of desperados to feet-first justice. "But I'd say you know that already."

"Indeed, sir."

Parker watched the landscape for a bit, then stood and nodded to me. "Indeed. Good night, Mister Poole." I watched as he left, and reflected that you meet all sorts of interesting people on trains.

§

I eventually finished my cigar and my third drink, and headed back to my compartment. I was surprised to run into *her* in the second sleeper forward, in the narrow corridor near the washroom. She must have been on her way back to her compartment from the dining car. Up close, her features were even more refined than I remembered. Her face was perfect, her skin smooth and clear, her ears delicate shells, her neck arched. Her eyes were a pale china blue, and they glowed with an inner fire beneath delicate brows. She was flawless, too flawless; and there was an air about her that aroused and intimidated me at the same time.

She paused when I made way for her, and favored me with a bold look and a warm smile. "I ney believe I have had the pleasure of meeting you, sir."

That was uncommonly forward for a proper lady in my opinion, not that she was just *any* lady, and there's no accounting for foreign tastes. "Ah...Poole, miss." I tipped my hat awkwardly in the narrow space. "Nathaniel Poole."

Her eyebrow inched up, and she studied my face curiously. "The heavyweight boxer?" The fire in her eyes was disturbing, and I was embarrassed by my physical response to her.

"Yes, miss."

"Indeed? Most curious." She surveyed me boldly, pausing below my waist. "Well, Nathaniel Poole, I am grateful that you would have come to my aid in the dining car, earlier."

"I...um...only did what was right. Thankfully you weren't hurt."

"Thankfully." She smiled again. "I would like to show you my appreciation. I am in the first compartment of this car, and I promise ney to throw you through the window." Her eyes locked on mine with a predatory gleam. "Unless you disappoint me."

§

Back in my compartment, I slumped in one of the plush seats, stared absently out the window at the passing landscape, and wondered over this latest run-in. My earlier confusion surfaced again, drawn up by her odd behavior. It seemed she took an interest in me right from the start there in Omaha, and if I took her invitation correctly, she wanted more than dinner conversation. As flattering as that was, I couldn't see the reason for it. She was a rare beauty the likes of which doesn't exist in the real world. Why would she take an interest in a banged-up prize fighter? She didn't seem like the sort of woman who is drawn to strong, violent men. She was no weakling, and those eyes...this was a hungry she-wolf. It was like she stepped out of an erotic dream and was determined to fulfill my deepest longings. Juvenile fantasies aside, that *just* didn't happen. I couldn't understand her, unless perhaps she was drawn by the implied violence of my calling. I knew women like that, but they were weak and fawning, nothing like her.

The day was getting on into an early evening made all the gloomier by the low clouds. Omaha was well behind us by then as the train rocketed along, and there was precious little but telegraph shanties and a few hardscrabble settlements between there and Ogden, Utah. The land was as flat as the proverbial flap jack, with nothing to see save an occasional creek and a few scattered trees. This was going to be a boring four days.

I watched the scenery absent-mindedly for a while before she came to mind again, unbidden. I was almost as startled by her bold invitation as by her fighting style, earlier. She came on like a shameless cathouse strumpet, which she certainly wasn't. I was flattered to be the object of her interest, but I wasn't sure I approved of her forwardness.

And she didn't fight by the Marquess of Queensberry's rules... How did a woman—and she was not unusually large or muscular —have the strength to toss that cowpoke around like a rag doll? I couldn't, and I was in top form. And her fighting style—street brawling, pure and simple: no rules, no quarter, put the other fellow down hard and fast so you could deal with the next one. But she was from refined society; where would she learn that? And why? It didn't add up.

And then there was her odd accent, her haughty bearing, and how she dressed. She was probably an aristocrat; her accent suggested Central Europe, perhaps Prussia? She was snooty enough. But that didn't make sense either. I met a few Prussians during the war—foreign observers here to watch the American rabble fight—and they were brutish barbarians whose only real talent was for attacking their neighbors. Their nobles were easily that arrogant, but a Prussian noblewoman traveling alone? Not to mention being so deadly a brawler? In the low form of street thugs? Their menfolk would never stand for that, or for her traveling unescorted, or for her making casual offers to men who caught her fancy. It made her all the more mysterious.

The car swayed and rattled as the train rolled over a short trestle, and the renewed rain pelted the window. The dim afternoon light was gone, taking an uninteresting world with it. Chill air was coming through the overhead vent, so I stood and closed it, turned the valve to admit steam into the tiny radiator, and settled in my seat again, brooding in the dark.

Wild Man McGurk wouldn't stand a chance against her, and even I would be hard pressed. Her mystery taunted me. I couldn't understand her, and I couldn't keep her out of my mind.

"Oh, what the hell," I muttered at last. I needed a break from boredom and frustration and this dismal weather, and she did make her invitation plain. A thorough gallop would do my mood some good. And if nothing else, maybe I could learn a bit about her.

§

Most of the open sections in the sleeper were made down and closed off by their curtains since folks were retiring early. There were still a few people about in the restrooms, and I carefully negotiated the narrow aisle, trying to keep out of Samuel's way as he prepared another upper berth.

The diner was closed and dark, deserted but for the scullery boy cleaning in the kitchen. The sleeper beyond was the same story; most folks were retiring early. I stopped in front of her door, and looked around self-consciously. Even a compartment wasn't exactly private in a crowded train, and no doubt tongues would wag in the morning. Not that I cared normally, but she upset all the presumptions, leaving me wondering what to do.

I finally got up my nerve, and rapped on the door. A muffled, imperious voice came from inside. "Enter."

The compartment was dark, lit only by the faint light from the window, which made the sight of her more provocative than any brazen display of nudity could. She was sprawled on the made down berth in a pose both demure and provocative, nothing about her hidden except by the shadows. In spite of my confusion, I felt my need stirring again.

"Well?" she demanded. "Close the door, unless you want the porter to join us?" Shaken out of my trance, I eased the door shut, and stood there dumbfounded. "Do you like what you see?" Her voice was silky, low, like the purring of a tigress. This woman was a man eater.

"Um...yes, I do."

Her breasts were full and firm, her nipples large and erect. Her abdomen was gently curved, and her legs were long and muscular. She was an athlete, in top form, and she was right there in front of me, close enough to touch.

"Why are you so shy, Nathaniel?" She reached out with one hand and undid the first button of my fly, and all of a sudden I was afraid of her. That never happened before, not with any woman I ever knew. It shook and confused me.

She undid the second button. "Touch me, Nathaniel," she purred.

I hesitated.

"Touch me, Nathaniel." That was a command, and I lacked the will to resist it. I yielded to her seductive power, and ran my hand gingerly over her stomach. She tensed. "That's right, Nathaniel," she sighed as she reached over and undid the third button.

My hand drifted upward and caressed her breast, evoking another sigh. "Ney make me wait for it, Nathaniel." She took my hand and placed it where she wanted, pressing my fingers home, and gasped in pleasure as my need became a burning agony. I was trembling, sweating, my mind submerged in a rising tide of lust like I never knew before. I fought temptation, afraid of the fire she had ignited, but my will crumbled under her caress.

"Your playing hard to get will only make me hungrier," she said with a wicked chuckle as she undid the last two buttons. Her touch drew an agonized whimper from my throat as my last shred of self restraint evaporated. "I am going to consume you, Nathaniel Poole."

*****

## "Day Two: Early Morning"

It was some time early, before dawn, when I finally collapsed and lay on her gasping for breath. I was soaked with sweat, shaking with fatigue, and my heart pounded like I'd gone fifty rounds with the great Ryan Mooney himself. Through my haze of fatigue, I wondered vaguely how I had lasted so long.

"Ohh, done so soon?" She ruffled my hair playfully. "I was just getting warmed up."

I managed to lift my head and look at her in disbelief. How she endured our relentless all night *manáge* was beyond understanding. For that matter, I couldn't imagine what got into me. I *never* had such an experience, never felt such uncontrollable, overwhelming lust. It dumbfounded me to think of what I accomplished that night.

"You ney giving up, are you?" she asked with a hint of disappointment. She ran her hands over me, which stirred my fires again, to my amazement. "Ney can I persuade you to go on?"

She wanted more? What's worse, my reaction to her caresses said she could get more out of me if she chose. It was high time to get out while I could still walk—if in fact I *could* still walk. My best effort to that end was to struggle up and sat on the edge of the berth, which took all my remaining strength. "I...guess you'll...have to...throw me through...the window," I managed at last as I gasped for air.

She let out a low chuckle, with hint of regret. "You tried hard, Nathaniel, so I will give you another chance tomorrow evening."

*'Tried hard'*, she said! I knew how to make a good impression, but bedding her was like being caught in a stampede. "The window would be kinder," I grumbled as I struggled to my feet.

Her answer was a deep sigh which might have been resignation. She lay sprawled on the berth as I left her, bonelessly limp, her body glistened with sweat. Her deep, steady breathing brought her ample figure to life; sensual mystery outlined by the pale predawn. Her womanly scent filled the compartment, calling to me, tormenting me. She was every man's darkest erotic fantasy; had used me—consumed me—in ways I never imagined from the

35

most wanton hussies.  I never knew such an incredible woman.  I wanted her and feared her as any man will who meets his match.

"I swear you've ruined me, woman," I groaned as I tried to balance myself against the swaying of the car.  It took what little coordination I had left to reach down and recover my clothes.

"You should be more optimistic, Nathaniel," she said, softly, as I dressed.  "A day of rest should put you back in form.  Go, eat a hearty meal, then sleep.  We can try again tomorrow night."

"If I'm still alive," I muttered as I wrestled feebly with my trousers.  Privately, as incredible as the experience was, I decided to pass on any further amorous adventures.

"Thank you, Nathaniel," she whispered as I left.

§

The train was rolling right along, determined to make up for the late start, and it was all I could do to steady myself against the swaying bulkheads.  Even at this hour, the passengers were stirring.  One older man sat in a made down lower berth with its curtains pushed aside a few spaces down from her compartment.  The annoyed glare he gave me said that the noise she made last night—and she was as enthusiastic as she was relentless—must have kept everyone awake.  My tattered state made my guilt in that plain.  I gave him a non-committal nod, and kept moving.

§

Getting across the open platforms between the two cars almost cost me my life.  It was raining hard, and the stiff wind of our passage buffeted the platforms with a blinding swirl of mist and smoke.  This is the part I always hate about train travel.  The platforms were narrow, and the footing treacherous from the rain.  One misstep could send me tumbling between the cars to be mangled by the wheels below.  I grabbed my bowler with one hand, gathered my nerve, and stepped gingerly across to the next car.  Despite my caution, my foot slipped.  My weakened grasp almost failed, and I clung desperately to the railing before I managed to pull myself to safety.  I wrapped my arms around the railing for a long moment, nervously watching the track whip past below, as I tried to calm my nerves and recover my wind.

§

The dining car crew were preparing breakfast as I came staggering through. I paused, and wondered absently if I should stop for an early meal since I was here. Lord knows some strong coffee would go down well. But they weren't ready, and I was too worn to wait for them, so I stumbled on down past the kitchen to my car beyond.

§

After an epic journey in my state, I finally reached my compartment, fumbled the door open...and stopped in confusion. There was a man sitting in one of the seats by the window. He was perhaps fifty, taller than me, burly and hard, clean shaven, and his pale hair was cropped close. Our eyes met, and there was something about his inhumanly cold stare that struck me with nameless dread. His suit and bowler hat somehow seemed as out of place on him as would a Roman toga. He watched silently with his arms crossed as I hesitated in the doorway, and his expression bore no welcome.

"I...beg your pardon, sir. Wrong compartment..."

"Ney, citizen Poole." He made an imperative gesture to the seat opposite. "Come in. We must talk."

Even through my fatigue, that struck me as ominous. This intruder had the same odd, vaguely German accent she did, and the ice in those eyes reminded me of a copper. And it seemed he knew who he was speaking to, which was more unsettling.

"Who are you, sir? What are you doing in my compartment?"

"I am Learnéd. I am here to speak with you about her." He gestured to the opposite seat again, more of a command than before. "Close the door, citizen. We have much to discuss."

I eased into the cramped compartment, settled reluctantly in the seat, and managed a quick glance around. Everything seemed in order. My two carpet bags were between the seats where I left them. If this Learnéd went through them, it didn't show.

"You still haven't told me what this is about." My exhaustion had me in a combative mood. "Explain yourself, sir!"

Learnéd gave me an annoyed glare, as if he was not accustomed to having his actions questioned. "Explanations are given ass needed. I will ask questions, and you will answer."

37

"I will, eh?"

Learnéd ignored that challenge. "You two put it in last night."

"...What..."

"You made sex with her, yes?"

"That is a personal matter, sir!"

Learnéd shook his head impatiently. "You ney realize who, or what, she iss."

"Nor is it any concern of mine, or yours. Why should you care, anyway? You're not a jealous husband, are you?"

"Ney!" I wasn't sure if he was alarmed or revolted by that prospect.

"Then what gives?" I shifted carefully in my seat so I could more easily reach my bags. "What's this all about?"

"I require your assistance to keep her under observation during this journey."

"You do, hmm? Why?"

"That ney iss your concern. All you must know iss my interest in her iss official."

Arrogant like a damned Prussian, all right. I was getting fed up with this character, and my aching exhaustion had me on a short fuse. I shifted slightly toward my bags. "Official, eh? Official how?"

"That ney matters to you. All that iss required of you iss that you do your duty..."

...I dove into one of the bags, and came up fast with my Colt revolver...

...and Learnéd snatched the pistol out of my hand so fast that I didn't see it happen. He examined it curiously as I nursed a sprained thumb, then gave me a bemused shake of the head, took the pistol in both hands, and *bent the barrel* as I watched in google-eyed amazement.

"I...w-what is going on here?" I managed at last. "Who are you?"

Learnéd considered me with no favor. "I suppose you need to know the basics, at least. She iss from the future, a dangerous fugitive. I am what you know ass a policeman, although I am more than that. I have come back to this past to apprehend her."

I stared at him incredulously. "The future?" Learnéd nodded, solemnly. "The future, you say? Do you take me for a fool, sir?"

"Are you a fool, citizen Poole?"

"I am not, sir! And I refuse to accept your wild tale."

Learnéd held up the bent pistol. "Then how do you explain this?"

I stared at it for a moment, confused and disconcerted. That bent gun barrel knocked all my presumptions out the window. "How did you do that?" I muttered at last.

Learnéd considered, then apparently thought more explanations were in order. "I am augmented with retroviruses."

"Um..."

"There are...a kind of life called viruses. The ordinary cold iss caused by any of several strains. They reproduce by entering the cells of a body and modifying them, using them ass hosts. Viruses can be modified—genetically engineered—so that they have new effects on the host body." He played with the ruined pistol, making sure I saw the bent barrel. "I received an Armstrong ass part of my preparation for this duty." He took the pistol in both hands and wadded it up like a piece of cardboard. "This iss what 'retros', ass we call them, can do."

That demonstration knocked the fight right out of me, leaving me confused and apprehensive. "Well...that may be, sir. But you'll forgive me if I find it hard to believe."

Learnéd cocked an eyebrow, and gave me a cynical look. "You rode her all night, ney?"

"That, sir..."

"You rode her at a pounding gallop for hours. You were inexhaustible, and you ney could stop yourself. I saw how stiff you were when you staggered in here."

"Well...what of it?"

"She took an Aphrodite, ass they are called on the street. It iss a retrovirus which causes a woman's body to excrete hormones which give men an uncontrollable need and the energy, temporarily, to fulfill it. She gang-raped you, citizen."

That explained a lot of what happened last night, as incredible as it seemed. "But...why would she do that?"

Learnéd's eyes dropped to my lap. "Probably because you have an uncommonly large one. Plus in your shape you would last longer than most men of this time could."

I was nonplussed again. I was proud of my manhood, which was larger than average, but... "How can you tell that?"

Learnéd tapped his temple. "Red Eye: a standard issue military retrovirus. It allows me to see in the dark, to see your body heat. Your clothes ney offer any concealment."

I tried to get a grip on this incredible tale while Learnéd watched patiently. This was unbelievable—it was madness—but it explained too much, answered too many riddles to be a mere concoction.

"Ah...well, assuming what you say is true, how does this involve me?" I managed at last.

"She takes a fancy to you, probably to keep her entertained during the journey." Learnéd shook his head in bemused wonder. "Four whole days to SaFrisko. These trains are dreadfully slow. Ney matter. Since you are in her confidence, you can observe her closely, and report anything she says or does to me."

"But why do you need me?"

"Because she ney suspects you. You can observe and report while I remain out of sight and wait for the opportune moment to move against her."

"This all seems too clever by half. Why not just call the local sheriff at the next town?"

"You ney understand the risk, and you ney are in law enforcement, so we shall do this my way."

"That's another thing. Why involve me when I'm so completely outclassed? If you're the law, she's your problem."

"I require your assistance, citizen. The details ney concern you."

"Well I'll tell you, *citizen*, what you require is no concern of mine. You don't even have jurisdiction here!"

Learnéd gave me an angry glare which chilled the fight right out of me. "Since her actions in this time can affect the future, we have jurisdiction. Even here, now, I have the authority to require your help!"

"I do not recognize your authority, sir!" I said in a shaky voice. "Nor does the United States of America."

"We do," Learnéd said, simply, and the chill in his eyes said it was not wise to press the matter.

There was a tense silence as we regarded each other, then, "What...did she do, anyway?" I asked.

Learnéd thought on that before deciding to answer, and the look in his eyes was scary. "She was part of a conspiracy which made illegal 'retros'," he said at last. "Retroviruses are dangerous, especially the street doses. We recently broke her conspiracy and captured their laboratory, but she got away."

"Well, then, why all this sneaking around? Why don't you go over and arrest her?"

He shook his head. "It ney iss that simple. She had access to an array of retros, so there iss no telling what she can do. Aside from that 'ditie', she took four Smarts that we *know* of, plus a Red Eye, at least three Vipers, and who knows what else. And judging from how she mangled that man at the station, she took two, perhaps three Armstrongs."

"Um... I'm afraid you have lost me, sir."

"What that all means iss that she iss inhumanly strong, inhumanly fast, and inhumanly intelligent," Learnéd explained patiently. "If I try to storm her, she would tear the train to pieces."

"Good Lord! You can't be serious!"

Learnéd nodded grimly, and gestured with the wadded up pistol. "You have no idea."

"Well...why not simply shoot her?"

"That iss risky, too." He played with the remains of the pistol, examining it curiously. "Even if you manage to get a shot at her, your chances of dropping her with this are low. And you ney would live long enough to get a second shot." He laid the pistol aside and took a strange-looking weapon out of his jacket. It was all curves, molded to fit his hand, and in place of a muzzle, there was a round, flat mirror. He pointed it at me, and a thin line of faint red light appeared between the mirror and my chest. I looked down and saw a red dot glowing on my breastbone. The dot vanished.

41

"This delivers far more punch than anything from this period. But she iss deadly at close quarters, and I suspect she iss armed. With that many retros, she might survive long enough to retaliate. The one thing we ney want iss a fire fight down the length of this train."

The sight of that strange weapon convinced me at last. "Good Lord, man, what can you do? Should we send for the Army?"

Learnéd shook his head. "We ney must involve the local authorities, or come to the public attention in any way."

"Um? Why not?"

Learnéd mused on that. "I suppose you need to know," he said at last. "It involves what we call the Executioner's Paradox. Imagine if you go back in time and kill your earlier self. What would happen?"

I puzzled my way through that bizarre notion for some time before I began to grasp it, and to get truly scared.

"The big risk in any temporal operation iss changing the course of the future...your future, our present," Learnéd went on when he saw my features pale. "Calling attention to uss will cause many people to change their activities. Whenever our presence changes someone's activities, it puts strain on the course of the future. If too many unplanned changes take place, the effect could be catastrophic."

"What...do you mean, sir?"

"If I should suddenly disappear into thin air, that means the temporal line has been significantly altered. The future will have changed so that I ney came here. Since my coming here set that change in motion, the paradox could result in a temporal causality loop. The consequences are unpredictable: there might ney even *be* a future if the damage iss severe enough. We must act alone, and we must be discreet."

I was completely lost, but what little I grasped of that bizarre explanation was unnerving. "But...how can she move through time? And why come here, er, now?"

Learnéd gave me another forbidding frown, then decided to answer. "Ass to why, it ney iss easy for one to hide in our day. Once a person iss identified ass a criminal, finding them iss inevitable. We were pursuing her, and she took the only escape she could find. Ass to how, I ney am at liberty to discuss that."

"Is there any hope for you, sir?"

Learnéd nodded. "My gestalt has been notified, but we are scattered across this continent searching for her. It will take days before any of them can rendezvous. Until then, we must avoid detection and observe."

"But how can..."

"Our strategy iss to wait until we reach SaFrisko, where my gestalt can corner her in some safe place and move against her in force with proper technical support."

I was flabbergasted by this bombardment. "Well...you have my sympathy, sir, but I don't see how I can be of any help. She is far more than I can handle."

"You must be careful, but if you do your part properly, she ney will suspect."

"I'm not sure how much more of her attention I can endure."

"She will drain you empty." This future copper was no harbinger of good cheer, that was certain. "Ney doubt she will ruin you, if she ney kills you, citizen."

"A very real danger, if my experience thus far is any sample. Is it proper to place a hapless civilian in harm's way like this?"

Learnéd glared at me with growing impatience. "Citizens must serve the Movement even at risk of their lives. It iss the same in your time, ney?"

Put it that way, he had a point. I saw far too many young lives snuffed out for the good of the politicians in the Civil War. But this was not my fight, and I wasn't sure if I was more afraid of him or her. "Well I for one see no reason why I should put my life in jeopardy when it's your job to deal with these things," I said, petulantly. "For that matter, I don't see why I am involved at all."

"I tire of your petty whining!" Learnéd snapped. "You will serve the Movement ass directed, or be judged ass one of the Broken!"

The implications of that were plain and ugly. This fellow was the distilled essence of every copper and Pinkerton man I ever met, and there was something about him that said *'give me a reason, any reason, and I'll hand you your head'.* He was scary to look at, and I had enough experience with coppers in general to know that I was pushing my luck.

"I can't match your abilities, or hers. What good could I do?"

"All you need to do iss entertain her, and report on what she says. But you must be careful. She iss strong enough and fast enough to tear you limb from limb. You ney dare arouse her suspicion."

"I saw her in action. You're right: she *could* tear me limb from limb. What do I do if she turns on me?"

"Die ass a proper citizen should, and ney reveal anything about me or the gestalt's plans."

"You are no comfort, sir!"

"I ney am here for your comfort." Learnéd paused, as if debating whether to offer more explanations. "And there iss more," he said at last. "Smarts increase neural connectivity, improve the flow between synapses in the brain. One Smart will raise a person's intelligence by an average of twenty-five percent. She used at least four."

"So?"

"There iss a thin line between genius and insanity. We have mapped out the neural process, and it iss definitely there. A Smart makes one more intelligent, and more unstable. She took four of them, enough to double the average intelligence."

That hit me like a punch to the gut. "She must be stark, raving mad!"

Learnéd shook his head. "Ney, she iss too smart for that. But with her intelligence, she ney iss easy to fool. She will be unpredictable ass well. You must be careful at all times."

"Do you expect me to go against a madwoman with her power?"

"The Movement requires your services, citizen. You must take your chances ass anyone would."

"You're simply full of good cheer, aren't you?"

"I have been on worse assignments," Learnéd said bluntly. "It iss time for you to do your duty to the future, citizen. I ney will accept further excuses or arguments."

"Oh, for crying out loud!" I groaned. "Enough, already! We can straighten this out tomorrow. I am exhausted, and I would appreciate it if you leave so I can get some sleep."

Learnéd shook his head again. "I will remain here, where she ney iss likely to see me." He was clearly not willing to debate the question.

"Oh, do as you please and be damned, then. But at least let me open the berth."

"Very well." Learnéd stood and pressed against the door of the tiny compartment while I managed to pull the two seats together to form the lower berth, peeled out of my sweat soaked outer clothes, then collapsed into exhausted slumber.

\*\*\*\*\*

## "Day Two: Afternoon"

It was midday before I awoke from a dead sleep. I lay on my back and stared vacantly at the curved berth overhead, trying to ignore the many aches and pains, and to make some sense of last night. I still didn't understand why she invited me in, to say nothing of giving me such an unbelievable gallop. Only a doxy would make such a bold offer like she did, and I was certain she had never seen the inside of a cat house. She would command a stiff price if she chose, but money was never mentioned. I had no idea what she wanted; she must want something from me, if not money. Else why that amazing night?

Then there was my performance, which I still couldn't believe. The ache in my groin proved it happened despite all common sense, but where I found the desire, not to mention the endurance for it was beyond me. I stared at the berth above my head and let the gentle rocking of the car and the steady clatter of the wheels lull me as I wondered about her. The crisp air, chilled by the window glass, drifting across my face was strangely relaxing. It brought to mind the memory of her laying on a made down berth in the frosty moonlight. The thought of her haunted me. There were so many questions I wanted to ask, but we did precious little talking last night, most of which was a vague blur in my memory. These 'retros' Learnéd told me about—did that really happen?— must be a miracle drug.

I caught movement out of the corner of one eye, and turned my head a bit to watch the scenery flowing past the window.

"So, you live. I was beginning to wonder."

That snapped me out of my funk, and I rolled over with an aching grunt. Learnéd sat in a dining car chair, which pretty much filled the open space in the compartment, his arms crossed, regarding me with no favor, as usual.

"Are you still here?" So it did happen. I ran my palm over my sweaty face with a weary sigh. "I hoped this was all a bad dream."

"Including your time with her?" Learnéd asked, pointedly.

"I'll...get back to you on that." I struggled to sit up and swung my legs around so I was sitting on the berth. My arms were shaky, I was still short of breath, and I felt like I was kicked in the groin by an Army mule, then trampled by a whole wagon team of them.

"You are a disgrace," Learnéd grumbled. "Such loose behavior iss undignified."

"Well, I am not one to stand on dignity when a beautiful woman throws herself at me." My attempt at humor fell flat under Learnéd's disapproving frown. The fellow was a terminal hard case, and the look in his eyes was scary. "You don't like it, go arrest her and have done," I told him. "I never wanted to be part of your posse in the first place."

"You are ney the expert in these matters, so we will do this my way."

"I guess." I struggled to my feet, and tried faint-heartedly to make some order of my clothes.

"Did she say anything last night?"

I gave him a glare that was equal parts annoyance, pain, and hunger. "Nothing you'd find entertaining."

"I doubt if you would remember anyway, the way she ravaged you. I am surprised you survived at all."

"Huh?" Learnéd gestured at the shirt in my hand. The back of it was bloody, which brought the stinging itch in my back to mind. Then I noticed that the bedding was bloody too.

47

"Marking her territory, I see," I muttered.

"You are lucky she ney tore your spine out."

"Yeah...I guess so." The sight of those streaks of blood was sobering. With her strength, when she was taken by the fever of the moment... I turned back to him. "That's another danger you failed to warn me about!"

He gave me a contemptuous snort. "I ney have time to instruct you in every hazard you face. You must use your common sense and hope for the best."

"Well that's a fine how-do-you-do! Aren't you supposed to protect people instead of putting their lives at risk?"

He was on his feet, and confronted me eye to eye. "You ney tell me of my duty!" he snarled. "I have my duty to the Movement, ass do you! The Movement iss all that matters. You are expendable, if it comes to that."

"I don't think much of your attitude!"

"What you think ney concerns me!"

A hint of caution crept into my mind just then. There was no sense provoking him, and he was beyond reason, anyway. I knew best to pick my fights; this was one I couldn't win and didn't want to start, with his strength. "Oh, to hell with it," I grumbled, and went back to dressing myself. "I can think of worse ways to go."

"Ney doubt." He settled in his chair again, and watched coldly as I made ready.

*'Of all the arrogant, self-righteous bastards,'* I thought as I fought with my suspenders in a cold temper. It was bad enough to be put upon like this, but he clearly didn't care if I was hurt, or even killed. *'Give me some Prussian high-muckety-muck instead of this... policeman...any day.'* I was tempted right then to go straight to her compartment and warn her just to spite him.

It took some effort despite my temper, but I finally completed dressing, took my hat in hand, and reached for the door.

"Where are you going?"

"To the dining car. I need something to eat."

Learnéd looked me over suspiciously, then, "Very well. Bring food back with you."

"You can feed yourself, citizen."

Learnéd jumped to his feet, grabbed my arm with a painful grip, and shoved me against the wall. "Ney offend me, citizen Poole! You will show proper respect at all times!"

I was surprised and shook by his reaction. "What?"

"*You* are the citizen! You ney will use that tone to the Learnéd!"

"C-citizenship isn't what it used to be, I take it?"

"Ney!"

I tried to stare him down coolly, without much success. "If you break my arm, I won't be able to entertain her."

Learnéd fumed at me, his eyes burning with rage, and for a moment I thought he would attack me...but then his attention wavered. His face softened, his eyes drifted, and he stared at nothing as I wondered if I could fight him off and escape the compartment. After a few seconds, he came back from wherever his mind drifted off to, and released my arm. "I must remain here, where she ney might see me," he said in cold contempt. "You will bring food, especially carbohydrates. Bring large quantities."

"You say so." I was shaken by Learnéd's unexpected violent outburst, and in no shape to argue the matter.

"And if there iss a doctor on this train, have your back looked at," he said as I left. "You must remain fit to serve the Movement."

"What? And call attention to myself?"

§

A quick wash with a cold towel in the restroom next to my compartment helped me feel a bit more human. I needed it. My hands were shaking, and my wind was up from how close I came to him turning on me. This deal was getting worse by the minute. Not only was I dragooned into a fight I had no interest in, and caught between two people who were way out of my class, but she was unstable, and Learnéd was proving to be foul-tempered and didn't give a rat's ass for who got hurt. What he did with that pistol last night scared me juiceless. I shuddered to think of what he could do to me in a rage.

The mirror confirmed what he said: she did all but claw my spine out, which didn't help my mood in the least. I was in as much danger from her passion as I was from his temper, and it looked like there wasn't a damned thing I could do against either of them. I longed for my Colt, and wondered idly if I might buy another one on the train. In the back of my mind, I began to wonder what my chances were of getting out of this mess alive.

I finished my toilet, and thought about going back to the compartment for a fresh shirt, but it didn't seem wise to dare Learnéd's anger again. I decided to lay low in the lounge car, and give him a chance to calm down. But first I needed something to eat. The scratches weren't bleeding, so I rinsed the blood stains out, then put my shirt on damp and headed for the dining car.

§

She was sitting at the same table as yesterday, at the far end of the car next to the kitchen, when I came staggering in. The lunchtime rush was past, and the crowd was thinning out to a few lingerers like us. Her waiter hovered nearby watching her with a bemused look as she worked her way relentlessly through a large steak. She gave me a warm smile when she saw me. "Good afternoon, Nathaniel. I trust you slept well?"

"Yes, I did, thank you," I said, cautiously.

"Thank me for what?" Her face lit up with an impish chuckle. "For asking about you, or for a good night's sleep?"

I grinned sheepishly in spite of myself. "For both."

"Come, please join me. I enjoy your company, and you must be starving." She waved at the opposite side of the table, and took another bite of her steak as I slid hesitantly into the chair. "I ney have had buffalo meat. It iss tasty, but we ney have it where I come from."

I caught the look in her eyes: for all her friendly warmth, she was wary, even frightened. She was different than yesterday, and something in the back of my mind was sounding alarms. The imperious noblewoman was gone, together with the wanton she-beast. In their place was someone warm and open and rather coquettish—and scared. Something was wrong here. I decided to play it close to the chest until I understood the game. "Well, you don't have buffalo over in Europe, so that's not surprising."

She eyed me curiously, then gave me a nod and a knowing smile. "So, where in Europe do you think I am from, Nathaniel?"

50

That put me on the spot, and I thought fast to talk my way out of it. "I'm guessing Prussia, maybe Poland? It's the accent."

"You picked up on that fast. I am impressed." Her voice was relaxed and intimate, while her eyes were cold and afraid, and searched the room warily. She must be worried about Learnéd; easy to understand if his story was true.

"All I know is that you are a mysterious lady from some far away country." If she wanted to use that as cover, I would oblige. I didn't want to be caught between the two of them to begin with, so I would watch my tongue until I saw a way to get myself out of this. "I am curious about why you're here, though."

She frowned at that and eyed me suspiciously, then took a small object out of her pouch, and tilted it up and down in front of me almost as if she was studying me with it. "You should have a steak, or perhaps two." she said lightly while she went through this mysterious ritual. "It will help you rebuild your strength. You ney want to disappoint me, do you?" She quit waving the object and studied it, which seemed to mollify her, then set it next to her plate, and attacked her meal again.

What was that little thing? I studied it out of the corner of one eye as I pretended to read the menu. It was about an inch by two, with a dull silver case and some small buttons. I'd never seen the like. I couldn't imagine what purpose it served, and the make of it was utterly alien. She noticed my curiosity, discreetly palmed the object, and slid it back into her pouch.

The waiter returned with another large plate of meat and a wicker bowl of rolls. She snatched one of them and downed it in four bites, then attacked the new steak relentlessly while the bemused waiter watched. She not only fought like a street brawler, she ate like one, too.

"Would you care for something, sir?" the waiter asked at last.

That snapped me out of my distraction. "Um...yes, I'll have a steak, please." In truth, I was famished.

"You could be a gentleman, and order a bottle of wine," she said with a warm smile and cold eyes.

"Um, yes, that too." The waiter nodded and withdrew.

§

We went on like that all through lunch.  She evaded my questions and kept up a steady chatter of small talk while questioning me discreetly in turn.  It was no polite dinner conversation between friends: we probed and maneuvered around each other in a careful dance, each trying to unmask the other.  I made precious little headway in that, as she was skilled at evading my questions, and she managed to get a lot out of me in turn with her disarming charm.  It wasn't a casual conversation at all, but somehow it didn't seem hostile, either.  She wanted something again, and was determined to learn more about me, about my past.  I had no idea why.  I was sure there was some hidden reason, but I couldn't see where this was going.

She was interested in my family in particular, and questioned me about them at length.  "And you ney have anyone back in Illinois?" she asked during her third steak.

"No.  My folks are dead.  My two brothers died in the war.  There's no one."  I couldn't see why we were on this; it was not a happy subject.

"Ney anyone?  Ney children?"

I shook my head.  "I've never married."

She seemed strangely relieved at that, but then she considered for a bit, and asked, "But ass manly ass you are, you must attract women.  Ney have you...fathered...any by accident?"

Why would she bring *that* up, I wondered?  "None that I know of."  I was too surprised to be offended at such a liberty.  "I've been cautious about that, since I don't want to come down with a dose of the French Malady."

She seemed confused for a moment, but covered it quickly.  "That iss good of you, Nathaniel.  Very responsible."

A bizarre notion struck me: could she be a distant descendent of mine?  Was I bedding my who-knows-how-many-times-great granddaughter?  That was a disturbing thought, as it would be for any decent man, but it made as much sense as anything.  But that seemed unlikely.  We were nothing alike in looks or personality, and if she knew we were related I was sure she would not have bedded me.  And the odds on such a chance meeting must be beyond reckoning.  I forced that thought out of my mind.

Our game of hide-and-seek continued as we ate. She knew a lot about me over all, and was trying to fill in as many details as she could. That began to worry me after a while: why did she know so much about someone from the distant past? And why was she so interested in the details of my life? Did she come here seeking my help to escape the law of her time? That didn't make sense; what could I do for her? She must know I was defenseless against their retros. For that matter, I couldn't see what good I could do Learnéd, or why he kept me so close under his thumb.

I couldn't see rhyme nor reason for their interest in me, but I knew it couldn't be good. I needed to know a heck of a lot more if I was to figure a way out of this. I needed to know why they were here instead of there, and why I seemed so important to them. With my luck, I knew I wouldn't like the answers.

§

After two hours of hard eating and four steaks that I *knew* of, she set her fork and knife aside with a contented sigh.

"How do you do that?" I asked. As hungry as I was, I tapered off in my second helping long ago.

She gave me that impish grin. "A good night's exercise gives one a hearty appetite, ney?" It seemed she wasn't about to change.

The dining car was empty by then, and the waiters were cleaning the place and preparing for the dinner rush. It was well into the afternoon, and the westering sun painted the prairie with faded reds and grays. The window frame was dusted with snow, and the ground along the track showed dirty white among the withered clumps of grass. Bleak and lonely: like my mood.

She mopped her chin daintily with a napkin, then gave me a calculating look. "I think I will retire for a while. Will you be kind enough to escort me to my compartment, Nathaniel?"

"Um...yes, certainly."

I wasn't thrilled. It looked like she wanted another romp, and *where* I would find the strength for it I couldn't imagine. She could get me to perform soon enough; I felt my manly tension growing in the pit of my stomach just thinking about it. But I didn't think I would last long, as sore as I was, and I worried about how she might react if I failed after a short time.

Nothing I could do about it. I stood and offered her my hand, and helped her to her feet. As we walked down the narrow aisle past the kitchen, I noticed her hand was tucked under the flap of her pouch again.

§

The train was rolling along at a good forty miles per hour, which sent a blustery gale of dust and smoke over the open platforms between the cars. The bleak, featureless prairie rolled past without any sign of civilization other than the track itself and the row of telegraph poles marching along side. The temperature was dropping, but at least we had left the rain behind. I grabbed my hat with one hand and forced the door shut with the other, then clung to the handrail as I studied the open gap between the platforms. The handrails were icy, and I didn't trust the footing either. After a moment's hesitation, I stepped carefully across and caught myself on the opposite handrails, then turned and offered my hand to her. She stepped lightly across the gap, then blocked the door when I tried to open it.

"Who iss he, Nathaniel?"

That caught me off guard. "Who?"

"The man in your compartment. Who iss he?" The coquette was gone, replaced by deadly earnest.

I tried not to show my alarm that she knew my unwilling secret. This was not someone to trifle with, and there was no telling how she would react to Learnéd. "I don't..."

She grabbed my lapels with one hand and lifted me effortlessly, holding me suspended at arm's length as I struggled in panic. "Nathaniel," she said in a level voice as if she was talking to a child. "This iss important. Talk to me, Nathaniel. Who iss the man in your compartment?"

I struggled helplessly in her grip, clutching her extended arm with both hands, thrashing and kicking, heart racing.

"Nathaniel?"

"He's..." I faltered, realizing I just gave myself away. "...he's a copper..."

"Ass I expected," she said at last. Her eyes narrowed on me. "What did he tell you about me?"

"I...n-nothing..."

She turned and leaned out over the side of the platform, dangling me helplessly at arm's length over the track whipping past below. My derby blew off, and she snatched it out of mid-air as it flew past. "Nathaniel, what did he tell you about me?" Her voice was as cool as her icy blue eyes.

"...he...you're...a criminal...from the future..."

She nodded thoughtfully. "Typical. They actually believe their lies." She set me gently on the platform next to her, and steadied me as I clung in terror to the handrail. "Did he tell you his name, Nathaniel?"

"Uh..." I was shaken by my close brush with death, and by how easily this woman—this monster—manhandled me. "...he...said his name was...Learnéd."

She nodded at that. "Some of their best." Her voice was tight with tension. "You should feel honored, Nathaniel. The Learnéd are among their elite."

"Elite?" I wasn't too focussed after that ordeal. "Of what?"

"The Pure Of Thought: the secret police." *That* got my attention. "I ney am a criminal, Nathaniel, regardless of what he told you," she said. "I am a revolutionary."

If I thought I was shaken by my brush with death, her words proved me wrong. I stared at her stupidly for a long moment as my innards turned to liquid once more. "...ah...r-revolutionary?" I was at a loss as I tried to collect my wits and get a handle on this bit of news. "Then...you really are from the future?"

"Yes. I came here on a mission, but the Learnéd are after me. I need your help, Nathaniel."

"*My* help?"

"I know it ney iss easy to understand, Nathaniel," she said, earnestly. "There iss so much to explain..."

The door to the next car opened abruptly, and the savage blow she threw at Conductor Doggett's throat was just a blur. As fast as she struck, her incredible reflexes stopped her with inches to spare, and she stood staring at him, wire tense and shaking. Doggett halted in wide-eyed alarm, then muttered, "Pardon me," and eased past us across and into the next car.

"We ney can talk here," she said once he was gone. "Nathaniel, *please* trust me. There iss more going on here than you know."

"*Trust* you?" She was on a hair-trigger edge, and her abortive attack on Doggett scared me almost as much as it did him.

"Please, Nathaniel. I am sorry I had to be rough with you, but the danger to uss both iss great. Come to my compartment this evening, and I will explain everything." There was genuine fear in her eyes. "And *whatever* you do, ney give him a hint of what I have told you. He will kill you out of hand if he decides you ney are of any further use to him."

*****

## "Day Two: Afternoon And Evening"

I made it back to my compartment after a stop in the washroom to compose myself. Learnéd was right where I left him: sitting in his chair, arms folded, waiting patiently for something to happen. "You ney brought food ass you were told," he accused me when I entered. His temper hadn't improved while I was gone.

"Huh?" I stared at him in confusion for a moment. "Oh. Sorry." Like I don't have enough on my mind. I did an about-face, and called Samuel.

Samuel hesitated when he saw Learnéd. "Yassuh, what can ah do fo' you?" he asked doubtfully.

"I need you to run to the diner and bring back a plate of food." I looked pointedly at Learnéd, but he made no effort to offer payment, so I finally dug a couple dollars out of my pocket.

"Suh?" Samuel eyed Learnéd uneasily.

"Bring lots of food, whatever they have," Learnéd said.

"Yassah." He gave me a dubious look, and left.

Learnéd rounded on me as soon as he was gone. "Where have you been all this time?"

"With her, at lunch. I've never seen anyone pack it away like she can."

That mollified him a bit. "There iss that." Then he gave me a sharp look. "What did you talk about?"

"Mostly small talk."

"It iss important that you learn whatever you can about her plans. Ney waste time with small talking."

"We talked about a lot of things. She wanted to know how long this journey will take, and what San Francisco is like." It didn't seem like a good idea to mention her interest in me.

"That ney iss enough," he said, angrily. "You must question her more. Be thorough, and stay on subject."

"I'm trying, but she keeps sluffing me off. I can't press her without arousing her suspicion."

Samuel returned with a plate heaped with bread, cold ham, and green beans, which Learnéd accepted with no favor. "This will do," he said after Samuel left. "But ney forget next time."

By that point, I was so frazzled that all I could do was hang my jacket on one of the hooks, plop down on the lower berth, pull the cover up, and stare out the window.

This was one fine hell of a fix! I had no idea of which way to jump. Normally I should help the authorities to apprehend a dangerous revolutionary...but if Learnéd was any example, then a little revolution might be a good thing, as Thomas Jefferson famously said. The hell of it was that I had nothing to guide me— no newspaper accounts, no announcements from Washington, not even rumors or gossip. I was completely in the dark.

The afternoon sun was sinking ahead of us through thinning clouds. The passing prairie was dusted here and there with snow tinted deep orange by the wain light and dull mauve by the shadows. It was bleak and cold and beautiful in its own way, and far from any sign of civilization. A herd of buffalo came into view, stretching to the horizon where they were lost in a kicked up haze of their own making.

I watched the prairie roll by, and tried to get a handle on this mess. What was their future like, anyway? All I had was Learnéd's begrudging account of a pursued criminal, and that criminal's claim to be a revolutionary, which was damn-all to go on. But I had an ugly feeling about Learnéd. The guy was inhuman, cold as ice, filled with arrogance and contempt. I couldn't presume anything.

For that matter, aside from her extraordinary strength and fighting skills, she hardly seemed the revolutionary type. And compared to Learnéd, her abilities didn't seem so extraordinary after all. What must her world be like if she would raise arms against it? The few answers thus far confused me as much as my ignorance did before.

Something outside distracted me: a crude sod hut with a smoking chimney made of piled stones. The train was slowing. There was another hut, then a group of conical Indian tents. A few Indians sat wrapped in blankets around a fire, or trudged dispiritedly back and forth. The train slowed more, and finally stopped near a wooden stockade. There were a few cavalrymen busy with various chores, and a few rough civilians around a board-sided tent which served as the local emporium. In the distance, a wagon filled to overflowing with buffalo pelts made its unsteady way across the prairie toward a box car set on a siding. The train stopped at this forlorn outpost for only a moment to drop off some mail perhaps, and we were moving again.

"You must go to the dining car," Learnéd demanded.

"Hmmm?" That shook me out of a half-sleep, and I turned to him in confusion. "Diner already?" Several empty dishes and a couple of wicker baskets used for rolls were piled under his chair. I must have dozed off, and he ordered more food while I slept. "How do you manage to eat so much, anyway?"

He gave me an annoyed look. "Retros accelerate the metabolism, so we need more intake."

"I...see." I struggled to my feet, retrieved my jacket, and gingerly worked my way around him to the door. Out in the corridor, I hesitated, wondering what to do. I didn't know enough to judge either way, or to see why I should help either side, but instinct had me leaning in her favor. She didn't seem like a revolutionary, or what I imagined a revolutionary to be, at least. I wondered how she must feel: trapped in the distant past with no one to turn to, stalked by an inhuman copper. It was hardly surprising if she was desperate. At least she promised explanations, which I needed badly. But for now I needed to get away from both of them, and try to put it all together.

59

I stopped in the diner briefly to tell them to send food to my compartment. It was still early for dinner, although the room was partly filled with people gossiping and playing cards. She wasn't there, but her favorite table—the single table at the end by the kitchen entrance—was not being used. The furtive glances and whispers told me how superstitious these people already were about her. I wasn't hungry right then, and didn't want to put up with their cattiness, so I headed for the lounge car.

§

The lounge car was busy with cigar smoke, card games, and loud talk a-plenty. I ordered a beer, and settled in one of the seats at the rear of the car. The track sliding away behind us was hypnotic, and my fatigue soon had me nodding off. I shook myself awake for the umpteenth time, and sighed in weary frustration as I wondered what to do. The train made a brief stop for water at another hardscrabble settlement, and Doggett interrupted my second beer shortly thereafter.

"Gentlemen, may I have your attention, please?" he announced from in front of the bar. "We have received word from up the line that Donner Pass is being hit by a heavy blizzard." That evoked an uncomfortable stir among the passengers. None of us was happy at the thought of facing a storm in the Sierra Nevadas.

Doggett must have expected that. "It is possible that we may be delayed, but I can assure you that every effort will be made to get us through to San Francisco. The company has a steam plow working around the clock to keep the track clear."

"Likely get stuck up there," someone said. Doggett confronted him, and the stranger added, "My pappy and me was with the Donner party back in '47. I been over that pass a dozen times, man and boy, and its a mean ol' place in winter, especial when the big snow comes down."

"Well I can assure you, sir, that we will do well enough to suit your 'pappy'," Doggett lectured him. "We are in a modern steam train, not covered wagons. If we do get stuck, we have plenty of food on board, and the railroad will send a relief train at once."

"You say so," the man muttered.

§

She was at her usual table near the kitchen when I returned to the dining car. The table was piled with the remains of two roast chickens, and she was busily attacking the third. She gave me a wane smile when I came in.

"Hello, Nathaniel," she said, somberly. "I am pleased to see you. Are you feeling well?"

"I survived a night with you, so I doubt anything can kill me now," I said coolly.

Her response was a nervous chuckle. "One can hope, since we have several more nights ahead of uss." Then she offered me a solemn look. "I am sorry if I was abrupt with you earlier, please ney hold it against me."

"No harm was done." I slid into the seat opposite her, and decided to sound her out. I was caught up in something huge, and I urgently needed to know more: my life depended on it. "I hope we could spend some time chatting. There is so much about you that I'd like to know."

She studied me for a moment. "I understand your curiosity; I must be quite a puzzle to you, ney?"

"You could say that."

She set her fork aside, picked up that small object she was fiddling with earlier, and ran it up and down in front of me. Something about it displeased her. She eyed me cautiously, then set the device aside, took a pencil and note pad out of her pouch, and began writing.

"Unfortunately, we seem too preoccupied to chat when we are together," she said as she wrote. "I am sure you have many questions to ask, and I will be happy to answer them when we find the time. This evening, perhaps?"

"I wouldn't know where to begin." I was puzzled over her actions, and with her the unknown was worrisome, so I decided to play it close.

"Do you think we can continue to see each other until we reach SaFrisko, Nathaniel? I know I ask a lot from you, and I appreciate your patience." She paused for a moment and gave me a look which said that was more than an invitation; she was sounding me out to see if she could depend on me.

61

"I'll have to see how I feel tomorrow," I muttered. "You put a strain on a fellow." Something was sounding alarms in the back of my mind again. The coquette had joined her two sisters: in her place was someone cool and focussed, and I didn't know what to make of that thing she kept waving at me. She finished her scribbling, and turned the note around so I could read it:

HE HAS PLACED A LISTENING DEVICE ON YOU. NEY SAY ANYTHING YOU NEY WISH HIM TO HEAR.

"Um..." I glanced from the note to her, trying to grasp the idea of a 'listening device', and to come up with something innocuous to say. "You see...I'm not sure if I'm the man for you." I looked her in the eye. "Not that I don't appreciate your interest, it's...I'm not sure I have the...enthusiasm...for the rest of our journey."

She nodded, knowingly. "Rest assured, Nathaniel, this evening I will entertain you to your heart's desire, which should improve your 'enthusiasm'." The look behind those words said there was a lot more than a carefully improvised act.

"Well, I hope my *enthusiasm* won't get the better of me."

"Have faith in yourself, Nathaniel." She gave me a calculating look as she tucked the note away in her pouch. "Tonight will be interesting, which brings to mind that you should eat. You need your strength for later."

§

The train rolled into Cheyenne early in the evening of that second day, and that's where it stopped. I was in the lounge car again, digesting two buffalo steaks and drowning my sorrows in a cold beer, when Conductor Doggett turned up with more bad news. I was starting to get really annoyed by that pompous little man.

Doggett took station in front of the bar, and addressed the crowd. "Gentlemen, your attention please! We have received word that Donner Pass has been closed due to the blizzard, and that it will be another twenty-four hours at a minimum before it can be reopened."

That produced a round of groans and muffled cursing.

"Due to the backed up traffic, we will be stopped here at Cheyenne until tomorrow." Another round of dismay; Doggett turned prissy at his reception. "Rest assured this is only a prudent precaution. We can replenish our food stocks while we wait, and this should be no more than a minor inconvenience."

"Hell of a way to run a railroad," someone grumbled once he was gone.

I couldn't blame them. I wasn't thrilled to be stuck on this train for another day, especially in the mess I was in, but it was inevitable. Once the winter storms came down, getting across Donner Pass could take days as they laboriously dug the track out for each passing train. That was just what I needed: to be here for who knows how long, caught between the two of them with no idea of what was what. The annoyance was too much; I grabbed my coat and headed for the station to try to walk off some of my frustration.

§

Cheyenne's station was another ramshackle affair like Omaha, although the foundations for a large brick station were visible in the gloom nearby. Around them, a substantial railroad yard was clogged with rolling stock, and beyond that was another rude frontier settlement of board houses and dirt streets. The nearby roundhouse was hidden in a fog bank of wood smoke and steam from all the locomotives waiting.

The 'Overland' seemed like it was rooted there for all eternity. The locomotive was gone, its place taken by a steam line from the roundhouse. Two car toads, bundled in so many layers that they seemed almost round, were tinkering with the diner's brake gear by the sputtering red light of a fusee, while one of the kitchen staff leaned on the Dutch service door watching them. Aside from that and a few passengers taking the air, the place was forlorn and empty.

I paced back and forth on the station grounds, rubbing my hands together and shivering from the cold as I tried to walk my tension and frustration off. The worst agony was not knowing what the hell to think. I instinctively felt that I couldn't trust Learnéd or whatever he might say about the future. At the same time, I didn't know what to make of her—wearingly amorous, mercurial, inhumanly strong, self-confessed revolutionary. I couldn't really know what to do—whether to side with him, or her, or simply jump off the train.

The last of the twilight faded, and the cold was getting to me. "God, what a mess," I grumbled as I headed back to the train.

§

"What does she talk about when you two are together?" Learnéd demanded when I returned to the compartment.

"Not much," I said, wearily. "Mostly small talk. I've tried pumping her like you said, but she doesn't rise to the bait."

Learnéd considered that, then, "Good. Anything you can learn iss important. But be careful; she iss ney easy to fool, and you saw how she reacts to danger."

"Yeah." I sat on the berth and tried not to show my nervousness.

"You will go to her again tonight." That wasn't a question.

I decided I wasn't so eager. "I don't know. She wears on a fellow."

Learnéd frowned. "This iss important. Your discomfort ney matters next to your duty."

"My duty, huh?" My sigh of exasperation was all too genuine. "It's always duty with you, isn't it? Don't you ever relax and have some fun?"

"Ney when I am chasing heretics," he snapped. "Ney do you when the Movement calls on you to serve."

I was careful not to react to that word 'heretics', but it caught my attention. Was Learnéd's Movement some sort of religion? I knew there was a lot more going on here than he let on, and that newest clue didn't sound good.

"You must question her more," Learnéd insisted. "But be careful ney to arouse her suspicions. Remember what I said earlier; we ney want a fire fight on this train."

"Lord, no," I said, fervently, as I rose to my feet. "All right, I'll take another one for the team." All of a sudden, I needed to get out of there, and find some quiet corner away from both of them.

§

I went to ground in the dining car, which was closed for the night. The place was dark and empty, free of distractions. I collapsed at her table with a sigh and rested my aching head in my hands. The car was eerily quiet without the subdued click-clack of the wheels, and I missed the gentle swaying as it rolled along the track. It seemed forlorn, somehow. I stared at nothing while my mind raced.

'Heretics,' the man said. And then there was this 'Movement'. That did sound like some sort of religion...a fanatical religion which tolerated no deviation from Scripture. Was the world of the future ruled by a ruthless theocracy?

The memory of old John Brown, the rabid Abolitionist, came to mind. John Brown: the crazed stump preacher who touted Sharps rifles as a 'moral force' in the slavery debate, and who tried to stir up a slave revolt in Virginia before the war. I shuddered at that memory. If Brown's mad dream of God's will had been made real, the slaughter would have been unspeakable. What was the future like if such insanity was the state politic?

Now more than ever, I needed answers. It was getting late, and she was expecting me. As much as I was reluctant to trust her, she was willing to give them.

§

She was fully dressed when she answered my hesitant knock at her door, and she carried another of the strange pistols Learnéd showed me. Her panicky edge brought back the memory of Doggett's near-fatal run-in earlier.

"Well, hello, Nathaniel," she welcomed me with her most predatory purr. "I was beginning to wonder if you would come." She gestured to me to be wary as I entered her compartment.

"I...um...I wasn't sure if I felt up to it."

That got a wicked chuckle that was completely at odds with her tension. "Well, I am sure I can make you feel better," she said in that sultry tone which pulled my chain. She scanned the hall quickly, then slid the door shut, pulled my jacket off, and threw it on the bed. "Why iss the train ney moving?" she asked as she produced the small box she used in the dining car earlier, and ran it up and down me.

"Um...the mountains up ahead are being hit by blizzards. Things are backed up, but it's nothing to worry about."

She gave me a nervous, frustrated look. "How long will we be delayed?" She knelt down to search my trouser inseams with the device.

"I...ah...guess another day."

"Such terrible weather," she sighed. She finished searching my trousers, and I helped her to her feet. "You look well, Nathaniel." She held the object up to bring it to my attention, and gestured for silence.

"Um...well, that's good to know."

She picked up my jacket, and ran the small object up and down, searching for something while we made awkward small talk. Finally she showed me a spot in the seam of the lapel, and a tiny black speck imbedded in the fabric. I would have thought it nothing but a bit of dirt or a cinder, but she pointed her box at it, and a red light glowed.

"Mmmmmmm," she purred as I studied the device in dismay. "I see you are beginning to understand my needs." She laid the jacket carefully on the berth and pocketed the small object. It was bizarre: her voice was the predatory seductress while her actions were those of a hunted animal, and the tension in her eyes said she was ready to kill. She picked up a slightly larger box with an array of tiny buttons on one side, gestured urgently for silence, and pressed one of the buttons.

"Do you like what you see?" Her voice came from the box.

"Um...yes," my voice answered, hesitantly.

I stared at the tiny box, dumbfounded.

"Touch me, Nathaniel."

I looked at her in amazement, but she gestured for silence again.

"Mmmmmmm, yes, that iss right, Nathaniel."

I listened in disbelief as her voice and mine made passionate love from the bowels of that small box while she checked the hall, weapon at the ready, then gestured for me to follow.

"Oooohhhhhh!" the box moaned.

§

The lounge car was empty and dark, the bar closed. Doggett and the brakeman were sitting at a table near the door playing cards. The brakeman gave us no more than a passing glance when we came in, while Doggett glared at her, but said nothing. I lead her down car to the far end near the door to the rear platform. The car was dimly lit by the red glow of the brakeman's lantern, but the shadows at that end of the car gave us some concealment.

"What is going on here?" I demanded in a hushed voice. "What is this about you coming from the future?"

"It iss true, Nathaniel. We are ruled by a ruthless totalitarian state. I am part of the resistance. I was sent here on a mission, but the Learnéd have located me. Now I can only hope to escape."

"Here? In the past? Why here?"

She glanced around nervously. "The Movement iss so effective that we have to operate in our past where they ney arc all-powerful."

"But...how? How did you get here?"

She seemed confused. "I ney understand such things, Nathaniel. We have a machine. How it works, I ney know."

There were other urgent matters at hand. "So he plans to arrest you and take you back to the future?"

She shuddered. "The Pure Of Thought have passed Judgment on me. If they capture me, I ney will see the future again."

"They can pass judgment on people? What about a trial?"

She gave me an odd look. "They are the law, Nathaniel."

That wasn't good, but there was nothing I could do about it. "How did you know he was here?"

"I have an instrument to detect the microwave burst of a temporal displacement. Microwaves ney are used now, and we ney have other missions going, so I knew they were here to hunt me."

That made no sense, not that it mattered. "So why did he decide to pick on me? What does he want?"

She hesitated, and gave me a guilty look. "I used you ass bait, Nathaniel," she said, softly. "I drew you to his attention so he would go to ground in your compartment. He will remain out of sight and monitor me through you, which will give me time to find a way to escape."

"I don't appreciate being Shanghaied into your fights," I grumbled. "Especially seeing how outclassed I am."

"I am sorry, Nathaniel." She took my hand and gave me an imploring look. "I did what I must to survive. You ney would begrudge me that, would you?"

"Well...I guess not." I felt guilty in spite of myself. "But how could you be so sure this would help?"

"There iss one good thing about Secret Police anywhen: they think everyone iss ass mentally lock-stepped ass they are. Stalking their prey through proxies iss standard procedure for the Pure Of Thought. Ass long ass things go smoothly, he will use you ass his shadow while he waits for the moment to strike."

"Wonderful."

"Iss he alone, Nathaniel?"

I hesitated for a fleeting second, and wondered if I should back away and do my 'duty' as Learnéd demanded. The future wasn't my concern, and I didn't want to get on the bad side of that future's lawmen. But right then she wasn't the imperious temptress, or the wanton hussy, or the coquette, or the cool professional. Right then she was lost and afraid and vulnerable. And the shadow of John Brown hovered, unseen, in the background.

I took the first step without willing it. "He's...alone as far as I know. But he said something about a gestalt. He's waiting for them to join him."

She nodded thoughtfully. "Standard procedure. They initiated a wide search to get a lead on me. Thankfully, that gives uss a chance since he iss alone for now."

"What? There are more of them running around in this time?"

"Yes. They work ass a hunter-killer team."

"Wonderful. How much worse can this get?"

"It can get much worse, Nathaniel," she assured me, solemnly. "A gestalt iss a formidable enemy, far more than so many men. They are genetically engineered clones."

"Um...clones?"

She hesitated, with a look like someone about to explain the birds and the bees to a ten year old. "They are exact genetic copies, duplicates stamped out from a specially prepared gene

68

sequence," she said at last. "They are identical in every way, and specifically engineered for their role. Their minds are altered to make them politically reliable, and they are loaded with retros." She was worried, as well she should be if that gibberish was as bad as it sounded. "One special advantage of clones iss that they are telepaths. That iss how he was able to summon his gestalt. It also gives them a deadly tactical advantage in combat, since they move and think ass one."

I couldn't understand half of what she said, but it sounded bad. "How many of them are there?"

"The usual gestalt iss nine, although we *think* the Learnéd lost one last year—my time. Ass to how many we will face, hopefully there ney will be more than two or three of them. More than that, and we ney have a chance."

"And what's this 'we'?" I demanded, peevishly. "I never wanted to get caught up in this to begin with."

"Nathaniel, I understand if you ney want to help me," she pleaded with me. "My mission has been interrupted. All I can do now iss try to survive, to escape. This ney iss your fight, but I need your help...if you will give it."

That put me in a bind. As much as I disliked the idea of rebellion, I didn't care for Learnéd and the world she described. And she seemed very much alone and afraid, as I would be in this situation. Maybe it was an act, like her arrogant noblewoman, but she was in real trouble, and however they did things in her time, the world I was raised in said I should come to her aid.

"But what good can I do? Either of you is far more than I can handle."

Her face brightened with hope. "You can keep him occupied, Nathaniel. He uses you to stalk me. Ass long ass he believes you are useful to him, he ney will move against me for now."

"But how long can we keep this charade up?"

"Ass long ass we must, Nathaniel. He ney will move until he has more of his gestalt on hand. The earliest they can join him would be in SaFrisko."

"And what happens when we reach San Francisco? What happens to you?"

She shrugged fatalistically. "If I can elude them, I will have a chance to reach safety. If ney, they will kill me..." She studied my face closely. "...and probably you."

"Why kill me? I'm supposed to be helping them."

"Perhaps they will think you are tainted by associating with me; perhaps they will think you know too much. The Pure Of Thought are quick to declare Judgment, and ney merciful with those they declare Judgment on. Killing iss all too natural for them."

I was not thrilled by the thought of three more days and nights bearding the lion in his den. "What happens if he figures it out?"

She sighed. "Hope ney it happens, Nathaniel." She glanced at a small watch strapped to her wrist. "We must get back. My recorder iss only good for an hour."

"What is that thing? That talking box of yours?"

"It iss a telephone...like your telegraph, but it sends sounds. It was made in the early Twenty-first Century, and has a recorder for messages." She smiled impishly. "You are supposed to be with me in my compartment. Let us ney keep him in suspense."

§

Later, in her compartment, I paused to catch my breath after one strenuous bout, and lay there wondering about her. Her face was faintly lit by the moonlight, glistening with sweat, and her eyes glowed with pleasure. The warmth of her body and the chill off the window set my skin tingling. Tired as I was, my need burned in me so that it was hard to think. Whether it was the tight knot of fear in my gut, or the Aphrodite Learnéd told me of, her scent was devastating.

"Iss something wrong, Nathaniel?"

I sighed. "Well...no. It's just, I find this all so hard to understand." I remembered to be careful since Learnéd was listening, which annoyed me no end. At least he would think I was pumping her for information. "I mean, you're so different, so mysterious. I don't know what to think."

Truth is I didn't know what to make of her. She seemed dangerously erratic, seeing how things were. What was she was really like under all the masks she wore? I could understand a hunted revolutionary not showing her true face to the world, but it was hard to understand her erratic moods, or make sense of her actions. It wasn't wise to stand out or let her guard down with Learnéd a few hundred feet away, but she did, with abandon. I was never quite sure which way to jump around her. I wondered if she truly was sane or not.

She must have felt my uncertainty. "Nathaniel, what is there to understand?" She ran her fingers through my sweaty hair. "I am only human. I live my life ass best I can, and I try to do the right things. The world ney iss perfect, and ney am I. At times, we are battered by the winds and waves of life. You should take each day one at a time, and trust your feelings."

"Carpe Deum, eh?" In a way, her words were a relief. Evasive as they were, she sounded human for once. I nuzzled her cheek. "Seize the day. Eat, drink, and be merry, for tomorrow we..."

She pressed her fingers against my lips. "Ney worry about tomorrow, Nathaniel," she said, softly. Then, in her lecherous growl, she added, "Worry about tonight. I am aroused, and the window iss right here." She gave me a passionate kiss and ran her hands down my back, which ignited my fire once again, to my amazement. "You ney want me to feel...unsatisfied."

*****

# "Day Three: Mid Day"

*...He was lost somewhere in space or time, he knew not where, wandering over a desolate, fever wracked landscape. John Brown towered over him like a mountain, head wreathed in storm clouds, eyes blazing with righteous hellfire. His shrill voice roared out endless damnation upon all and sundry, while all around him disjointed scenes and fleeting images of bloody slave revolt...genocidal slaughter...war to the knife...raged...*

*...Everywhere he went, the butchery was gruesome, the devastation total. And everywhere he went in this fever land of burning ruins and dangling corpses, he ran into Learnéd, or her, or both...*

*...He came to the looted remains of a large plantation manor. The stately drive leading to the front entrance was lined with dangling corpses—whites on one side, blacks on the other—all glaring at him with hatred and contempt...*

*...In the back, in the slaves' quarters, she appeared as an arrogant Southern aristocrat lashing a trembling black Learnéd with hysterical glee. As he watched, uncomprehending, she turned on him and began lashing him with the bull whip, crying, "Traitor! Citizen!" while Learnéd stood by, nodding in calm approval...*

*..."It's me!" he cried to her as he reeled under the stinging whip. "It's Nate! I'm here to help you!"...*

*..."Stinking broken trash!" She dropped her whip, drew one of Learnéd's strange weapons, and blasted away at him as he fled into the woods...*

*...He emerged from the woods on the grounds of another ruined plantation. She appeared again in the slave quarters as a comely black wench being blood ravished by an endless throng of Learnéds. He tried desperately to intervene, but he was helpless against their numbers and strength. They turned on him with sadistic glee with screams of "Kill the nigger!", "Get him!", "String him up!" while she cheered them on...*

72

*...To his horror, he realized that he was now black, and fled into the swamps with the sound of baying dogs and her screams of agony echoing in his ears...*

*...And John Brown towered in the background, urging them on with insane rage that fell on them as thunders and lightnings...*

§

...I woke some time after noon, and lay staring at the compartment ceiling, trying to still my pounding heart and put the latest nightmare out of mind. I was soaked in sweat, my breathing was fast and jittery, and I ached from head to toe; spooked by that horrid dream. I gradually got my panic under control, but I was still shaken with doubt and uncertainty. I hadn't forgotten my conversation with her last night, and the fantastic things she told me about the future. I wasn't sure if I dared to believe her, and I had no idea what to do if her story was true.

The scene outside the window caught my eye, and I lay on the berth, lethargic and drained of emotion, and watched the random movements of people and baggage carts without really seeing them. The chill off the window was bracing and strangely calming. It was the feel of the reality outside. I clung to that as I tried to calm my nerves and get a handle on this bizarre situation.

What really dismayed me was how shaken and uncertain I was about all this. Self confidence always was my strong point, and right then I wasn't confident about anything. The worst of it was an aching suspicion that I was *meant* to play some part in her struggle. The sensation was uncanny, like some kind of foretelling or Divine Revelation. I felt like I had rehearsed my starring role in this struggle between good and evil again and again, for ever. But I was still vague about what was what, or who I could trust, or why I should get involved in the first place when it could well lead to a violent death. There were no answers; just the faint echos of the lashing bull whip, and the baying hounds, and that haunting certainty.

After a time, hunger distracted me. Soon I was thinking dark thoughts about a huge stack of flap jacks and bacon. And coffee. Lots of coffee. That motivated me enough to struggle to a sitting position and rub my face with both hands, trying to fully wake up. Learnéd was still seated in his purloined diner chair, watching me stoically.

"Don't you ever sleep?"

Learnéd gave me an annoyed look. "I can manage without for several days, if needed."

"You sure don't have much of a life, do you?" Learnéd frowned, but didn't make anything of it.

I settled on the berth and thought about my next move. Learnéd seemed fairly calm at the moment, and now that I heard her story, I wanted to hear his side of it. Breakfast could wait for a few minutes: I had to know more if I was to understand what to do, and my own aching bewilderment needed answers like a sinner needs salvation.

"What is the future like?" I asked at last.

Learnéd studied me in confusion, then, "The future iss ass it iss, ney more, ney less. It iss ass it was meant to be."

That stuck me as the parroted party line. "So...how far in the future do you come from?"

"I ney am at liberty to discuss that."

"Oh, come now. You're telling me that the *date* is a state secret?"

"It ney iss your concern!" Learnéd snapped. "You have your duty, citizen. Be content that the Movement has need of you."

"I suppose I should be flattered," I mumbled. Learnéd was touchy about the Movement; not surprising if what she said about their being conditioned to obedience was true. I wondered fleetingly how they did that, and what his thoughts and hopes and dreams must be like. This was getting uglier with each passing comment, but his outburst gave me a wedge to get under his skin.

"So...is the United States still the greatest nation in the world in your time?"

Learnéd was confused again. "The...states were rationalized. All of the states, everywhere. There iss the Movement, and it iss everything."

Another party line for sure. "Still, you have criminals in your time, so things can't be perfect, can they?"

Learnéd was on his feet in a hot rage, and snatched me up by my jacket before I could defend myself. "Ney question the Movement!" he snarled. His face was livid, his eyes, inches from mine, were filled with blood rage. "It iss heresy..." Then he faltered, his eyes drifted, and he stared at nothing for a few seconds as I watched him in stunned surprise. When he came back from his daze, he shook me in disgust, then dropped me. "You ney need to ask so many questions," he said sternly. "You have your duty to the Movement; you ney need anything more."

I sat quietly on the berth until my shakes passed, and wondered at the fury in Learnéd's reaction. It seemed I'd tread on delicate ground, and it might be best not to press him about the Movement after all. Still, his reaction told me volumes, not only in what he said, but in what he didn't say. Add that to what she said last night, and it painted an ugly picture of the future.

I finally got over my shakes enough to dig some fresh clothes out of my bags and headed for the washroom. "Where are you going?" Learnéd demanded.

"Out."

"And when will you be back?"

"Eventually." I gave him an annoyed look in turn. "It's not like I have anywhere else to go, do I?"

§

After freshening up in the restroom, which didn't help much, I stumbled toward the dining car. The brisk weather on the open platforms between cars snapped me out of my funk, and I paused for several deep breaths of bracing, smoke-tinted air, reveling in the sensation and the illusion of freedom it brought. For a moment, it made me feel half-way human again.

The railroad yard was busy with messenger boys running back and forth, and locomotives moving out of the roundhouse. My old railroader's instinct told me the log jam would burst soon. Ahead lay Ogden, Reno, then Donner Pass, and finally Sacramento, and a riverboat to San Francisco. Sometime in the next two or three days, the final confrontation between Learnéd and his prey would happen. How many would die then? Would I be among them? I had a dark premonition that I would.

The bracing air didn't feel free any more, it just felt cold. I sighed in resignation, and headed into the dining car.

§

The diner was pretty much empty at this time of day, so I had no trouble claiming a seat at her table. The waiter was the same one who usually served her. "Has the lady been here today?" I asked.

The man hesitated. "Yessah, she was, an' she left jus' an hour ago, ah reckon." From his tone and the awed look on his face, she must be creating legends of fear and loathing among the kitchen crew. "Is there anythin' ah can get fo' you?"

Right then there was so much on my mind that I wasn't hungry, but I had to eat; I had to keep up my strength if I was to serve the Movement. I put the future and revolution and the Movement firmly out of mind, and dug into a huge plate of flap jacks and ham —more generous than the usual portions—while the waiter stood by and plied me with cup after cup of coffee. Evidently some of her reputation had rubbed off on me.

§

The lounge car was busy as usual. Gentlemen of high and low pedigree were killing time by drinking, smoking, and gossiping...that is, 'discussing the issues of the day'. Those 'issues' made for lively, envious talk, with more than a few glances my way. The air was thick with cigar smoke, and the bartender was busy.

Parker sat in one of the lounge chairs, drink at his side, indulging in a cigar. He waved his mug in salute when I came in. "Well, Mister Poole, good day, sir."

"And to you, sir." I settled in a nearby chair and swiveled around to look out the windows. Right then I was in no mood for company or idle chatter. Parker considered me for a moment, then nodded cordially and went back to following the gossip around us, which was about her and precious little else.

I ignored the hubbub, and sat for some time pondering the smoke from my cigar and idly watching the scene beyond the windows as I mulled over what little I knew. I was hard put to grasp the concept of time travel to begin with, not to mention fighting a revolution up and down the centuries. I didn't doubt that they came from the future; not after what I saw both her and Learnéd do. And as hard as it was to understand what she told me, I could tell it was the grim truth. Bad news does not need confirmation. But the whole thing was so fantastic, so bizarre that it left my head swimming.

Above all, I resented being dragged into their fight. She had no right to use me like that, to make me her stalking horse, just as Learnéd had no right to impose on me so. Her I could understand and forgive: she must be terrified with Learnéd on her tail, so it was no surprise if she grasped any straw she could find. As for Learnéd, he was doing his duty as he saw it in his time...and for all I knew, crime may have changed so much that their harsh methods were necessary.

I couldn't make heads or tails of it, and my first—sensible—instinct was to run, forthrightly and without shame. I couldn't imagine how this mattered to me in the least, and the only outcome I could see from it was the very real risk of violent death. But the epic scale of it...the sheer magnitude of a revolution waged throughout time itself...the little I knew appalled and intrigued me. And the issues she fought for...

"Your attention, please, gentlemen!" Doggett was at it again in his usual spot in front of the bar. "We have received word that we will be getting under way again in about an hour." That brought a mix of joy at the pending end of our exile, and more grumbled cursing at the delay. "We are now loading further food and liquor stocks..."

Then he tapered off in obvious dismay, which alerted me, and I spun around to see what was happening. A woman invading this masculine holy-of-holies was unheard of, not that she was just *any* woman. The room went silent, and the nabobs of San Francisco watched with mixed bemusement and more than a little fear as she passed. Those who came to her attention were polite and poker faced, and she ignored them for the most part aside from an occasional courteous nod. The three ranchers she tangled with on the first day were at one of the card tables. They avoided meeting her eye. The tension rose as she walked the length of the car.

77

Doggett turned all hissy at the sight of her. "Young woman, this car is reserved for the gentlemen!"

"Oh?" Her expression implied a bad smell in the air. "Then what are *you* doing here?" The tension broke, and Doggett was laughed out of the car.

"Hello, Nathaniel," she said to me once the ruckus died down. "I missed you at lunch."

"I was...attending to something important," I said, cautiously.

She nodded, and gave me a knowing look. "Well, I hope everything iss in order, and that I might see you for dinner."

"I...believe so, for now. I'll try to make it."

"Until then." She gave me one of her coquettish smiles as she headed to the door.

Parker considered her over a fresh cigar, then looked at me. "A remarkable woman."

"She is that, sir." I wondered if Parker could grasp how remarkable she was.

Parker nursed his cigar as he watched her go, then leaned toward me. "It seems she takes an interest in you," he said, confidentially.

"Hmph."

Normally I wouldn't mind the attention she drew. Being a rake added to the manly image, made men envious and women curious, built the mystique that was part of a prize fighter. But next to her I must look like a poodle. I was mortified at the thought. After all the noise she made last night, the entire train must be gossiping about the outlandish hoyden and the supposed man she claimed for her pleasure.

"I was wondering about that accent," Parker said once she was gone. "Some kind of foreigner, I reckon." He glanced at me with studied nonchalance. "Did she mention where she comes from?"

I was distracted by my brooding, and had to focus on him to reply. "Eastern Europe. Prussia."

"Is that so?" Parker thought about that for a bit, then, "She seems high class; some kind of petty nobility, maybe?" I was on my guard by then, and didn't answer. "I met a couple of them Prussians during the war," he went on, musing to himself.

"Mercenaries, they was: staff officers come over to teach our boys how to fight scientific. You never saw such a pair of self-righteous bastards. Each was more arrogant and in-your-face than the other, and the way they took on about coloreds..." He shook his head in bemusement, and glanced at me. "Odd, that they'd let their women folk go galavanting off on their own. Don't seem natural somehow."

"I don't pretend to understand her either, sir."

Parker chuckled. "Not surprising. She is a caution, no mistake." He settled in his chair and went back to contemplating his cigar.

I went back to staring out the window, and tried to relax without much success. It wasn't bad enough being trapped between Learnéd and her in a struggle I could barely understand; Parker's nosing around made things worse. The man was the law in a land where the law played rough, and he was not one to take lightly. I hoped he would limit himself to idle curiosity. Some Texas hotshot butting in could upset everything, which could be fatal...to a lot of people.

§

"I ney am surprised at this inefficiency," Learnéd said when I told him of our pending departure. The man had precious little curiosity, which made him seem all the more unnatural, somehow. "It iss a wonder that your society functions at all."

"You'll get to San Francisco all right," I grumbled. "You'll just have to rough it, like real men do."

He gave me a hostile look. "We *are* the real men. You primitives ney can match the people of our time. We are superior in every way."

I flopped on the open berth with a weary sigh. "Yeah, I guess so, with all your fancy medicines."

"It was us who made those medicines! The Founder showed us the way. He showed us how to build the perfect world. We ney are wild animals like you are today."

It seemed I'd touched another sore spot. I gave him a hostile look. "So you say you've been tamed, then?"

"We have become civilized!"

79

He was starting to get heated again, and after his outburst earlier, it didn't seem wise to goad him any further. "Well, I guess it's how you look at it," I said cautiously, and rolled over to face the window.

"Has she said anything?"

"Hmph?" I looked at him again. "Nothing much. She just prattles on about San Francisco."

"You must question her more thoroughly. Anything she reveals may be significant."

"I'm doing the best I can. She has a mind of her own, and I'm not going to risk her turning on me."

He fumed at me. "You are a sorry excuse for a citizen; insolent and careless. You ney make this job any easier."

"And I'm all you've got," I said, hotly. "So live with it."

"That iss the only reason I put up with you! You need to take your duty to the Movement more seriously."

My exasperation got the better of me. "To hell with this," I grumbled as I grabbed my coat and reached for the door.

"Where are you going?"

"To take a stretch. I need the fresh air." More than that, I needed to get away from the two of them and *think*.

§

The weather was clear and bracing, with a mild breeze that chilled me as I climbed down from the car's platform. The sky was autumn pale, with high, fleecy clouds glowing orange and red by the westering sun. I pulled my coat tighter, dug my hands into my pockets, and looked around to get my bearings.

A new locomotive was standing by at the head of the train while the brakeman fiddled with the roundhouse steam hose. I had nothing better to do, so I idled over to watch. It was a heavier engine than our last one, which said we were headed into hill country where more power would be needed. It wasn't as fancy as before, painted plain black, and the tender was filled to overflowing with cordwood.

There was a loud '*clunk*' and a spurt of wet steam as the hose from the roundhouse cut off. The brakeman gestured, and the locomotive backed down to the train with clouds of steam and the rhythmic clanking of its mechanical parts. The brisk autumn air was tinged with wood smoke and the pungent scent of hot oil. The cloud of exhaust steam was warm and damp, with a heavy, dead smell; an unnatural fog from some other world.

The station grounds were busy with passengers coming and going, or simply taking the air. A few chatting among themselves were drowned out at times by passing engines and the shouts of workmen making last minute preparations to leave. The car toads were busy checking the brakes and couplings, and a cart load of food was being transferred to the diner. Doggett was by the diner checking the tickets of a couple of local passengers. The new locomotive backed into the train with a metallic *crunch*, and the brakeman busied himself with the steam and brake line connections. He nodded to me briefly when he was done, then climbed into the locomotive's cab. We would be leaving soon...for San Francisco.

I shrugged it off that thought, helped myself to a badly needed cigar, and paced back and forth in front of the station, trying to put it all together in my mind. The whole thing was fantastic, but what I had seen thus far said it was all too real. In some ways, it was worse than my late nightmare; all too real and liable to explode at any time.

I was not pleased to be dragged into her fight, although I understood how desperate she was. And I could see why she would turn to me for help—the only man she knew in this time. Should I get involved or not? Should I help her—a fugitive, a revolutionary—or should I be a 'good citizen' and do my 'duty' to the future? From what they said that future sounded harsh, but how could I judge based on a few hints by a confessed criminal and her pursuer? And even if it was as horrid as she claimed, why did that involve me here in the 19th Century?

A yard bull was patrolling the station grounds to keep order. Our eyes met briefly, and he gave me a suspicious once-over before moving on. He had that same look, that forbidding stone face of a copper that Learnéd did, but he was a pale imitation of that grim future policeman. *'Genetically engineered'*, she said. That sounded almost like people were made to order. How could they do that? I brooded for some time over what a made-to-order Pinkerton man would be like. From the evidence, it wouldn't be pretty. I didn't want Learnéd after me; justice in their time must be harsh, indeed.

Another cart rumbled past and drew up next to the diner, and the two men pushing it helped the diner crew transfer more boxes and bags of food for the rest of the trip. Further up, another cart stood next to the baggage car, where suitcases and trunks were being loaded. A train rumbled past on the other track, leaving a trail of smoke and cinders.

Learnéd was a hard-nosed bastard if ever there was one, but he was upholding the law of his time. As ugly as the future sounded, I couldn't be sure of what it was like from what they told me. There were harsh and ugly things in these United States, but the country as a whole was a decent land with decent people. Her viewpoint was probably biased. Could I trust her words?

She claimed to fight for liberty, trying to overthrow a state which came across as totally evil. She didn't seem like a bad person. She was beautiful, vivacious, and her independent spirit appealed to me. This was no meek and subdued lady; not the way she handled that cowpoke. And the passion we shared...

I put that thought firmly out of mind. She was erratic and manipulative, and was driven by an insatiable need which had to influence what common sense she may have. She was also a revolutionary, a fugitive, and she could tear me apart like a roast chicken. In spite of myself, I longed for her, and feared her.

*'What do I do?'* I thought in dismay. What was the future like? The simple fact was that I didn't know enough to judge, or who to side with.

"Everyone aboard!" Doggett came striding down the boardwalk shouting, "Passengers for the 'Overland' please board. Train's leaving."

There was a minor surge of passengers who were also taking the air. Up ahead, the locomotive started smoking heavily as the fireman made ready to leave. I watched sourly as Doggett reached the front of the train and consulted with the engine crew. Right then, that train felt like a prison.

"Damn it," I muttered.   I should stay here, stay on this boardwalk. I could say I missed the train, and continue my journey tomorrow.  I was mortally tempted to be shut of them, shut of the danger and annoyance, shut of the moral qualms.  But she needed my help, and despite my misgivings and that uncanny sense from some other place, I knew I should help her.

Doggett came back, shouting, "Last call for the 'Overland'! Please get on board!  Last call!"  The breeze picked up a bit, chilling me.  I took a quick look at the sky; there was bad weather ahead.  The thinning crowd parted; railroaders heading back to the station, and the last few passengers scurrying to board.

"I don't need this," I muttered.  I could be shut of this whole impossible mess, just stand right here and leave them—leave her— to whatever fate waited in San Francisco.

Doggett reached the rear of the train, mounted the step, and waved his lantern.  The locomotive gave two toots in reply, and erupted in clouds of steam.  I watched impassively as the cars clanked and groaned and began to roll.

No, I couldn't do it; not and keep my self respect.  Cursing in frustration, I caught the next to last step as it went by.

*****

## "Day Three: Night"

"You go to her again?" Learnéd demanded as I headed for the diner late that afternoon.

I paused in the doorway. "Isn't that what I am required to do?"

"It iss." Learnéd had no sense of sarcasm, or didn't care what mere mortals thought. "When you pass through the dining car, tell them to send more meat and bread here."

I was already on a short fuse, and Learnéd's endless presumptions were getting on my nerves. "Why do I have to feed you? Doesn't your Movement provide for your operating expenses?"

Learnéd erupted at that. "You ney concern yourself with what the Movement does! Focus on your duty!"

I backpedaled cautiously and tried to show a bold front. "My funds are running low. How can I do my duty when I'm broke?"

Learnéd considered me coldly, then dug in his coat and produced a small purse, which yielded a dozen twenty dollar gold pieces. He grabbed my outstretched hand, all but yanking me off my feet, and pressed the coins into my palm. "This will cover my expenses for the rest of our journey," he growled as his eyes burned with barely contained rage. "And you ney test my patience again!" He shoved me back sprawled against the wall, and we stared at each other in tense silence while I tried to compose myself. "Well? Iss that enough?"

I fingered the coins distractedly: brand new double eagles, probably made up there in the future. "Yeah, these will do."

§

Once out in the passageway, I sagged against the wall until my shakes were under control, then headed for the diner with a weary curse. As I passed through the open sections in the center of the car, I spotted the familiar white short coat of the porter, Samuel, who gave me a nod and a friendly smile as I approached.

"Evenin', suh. Ah hope everythin' is fine fo' you."

Then inspiration struck: it was high time I started playing my own game, and Learnéd's begrudging handout gave me something I needed for that. "Fine, thank you, Samuel. May I have a word with you?" Samuel nodded, and followed me to the restroom at the far end of the car. Learnéd's listening device worried me, so I peeled my jacket off, tossed it on the restroom vanity, and returned to the hallway before I dared to speak.

"I have a job for you, Samuel."

"Suh?" Samuel eyed me uneasily, wondering at my strange behavior.

"You know about the gentleman in my compartment?"

He seemed even more uneasy at being reminded of Learnéd. "Yessah. I was wonderin' about him. Seems he got a berth in the first car, but he say he'll be stayin' with you."

"Yeah, well, that's fine, but there is a problem with him."

"Suh?" Samuel was more alarmed than seemed reasonable, which worried me. What happened during his run-in with Learnéd?

"You know the lady I've been seeing?"

"The one what threw that feller through the window? Yessah, I seen her."

"Look, Samuel, that fellow in my compartment is her ex-husband. She left him, and he's after her. He wants to hurt her, but I've managed to keep them separated so far." I dug in my pocket, and handed over one of Learnéd's double eagles. "This is important, Samuel." His eyes bulged at the sight of so much gold; more money than he earned in a month of tips. "I want you to keep an eye on him. Don't get near him or try to interfere, that way you won't get in any trouble. But keep on the alert, and let me know if he does anything unusual. You with me?"

Samuel studied me doubtfully. "Suh..."

"She's counting on you, Samuel."

"Yessah." He rubbed the gold coin between finger and thumb, then pocketed it. "I'll do that fo' you, suh. You can count on ol' Samuel."

"Good man."

As I headed for the diner, I wondered idly if those double eagles were real gold.

§

It was getting late, and the diner was nearly deserted, but she was enjoying a cup of coffee at her favorite table by the kitchen as her regular waiter cleared away the remains of a huge pot roast. She paused in her coffee and gave me a warm smile. "Hello, Nathaniel. Are you feeling well today?"

"Well enough, I suppose." I slumped in my chair.

"Would you care fo' somethin' suh?" the waiter asked.

Right then I was too distracted to be hungry. "Coffee, I guess."

"An' would you like somethin' else, miss?"

She drew a small purse out of her pouch and fingered through it, then eyed the check laying on the table between us. From her glum expression I realized that her funds were dwindling. She must go through her resources fast with as much as she ate, and she was nursing what she had left.

"What sort of pie do you have?" I asked the waiter.

"Apple, suh. They was baked fresh jus' this afternoon."

Right then that sounded good, and I decided I really did need to eat. "Fine. Bring us a whole pie, warm please." I slid the check across the table as I spoke, which brought a grateful smile from her and a startled look from the waiter as I laid another of Learnéd's double eagles on it. *'Might as well get some good out of the Movement's blood money,'* I thought.

86

"You ney look happy, Nathaniel," she said once the waiter left. She eyed the double eagle, then looked at me, and I could tell she knew where it came from. "I know you have a lot on your mind, but your problems will pass if you are patient."

"I hope so."

She studied my face again. "Are you feeling sick?"

"No..." It took an effort to focus, as weary and distracted as I was. "I'm just...tired. It's been a hectic trip. I'll manage."

"You poor dear!" She took my hand in sympathy. "I have asked so much from you. I know I am a burden, and I am thankful for your kindness."

That helped pick me up a bit. She was an attractive woman, and her warmth was encouraging when she showed it. But we were both mincing around the hidden listening device in my lapel, and I could see from the look in her eyes that there was much she wanted to talk about. That was reassuring in a way, since she seemed far more human than Learnéd.

"I'll be all right, I suppose. Any trip with you is an adventure. I need to catch my breath, is all."

She smiled uncertainly as the waiter returned with a steaming pie topped with grated cheese, and more coffee. We dug in, and it turned out that I was ravenous.

We spent the next couple of hours making careful small talk until the steward politely chased us out. After that, we retreated to her compartment, where we spent some more time keeping up pretenses until it grew late. Once I felt sure the lounge would be empty, we left Learnéd's listening device behind and headed for the lounge car.

§

Once again, the lounge was dark and deserted but for the brakeman, who sat at the rear of the car and ignored us. By time we could really talk, I was bursting. I was still vague on most of this, and had endless questions for her, especially now that I was more or less committed.

"Tell me about the future," I asked once we were seated.

She considered that. "There iss so much to tell, and I know so little of it. I will tell you what I can if you ask."

87

"I hardly know where to begin. All I have are bits and pieces from you and Learnéd to go on."

"Oh? So what did he say to you, Nathaniel?" She leaned on the table and gave me her undivided attention, which was both flattering and disconcerting. Her cleavage was provocative, as was the glow in her eyes. "Did he tell you much that you can believe?"

"Not a whole lot." I had to think that one over, which wasn't easy as her presence was affecting me again. "What year is it where you come from?"

She seemed a bit confused. "It iss the four hundred and fifty-third year of the Temples. I ney know what year you would call it. The time machine's operator might."

That was a dismayingly long time: longer than since Columbus sailed for the New World. Add in maybe another two hundred years between now and the coming of the Movement...

"I asked him about the future, but he got angry when I mentioned the Movement." She frowned at that, which brought the incident earlier to mind. "All I did was ask a simple question, but he practically exploded. He was in a rage...but then...he drifted off. He stared at nothing." It was hard to find words for what happened. "I've seen him do it a couple times, always when he gets angry."

She nodded. "He was linking with his gestalt. You did the unthinkable by questioning the Movement. The others linked with him to calm his reaction." She took my hand. "You are lucky to be alive, Nathaniel. That iss the act of someone who iss Broken, and the Pure Of Thought are programmed to react violently to any deviant behavior. Ney question the Movement again."

It was a shock to realize how close I came to being hurt, if not killed. "And those people are judge, jury, and executioners? Is there no justice in your time?"

She shook her head, and her flirtatious air vanished. "There iss only the Movement, and the Pure Of Thought are the visible hand of authority. Their word iss law, and those they condemn are killed out of hand."

"But... Why do your people tolerate that? We would have risen in revolt long since."

Again, she thought about it before answering reluctantly. "You ney understand the power of sheep-think. You ney realize how completely the Movement controls uss, or how helpless ordinary people are against our own technology." She shook her head at that with a bitter sigh. "We...are conditioned ass part of our breeding; programmed to obey the Movement. It can be done, Nathaniel," she added in reply to my startled look. "Done in mass. Revolution ney iss possible because ney wish to, ney can they find the will if they do."

"But...what about you? How did you escape?"

Her face sagged, and she withdrew into herself a bit. "Such conditioning ney iss perfect," she muttered. "Anything made in mass iss cheapened, including the masses. The Pure Of Thought receive better conditioning, and ney have ever broken. But for the common people, the drones, sometimes—rarely—the conditioning fails."

"You became a free thinker?"

"Iss that what you call it in this time? Yes, I was starting to think for myself." She stared at nothing and shuddered. "I was terrified," she whispered. "I ney could trust my own mind. Without the Movement... I was lost, Nathaniel." She looked at me solemnly, and there were tears in her eyes. "I was insane, ney conditioned, which iss insanity in my time. I ney knew how to take care of myself, how to make my own decisions, my own value judgments."

"Couldn't you go to them for help?"

"Ney." She shook her head emphatically. "Once someone breaks conditioning, the Movement ney tolerates their existence. The Broken ney can be made whole; they will break again. Citizens ney are worth the effort, anyway."

"What about your resistance? How could they function with this conditioning?"

"We are the Broken, mental outcasts who fight to overthrow the Movement so that we may survive. What more iss there to know?" She seemed reluctant to talk about that, too. Perhaps it was ingrained in her, considering her past.

"How did you wind up with them?"

"I...was a drone, a worker. When I realized I was breaking, I seduced a manager to help me escape. I hid in the ruins with the other Broken. One of the men I met there was in the resistance, and he recruited me. I was lucky: most of those who break are eliminated by the Pure Of Thought."

"Your people are conditioned so they can't disobey?"

"Yes."

"But how can your resistance win if everyone is cowed?"

"We ney can overthrow the Movement," she said, firmly. "We hope to change the past to keep the Movement from happening."

"Well, I wish you luck with that!" Then I remembered something Learnéd told me that first morning. "He talked about changing the future. He said if we aren't careful, we could make changes so great that the future would never happen."

She gave an unladylike snort. "Changing the temporal structure iss ney that easy. But he iss right: there iss danger in time travel. Anything can cause change. Even the fact that you are sitting here instead of in your compartment iss a change in the time line. But small changes like that ney matter; they cancel out. The danger iss in paradoxes."

"The Executioner's Paradox," I muttered. I was a bit unsettled to be changing the future just by sitting there.

"He told you about that?" She studied me carefully. "Then he ney cares what you know. That iss bad, Nathaniel. The Learnéd are specifically configured for time travel so they can function among the ney conditioned people of this time. He told you the little he has to insure your cooperation, something they ney have to do, usually. To him you are unnatural, and you know more than he will think safe. He ney will hesitate to kill you."

"That wouldn't surprise me," I grumbled. "Not that he's told me much. What about these paradoxes?"

"Any change in the cause matrix—the past—puts strain on the fabric of space-time. Usually the strain will dissipate by hysteresis." She must have known I didn't understand. "Hysteresis iss when small changes either ney have an effect, or trigger other small changes which gradually relieve the strain."

"Uh...yeah. And these paradoxes?"

"I was told that if the strain iss too great, time will become...think of it ass becoming knotted. That segment of time will split off and form a closed loop: a temporal causality loop. The cause and effect of the paradox cancel each other out continuously, which isolates the paradox from the time line. The time stream would be safe. The risk iss that we could be trapped in time, doomed to replay these events forever."

"That's a scary thought." I could barely understand even her simple explanation, but what I could make of it sounded like they were tampering with the cosmos itself.

"Oh?" She grinned wickedly. "Iss being trapped in my compartment forever such a terrible fate?"

"You know, Learnéd asked me that same question."

Her eyes sparkled. "And what did you tell him?"

"I said I'd get back to him on that."

She actually blushed. "I will be interested to hear your opinion when you decide."

There was a moment of silence, then I said, "You know, I don't even know your name."

She smiled. "I am Arda."

"Is that all? Just Arda?"

Her smile vanished, and she seemed a bit miffed. "Arda-one-seven-two-eight-four-alpha-epsilon-seven-nine-three-delta-eight-eight-zero-seven-one, if you must know."

That took a moment to sink in. "You have a number instead of a name?"

She shrugged. "We are property of the Movement. Property must have serial numbers."

"But what about your family? Didn't they give you a name?"

She hesitated, and looked at me with bleak eyes as her life seemed to drain out of her, and she sagged within herself. "We ney have families ass in this time, Nathaniel," she said at last. "I was produced at a Life Center."

That took another moment to sink in, and when I finally grasped it, my hackles rose. "You were *manufactured?*"

She nodded, solemnly. "The Movement breeds the necessary workers by artificial means."

"That...is...horrible..."

"Now you begin to see what the resistance iss fighting."

"How can they get away with that?"

"Why do you have black people ass property now?" she demanded. "Why do you murder the natives? Because you can. Power iss its own truth, Nathaniel. The Movement iss ass it iss because they have the power. There ney iss any power which can defeat them. The only way we can end their power iss to take their past away from them."

"But...how? How can you change the future?"

She hesitated. "It iss hard to explain, Nathaniel."

I suspected that was an evasion, which made me wonder just how one *could* change the future? "What happens then, after you prevent the future from happening?"

She sighed, and stared at nothing, shaking her head in sorrow. "Some of uss think...that if we prevent the Movement...something else will come that iss just ass bad." She was silent for a bit, then, "Some of uss hope that the future will be better, somehow; ney know how. And some of uss simply feel that anything iss better than what we have now, so they are willing to gamble. In any event, we are the Broken; we ney have anything to lose."

I slumped in my chair in dismay as she sagged again and stared dejectedly at nothing. They were wagering the fate of humanity by blindly tossing the cosmic dice; literally playing God with powers beyond comprehension. The very concept was mind boggling. If their plan wasn't a desperate Hail Mary move, I couldn't imagine what would be. What was worse, they appeared to have precious little hope for success and no real alternative. And the way she described it, their resistance sounded like a pack of orphans, deprived of the chains they craved and hated, lost even in their own time and place.

"What do you feel, Arda?" I asked, softly.

She didn't respond at first. "I...ney know, Nathaniel. I ney am expert at these things, if any such even exist. But we have to do something, whatever the result. The human race iss depending on uss. We Broken have fallen through the cracks, and are the only ones who can change our fate."

92

We sat silently for a few minutes, neither looking at the other, both drawing comfort from the other's presence. I struggled to piece all this together, but the future she came from was so alien that I could hardly comprehend it.

"What is it with this Movement, anyway?" I demanded at last. "Why did they create such a hell on earth?"

She thought about that for a bit. "We ney know much. Information of any sort iss ney shared unless necessary. It iss a distraction from our true calling, ass they say."

"Especially knowledge of your past, I imagine."

She nodded. "The smell of the sewers—rumors and legends— say that the Founder thought the human race was imperfect, so He set out to improve uss."

"Some improvement! What went wrong?"

"We ney know; there are few records of that time, and all knowledge iss controlled by the Movement. What we do know iss that the Movement became all-powerful."

"How could they do that? Didn't humanity rise up against them?"

"They must have. The Temples are all that iss left now. The rest iss shattered ruins. Those were dark times, Nathaniel. According to the Writings, the world was overpopulated, the ecosystem collapsing, millions were starving and killing each other. According to the Writings, He used the opportunity to create His improved race. We ney know how."

"And the Movement conquered the world? How?"

"The Movement has the Life Centers and the conditioning. With the armies they bred, they took control of the natural resources. The rest of the race were allowed to die out."

I slumped in my chair, breathing hard and hands shaking. This was beyond comprehension! "Allowed?"

"Ass they tell it."

"How...many are left?"

"I ney know. I heard someone say once that there are a million citizens in SaFrisko. I ney know how many Temples there are, but it ney iss many." Her voice was bleak and faint. "The ecosystem ney can support any more."

"As they tell it."

"Yes." She sniffed, and dabbed a tear with her sleeve. "Ass they always tell it."

We sat silent for a while as I tried to put it all together. My pity rose for the people of Arda's world: ruled by fear and conditioning, doomed to empty lives of labor, knowing they would be disposed of when no longer needed. Surely they must see the nightmare of their existence, but were unable to refuse, unable even to resent their dehumanization; conditioned to obey even in the face of that evil, knowing it was wrong. How desperate must they be? What were their dreams be like? I shuddered at the thought of it.

"What about all these changes?" I asked at last. "Making people in factories is not now it's supposed to be!"

She closed her eyes and sat rigid, head down, as of she was trying to suppress an intolerable thought. "They remade uss in the Founder's image," she whispered at last. "Now we are perfect, so they say. Each of uss iss created on a quota system for a specific role, bioengineered for one task. When we are no longer needed, we are discarded and replaced. The race goes on; a perfect harmony of order and function."

"Ants." I was appalled beyond anything I could have imagined. "He turned us into a race of ants!"

She looked at me, startled. "Yes, He did, ney? The...ant iss sacred to them."

"He must have been mad!"

She started to break down, her face contorted in misery. "It...iss so wrong! Why does life have to be so cruel, Nathaniel? Why iss there so much evil?"

"I don't know, Arda."

"Why was I ney born like you?" Her tears flowed as she finally broke through her shield of self denial.

I squeezed her hand gently. "Don't dwell on it."

"I...I sometimes wonder...what it would be like...to have a baby..." She collapsed on the table and wept like a lost child.

I tried to comfort her, not knowing what to do or say. "Let it go, Arda."

94

It took her a while, but she finally got herself under control, and took deep, slow breaths to calm herself. As the worst of it passed, she sniffed a few times and shook her head in her misery. "You are wise, Nathaniel," she managed at last.

§

Later, in her compartment, she cuddled close to my chest and murmured, "Please hold me, Nathaniel."

I held her close, gently rubbing her back as she sobbed softly, and wondered what to do. It was clear now that Learnéd and the Movement were an unmitigated evil, a horror beyond horror. It must have taken centuries to reach its full flowering, to conquer the entire world, and crush all traces of humanity. For the life of me, I couldn't see how such entrenched power could be overturned.

Icy rage built up in me as I thought of what they did to her, to all of humanity. But I also felt an ugly sense of guilt, since I could see that the Movement's foundations were here in this time. She was right: the chattel slavery I fought against, and the butchery of the Indian tribes were possible because there is something dark and terrible in mens' souls. These things happened because the power which willed it went unchallenged; because nobody bothered with the fate of the poor Negro, or the hapless Red Man.

I was dismayed to realize that the Civil War, where so many of us gave our all, was a defeat. Even though the rebellion was crushed and the slaves freed, the evil in mens' souls does not die. Slavery was still with us; subtle, in the background, but still there. And no one cared. No one saw it once the Rebel flags were torn down and the plantations burned. But those were the visible symbols of evil, just as Learnéd was a visible symbol of the Movement. The evil itself was untouched, festering anew. It would take centuries for the coloreds to find justice, if ever. What would it take to bring justice to the victims of the Movement?

And what would be the price of that justice? Challenging the power that willed slavery lead to years of slaughter. What would it take to defeat a power that conquered the world? No, tearing down the Movement was not possible. Arda's quixotic resistance was humanity's one feeble hope, but they didn't even know what would happen if they succeeded—which seemed unlikely. If they did change the future, anything might happen, ranging from trading one horror for another to destroying time itself. I didn't understand time travel, but I had little faith that some kinder, gentler world would emerge from the ruins. As she said, science is power, whoever controls it; and I knew the evil results of power all too well. Would it matter if the real economic power in this country was controlled by someone other than the Morgans and Goulds and Tweeds? We would still have poverty, still have injustice. Power corrupts: and science, even the primitive science of this time, is power.

I sighed and stared out the window at the passing dimly moonlit landscape. One thing was certain: I couldn't side with Learnéd. And as wise as it would be to walk away, to get off the train at the next stop and leave them to their fates, I couldn't do that either.

I lay for a time, rubbing her back and staring sightlessly out the window. The gentle swaying of the train, and the steady click-clack of the wheels on the rails was hypnotic. The cool draft coming off the window evoked some visceral dread in me: an icy portent of the future, a chill wind from tomorrow.

John Brown. The memory of that nightmare came back. There are some evils so great that no price is too dear to be rid of them. Monster though John Brown was, he knew the right of it. The Founder must have been thoroughly mad, as mad as John Brown was, and controlled knowledge and power far greater than anything I could understand. There are some evils so great... How could I walk away from her and the resistance, as hopeless as their plight may be? But at the same time, it seemed futile to openly defy the Movement. I sure didn't want to confront Learnéd. There must be another option, but what it could be was beyond me.

She stirred in my arms. "Please love me, Nathaniel," she murmured. I answered her without words. Right then, I needed the distraction too, and tomorrow could take care of itself.

*****

96

# "Day Four"

Despite that emotionally wearing night with Arda, I woke after only a few hours of sleep. I was too preoccupied with the mess I was in to rest, so I lay staring at the roof, alternating with brief glances at Learnéd in his chair. There was a lot to think about.

I didn't know what to make of Arda. For all her formidable strength and abilities, she was erratic and flighty, and seemed awfully unsure of herself at times. If she was the best their revolution could offer, they must be in a bad way. As much as I wished them success, they seemed unlikely to achieve much against the likes of Learnéd. And I couldn't see what her part was, since she seemed so ill-suited for this. Was she expendable? Did they want her to fail for some reason? That seemed even more inhuman than Learnéd and his Movement. Most likely she was here for some minor routine matter, and was in way over her head. It was the only thing that made sense, and I couldn't even trust that.

To hell with it. I was starving. I struggled to my feet with a weary sigh, and dug into my carpet bag for fresh clothes. Learnéd watched as I dressed, and stopped me when I reached for the door.

"You are going to the dining car?"

"Yeah, yeah, I know. Send food. Lots of carbohydrates."

Learnéd gave me a cold look. "Correct. And ney be so stingy this time."

"Why not? It's on your tab, for once."

§

It was snowing lightly, enough for the raw wind to blow into small drifts half hidden in a low-laying haze. The train rumbled along slower than usual, and I paused for a second on the platforms, wondering if there was a problem. The prairie was desolate and featureless except for a small herd of buffalo in the distance; a Godforsaken wilderness if ever there was one. The thought of a breakdown out here... The train rattled across a trestle over a shallow creek, breaking my distraction. It was probably just traffic up ahead; the snow wasn't enough to slow us down. No need to borrow troubles.

§

The diner was fairly busy with the late morning crowd relaxing over coffee and card games. The bright gas lights and the warmth of the kitchen made the dreary scene outside all the more remote and hostile, not that I really cared. Breakfast was routine, and I was too weary to notice what I ate, other than cup after cup of strong coffee. She wasn't there, and I wasn't sure if I should be relieved or worried. Her regular waiter attended me, refilling my cup repeatedly. He seemed to sense my mood, did his job without fanfare, and faded into the background. I ignored him and the cozy chatter around me, and brooded.

"Well, good morning, Mister Poole," a voice broke through my distracted haze after a while. It was Parker, dressed in his accustomed vest, string tie, and revolver on his hip. "Would you care for a bit of breakfast company?"

"I would indeed, sir." Right then, I needed it. As much as Parker's nosiness worried me, his strength was a comfort, something familiar to hold onto in the storm of my life.

"Bless me, but this trip seems to drag on forever," he grumbled as he settled into the other chair.

"It feels like we have all the time in the world out here," I muttered in grim humor.

"It does that." The waiter brought a heaping plate of ham and flap jacks, and Parker dug in with gusto. "You look like a lost soul," he mumbled. "Did you have a tiff with your lady friend?"

I eyed him suspiciously. "No. It's just that she kind of overwhelms a man."

"Remarkable lady. Where is she, by the way?"

"In her compartment, I guess." Now that I thought about it, that worried me. Did Learnéd act while I was asleep? And if he did, what could I do about it?

"Did she mention where she comes from in Prussia?"

I shied away from that. "She didn't say, exactly."

Parker made a show of consuming a fork full of ham, and studied me closely as he chewed. "Maybe she's one of them *stateless* types, a political refugee?" he asked at last. "I hear-tell they had some revolution over there a few years back. That might explain why she didn't fill the whole train with servants."

98

"You may have it." If he wanted to believe that, fine. It would ease Learnéd's suspicions too, if he was listening at the moment.

We ate in silence for a bit as I brooded. I was too at sea about Arda's revolution...the Movement...tampering with time itself...to know what to do. The temptations were obvious, and the risks frightening. My confidence was shaken by all this...and here was a man who stared death down for a living. Right then I needed someone to talk this out with, but how could I ask his help without revealing Arda's secret? I finally got the nerve up to give it a try, but first I needed to keep Learnéd from overhearing. I made a show of standing to stretch, then pulled my jacket off, carefully folded it and sat on it while Parker watched curiously.

"Would you mind if I pose a hypothetical question to you, Mister Parker?"

"That would depend on the subject."

"Law enforcement."

Parker thought about that, then said, "Ask away."

"Well, sir..." Now that I was doing it, this didn't seem like a wise idea, but I had to ask. "...I was thinking earlier about a situation I found myself in briefly...several years ago. I'm wondering about the ethics, I guess you could say, of it."

"Indeed?"

"Suppose a revolutionary, purely hypothetical, mind you, and this revolutionary is being pursued by a policeman."

"A hypothetical policeman?"

"Yes. Normally, I would side with the policeman, but...what if this revolutionary was fighting a vicious tyranny? What if the policeman was a monster, thoroughly evil...what's a man supposed to do?"

Parker eyed me skeptically. "You would do right to uphold the law regardless of your personal doubts," he said, evenly. "Lord knows this land has suffered enough revolution...to say nothing of Mexico...and elsewhere." He sat for a time sipping his coffee, and studied me. "But...if the cause this revolutionary was fighting for was honorable...that's a hard one to call. I suppose it would depend on your judgment, on what you think the right and wrong of it are."

That helped somewhat, anyway. "I was an outsider. I wasn't sure what to do, or if I should have done anything."

"Well, I'll tell you a little story." Parker nursed his coffee for a bit, then, "There were these two boys down in Amarillo, the Arley brothers. Farm boys; a little wild, but good folk, mostly. Well, sir, one day this drunken galoot went and shot their pa, left him in the street dead as a nail." Parker contemplated for a bit. "Them two brothers came to town and shot him dead right there in the jail. They had every right to, I reckon, but they did a wrong thing, so I had to go after them."

"I cornered 'em finally. They pleaded with me, said they were sorry, but they had to avenge their pa." Parker stared at nothing for a bit, remembering. "Just between you and me, I pointed 'em south toward the border, gave 'em an hour's head start, and told 'em if I ever saw 'em again, I'd shoot 'em on the spot." He gave me a solemn look. "They did the wrong thing for a good reason, which is why I gave 'em a second chance. Sometimes you have to look at the backside of something to see the truth of it, to know what's right."

Parker finished his third cup of coffee, and signaled to the waiter for his check. "Well, Mister Poole," he said as he stood to go, "it's been a pleasant chat. I wish you a good day, sir."

"And to you, sir."

I dawdled for a while, poking at my plate as it grew cold, and worried about Arda. After brooding on it for some time, I decided that if Learnéd did something to her, he would have dismissed me; not to mention I would have noticed the train wreck which resulted. That was one load off my mind, at any rate. I had no idea what to do about the rest of it. Parker had it: the right and wrong of Arda's rebellion followed a higher truth than the letter of the law, and I had to deal with it on principle. That was the easy part; what to do *about* it still perplexed me. I gave up on breakfast, and headed for the lounge car.

§

For a while, I wondered if we'd even make it to Ogden. The 'Overland' slowed to a crawl by midday, probably stuck behind a freight train, and we stopped every now and then for no apparent reason. One such stop lasted over an hour, stuck out on the wind-blown prairie with nothing but a crude telegraph shanty, its train order semaphore, and a row of telegraph poles marching into the distance for company. How the lines were still up with all the ice they carried was beyond me. I shuddered to think of what the the signals crews went through to keep them going. The bleak and lifeless prairie spread around us as far as the eye could see. The snow wasn't that heavy, but a raw wind piled drifts against the shanty, the train, and everything else.

I sat at the rear of the lounge car, ignoring the chatter around me, and worried. I was desperately tempted to go looking for her to be sure she was all right. I fought that temptation down, since I didn't want to arouse Learnéd's suspicion, and stared listlessly out the rear windows, pondering the track that stretched away behind us to the vague horizon. Right then, I wished I was still in Omaha, or better yet, New York City.

Eventually the station agent came out of his shanty, and passed orders up to the train crew before beating a hasty retreat. A short time later, we started moving again.

§

I finally broke down by mid afternoon. I couldn't resist not knowing what happened to Arda. Her compartment door was closed when I got there, and I couldn't hear anything from within.

"Arda?" I tapped on the door gently. "It's Nate. Are you in?"

The door opened after a bit. She was solemn and weary, and she'd been crying. "Hello, Nathaniel."

"I missed you for breakfast. Are you all right?"

"Yes." She sighed, a half sob, and stepped back to invite me in. "I was resting."

I knew she was brooding over what she told me last night, about her life, and how the Movement blasphemed her very existence. She had every reason to be sad, and I pitied her. I carefully left my jacket in the hall, closed the door, and took her in my arms. "Would you like some lunch?" I asked, softly.

"Thank you, Nathaniel. I had them send something to me." There was a tray on her berth: she was eating light, for her. "I will be all right, Nathaniel. Thank you for caring."

I hesitated for a moment, then decided that she needed to be alone. I gave her a comforting squeeze, then turned for the door. "Well, I guess I'll see you for dinner then?"

"Please...hold me, Nathaniel."

I took her in my arms again and tried to comfort her. "I'm sorry about what happened to you, Arda. I'm sorry about how the Movement used you. You can't let the past hurt you. You have to go on with your life."

"You are right, Nathaniel. B-but how can I leave the only life I have ever known?" She looked longingly into my eyes. "Freedom iss an alien world to me, ass alien ass this time iss. I ney know how to function on my own."

That reminded me that, broken or not, all she had ever known was mindless obedience. I'd seen this before in the slaves we freed during the war: once they got over their joy at being liberated, they were lost. They were never subjected to the mind control of Arda's time; how could she cope with being freed from a power greater than any overseer's whip?

"This mind control? They do that with retros, don't they?"

She nodded. "Their uses are almost unlimited. They are the key to most modern medicine of my time." She gave me a wain smile. "We lowballed a shipment of three hundred retros, and used them to improve ourselves. It was a major victory. They gave uss a fighting chance against them."

I hesitated before broaching the next obvious question. "He...said the 'Smarts' may have driven you mad."

She looked away with tears in her eyes. "That iss true. Citizens are only given ass much intelligence ass needed for our assigned roles; it iss easier to control uss that way." She clutched herself and shivered. "My duties ney required much intelligence. I took the Smarts so I could function, but they have a price."

"Arda..."

"Nathaniel, the only way we can match the Pure Of Thought iss to be ass tough ass they are. Their minds are stabilized by their gestalt. Mine..." She sighed, and turned away again. "I ney am perfect, Nathaniel. Truth, I ney entirely sane, although I control it most times. It iss the price we pay for freedom."

I had a sudden suspicion. "Is that why you took me to bed, Arda?"

She nodded. "Yes, Nathaniel. I gave in to impulse. I ney should have, but I am only human."

"I...can't fault you, Arda."

"Sometimes I wish I ney was made," she sobbed. "Sometimes, I see what the Movement has done, and I want to die. And other times, I am so filled with hate that I ney can control myself."

"That's why you joined the revolution?"

"They gave me a place to hide. They gave me the retros I needed to function. They gave me a chance to strike back at the Movement." She stared silently for a moment, then, "I was Broken; I had ney other choice if I was to live."

We held each other for a while in a room full of aching silence, and wept. I was shaken by the horror of her existence, and it took some time for me to pull myself together.

"Look, this mission of yours can't be all that important, can it?" I said at last, and gave her a little kiss. "Right now you're in a bad spot. Focus on getting to San Francisco and safety. Your mission can wait for another day."

She shook her head emphatically. "Ney, Nathaniel. My mission iss key to our strategy, and it can only be done now. I ney can fail."

I cursed silently in dismay at that. Were they so desperate as to rest all their hopes on this one frail woman? "Why did they send you, Arda? You don't really seem cut out for this sort of thing."

She was silent, cuddled in my arms. "I was the best qualified for the mission," she muttered at last.

They *were* desperate. "Can't you do this mission later after you've escaped from Learnéd?"

"It ney works that way," she said in a soft, almost resigned voice. "The fractal anomaly in the temporal structure creates a finite time frame where action iss possible. Operating outside that frame would cause an uncontrolled change. Duplicate missions in that frame would trigger a paradox. We have already entered the anomaly's perimeter, so I ney can abort. I have to act now regardless of Learnéd."

That was even more disconcerting. I tried to imagine a rift in the fabric of reality itself, but the very concept made my head swim. Whatever they planned, it had to happen soon, probably right here on this train, and there was no way she could get out of it. We were both running out of time.

"How long do you have?"

"I have from yesterday until four days after our arrival."

That gave us some slack at any rate, but the delays in our journey were eating up her margin for error, and the confines of this train gave her precious little room to maneuver. And who knew how many more Learnéds would turn up if she waited. The odds were simply too great. Her only hope was to abandon her duty and run for cover...but she couldn't do that without dooming the future. No wonder she was so shaken.

"You can't let all that get to you," I told her. "If you have to do this now, then you need to stay focussed." We looked at each other for a long moment, then I said, "I'll do whatever I can to help you."

She sobbed, and looked away.

"You can do this, Arda. I know you can."

"My mission..." she muttered, hollowly.

"Be strong, Arda, for your own sake, and for the future."

She turned away and wrapped her arms around her middle. "You are wise, Nathaniel. But I ney am strong, ney like you."

"The resistance wouldn't have sent you if you couldn't do the job." I wrapped my arms around her waist, drew her against my chest, and gave her a little kiss on her cheek. "Have faith in yourself. I do."

She fought back her tears, then said, "I...will try. I need to rest now, Nathaniel. Thank you."

§

Ogden, capital of the Utah Territory, was the largest town we'd seen since leaving Omaha, not that that was saying much. It was well after dark when we arrived. I was in the lounge car digesting an early dinner and brooding, as usual. Parker showed up a bit later, we spoke briefly, and he settled in a nearby seat with a beer and a cigar. I wasn't in the mood for company, so I went back to staring out the window and wondered what would go wrong next.

104

Sure enough, Conductor Doggett showed up as regular as clockwork, and took his station before the bar. "Your attention, please, gentlemen! We have received word that the weather to the west of us is slowing traffic, so we are going to hold here for a while. You can rest assured that this is purely routine, and we are in no danger. We will use the opportunity to refresh our stocks, and we should be leaving again in the not too distant future."

That brought on another round of complaining from the crowd, not that there was anything they could do but order another beer and go back to gossiping.

"Damn, I swear we'd do better in covered wagons," Parker grumbled.

"Maybe," I said. "But then there'd be no beer."

Parker chuckled. "You got that right. We should count our blessings."

I put the noise around me out of mind, went back to my window, and worried over what to do. Learnéd, both here and the ones waiting in San Francisco, either had to be eliminated or outmaneuvered. The one here was a very real threat, and whatever we did, he had to be dealt with soon. But even armed as she was, it would be foolish for us to go against him, and if more of them came, it would be suicide. No, we had to avoid them, get to San Francisco, and complete her mission before they picked up our trail again. The problem was how?

I stared gloomily out the window at the dimly lit streets of Ogden as I played with the gold coins in my pocket. That drew a nearby hotel to mind, and my hope rose as I saw a possible solution to our problem. There was more than enough gold to put me and Arda up for the night. We could wait until the last second before the train left, then duck out and go to ground in the hotel. We could take the next day's train, and with reasonable luck, she could avoid Learnéd long enough to reach San Francisco, complete her mission, and safety.

The more I thought about it, the more it seemed that I could best help her by getting her away from Learnéd. It was a plan, and an easy solution for me. She would be free to continue their fight, and I wouldn't have to worry about Learnéd.

That was a huge load off my mind, and the more I thought about it, the more optimistic I felt. But I would miss her, I realized after a bit. She was erratic, flighty, nigh-on impossible to predict, but there was no denying that she made life interesting. For all the problems she brought into my world, she would take the light away when she left. It was silly to pine over her, but I couldn't help wondering.

I sat staring out the window at the distant hotel, watching people pass on the station boardwalk without seeing them, and mulled it over. If I helped Arda avoid Learnéd and complete her mission, then she would be free, her duty to the future done. If I understood half of her futuristic babble, Learnéd and his Movement—and her resistance—would no longer exist. Perhaps she would be cast adrift in this time, and would have to start over? She would need a friend in this strange world, and we could think about making our own future.

I was fooling myself; we had only just met, and I was nothing more to her than a way to contain her overwhelming lust. I was a primitive brute from her distant past, and while she seemed fond of me, I had nothing to offer her. For one thing, it would be impossible for me to satisfy her and still have the strength, not to mention the time, to earn a living for us. But then...

"Missa Poole, suh!" Samuel's cry snapped me out of my daydreaming, and I spun around in alarm as he came hustling up looking all agitated. "Missa Poole, you need t' go to yo' lady friend. She in trouble!"

That shook me, thinking my worst fear had come to pass; Learnéd must have made some move against her. She might be hurt, or even dead. "Is she all right? Did he do something to her?"

Samuel was jittery in excitement. "No suh. It's the sheriff come to take her to jail fo' killin' that man in Omaha!"

§

The corridor outside her compartment was a mob scene when I arrived. Doggett was there, looking smug and pleased as he watched from the background along with a half dozen curious gawkers. The local sheriff was a hard character with a scraggly beard and cold eyes, backed up by a hulking brute of a deputy.

106

They had blocked the corridor from both directions, with Arda trapped in the doorway to her compartment between them.

"Nathaniel!" She was frantic, trembling, with tears rolling down her cheeks, not surprising with her ingrained fear of authority.

I pushed past the sheriff and took her hands to comfort her. "It's all right, Arda. We'll get this straightened out. Don't you worry."

"Who are you?" The sheriff demanded.

I gave him a distracted glance and muttered, "I'm a friend of hers," then went back to comforting her. I was terrified that she might panic. A lot of people could get hurt if she lost control in this narrow corridor.

"That so? Well I got a message from Omaha says this lady is wanted." He waved a telegram at me. "You'd best not interfere."

"Let me see that." I was so preoccupied that I hadn't noticed Parker tagging along. The sheriff sized him up, including the tin star on his lapel, and handed the telegram over. Parker studied it, then turned to me with a grim look. "Seems that feller she fought with went and died." He handed me the telegram:

OMAHA / OGDEN URGENT 102276 1535
SHERIFF OMAHA REQUESTS SHERIFF OGDEN
ARREST MISS ARDA NO FIRST NAME ON
OVERLAND TRAIN WANTED FOR MURDER X
ADVISE EXTRADITION X

The sheriff in Omaha was intimidated by her at the time, but now he had a body on his hands, which must have made him rethink that. I cursed this latest bad luck as I wondered how Learnéd would react.

"You have to come along, miss," the sheriff said. He nodded to his deputy, who came out with a set of shackles. At the sight of them, Arda whimpered and clung to me hard enough that it threatened to snap my spine.

"You won't need those," I grunted. "I'll walk her over." The sheriff considered for a moment, then waved his deputy back.

It took a lot of coaxing to get her to release me so I could breathe again, after which it took more coaxing to get her to move. She was petrified in sheer terror, but I finally got through to her, and she let me lead her out of her compartment on my arm.

"I'll take care of your things for you, Arda," I said as I pulled off her pouch and tossed it on her berth before closing the door. One thing we didn't need was for them to find her strange weapon and her other future trinkets. This situation was bad enough already.

"It looks like your lady friend has a whole lot of troubles," Parker said to me as we left. He didn't know the half of it.

*****

## "Day Four: Evening"

The Ogden Township jail was a solid brick building a few blocks from the station along one of the town's few main streets. The inside was typical of the like; bare and functional, lit by oil lamps, with a board floor, a Sears iron stove, a rack of rifles on one wall, and the cell block through a barred door to the rear. The Justice of the Peace looked like the local preacher, which he probably was; thin, stoop-shouldered, and balding. He was waiting for us, sitting at the sheriff's desk studying another telegram when we trooped in, and he blinked at Arda in surprise as she stood before him.

"As I hear-tell, you got into a scrape with a man in Omaha?" He paused to adjust his spectacles and read the sheriff's telegram again, then pondered the second telegram which must have been a follow-up with more details. "Seems you beat him so bad that he finally went and died." He eyed Arda skeptically. "But that don't make sense. How a mere woman could..." His gaze shifted to me. "I wonder if they're talkin' about the right person."

"She done it, all right," Frank said. He and his two friends turned up right behind us, alerted by Doggett no doubt. "I ain't never seen the like. She bounced him all over the place, an' threw him out the window like nobody's business!"

"That's right," Doggett said. "She did it."

"He grabbed me!" Arda sobbed. "I panicked. I...I ney meant to kill him!"

"She don't seem like the violent type, your Honor," Parker said. "But she she does seem a mite panicky from what I hear. It might have been an accident."

The justice squinted at him. "And who are you, sir?"

"The name's Ned Parker, your Honor. Texas Rangers. And I can tell you that mister Doggett here don't know beans about it. He was on the station grounds collecting tickets when this happened."

"She admitted it!" Doggett yelped. "She said so right in front of the sheriff!"

"But you didn't see it?" the justice demanded.

"Well, no." Doggett faltered under Parker's stern look. "But she said so, and you heard her again, just now! Anyway, the diner steward was there. He can testify."

"So can we!" Frank added, hotly.

"And what about you?" the justice demanded of me. "Were you there? What did you see?"

"Yes, I was, and he grabbed her first. He was drunk. She was defending herself."

"It don't make sense," the justice grumbled as he studied the telegrams again. "Why'd they let her go in the first place?" He looked the three cowpokes over skeptically. "I don't see how a mere woman could..." His eyes drifted to me, then back to her again. "I don't see heads nor tails of it, but we got plenty of witnesses both ways..." He brooded over the telegrams once more. "...So, Tom, I guess you better lock her up for the night," he said to the sheriff. "We'll ship her back to Omaha an' let them figger it out."

Arda whimpered at that, and clung to me as I tried to comfort her. "Serves her right," Frank crowed as the three left. I almost went for him, but she needed me right then. Doggett lingered as the others drifted away, gloating over her misfortune until I gave him a look that made him cringe, and he left quickly. Soon all that remained was us, the sheriff and his deputy, and Parker.

"Don't be afraid, Arda," I said to her. "It'll work out."

"They will send me back?"

"Don't worry. I'll take care of it."

She watched me with wide eyes. "This...will delay my journey. I ney will get to SaFrisko in time."

Her damned mission again, not that there was anything we could do about it if she did miss her deadline. I nuzzled her cheek and murmured, "It'll work out. I'll be there to testify. You'll get off."

If anything, that seemed to upset her even more. "You will come with me?"

"Yes, of course I will." In the back of my mind, I wondered if we could use this to throw Learnéd off the scent, as I had planned earlier.

I noticed Parker standing by, obviously wanting to meet her at last. I wasn't thrilled about it, but there was no way I could refuse without offending him or arousing his suspicion. "Arda?" I took her arm and turned her to face him. "This is Ned Parker. He's a famous lawman...our law!" I added hastily as she recoiled in panic. "He's not like the law where you came from."

Parker considered her as she stood trembling, wide-eyed, and breathing hard, then tipped his hat to her gravely. "I'm pleased to meet you, miss Arda. Shame it has to be under these circumstances."

She clung painfully to my arm, unable to speak for the moment.

"I've heard a lot about you." Parker smiled and shook his head. "The rumors don't tell the half of it."

"What...what will they do to me?" she managed at last. "I ney meant to kill him. Ney can they let me go?"

"Folks have to face up to what they did," he said, firmly. Then his tone softened. "But you was defendin' yourself from what I hear, and that makes a difference. Anyway, I'll put in a good word for you."

"Thank you," she whispered.

Parker gave me a sympathetic look as he turned to go. "I hope this works out all right, mister Poole."

"Thank you." He nodded, and left. The sheriff eyed me skeptically, then pointed her toward the cell block.

§

Arda's new home was a six by eight foot brick cell with a barred door, a rough wooden cot, and a bucket in one corner. She froze in the doorway, trembling, and it took some coaxing, but I finally got her to enter. The sheriff locked her in, leaving her clinging to the bars with a woebegone look, and left me alone to comfort her.

"Everything will be all right, Arda," I said, softly.

"I am sorry, Nathaniel," she whimpered.

"You couldn't help it." It struck my heart to see her like this, in this rude lockup facing trial for murder. I wondered whether her resistance ever thought of such an unpleasant mischance.

"I ney should have done that. It was an unplanned change..." I gestured urgently for silence; in her distraught state, she'd forgotten Learnéd's listening device. She faltered, then said, "...something like that could upset everything. That was stupid of me."

"I'll do what I can to get you free." I caressed her cheek. "I'm with you all the way. Promise me you won't do anything rash." I gave her the best smile I could. "I'll be back in the morning. Until then, try to get some sleep, and don't worry."

"I will try, Nathaniel."

I gave her a peck on the cheek. "Good night."

"I...must stay sane," she mumbled as I left.

§

The night was frosty and tinged with wood smoke, and the sky above blazed with stars. The ground under my feet was half frozen, and crunched as I walked. The streets were quiet, although a piano was playing somewhere in the distance.

This was a fine pickle! I fretted as I headed back to the train, wondering how we would cope with this latest mess. Learnéd must know what was going on from his listening device, and he would figure that she was disarmed. What would he do? He was content to wait up to now, not wanting to risk a confrontation on the crowded train, but with her cornered in the jail, would he make his move? I stopped in the middle of the street and looked all around, carefully searching the shadows. He could be anywhere, and I was no match for him physically, that was certain. Then I remembered her strange future weapon: if I could figure out how to use it, it would give me a fighting chance. It occurred to me, as I ran for the train, that they would be in for an ugly surprise if they did try to hang her.

§

I went to ground in Arda's compartment, and dug into her pouch and came up with a half-dozen items including her future weapon. The thing was surprisingly heavy, and as I examined it, I began to lose heart. There was no trigger, no sights, no screws, no release catches, nothing except that smooth mirror for a muzzle and the outline of an opening in the butt. I toyed with it for a while, but the more I thought about it, the more it gave me the hebe-gebees.  Seeing the horrors of their future science, I had to wonder what their weaponry must be like.  I couldn't figure out how to fire it, and since it didn't have a trigger, I couldn't even be sure what would set it off, so I put it gingerly back in her pouch along with the rest, and sat on her berth trying to think of something.

Should I smuggle her weapon to her, I wondered?  If I did, could she use it effectively in her present state?  After seeing her reaction to any sort of lawmen, I was afraid she would come unglued simply at the sight of Learnéd.  No, she was too close to the edge to trust with a weapon.  The only thing I could do was keep an eye on him, and somehow head him off if he made a move.

There was also the matter of getting her out of jail.  One thing was clear: she couldn't go back to Omaha.  Not only was she in very real danger of being hanged, but it would give Learnéd plenty of opportunities to strike.  Why he hadn't done so yet was beyond me, but our luck wouldn't hold much longer.  I had to get her back on the train and, mission or no, get her to San Francisco and safety.  But could we break her out without killing the sheriff and his deputy?  And if she did break out, how far could we get before the authorities down the line intercepted us?  No, I had to convince them to let her go.

The train could leave at any time, so there was precious little to waste, but I had to wait for morning before I could do anything.  For the moment, all I could do was check up on Learnéd.

§

"Where have you been?" Learnéd demanded when I returned to my compartment in a weary funk.

"With her," I muttered.

"Has she said anything important?"

I looked at him in surprise, wondering why he didn't say anything about all the commotion.  "Um...no, nothing.  We've been kind of busy, you know?"

Learnéd snorted in contempt.  "I ney suppose I can expect any better from you."

"Probably not," I grumbled.

113

I didn't know what to make of his seeming indifference. This was *so* obvious an opening that he should have been demanding answers and getting ready to go after her. What was he up to? Could he somehow not know? I thought about sticking close to him so I could counter anything he tried, but decided it would be best to keep up appearances in case he didn't realize what happened. I needed to get out of there in any event before I burst.

"You go to the diner?" he asked as I headed out again.

"Yes, yes, I'll send you food."

"It iss about time. I hope for your sake they ney are closed."

§

The after dinner crowd was already thinning out when I got there, and the kitchen didn't have much left. They put together something for me, and I ate listlessly while trying to figure Learnéd's game. Why did he pretend not to notice the commotion over her arrest? That black speck in my lapel must have let him listen in on the whole thing. Was he figuring out his next move? Or was he trying to lull me with his act so he could move against her later that night? Did that mean that he suspected my disloyalty? Whatever he was up to, it was an unexpected turn which could only be bad news for us.

My train of thought was interrupted when Doggett came into the diner. His jacket and vest were unbuttoned, and he had a sandwich in one hand. From his weary look, it seemed likely he was headed to bed himself. I stopped him as he went by.

"Mister Doggett, I was wondering how long we'll be here?"

He gave me a hostile glare. "Probably until tomorrow morning at the earliest. *Hopefully* we will have some peace and quiet tonight, for a change." He prudently retreated after that.

That was one small relief, at any rate. I still didn't know what to do about Learnéd, or whether he would try anything tonight, but without a weapon, there was nothing I could do but hope for the best. After dinner I sent something to him, then went back to Arda's compartment for the night, too tired and depressed to put up with him right then.

*****

114

# "Day Five"

I headed out bright and early the next morning after a sleepless night. My first stop was the diner, where I grabbed a quick bite, ordered a large basket of food for Arda, and sent something to Learnéd as an afterthought.

It was brisk and clear when I climbed down from the train and sized up the situation. Our locomotive was gone, sent to the roundhouse, and apparently they didn't have a steam line here since an elderly yard goat took its place to provide train heat. That was promising, so my next stop was the stationmaster's office to find out how much time we had.

The stationmaster was a sorely tried soul whose office was a Bedlam of irate trainmen, scurrying messenger boys, and the endlessly clattering telegraph. He sat at a desk littered with open account books, dirty dishes, and piles of telegram forms and train order copies which kept spilling onto the floor. "Well, that's hard to say," he answered my question after some deliberation. "There's been weather and breakdowns, so things are clogged up bad west of here. The line is running, but it's as slow as molasses."

That was good news for a change. "Any word on the eastbound passenger train?"

He fought off an enormous yawn, and rubbed his neck. "Well there you're out of luck. They were delayed getting over Donner Pass. Reno cleared out their yard to hold westbound traffic, so they got stuck behind a half-dozen freight trains. The whole she-bang's headed this way, but it'll likely be tomorrow before the last of them gets here. As for your train, it probably won't move until that eastbound pack gets clear. We don't want all you people stuck in the hole out there in the middle of nowhere."

A train came crawling past as I left the station, and I paused to size it up: two large locomotives straining with perhaps eighty freight cars. If they were forced to clear out Reno, then the rest of the eastbounds would be every bit as big and slow, and clearing the line could take for ever. Ordinarily, I would have been annoyed no end at the delay; for the moment, I was thankful.

§

The sheriff was at his desk working on a mean plate of bread and beans when I came in, while his deputy was busy cleaning his pistol with an oily rag. I sized the two up, wondering if I would have to tangle with them to get her out, and was not happy. The sheriff was a hard case, and the deputy was a hulking brute whose battered features said he'd seen plenty of desperate scrapes. Either would be a tough fight, and together they were too much to handle even without all the firearms in the place. No, a jailbreak would be a last desperate option.

"What's in the basket?" the sheriff demanded. The deputy scowled at me.

"I brought her something to eat."

"She's been fed." He set his plate aside, came over and took a look under the napkin. "Might fancy," he grumbled. So much for any hope of smuggling Arda's weapon to her. "All right, go on and see her." He waved me toward the cell block, and went back to his breakfast.

Arda was curled up on the cot staring at the wall when I came in. She was utterly woebegone, and she'd been crying, but her face lit up when she saw me. "Nathaniel!" She bounced off the cot and clung to the door bars, almost giddy in her joy. "You came back!"

"Of course I did." I was a bit hurt that she had seemingly given up on me. I held the basket up to her and pulled the napkin away. "And I brought you some food." She grabbed the bread and attacked it with such a fever that it made me feel guilty. She finished that fast, then attacked the piece of ham, and hardly slowed when she got to the potato fritters. A tin plate and cup lay on the floor by her cot, but jailhouse fare would hardly put a dent in her appetite.

"I'm going to see the Justice of the Peace," I told her while she ate. "Hopefully I can talk him around and get you out of here."

She paused and gave me a worried look. "Do you think they will let me go?"

"I don't know," I told her, honestly. "But I won't quit on you; I promise."

"But I must..." she muttered in confusion, then, "You...are very kind, Nathaniel, more than I deserve."

116

"Don't ever think like that." I caressed her cheek with one finger. "I will do everything I can for you."

She studied me solemnly. "You are right, Nathaniel; I ney should give up hope."

§

The Justice of the Peace turned out to be the town doctor, whose office and home was a few blocks from the jail. He was a methodical sort who took his time to get everything just so, and I waited with growing frustration as he treated a woman with a burnt hand.

"You said yourself that it doesn't make sense," I pleaded with him. "That fellow was bigger than I am, and a tough sum-buck. How could she beat him to death?"

He considered me, then shook his head in confusion. "It don't make sense, but there *are* all those witnesses. Something must have happened."

"He grabbed her, she slapped him, and he slipped and fell out the window."

"And he died later of a brain injury from the fall?"

"Might be. If so, it was an accident. You don't think she could actually beat him to death?"

"She certainly couldn't," he said after pondering it. Thankfully looks were deceiving in her case; I prayed she wouldn't lose control and do something to dispel that notion. "But then why did those three say she did, as well as the conductor?"

"They were getting back at her for their pal, and that conductor is an annoying pain in the ass; we've had no end of run-ins with him, this trip."

"Can't say as I take to him," he muttered.

That was promising. "Look at the common sense of it. Who are you going to believe? Them? Or your own eyes?"

He agonized over that one. "I still can't help wonder if they got the wrong person?"

I grabbed for that. "Maybe he got in a fight somewhere." I prayed he would buy it; it seemed reasonable on its face. "He was drunk and looking for trouble, and he would have been angry after his run-in with her. He must have tangled with someone else."

117

"Well...yeah. I suppose that could have happened," he said after more deliberation. "It makes more sense, anyway." For a moment my hopes rose, and I thought he might let her go. "But still, we don't know what happened, and it's Omaha's problem anyway," he went on. "So I guess she has to go back." He gave my arm a reassuring squeeze. "I'm sure they'll figger it out, and she'll get off."

§

After that failure, I was at a loss. I stood on the street outside the doctor's house, ignoring the townies that walked or rode past, and wondered what to do next. All the legal angles were exhausted, and as much as I hated it, a jailbreak was all we had left. That would be risky, and even if we pulled it off, we would be on the run in a land with few options. And what about Learnéd? Would he act once we were loose even when he hadn't while she was in jail? What would our chances be caught between him and the locals? I still couldn't figure why he did nothing thus far. Could he possibly not know? Once again, I had to wonder if I would live to see San Francisco. I wasn't optimistic about that.

Another eastbound freight train rumbled slowly past in the distance. How many more were there?

§

"I had no luck with the locals," I told her when we were alone at the jail.

She was crestfallen at that. "Then they will send me back?"

"Not if I can help it." I glanced nervously at the doorway, then peeled my jacket off and laid it on the floor at the far end of the cell block before continuing. "Can you break out of here if you have to, Arda?" I asked, softly.

She gave me a solemn look, then took two of the bars in hand and tugged on them. They bent slightly. "Yes, Nathaniel."

"All right." I looked around again. "We have some time yet. I'll come back for you right before the train leaves. You'll have to be ready to break out fast, and we'll run for it."

"You ney will get in trouble?"

"I'll worry about that later."

§

Back on the train, there was nothing I could do but go to ground in the lounge car, where I sat staring out the window and wondered at how bizarre my life had become. The lounge car was busy as usual since there really was nothing else to do on board, and Omaha long since lost its charm. The air was thick with cigar smoke and idle chatter, and for a change there was more grumbling than gossiping. Everyone was upset about the delays since we should have arrived in San Francisco by then, and there was no telling how long the trip would take.

Morning moved on into midday as I sat brooding over the next step. I was not thrilled about a jailbreak, especially with the fast timing it would need. Hopefully it wouldn't come until after dark, so there wouldn't be so many townfolk around to get in the way. This could easily turn into a disaster, but there were no other choices left. The bar was busy, and I wanted a beer in the worst way, but decided I'd best lay off the booze for now. Another freight train crawled past doing all of ten miles per hour. The car roofs were heaped with snow.

Parker drifted by sometime after lunch, and stood staring out the rear windows for a while, lost in thought as he nursed a cigar. Then he glanced at me. "I guess you'll be going back to Omaha, mister Poole?"

"Perhaps," I said cautiously. "I'm still trying to get this mess straightened out."

"Lord, I hope you can. She seems like a decent sort, if a bit high-strung. And from the look of those three yahoos, she likely did this ol' world a favor." He stared off into the distance for a bit, then shook his head. "I can't imagine how she could kill him, though. Remarkable woman," he added as he turned to go. "I wish you the best of luck, mister Poole."

"Thank you, sir," I said as he left.

A remarkable woman; she was that. I thought about her for a long time after he left, and came to realize that my interest in her was personal. It was a foolish notion, but I wanted her sincerely, for all her faults. Afternoon drifted into an early evening, and another eastbound freight train came rumbling by shortly after dark. I'd lost count of them by then.

"Gentlemen, your attention please," Doggett's shrill voice snapped me out of a half-doze. He was back at his usual place in front of the bar. "We just received word that we can leave, so we'll be on our way momentarily." That caused an excited stir in the room, which covered me as I made for the exit.

§

They were coupling a new locomotive to the train as I climbed down from the lounge car, which meant there was still a precious few minutes, but I would have to move fast. I slipped around the far side of the station, trying not to draw notice, then ran for the jail. As I ran down the dark street, I tried feverishly to come up with some clever way of pulling this off, but no brilliant ideas came. There was just one thing to do: I had to grab one of the rifles on that wall rack and pray that it was loaded; that they didn't start shooting; that I could lock them in Arda's cell and we could get back to the train and leave town before they got loose. How far that would get us was doubtful. We would have to change trains as soon as possible to throw off pursuit, but the earliest we could do that was at Elko, Nevada, a half-day ahead. The odds were that a posse would be waiting for us there.

I reached the jail, took a moment to collect my nerve and a deep breath, stepped through the door...and stopped in confusion: Arda was standing by the sheriff's desk. "Nathaniel!" she cried when she saw me. "I am free! They let me go!"

"Her bail's been paid," the sheriff said. Then I noticed a large stack of shiny new gold double eagles on his desk, which made my heart skip a beat. Murder suspects never get bail, since they have every reason to flee to avoid the noose.

"Is it ney wonderful, Nathaniel?" She swept into my arms and hugged me. "We must hurry to catch the train."

"The charges against you haven't been dropped, miss," the sheriff told her, sternly. "You still need to go back to Omaha to stand trial."

"Nathaniel?" She wilted as she turned to me in confusion.

"You can put up at the hotel for the night, but don't try to leave town." The sheriff studied her. "You got some money on you?"

"I'll help her out," I told him.

He pondered me for a moment. "All right." Then he turned to his deputy. "You take her on over to the hotel for the night, Earl." So he had a name after all. "We'll put you two on the eastbound train in the morning. If he wants to tag along, that's fine."

"Right, boss." Earl gave me a look that said he knew what I was thinking, and he was ready to do something about it.

I was a bit flustered now that my desperate plan came to nothing, so for want of a better idea, I took Arda's arm and held her close as we left with Earl a couple paces behind. "Thank you, Nathaniel," she murmured.

"It wasn't me," I said. She gave me a worried look. "We both know who, though."

Those gold double eagles were a bribe, pure and simple: there were precious few lawmen who couldn't be bought for the right price, and Learnéd's shiny gold and forbidding presence would do the trick for some small town sheriff. Something was wrong here: why would Learnéd do this? What was his game?

§

We had to turn left to go to the station, but Earl pointed us to the right. The hotel loomed at the end of the street, and I cursed in frustration at the sight; we should have been checking in as part of my plan to evade Learnéd. As we walked, I tried to figure a way to jump Earl, but he was too far back for me to surprise him. I couldn't count on Arda's strength; she was too shaken by any sort of lawman to put up a fight. I'd have to go it alone, and quickly. A standup fight couldn't end well; my only hope was to ambush him, and he was too wary a brawler to let that happen. I sized up the street ahead, and it looked like my one hope would be at the hotel door; if we stalled for a second, and he got careless...

As we passed an alley between two buildings, there was a heavy *'thud'* followed by a groan from behind us, and we spun around in time to see Earl collapse in a heap.

"What...?" Arda gasped.

"Run!" I grabbed her arm and dragged her down the street. There was only one person I knew who could take a man like Earl down in a single punch, and we didn't want to meet him in a dark alley. Arda collected her wits, and we ran.

121

We went to ground two blocks over, and ducked into a doorway. Arda clung to my arm with a painful grip as I watched the street for any sign of Learnéd. The street was empty except for Earl, still laid in a heap, but there were no end of shadows and dark corners where Learnéd could be hiding. What was he up to?

"What iss happening, Nathaniel?"

"It's him," I whispered as I searched the endless shadows. She whimpered and cringed. "I can't see him. Can you?"

She whimpered again, and clung even tighter.

"Dammit, Arda!" I hissed. "You have night vision, use it! Is he out there?"

She stirred nervously, and looked around. "There...there are many heat sources...I ney see him." She buried her face in my chest. "What are we to do, Nathaniel? He will kill uss!"

"No, he won't." She turned to me in surprise. "He helped us escape, remember? He bribed the sheriff and took down the deputy. He wants something."

"What?"

"That doesn't matter now; getting to the train does."

We ran for it, cut over to the next street, and sprinted for the railroad. Up ahead in the gloom there were two brief toots of a steam whistle. We came to the corner of the street leading to the station, and the train came into view just as the locomotive emitted a cloud of steam and started moving. "Damn it!" I cursed as we ran. Then there was a sharp *'crack'* and the hiss of escaping air, and the train lurched to a halt. "What the...?" They'd big-holed!

There was a stir of curious people along the train, so I pushed her to the left, and we circled behind a box car where we stopped, gasping for breath as I peeked cautiously around the car. The head end brakeman was working his way back along the train, stooping to check the undercarriages, while the hogger and fireboy watched from the cab. No one was looking this way.

"Come on!" We picked our way across the track, keeping to the shadows as much as we could, and came down the far side of the locomotive. We were nearly to the end of the baggage car when the door opened, and a figure stepped out onto the platform. He was obscured by the light behind him, but I knew who it was.

"It's Doggett!" I hissed, and we flattened ourselves against the side of the car. There was an anxious moment as he leaned out to look back down the track, then he vanished, and his legs appeared under the car as he headed along the other side to where the brakeman squatted looking at the coupling between the next two cars. I gestured to her, and we paced him, creeping along in the shadows, trying not to slip in the treacherous slush, and making as little noise as we could. We stopped short of the next car, and I peeked around the edge carefully.

"What happened?" Doggett demanded.

The brakeman turned away; I grabbed her hand, and we slipped by as quietly as we could, me hoping they wouldn't see us pass. "We got a broken air hose," the brakeman told Doggett. "Must-a been frozen. It'll take about ten minutes to fix." A length of heavy rubber hose, the kind used to connect the cars' brake systems, lay on the track.

"Well then, get to it, man! We're late as it is!"

"You say so." He headed for the locomotive while Doggett fumed.

I didn't wait around for them to make repairs; I hustled her further down the train to her car, and we took cover in her compartment where we waited nervously for any sign of pursuit. It seemed like forever before the air brakes sighed, and with two toots from the locomotive, we began moving.

"We were lucky the train ney left," she said softly as she cowered in my arms.

I didn't say anything, but I knew that breakdown was no coincidence, as was Earl's misfortune. Learnéd wanted us on this train, and ripping out a rubber air hose would be no trick for him.

*****

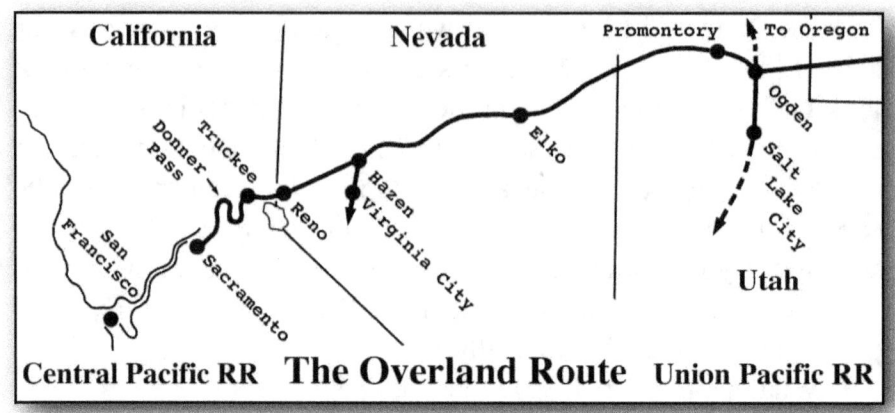

Central Pacific RR **The Overland Route** Union Pacific RR

## "Day Six"

I spent the rest of the night with Arda trying to calm her, which took some doing since she was an emotional wreck. Her ingrained fear of the law all but ruined her, and she needed a lot of comforting. I buried my jacket under the mattress since she was so unsettled that she might say anything, and we wound up stretched on her berth in each other's arms, her trembling and sobbing in a full blown panic while I rubbed her back and spoke gently to her.

"Everything's all right, Arda...*easy!*" She was clinging to me with desperate strength. I fought for air and said, "We got away from Ogden. You don't need to worry about going back."

"He iss still here!"

"He's in my compartment. You said yourself that he'll stay there for now."

"He will kill uss!"

"He hasn't yet. *Arda...*" I was getting woozy from lack of air. "...*easy*..." She relaxed her grip a bit, and I was able to breathe with some effort. "He could have done it back there in Ogden, but he didn't. He's waiting for his pals to join him in Frisco."

"They will kill uss!"

I grunted from the pain of her renewed stranglehold, and managed to wrestle her arms down to my waist so I could at least breathe. "Don't let your fear rule you, Arda. There's time yet, and I have some ideas for how we can evade them."

She fought back her tears, and looked up at me. "I...I ney can do this...I ney am strong...ney like you."

"Think, Arda! Use your intelligence. Don't let their conditioning take over again."

"But we are trapped here. We ney can avoid them."

"I'm working on that. We still have time. Things will work out somehow."

She buried her face in my shoulder as her panic subsided a little. "You are wise, Nathaniel," she murmured. "I trust you."

Her panic ebbed slowly, and she finally relaxed enough that I was able to peel her off me. I lay with her in my arms and stared out the window at the passing landscape without really seeing it, and wondered about what happened back in Ogden. Something was seriously wrong: Learnéd's actions yesterday didn't jibe with what he told me of his plans originally. Of course I was a fool to put much faith in his word on anything, but if he didn't simply want to arrest her, what did he want?

Something she said the other day came back to me: *'There iss one good thing about Secret Police anywhen: they think everyone iss ass mentally lock-stepped ass they are.'* But Learnéd was hardly acting like an old-time routineer; he was up to no good, and I couldn't see what he planned. What I could see, now, was that she seriously underestimated him. And as I thought about it, I recalled other instances where she was thoughtless, or gave in to impulse, or failed to see the obvious.

*'Smarts make one more intelligent,'* Learnéd said at the beginning. *'She took four of them, which more than doubles the average intelligence,'* If so, she was no more than average now, and spotty at that. She may have had the brain power, but she wasn't in the habit of thinking. I caressed her head gently, and wondered how much brain power she had to begin with? It was bad enough that the Movement created her to order for their purposes, but to deliberately make her as a half-wit grated on my soul. I promised myself an accounting for that sometime soon as I comforted her. As for now, it was clear that I couldn't trust her judgment for a number of reasons. I would have to take the lead in our efforts if we were to get out of this mess.

125

The gentle swaying of the car, and the rhythmic *clickey-clack* of the wheels was hypnotic. Sometime in the wee hours exhaustion got the better of our terror, and we drifted off into troubled sleep.

§

Morning, to my surprise, did not begin with a heavy knock on the door. The wain sunlight streaming through the window dragged me back to the here and now, and I idly watched the passing landscape. We lay together, drowsy and half-awake, with her head on my shoulder as I rubbed her back gently and wondered what would happen next.

"Good morning, Nathaniel," she muttered at last.

I caressed her cheek with one finger. "How do you feel this morning?"

"I suppose I am all right." She hugged me closer, but not as hard. "I could lay here in your arms forever, Nathaniel," she sighed. She still sounded shaky.

"How about some breakfast?" My stomach was sounding off irritably. "You'll feel better with some hot food. Are you up to going to the diner?"

She gave me a worried look. "Ney can we stay here?"

"We can't stay hidden forever. We both need food, you especially."

"But people will see uss. They will know I ney am in jail in Ogden. Will they become suspicious?"

"It won't take long for people to figure out that we're on the train, so our best bet is to pretend like nothing happened. In any event, you need to pull yourself together for the rest of our journey. You need to get this over with."

She was still trembling slightly, and her voice was weak. "You are right, Nathaniel. I will do the best I can."

As luck would have it, we no sooner left her compartment then we ran head-on into Doggett, who stared at her in amazement. "You!" he gasped. "What are *you* doing here?"

"I am on my way to breakfast, if you *must* know," she rebuked him in her most arrogant regal tone, and swept on past as if nothing had happened while I looked on in bemusement.

126

Doggett watched her go, then shook his head in dismay. "This has been one hell of a trip," he muttered. "Weather, breakdowns, all these delays, and now her." He eyed me bitterly. "You two are my cross to bear."

"Yeah, well just remember; you can never hammer the last nail in by yourself."

§

We were headed into the foothills of the Rockies. The region was barren, rolling sagebrush country with a forbidding line of mountains in the distance ahead. There was a chill wind blowing from the north as we crossed between the cars, and the sky was starting to cloud up, although it felt more like rain than snow.

Breakfast was routine and the fare was plain, with flapjacks, potato hash, and whispered gossip in the background. The diner long since used up its supplies, and was improvising with what they could get locally. She was to all appearances completely calm and self-possessed, and I marveled again at her quicksilver personality. Neither of us was in a talkative mood, so we plowed through in silence, each of us taking comfort from having the other there. Her regular waiter served us with more than the usual courtesy and a hint of fear, since her reputation now included that of an accused murderer. Those three cowpokes came in while we were eating, and carefully avoided her.

She ate like a lumberjack, going through three plates full before she tapered off. We sat for some time after, nursing thin coffee and waiting for someone to say something. "What can we do, Nathaniel?" she asked at last, softly.

I took her hand and gave it a comforting squeeze. "It's like we used to say in the Army: get through today, worry about tomorrow when it gets here."

"Tomorrow...iss all too close."

"Things are all right for now. Don't borrow trouble. We'll get to San Francisco, and your journey will be complete."

"My journey..." She gave me a stricken look. "I...suppose it will." She dropped my hand and busied herself with her napkin. "Will you please escort me to my compartment, Nathaniel?"

§

I was afraid to return to my compartment after dropping her off, but I had no choice. After last night, we faced a whole new situation, and I needed to keep up pretenses until I could sound Learnéd out. Hopefully I could learn something of what he was planning, and perhaps forestall any further moves by him.

"So, has she said anything?" he demanded when I came in.

"Nothing much. She's pretty close-mouthed."

He sneered in contempt. "Well I hope you gave her a good time, at least, since you seem to be accomplishing little else."

"Honestly, it wasn't all that pleasant. I'll be glad when this is over."

"Ass will I, ass I ney will have to rely on you any further."

It looked like he wanted to pick a fight, which I was in no mood for. "Yeah, well, what can you expect from a citizen, after all?"

"The Movement *expects* you to do your duties ass instructed," he snapped. "Once again, you have failed to bring food ass you were told to."

"Dammit!" I turned on him in frustration, then caught myself. "All right. I'll get your food, and I hope you choke on it!"

I stormed out of there in righteous outrage, and paused in the washroom to pull myself together. I was starting to lose it from the endless tension, which dismayed me when I thought about it. I studied my face in the mirror; my reflection was strained and weary. I took a couple deep breaths to calm myself, then splashed some water from the sink on my face.

"Is yo' all right, suh?" Samuel asked from the doorway.

"Huh? Um...yeah. Just a minor disagreement, is all."

"Ah hope it ain't no mo' then that, suh. That man scares me somethin' awful."

I looked at him in surprise, then realized the thin walls did nothing for privacy. If he was listening to our confrontations, it'd be no wonder if he was nervous. "He's good at that," I told him.

Samuel fidgeted for a bit, then, "He come out of yo' room last night, suh." He hesitated some more. "He got off the train just fo' we left, an' then we pull out, an' then de brakes failed, and then he come back on an' goes back to you'ah room."

That confirmed what happened last night, not that it was any surprise. "Thank you, Samuel. You're doing a fine job." I was impressed by his devotion, especially with how nervous he was.

"Is yo' lady friend all right, suh? She seemed might shook, with de sheriff comin' fo' her an' all."

"She's pretty upset, but she'll be all right. We got that straightened out."

"Lawd, I hope so, suh. She got enough troubles."

I stood leaning on the sink for a time after he left, too weary to do anything. *'She got enough troubles,'* he said. Lord, that was the truth. We both needed all the help we could get, and Samuel's courage and support meant a lot just then. He was a good man; better than we deserved.

As for Learnéd, whatever he was up to, he was keeping it to himself for now, so I had to pretend like I knew nothing about his part in our escape. As I thought about it, I realized that he must have left the train several minutes before I did—before Doggett's announcement in the lounge car—for him to have the time to bribe the sheriff and disappear again before I got there. The only way he could know of our departure in advance was if he put a black speck on Doggett's uniform as well. How many of those did he have scattered around? Did he put one on Samuel? I wondered if I could borrow Arda's little detector box, but if Samuel was compromised, it was already too late to worry about it. For the moment, if Learnéd wanted to play the innocent and pretend that last night's jail break never happened, I was happy to cooperate.

§

I stopped in the diner to send food to Learnéd, then headed for the lounge car, so fed up that I couldn't stomach him for the moment. Parker caught me in the corridor as I entered the car. "I hear your lady friend is still with us," he greeted me.

That was Doggett's doing, no doubt, and there was no sense in denying it, so I looked him square in the eye. "Yes, she is."

"Last I recall, she was under arrest there in Ogden."

"We got it straightened out."

He pondered that, then said, "One can only hope. She seems like a decent sort, and I'd hate to see her in trouble with the law."

"Me too."

"What happened there in Omaha is pretty serious." He gave me a stern look. "Killin' a man ain't no small matter. I hope this *has* been settled, for her sake."

"She was defending herself, honest."

His eyes narrowed. "There ain't nothing *irregular* about this, is there, boy?"

After putting up with Learnéd, I shouldn't have been intimidated by his display, but I was. Nonetheless, I didn't want to lie to him any further, as I felt it was best to keep his respect, if possible. "If anyone has a problem later, I'll answer for it," I told him. His expression turned harder, if possible. "It's like you said the other day: sometimes you have to look at the backside of something to see the right of it."

He considered me with a hard eye, then nodded thoughtfully. "Sometimes you do. Good day, mister Poole."

"And to you, sir," I said as he left.

§

It was slow going on the long grades, but the rare opposing traffic was always in the hole for us. The line ahead was largely empty since they cleared it for the expected backlog heading west over the Sierras, so we slogged along making steady time.

We reached Elko, Nevada by mid-morning, and by time we got there, I half expected the sheriff and the territorial militia to be waiting in force on the station grounds. There was nothing unusual out there as we pulled in, which was a huge relief.

"So, we reach another bright light of your civilization at last," Learnéd said as he peered out the compartment window.

"Be thankful," I grumbled. I had returned to the compartment —I no longer thought of it as 'my' compartment—to check up on him. My excuse was sorting out a few items of clothing to rinse out in the restroom later, since I was fresh out. "At least there is a civilization out there to come to."

"I suppose I should be thankful. This iss taking for ever."

I paused digging through my soiled linens. "This is your past, shouldn't you know how long this trip lasted?"

He hesitated. "I ney thought to check that before we left."

130

"That a fact?" I was a bit relieved to see Learnéd was capable of error. "So maybe you need a native guide after all?" He frowned, but said nothing. "I'm going to look around," I said as I grabbed my coat. "Maybe I can get an idea of how much longer this trip will take."

§

I hit dirt to scout the area almost before we halted. My first look around was some relief; aside from a few railroad workers and some idlers gathered for what was probably the highlight of Elko's day, there was no one on the station grounds. That was no proof that a posse wasn't about to swoop down on us, but it was promising. It snowed here recently, and the chill rain was coming down now, so the station grounds were ankle deep in dirty slush.

Elko wasn't much: another crude mining settlement of dirt streets and false front board buildings, home to maybe a thousand souls, if that. The town's only claim to fame was as a division point where the crew could be relieved and the locomotive replaced. They didn't even have a proper roundhouse, and aside from a bridge across the Humbolt River, the railroad didn't have much to say in general. Other than the engine change and dropping off a sack of mail, there was no reason to stop here. The schedule allowed thirty minutes for business, but they would probably shave that in an effort to make up time. Nonetheless, I wanted to size up the situation in the worst way.

Like the town, the station wasn't impressive. The stationmaster's office was a bare wooden shack with whitewashed walls, a desk with the telegraph, and another cast iron stove which glowed a cheery red. The stationmaster was a lanky, excitable old codger who bubbled with crusty enthusiasm. While most of the railroad people I'd met lately seemed overwhelmed by traffic conditions, he was having a high old time of it.

"Shamus, if you aren't the sorriest of ingrates," he was lambasting a conductor when I came in. "You ought to be proud that we gave you a train at all."

That conductor, another burly Irishman, growled, "I would be, 'cept ye gave it to me. So how long will it take ye t' figger out which way t' send us?"

"Oh, dearie me." The stationmaster struck an exaggerated pose like he has lost in deep thought. "First I got to get rid of that passenger train—stink like a herd of sheep, the lot of 'em, I'll wager—an' then I got to get Billy Ferguson out of here. *Iffn* the Good Lord sees fit to remind me, I *might* let you loose after he's gone."

"But that'll be another hour, easy!"

"Well, then, that'll give you time to clean that pigsty you drive. Lordy, man, I never *seen* such a dirty locomotive!"

The Irishman chuckled at that. "Ain't no dirtier than your station's getting, with all these trains sittin' around smokin' up the place instead of out there on the road!"

"Ain't *that* the sorry truth?" The stationmaster turned on one of the runners lounging by the stove. "You, boy! Get over to the engine shed an' tell ol' man Perry to wake up! There's railroadin' to be done!" The kid laughed, and trotted out. Evidently they were hard up for entertainment here in Elko.

"So what about us, Cap'n?" the conductor demanded.

"What about you?" The stationmaster gave him a disdainful look. "Best I can be bothered is give you third after Ferguson and the sheep train."

"Welllll, if that's all t' *better* ye can manage..."

"At least you've got a nice cozy fire to warm you while you wait," he called as the man left, then he turned his sunny disposition on me. "If you come bringin' me woe, friend, I'll trade you turd for turd, an' give you full measure," he greeted me with a wry grin.

Sad to say, I didn't rise to his levity. "I'm hoping to receive a telegram from Omaha. Has anything come in lately?"

"No, sir, nothin' except railroad business, and a more pitiful tale of woe you'll never hear!"

That was a relief, although it wasn't the final word by any means. "So, anything new and exciting around here?" I asked carefully.

"*Hell* no," he snorted. "This town ain't big enough. There's just our regularly scheduled winter crisis, and even that's nothin' like what we've had here in the past."

Better yet; if the local law was stirring, this fellow would be the first to tell the world of it. Maybe the sheriff in Omaha decided not to say anything about our escape, which suggested that Earl survived his run-in with Learnéd, and that they knew better than to let her release be known.

"So what's the situation west of here?" I asked. "We should have reached Frisco by now."

He gave me a cold eye. "Sonny boy, there's many things that 'should happen' in this-here world."

"You got that right," I muttered, fervently.

He settled in his chair and pondered for a bit, and as he did, his weariness showed. "Most of the traffic's been cleared from the west, so most of what's running now is westbound. There's a few trains gettin' over Donner, so you'll meet some traffic, but it should be fairly smooth sailin' from here to Reno."

"That's good news. It's been rough out there."

"Shoot, boy, this ain't *nothin'* compared to what them poor barstids at Reno are stuck with. Heck-fire, I swear I'll quit this road an' go work for the Southwestern before I'll let them stick me in Reno! Why, I'm minded of a time when the *big* snow came down, and we was..."

"Speaking of which, I better get back." I edged toward the door.

"Sonny, when we first opened this line, it was hell out there at times. Trains would get snowbound or ambushed by injins..."

"Um...look, I got to run for my train." I headed for the door.

"...trains'd get stuck for *weeks*..."

§

I paused once I got out of there, and stood watching the station grounds for any sign of suspicious activity while I thought matters over. Tentatively, we'd left the troubles in Ogden behind, so all we had to do now was get to San Francisco, complete Arda's mission, and somehow avoid a horde of Learnéds in the process. Nothing to it. Some passengers were taking the air despite the steady drizzle while the car toads gave the train a quick once-over, and the diner received a skimpy load of supplies. Our new locomotive was being coupled on, so we would be under way shortly.

133

I stood watching as the new locomotive was coupled to our train, and wondered what the next step would be. We still had to lose Learnéd, which meant that my original plan to change trains was still in the cards. I looked around at Elko, and wondered if there was a hotel here. Nothing in sight looked vaguely like one except for a couple of old passenger cars on blocks nearby which were probably makeshift crew quarters; not promising. In any event, we hadn't had the chance to plan anything, so Reno was where we would make our move.

The locomotive let out two shrill whistle blasts, and the loungers on the station grounds headed for the train.

*****

## "Day Seven"

The train rolled into Reno under a nasty midday sky. The omens didn't look good to an old railroad man as we ground to a halt in front of the station. The Reno yard was packed with rolling stock. There was another passenger train parked next to us in the station proper, and the station grounds were thick with idlers. Our train occupied the last open track, which meant that the Overland Route was completely blocked. There wasn't much snow on the ground or in the air, but the bitterly cold wind sent a raw chill through the cars.

"The heater has quit," Learnéd said. True enough, the thin trickle of steam was gone, and I could already feel the advancing chill.

"The locomotive must have been cut off and sent to the roundhouse," I told him. Without that source of steam, we were at the mercy of a Nevada winter. "They'll put a new one on soon, and we'll be on our way. Hopefully."

Learnéd came over and studied the scene through the window, then gestured at the jagged granite range which formed an ominous backdrop ahead of us. "Soon we go into the mountains?"

135

"Yep. The Sierra Nevadas, no less."

"The snow has stopped, yes?" That surprised me a bit. Even this dehumanized future policeman was worried about what we would find in the pass.

"Don't count on it. Those mountains have some of the worst snowfalls on this continent, even this early." I took nasty pleasure at Learnéd's uneasy look. "I imagine the *horror* stories about Donner Pass are still told in your time. No?" Perhaps it was my imagination, but he seemed almost dismayed. "How the Donner party were trapped up there in the pass—about this time of year, in fact? How they had to resort to cannibalism? How less than half of them survived? How the pass was renamed in their memory as a warning to others?" Learnéd blinked at me in surprise. "Well, sir, now you get to find out for yourself."

"They were foolish," he muttered.

"Yeah, well, I *doubt* if we have anything to worry about. I'm going to scout around," I added as I reached for my coat. "Maybe I can get an idea of how long we'll be here." I paused to enjoy Learnéd's uneasy look. "I'll stop by the diner and have them send up a *big* plate of fried pork for you."

§

The chill took my breath away as I climbed down from the car, and I rubbed my hands together for warmth as I gave the area a good once over. The Reno station was smaller than the one at Omaha, and wasn't much fancier. The area along the tracks was swept free of snow, although the footing was treacherous. There was a train order semaphore, its signal arms horizontal to show a complete stop, and a commissary storehouse right up the track. The roundhouse in the distance was shrouded in a fog of wood smoke and steam.

A few passengers were wandering around taking the air. The light was wain even here at midday; the scattered lights of Reno glowed faint against the dark bulk of the mountains. The sky overhead was winter pale and cloudy. Scattered snow was falling, which the chill wind churned up into a thin ground haze. From the look of that sky, it was either snowing or had just snowed up in the pass. It would again.

I wasn't surprised that there was no other locomotive ready to couple on. Instead, two car toads were busy hooking a hose from the roundhouse boilers to the train. The steam hose was caked with ice, which they hammered away to make the connection. A couple more workmen with a baggage cart were loading food into the diner with frigid haste. It looked like we would be here for a while.

A freight train pulled in right behind us. I watched unhappily as the locomotive cut off, switched over to the yard lead, and headed for the roundhouse. There was no other locomotive waiting to take its place either, nor was there for any of the trains in sight. Yes, it seemed we were here for a while. I headed for the station to see what the problem was.

§

The waiting room was empty and dark, save for a messenger boy resting on one of the hard wooden benches. Two cast iron stoves against the opposite walls glowed a cheery red, which took some of the edge off the chill. The stationmaster's office was nearly as large as the waiting room. Reno didn't do much passenger service, being just another railroad division point and mining settlement. The place was long overdue for a fresh coat of whitewash, and the furnishings were a battered desk, a counter behind it holding the telegraph instrument, a couple of chairs, and two bulletin boards liberally plastered with paperwork. The feeble light of some oil lamps gave the room and its two inhabitants a sickly pallor.

The stationmaster was a thin, frazzled man in his forties. He was unshaven, and his bleary eyes and the remains of a sandwich on his desk said he'd gone for some time without sleep. The other was a train crewman; another burly Irishman whose bulky coat and sweaters made him seem to fill the room. His boots dripped, his coat was dusted with snow, and he was every bit as weary.

"Dammit, we're completely swamped," the stationmaster was saying. "The yard is full up, we've got trains standing on the main, and they've started shoving trains down onto the Virginia City line to have a place to park 'em."

The trainman sighed. "So what do we do, Cap'n?"

"Lord, I don't know." The stationmaster rubbed his eyes wearily, then stared at nothing for a bit, trying to marshal his thoughts. "You wait out there on the main until the work train clears, then you can have their spot."

"Ye say so," the trainman grumbled. "But ye best move right quick; we're running out of fuel."

The trainman ignored me as he left, grumbling to himself. The stationmaster finally noticed me. "Can I help you, sir?"

"I wanted to see what the delay is for the 'Overland'."

"You with the railroad?" he asked, suspiciously.

"I laid track for the Southwestern, a ways back."

The stationmaster considered that, then eased up a bit. "There's been a derailment up in the pass. It's hell up there, so there's no telling how long you'll be delayed." He paused for a jawbreaker yawn, then added, "You might want to settle in for a while."

The telegraph on the desk behind him started clattering. He turned, grabbed his pencil, and began recording the message, his visitor forgotten. Having got what I needed, I decided to take a look at Reno, Nevada.

"Shit," the stationmaster muttered as I left.

§

Reno was a typical railroad boom town like dozens sprouting up across the West; that is, a disappointment to someone familiar with more settled eastern cities. The town didn't even exist until a few years ago when the railroad came through. It couldn't have a population of more than 1000 or 1200 at most now, but it was what passed for a center of civilization for this gold and silver mining region. Like Ogden, Reno was a collection of ramshackle wooden buildings, with a few more substantial brick ones laid up and down a network of dirt roads. The most obvious was a fortress-like stone building with a sign reading 'Pinkerton Repository' next to the station. The Pinkerton agency was there to guard precious metal shipments leaving by rail, while the brothels and saloons clustered nearby were there to relieve them of that worry. The railroad's roundhouse, shrouded in smoke, was further down the track with a car shop next to it, along with a water tower and long piles of cordwood for the locomotives. And that was Reno, Nevada.

Two men came out of the Repository and walked up the street toward me.  Pinkerton agents: hard, dangerous men armed with pistols and shotguns and cold arrogance; very much a law unto themselves in this lawless frontier.  I wondered idly what they would think of Arda's future...whether they would aid her or side with the brutal law of her time.  One of them glanced at me as they approached, meeting my gaze eye to eye.  *'I can take you,'* was his unvoiced challenge.

*'No, you can't'*, was my unvoiced answer, and meant it.

The Pinkerton held my eye for a moment, then nodded. Pecking order established—or an unspoken standoff achieved— they went on down the street and vanished into a nearby saloon.

There a large hotel across the street from the salon, which brought to mind my plan to duck out on Learnéd.  We had put this off long enough.  It was time to get Arda off that train and safely to San Francisco and the end of her mission.  The question was timing.  We'd have to move literally at the last second, so the thing now was to decide how soon that second would arrive.

§

There was a work train on a nearby siding.  A row of flat cars loaded with ties and rails sat buried in snow, but a string of bunk cars were lit, and smoke poured from their chimneys.  They sure weren't laying rails in *this* weather.  The gandy dancers were up there in that Godforsaken pass trying to clear the track.  A large steam crane and its tool cars sat on the next track over.  Men hustled around it in a stygian gloom of smoke and blowing snow under the lashing tongue of an ill-tempered foreman, while a large locomotive coupled behind them sat ready to go.

Ahead of the big hook was a steam plow coupled to three large freight engines, with a couple of work cars and a caboose tucked in behind.  Even when it didn't snow, the wind would pile drifts high enough to bury a man, especially in the narrow cuts where the track ran.  In most cases, passing trains could keep ahead of it with heavy plows mounted on their pilot beams.  Donner Pass was the exception: storms routinely dumped seven or eight feet of snow at a crack up there.  It would be like this all winter; each train being escorted over the pass by one of these huge rotary snow machines.

139

Not much snow got over here in the lea of the Sierras, but it was a different story up ahead. Likely there was an avalanche, or a train hit a patch of caked ice that lifted the wheels off the rails. There was no telling how bad it was, or how long it would take to clear the wreck. And if they needed to repair the track in this weather...

There was a flurry of whistles, accompanied by clouds of smoke and steam. A switchman bent the iron, the snow plow train lurched and rolled slowly out onto the main line, followed by the wrecking train with its massive steam crane leading the way, all protesting with loud groans and squeals of metal on chilled metal. "Great," I grumbled. If they were only now sending the big hook up the hill, there was no telling how long we'd be here.

§

"One bit of good news," I told Learnéd. "You won't have to worry about going over the pass for a while."

Learnéd studied me for a moment. "I suppose that iss," he said, doubtfully. Then, "Do you think she suspects?"

"She hasn't said anything," I said, carefully. Learnéd didn't look convinced. "And even if she does, where else can she go? There's nothing out there but some little Godforsaken hell-hole of a frontier village."

"There iss that." Learnéd sounded suspicious, but he seemed content to wait for now. "And where are you going?" he demanded as I turned to the door.

"To the diner. The air in here is getting thick. And, yes, I'll have them send food."

He frowned, and settled in his chair. "That iss correct."

§

"Missa Poole, suh," Samuel called to me as I reached the car door.

I instinctively clamped my hand over the listening device in my lapel. "Yes, Samuel?"

Samuel sidled up to me, looking all around with conspiratorial caution. "I seen him come out of yo' room, suh. Jus' a while ago. He went off down train, maybe to the lounge, an' then he came back a short time later."

That wasn't good. It seemed unlikely that Learnéd would go for a casual stroll. Did he suspect something? Or did he decide to take his investigation into his own hands? Either way, it was another wrinkle in this already tense situation. I was thankful for Samuel's warning; that was a gold eagle well spent.

"Thank you, Samuel. Keep your eyes open."

"Yessah."

I tamped down my anxiety as I headed for the diner, and firmly resolved not to go rushing to her compartment like a panicky child. She was all right, I told myself: if Learnéd did make a move, panic and chaos would be the best *possible* outcome. Since the train was in one piece, she must be all right, I reassured myself. And I could see her for lunch in a bit. I could tell her of my plan then.

§

Arda was still skittish after our Ogden misadventure, so I was a bit surprised to find her at her regular table when I arrived. She and Learnéd must have missed each other somehow, for which I was thankful. Lunch was buffalo roast smothered in gravy and onions, with baked beans and biscuits. The kitchen staff were performing miracles with what they had to work with, but she was plowing along more from need than desire.

"How are you doing, Arda?"

She gave me a wain smile. "I am better, Nathaniel, thank you. And how are you?"

"Managing, I suppose." I peeled off my jacket, folded it up, and put it on my chair as I sat. We had urgent things to talk about. "There's a problem," I said, softly. "Learnéd left my compartment while I was off the train. He came down this way, but I don't know what he was up to." She gasped, and stared at me in wide-eyed terror, as pale as a ghost. "He's back in my compartment," I assured her. "We're safe for the moment."

"I...ney saw him," she managed at last. "Did he come here?"

"I don't know." I was doubly worried, since he must have gotten off the train to avoid her if he came this far back. What was he up to? "Can you think of what he was doing?"

"I...I ney know..." She agonized over it for a bit. "Unless he bugged my compartment while I was out?"

"Bugged?"

"Planted a listening device." She gestured at my lapels.

"Wonderful." That was *just* what we needed. "Look, we'll take care of it after lunch, okay?"

§

We made a quick lunch, after which I escorted her back to her compartment and stood anxious watch in the hall while she went over the place with her little sensing box. It took some time before she was convinced he hadn't been there. As an afterthought, she went over me again, and found that I still carried only the one black speck in my lapel. By the time she finished, our worry over his listening devices approached paranoia.

"What do you think he was doing?" I asked after I shucked my jacket in the restroom.

She collapsed on my chest with a sob. "I ney know, Nathaniel. It ney iss ass I was told they behave."

I gave her a reassuring squeeze. "That's not surprising. Your people are hardly experts at these things." She looked askance at me with one part fear and one part frustration. "We'll just have to be on our toes, and improvise as we go."

"What are we to do, Nathaniel?" she whimpered. "We are trapped here!"

I gave her a kiss, and held her to my chest. Right then she needed some good news, and, providentially, I happened to have some. "I have a plan to evade Learnéd. We'll wait to the last second before the train leaves, then we'll duck out and go to ground here in Reno." She looked at me in surprise. "We'll take the next train, tomorrow, and jump off just short of the station in Sacramento. From there, we'll avoid Learnéd and get to San Francisco as best we can."

"Nathaniel!" She was thrilled, her face lit up with an eager smile. "That iss wonderful!"

"Will that work, Arda? Will you still have enough time to complete your mission?"

Her face fell. "My mission..."

I was getting heartily sick of her damned mission. "I know you're already running badly behind with all these delays."

142

"I...ney, we knew the trip would take longer...I ney am behind schedule." That put her resistance one-up on Learnéd, not that she was thrilled about it, apparently.

I held her close, and she rested her head on my chest. "Look, all we have to do is get you to San Francisco and complete your mission. After that, the Movement won't exist any more, right? You'll be free."

"...I...y-yes..."

"Do they know what your mission is, Arda?"

"...Ney..."

"Then all we have to do is avoid them until we can get the job done. San Francisco's a big city; we can do it."

She stared at me silently for a long moment, her morale tottering on the verge of collapse, which perplexed and worried me. "You are kind, Nathaniel," she murmured at last, with tears in her eyes. "I ney deserve so much from you."

"Don't think that way." I held her close and gave her another kiss. "I'll see you tonight. It'll work out."

§

It turned out that Learnéd hadn't come to the lounge car either, which was perplexing. I questioned the bartender discreetly, then settled in my usual seat at the end of the car to brood over the situation. Hopefully my plan would work, and we would escape Learnéd. If we got free, our chances would improve dramatically, and once we reached Sacramento, our options increased just that much more. All we had to do was get off this train...

I was working on my second beer and staring out the window an hour later when our plans received a major setback. "These belong to you?" the local sheriff demanded of Doggett. He and a posse had manhandled the three cowboys back to the train after what must have been an epic bender in town. They were as drunk as so many Lords, and from the look of their torn clothes and battered features, they were in a hell of a fight.

Doggett was tight-lipped in anger. "I'm afraid that's so," he said. "They're a disgrace to this train and this railroad, and they've been a constant pain all through the trip. As far as I'm concerned, you can bury them under the jail."

"You gutless worm!" Frank lashed out at Doggett as he beat a hasty retreat, but was held back by two of the locals who threatened him with billy clubs.

Parker was watching all this from nearby, and decided to intervene. "Howdy, boys." He brushed his coat back, revealing his tin star. "The name's Ned Parker, Texas Rangers from down Amarillo way. So, what do we have here?"

The sheriff evidently heard of him, and nodded respectfully. "These three tore up Mabel's place, chased the girls out into the snow, and messed up a half-dozen of our citizenry."

Parker eyed them in ill-concealed contempt. "Hmmm, serious business, bustin' up the local house." He turned back to the sheriff. "What do you reckon the damages are?"

The sheriff hemmed and hawed a bit; he no doubt had an under the table interest in the local cat houses and some personal ideas about justice. "I'd say a hundred dollars ought to do."

"A hundred dollars, eh?" Parker walked down the line, looking each of them eye to cold eye. "And a half-dozen of your folks?" He glanced at the sheriff. "Let's say ten dollars a head for their troubles. That comes to a hundred and sixty. That sound about right?"

The sheriff nodded, reluctantly. Parker turned on the three again. "Okay, boys, here it is. You three need to pony up for the damages."

"A hundred and sixty?" Ed whined. "That's a lot-a bull!"

"May well be," Parker said, reasonably. "But it's that or the sheriff here throws you in the whose-cow for disturbing the peace." He idled back over to the sheriff, then turned and looked them over in mock deliberation. "Now I don't know how they do things around here, but down Amarillo way, you three'd get six months workin' on the roads."

The sheriff nodded again, with a grim smile.

"I imagine workin' the roads in these parts must be hard, with the weather and all..."

The three went into a huddle, and managed to come up with a hundred and forty-eight dollars between them.

"Ain't good enough, boys," Parker said.

144

"It's all we got!" Ed cried.

Parker shrugged. "Still ain't good enough. If I recall, didn't you boys have a Winchester when you got on at Omaha?"

"That's a hundred dollar rifle!"

"And it was Jim's, anyway!" Frank added.

"Hmmm...I don't suppose he'll be needing it where he's gone to." Parker turned to the sheriff. "Then I guess you can tip the girls for their troubles, too."

The bartender was sent to their berths to collect the Winchester, and the sheriff and company departed with snarls and dark looks at the three. "I ought to chain you up in the baggage car," Doggett huffed once the locals were gone.

Frank was the drunkest of the lot, and in a nasty temper. "You piece-a shit!" He advanced on Doggett, who prudently retreated to the bar. "You ain't no kind of man, nohow! I'll teach you t' respect a Texan!"

Parker stepped in the way with a hand on his revolver, and a look that stopped Frank in his tracks. "Let's start with respecting this Texan," he growled.

Frank was not easily daunted, even if the sight of Parker had his wind up. "You got no business buttin' in! No one asked you anyway!"

"You having second thoughts about my intervening, eh? Well that's fine and dandy. I'll call the sheriff back, and we can *reconsider* that whole thing." That took the wind out of the other two's sails, and even slowed Frank down. "I *trust* we won't have any more problems for the rest of the evening?" Parker gave them all a hard look. None of them answered, but their expressions said that the fight was clean out of them.

"Now, you boys go on back to your car and settle in for the night. You've had enough to drink for now."

Frank was drunk enough that he was still willing to argue, but his two friends, aided by Parker's forbidding frown, talked him down. They left after a few minutes to get sorted out, Frank muttering venomously, and giving all and sundry the evil eye. Doggett prudently hung around for a bit to give them a head start before he left.

I slumped in my chair once they were gone, frustrated and annoyed by this latest turn. What little we had to work with was gone: it wouldn't be wise to remain in town after this incident. Even the railroaders got into scrapes with the locals fairly often, and outsiders would get short shrift, especially if the rowdies were already worked up. Arda and me could take care of ourselves, but the one thing we didn't need was to draw attention, especially if she was forced to use her enhanced strength. I cursed in silent frustration, wondering what to do now. Those three yahoos made a fine mess of things! On top of which, Doggett would be insufferable for the rest of the trip.

*****

# "Day Seven: Evening"

"You go to her again?" Learnéd demanded as I made ready to leave later that afternoon.

"I guess so."

Learnéd shook his head. "I ney see how you have lasted this long. Perhaps you ney are putting your best effort to your duties?"

I managed to keep a straight face as I wondered if Learnéd was growing suspicious of our activities. "We don't have your fancy medicines," I said, carefully. "So we do things the old fashioned way, by muscle power."

"Primitive." Learnéd snorted in contempt. "It iss a wonder you survived at all before the Movement came. First you stop in the dining car, and have them send more food here."

"How long would you last if I stop feeding you?" I grumbled.

Learnéd's hard look sent a shiver down my spine. "Long enough. Perhaps you think forbidden thoughts?"

"Who? Me? I'm not even a citizen; what would I know?"

Learnéd glared at me. "That iss correct."

I got while the getting was good, thankful to be out of there. Learnéd's icy aura was unnerving, and having to constantly tip-toe around his conditioned temper was an endless strain. How could one design a human to be so intimidating? However they did it, it was damned effective. I had enough problems already, so I tried to put it out of mind, and focus on the here-and-now. At least the steam heat was back, although there was still no word on how long we would be stuck here in Reno.

§

The dining car was busy with the dinner crowd. The place was brightly lit, and there was a steady rumble of conversations, the rattle of dishes, and the inviting aromas from the kitchen; none of which helped my mood in the slightest. Parker was talking with the steward when I came in, and paused to greet me.

"Well, mister Poole, good evening, sir."

"And to you, sir."

"Looks like I'll have to wait a bit for a table. Oh, well. Life is hard, ain't it?"

"Hmph?" I was a bit distracted by my problems. "Sorry?"

"I trust everything goes well for you?"

"Yes. I suppose so."

Parker looked me over skeptically. "You couldn't prove it by me. You and your lady friend aren't fussing, I hope."

"No, sir. We're tired from this trip, is all."

"Ain't that the truth?" Parker sighed. "So, is she all right?" He gestured to her sitting at the far end of the room where she was poking half-heartedly at her dinner. "She seems a bit off her feed."

"She's well enough, just frustrated with these endless delays."

"One hopes so." He glanced at her, then turned to me again. "I wouldn't mind getting to know her, if I have the chance. She didn't seem in a *sociable* mood when we met there in Ogden."

I eyed him suspiciously. Parker's endless curiosity was getting on my nerves, and his relaxed look didn't hide his obvious interest. "She's as weary as the rest of us, and she was pretty unnerved by what happened. I'll mention it to her. Perhaps we can arrange dinner once we get to San Francisco."

"I'd appreciate that, son."

§

She greeted me with a wain smile, but she was subdued, and her single plate of roast beef and boiled potatoes was half eaten.

"Hello, Arda," I said, softly, as I sat down opposite her. "Are you all right?"

She took a moment to answer. "I suppose. I am just...worried about this journey." I could tell she was being careful around Learnéd's listening device, but I understood what she meant. "There have been so many problems, so many delays..." She shook herself in nervous frustration. "I am tired and anxious; ney worry about me."

"I do worry about you." I gave her hand a reassuring squeeze; she shuddered at my touch. "I care about you, and I want you to be happy."

She gave me a faint smile. "You are kind, Nathaniel."

"You'll complete your journey and reach San Francisco well enough." The look in her eyes said she wasn't convinced of that. "It'll work out."

Her face sagged, and she stared at me expressionlessly. "My journey..." Her gaze drifted. "I suppose it will."

She didn't know as yet about the setback to my plan, and she was troubled enough without that burden. I honestly didn't know what to do at that point. Leaving the train before Sacramento was still the goal, but the timing was up in the air. I swore to myself that I'd work something out. I would get her safely to San Francisco and help her complete her mission for her sake, and for my own revenge against Learnéd and his abominable Movement.

"D'you suppose I might see you again...afterwards?" That was impulsive on my part, and I knew how futile any hope of that could be, but I couldn't help asking.

She looked at me in surprise, then her expression closed down again. "I...ney have any plans after my journey's end. I ney know what I will do."

I wondered idly about her mysterious mission, not that I wanted to know. Whatever it was, the delays and Learnéd breathing down our necks were getting to her. "Look, there's no sense in agonizing over it. Relax. Have something to eat, and enjoy the company. Your journey can take care of itself."

That didn't seem to help. "You are right, Nathaniel. I ney should think about it now." She gave me a somber look. "I should enjoy your company while we have the chance."

The way she said that struck me as ominous too. I reminded myself that she was part of a conspiracy to change the course of the future, and I was a passing fancy... Then reality hit me: the change she intended to cause would mean that she would no longer exist. Without the Movement, where would Arda come from? No wonder she was so down: she was on a suicide mission.

The waiter brought me a plate of roast beef, and we ate in silence for a time, each consumed with our own thoughts. It was so unfair! I fumed as I ate, torn between pity and admiration for her. I could see why she went from the bold, self confidant aristocrat I first met to the nervous and withdrawn waif she was now. She must have psyched herself up for this mission, and her courage was slowly waning with these endless delays and Learnéd on her trail.

149

My thoughts drifted, and I wondered about that, trying to guess what change she might make that could unravel the next several hundred years. The very idea was unnerving. It was difficult enough to anticipate what the future might bring, to say nothing of how her change would affect that future. Whatever happened— would happen—tomorrow would be very different from today.

§

We hung around the dining car until the steward politely threw us out at closing time, then retreated to her compartment.

"I am getting so damned tired of all this waiting," I grumbled as I stretched out on her berth. She stretched out beside me and ran one hand over my chest as I cuddled her in my arms.

"What iss your life like, Nathaniel?"

That surprised me. "Curious how the other half lives?"

"There iss much about you that I find admirable." She sighed, and was silent for a while. "Do you mind if I ask?"

"No, not really." I held her and brooded on it. "Not that there's much to tell." There was no family, no close friends, nothing to go back to, no one to turn to. It struck me how alone I was in this world.

"We all have something to say of our lives, ney?"

"I guess so." I gazed into her eyes; she turned away. "I'd say everyone does. Don't you?"

"Perhaps so." She withdrew some, although she still clung to me. Her personal life must be a touchy subject, which wouldn't be surprising. In any event, that was an area we dared not enter with Learnéd listening.

She rested her head on my shoulder, and we lay in the dark for a time as I idly pondered her. Right then she seemed remarkably human; more so then when we first met. Maybe I was having some positive influence on her, or she was slowly losing the ingrained fear of her time. Or maybe she was coming out from behind the many masks she wore. I liked her this way, not that I wasn't drawn to the coquette, or the cool and collected aristocrat, or the she-beast. Her features were outlined by the pale moonlight through the window. The faint light filtered through her golden hair, creating a halo.

"Nathaniel?  Why do you fight?"

"Hmm?"

She raised her head and looked at me.  "I can understand if you fight to protect yourself, but why do you do it for a living?  Is ney it painful?"

"It is that," I muttered.   I struggled for a while to find an answer to that question.  I never was long on introspection, and she was pushing me into thoughts I had never entertained before.   "I guess...it's my nature.  I've never been one to back down from a fight."  I struggled with it for a bit, trying to understand a part of me that I always took for granted.  "When I face another fighter, I guess I'm testing myself.  I'm looking to see if I still have it, if that makes sense."

"It iss a ritual?"

That was an odd way of putting it.  "You might be right."  I sighed in exasperation.  "I must seem like an animal to you."

"I understand, Nathaniel."  She gave me a little kiss on the cheek, then cuddled on my shoulder.  "We are all animals.  We are all living beings.  We all struggle to find confidence in ourselves.  We all struggle to survive."

We lay together for a while, each drawing comfort from the other.  I stared over her shoulder out the window at the faint lights of Reno and the frosted ranks of the Sierras softly lit by a waning half moon, and thought about her.  She was so different from any woman I ever knew; neither the meek and self effacing proper lady, nor the wanton trollop.   She was something in between; capable and self reliant, frail and mortal.   And there were undertones of the meek lady—and the trollop—that kept me guessing.  Life was never dull with her around, that was certain.  I was impressed in spite of myself, and I wanted her like no one I had known before.

She raised up on one elbow and considered me somberly.  "Then you ney have a purpose in life?  Ney reason to live?"

I wondered why she would bring that up.  "No, I don't suppose I do.  It...never worked out that way."

"That iss sad," she said, solemnly.   "To ney have a purpose when life iss so brief and uncertain."

"Well, it's not that simple here. We aren't assigned roles like...in some places. That's what freedom is all about."

"Freedom has a price," she muttered.

"Yeah. It does that."

We fell silent again, and lay in each others arms after that while I reflected on this strange twist in life. I was mortally tempted to ask her to stay, to abandon the mission she was so ill-suited for, and carve out a new life with me in this time. And from her questions, I got the impression that she might respond favorably if asked. But that brought up the problem of Learnéd. He wasn't going to abandon the hunt just because she jumped ship. Could she vanish into this time—change enough that she wouldn't shine as a beacon for the Movement's assassins? Could we live our lives with the prospect of another Learnéd turning up at any time?

For that matter, was it right of me to be so greedy, to take away whatever slim hope the future might have in her? No. No man's greed could be that great. It was bittersweet: to find each other across the width of time only to be separated by time itself. All I could do was help her reach safety, and hope that she could find happiness in her altered future—if, somehow, she lived to see that future. Selfless love: something I never would have suspected of me, now that I thought about it.

The problem of our escape intruded again, and as I lay there brooding, an answer came to me. I poked at it for a bit, and while it was less than perfect, it would work. "Make love with me, Arda," I murmured as I gestured at the door. We needed to talk, and the lounge must be closed by now.

She looked at me for a moment, then nodded, and we crept carefully out of the berth. She arranged her speaking box for Learnéd's entertainment, and we headed for the lounge car.

§

As usual, the lounge car was deserted except for the rear brakeman sitting at the far end by the platform door, guarding his outpost from long habit even though the train wasn't moving. We took seats at the front of the car where he wouldn't overhear, and she looked at me expectantly. But as urgent as our business was, my resolve not to be greedy was slipping.

"Do you like this time?" I leaned on the table with both elbows, and took her hand in mine. "It must seem kind of raw compared to the time you came from."

"It...iss," She said, solemnly. "This period iss ney so built up ass in the future. SaFrisko was a huge city." That was tempting. Even if it was in ruins, San Francisco must be a sight after who knows how many centuries.

"I'm thankful you came here, Arda. I'm thankful I met you."

"You are a great help, Nathaniel." She gave me somber look. "I hate to think of what might have happened to me if you weren't here."

This was foolish, and I knew it, but I couldn't help myself. "You have made such a huge difference in my life. I want more than anything for you to be safe and happy."

She smiled tentatively. "Thank you, Nathaniel. You flatter me."

"Look...you're not cut out for this sort of thing...perhaps you can vanish into this time, away from Learnéd and the Movement." I was sweaty and short of wind, and tugged on her hand imploringly. "Your resistance can send another mission. You deserve to live free...here...now."

She hesitated, and her spirits fell. "I...I ney can, Nathaniel. The future iss too important for uss to think of ourselves. I must complete my mission."

"Please?"

She withdrew a bit. "It...iss painful, Nathaniel."

I sighed in resignation. She was right: the future was too important, and there was no sense in dwelling on it if it only brought her pain. And those urgent matters would not be denied. "We've had another setback," I told her honestly. "We won't be able to leave the train here as I planned."

Her face fell. "What can we do, Nathaniel?"

"There is another way we can do this. Let me have that talking box of yours. When the train leaves, I'll stay here and use that and his listening device to draw him away. You go on like we planned; leave the train just before you reach Sacramento, and make your way overland to San Francisco."

153

I would have to lead Learnéd on for as long as I could to give her her best shot at completing her mission. It meant that I would never see her again, but at least she would be safe. I avoided thinking of what Learnéd would do if he caught up with me.

She sat still and studied my face for a long time, clearly caught up in some sort of turmoil. "Verdamme," she mumbled at one point, then turned away and stared at the floor. Finally, she shook her head in dejection, and turned to me again with tears in her eyes. "Ney, Nathaniel," she said, softly. "If you do that, I must come after you."

"Why?"

There was a long, ugly silence. "You...are my mission, Nathaniel," she muttered at last as she turned away, half choking in sorrow. "I...I was sent here to kill you."

It took me a moment to absorb that, then my hackles rose as it fell into place: she was armed with futuristic weapons, and could toss me around like a rag doll, and she was an assassin!

"But...kill me? Why? What did I do?"

She turned to me earnestly. "Ney you: your great-to-the-eighth-grandson. He was the Founder, the one who set the Movement in motion. He created the police state which rules uss in my time. By eliminating you, we can prevent that from ever happening."

Great. I was the focus of their desperate scheme, of their slim hopes of destroying the Movement and saving humanity from itself. The future was coming after me from all sides. All of a sudden my wind was up, and my hands trembled. I stared at her wide-eyed, waiting for her to strike me down as I tried to get a grip on myself.

"But...why me? Why not kill my...grandson?"

She sat very still, hands folded before her, trying not to spook me. "You ney realize how well protected He iss. The Movement has placed in-depth defenses around him for over a hundred years before he was born. Ass for you, there are...structures in the flow of time. Change has to be made by altering certain key points in that structure. You are the only key point we can target and ney unleash temporal chaos."

As my mind reeled from the sheer terror of it, one thought surfaced: the monster who created that future hell was my descendant.  I would sire another John Brown...or worse.  Far worse.  That was why she asked so many questions about my family: she needed to know if she was too late to prevent the future.  Whether she killed me or not, I couldn't walk away from this now.

"Nathaniel..."  She took my hand in hers, gently.  "I am sorry.  Please understand; I am a soldier.  I ney enjoy killing.  I do what I must; the future iss that important."

"Why...don't you, especially with Learnéd on your tail?"

She studied my face, hers tight with fear and frustration.  "I ney am a machine; ney like them.  I am still human.  Too human, it seems."

"But what else can you do?"  As appalled as I was at bearing a death sentence from the future, the question riveted me.  *Nothing* else mattered any more.

"I ney know.  Right now I have to focus on escaping.  I hope I can find some way to spare you.  I owe you that."

"I..."  An odd thought came to me.  "You took me to bed knowing you have to kill me?"

She gave me a raised eyebrow.  "Morality iss different in our time, Nathaniel.  Sex ney exists except for the elite of the Movement.  It iss a privilege, ney a part of peoples' lives ass in this time.  I gave you a gift reserved for the select few."

"Still, that's...creepy...morbid."

"Waste not."  She shrugged, then gave me that lecherous grin.  "And it iss the least I can do for you, considering."

"Um...there is that."  Her sudden change was even more unsettling, if possible.  She was a superhuman killer with erratic mood swings.

She looked askance at my reaction.  "Ney be so shocked, Nathaniel.  It helps to have a release, and I ney am a monster."

I smiled humorlessly.  "No, you are simply a beautiful young woman made in some future factory and sent back through time to kill me, pursued by something not human.  What's to worry about?"

She frowned at that. "This iss serious, Nathaniel!" She sagged in dejection. "I ney know what to do. I have my duty to the future, to the human race, but I ney want to kill you. But I ney see any other way." She sobbed and clutched herself. "I ney am good at this, Nathaniel. I ney am good at making decisions. What can I do?"

From what she told me of the future, my first reaction was that she *should* kill me. Better steer clear of that line of thought. "Ah...look, let's not do anything hasty. I guess...if you have to...well, let's not cross that bridge until we come to it. There may be some way out of this for both of us."

"You are wise, Nathaniel, but I ney have any hope for an alternative. And with the Learnéd here, the longer I wait, the greater the risk." Her calculating look chilled me to the bone. "The obvious solution iss to do it now."

My heart fluttered with fear as she studied me with eyes that seemed as cold and blue as ice. I was defenseless against her...she could snap my neck with one quick flick of the wrist...she was emotionally unstable...running for her life from Learnéd...not all together sane... "Why don't you?" I asked with fatalistic calm. Sitting across the table from one's executioner was a daunting experience. It drained the will out of me, leaving me hollow.

"I hope I can think of some alternative, some way to change the future so that I ney have to kill you."

"So I have a little time, anyway."

"A little." She glanced at her watch, and stood to go. Then she turned back to me. "If I must, I will be merciful, Nathaniel."

§

I was in the lead as we headed back to her compartment, and was at the end of the short hallway past the restroom in the next car when I saw a figure in the gloom ahead. Instinct kicked in, and I flattened myself against the wall. "It's Learnéd!" She emitted a squeak of near terror, and her face turned white. I cursed at that noise, and peeked cautiously around the edge of the doorway. Learnéd didn't seem to have heard her. I couldn't see what he was up to, but we had precious seconds to get out of this. "Come on!" I whispered. "Move it!" In panicked inspiration, I shoved her through the curtain into the ladies' washroom, and glanced around frantically for some place to hide. The restroom was small, with no dividers or closets, and there was no other way out... "Quick!" I shoved her toward the toilet stall.

Learnéd came through the curtain a second later, weapon at the ready. I watched anxiously through the narrow crack of the stall door as he circled the room slowly. Arda and I were standing on the rim of the toilet trying to be perfectly silent. The footing was treacherous, and the stall was barely large enough for one. Learnéd paused and eyed a curtain on the opposite wall, then inched over with his weapon leveled, and yanked it aside. It was a bath stall, with a small radiator to provide warm water. Learnéd spotted it with his heat vision.

He gave a grunt of disappointment, and turned his attention to the rest of the room. There was a second radiator by the window to heat the room. He considered it for a bit, then his gaze locked on the stall door. He could see our body heat. I prayed that his hearing hadn't been improved too; my heart was pounding like a hammer.

Another moment of careful deliberation, then Learnéd grumbled something and slid his weapon back into his jacket. After a brief backward glance, he slipped out through the curtain. We hovered awkwardly in the stall, not daring to even breathe, until we heard the door at the end of the car slam.

"Let's go." We clambered down from our confined perch. It took a lot of courage to draw the curtain aside a bit to check the hallway. Learnéd was gone.

"What was he doing?" I demanded as we fled back to her compartment. "Is he on to us?"

"I ney know, Nathaniel." She was shaken to her core by that close scrape, so much so that I had to steady her.

We crossed over into the next car, and stopped to collect our wits. I peered through the window to see if he was following us, then sagged against the wall. "Damn, this being a revolutionary is a hell of a way to make a living."

"I ney recommend it," she said, shakily.

§

157

Later, in her compartment, we coupled in a frenzy, both driven by angst and fear, both seeking to escape this horrid fate in a rosy Neverland of passion. After a while, once our fever cooled, I rolled off her, lay by her side, and held her in my arms. She cuddled against my chest, sobbing softly.

I sighed in weary resignation, knowing I would not live to see San Francisco. Would my death help? If she did kill me, would that change the future? And would that changed future be any better? The sad part was that I understood what she had to do, and I agreed with it. If I must die to save mankind from itself...

What a monstrous joke the Universe played on us! Now that I thought about it, I really did like her. She was bright, mercurial, a complex puzzle of shifting moods and emotions; a challenge to the better side of me that had lain buried for so long that I all but forgot it existed. Despite her retro-induced instability, she had a lot to offer, and despite her strengths, she needed someone. She was more than a travelers' affair, I was mortally tempted.

I rubbed her back gently as she sobbed and cuddled closer, losing herself in my warmth. We lay together quietly as I watched the faint lights of Reno outside the window without really seeing them. Would she do it, I wondered? She could, right now: one quick jab could crush my throat or rip my heart out. After reflecting on it for a while, I decided she wouldn't; not like that. She was not cruel or vindictive. She would find some way to spare me, if any way could be found. I went over what she told me about time travel—what little I understood—trying to find some way around this paradox. Every which way I turned, there was the same insurmountable problem. If she didn't kill me, someone else would have to. And the longer she delayed, the greater the risk that Learnéd would make his move. The smart thing—the only realistic thing—for her was to get it over with now.

The strangeness of it all gave me a headache. I was cuddling and soothing a superhuman killer, a mentally unstable assassin who could crush the life out of me without half trying. I knew she cared about me, and would do whatever she could to spare me— but she was not entirely a free agent in this. For that matter, she wasn't entirely human.

I was bemused by it: earlier that evening, I asked her to abandon her mission and go away with me. Now that I knew what she had to do, I wanted her more than ever. A thought came to me of a moth dancing around a flame, drawn irresistibly to its doom in the glowing beauty it so desperately craved. I was that moth; drawn to her by her sensual charm, her quick wit, and her all too obvious mortal frailty; doomed to burn in her flame.

I sighed, and held her closer, listening to the faint sound of her heart. At least if she did do it, I was sure she would allow me to die in dignity. That was a small comfort, at least. It was all the comfort we could find, just then.

*****

# "Day Eight"

It took no small amount of nerve for me to return to the compartment the next morning, since I wasn't sure what Learnéd suspected—or knew—or how he would react. He was sitting in his chair with his arms folded, as usual. He looked up as I entered, but didn't say anything, which was a small relief. I could tell that he was weary; after seven days and nights without sleep, even that genetically engineered superman was starting to feel it.

"So, all quiet on the old homestead?" I said with feigned nonchalance.

Learnéd gave me an annoyed look. "Yes. I trust you are keeping her occupied?"

"Oh, I occupied her all right." I tried to be casual, hoping some crude humor would allay his suspicions. "You know, I think you were right; she may yet wear me down to a stump. I'd swear I'm a couple inches shorter already." I gave him a smirk I didn't feel. "Giving my all for the Movement, eh?"

He considered me sullenly, then nodded. "That iss correct."

It seemed he wasn't suspicious after all. Still, last night was far too close a shave for my peace of mind. What we would do for privacy was anyone's guess, but right then, I was too weary to care.

"I wish to know how much longer we will be here. You must reconnoiter again."

"Hey, you're the one who knows the future," I said in real exasperation. "Didn't you think to check before coming here?"

"Such random details ney are recorded. You are my native guide, so you must find out how much longer we will be here."

"I doubt anyone can say for sure. This is a priority train; they'll get us moving as soon as they can."

He frowned at me. "It ney iss like this in the future," he grumbled.

"Well, this is now, and that's how we do things around here. We'll worry about the future tomorrow." I sagged onto my berth with a heartfelt sigh of relief, not even bothering to pull off my jacket or shoes...

§

*...the devastation was total...the ruins stretched away as far as he could see...*

*...John Brown towered over him like a mountain, his shoulders and eyebrows frosted with glistening snow, his voice roaring thunder and lightning as he hurled his insane rage at the world below. As Nate looked up him in awe and horror, he realized Brown's features were changed. In place of the emaciated cheeks and feverish eyes, the face high above him was heavy, craggy, with battered brows and a scar on one cheek. His face. The face of his many times removed grandson. The Founder...*

*...That hideous face looked down on him, regarding him with Olympian disdain. Their eyes met, and Nate felt his soul being drained out of him. He fought against it feebly, but his arms, his will, his soul were no match for the power and wrath that descended on him from on high...*

*..."Inferior," the face said, scornfully. The words rolled back from the snow capped mountains all around them like an infernal chorus. "Weak. Flawed. A mere human, ney even a citizen." As he spoke, the Founder reached down with one vast hand that grew until it covered all the land, engulfing him in stygian darkness. "Ney worthy of living..."*

§

...I woke abruptly, and stared out the window as I tried to still my racing heart. It took a moment to realize where I was, by which time my fatigue reasserted itself. I was still groggy; from the shadows outside, I couldn't have slept for more than a couple hours. I fought a jaw breaking yawn. Between Arda and Learnéd, I was rapidly running out of steam.

"You ney are sleeping," Learnéd said.

I rolled over and looked askance at him. "Brilliant. Can't get anything past you, can I?"

"This iss your sleep period. You must regain your strength to continue seeing her."

"I can't sleep. Too much on my mind."

"Ney discipline," he grumbled. "How did you primitives manage without the Movement?"

"We got along," I snapped, irritably. Learnéd frowned, reminding me of Arda's warning about questioning the Movement. Right then I despised him more than usual, and would have taught him some manners if we were anything like equal.

Despite my weariness, I couldn't get to sleep again, so I struggled to sit up and rubbed my face, trying to wake up fully. I ached, my sinuses throbbed, and I felt greasy. Right then a trip to the washroom sounded like Heaven.

"You ney must neglect your duty to the Movement. Sleep iss necessary. You should continue trying."

"I'm too tired to sleep."

That seemed to confuse him. I allowed myself a weary sigh, then struggled to my feet and rooted through my bags for some fresh clothes.

"Where are you going?" Learnéd demanded.

"To get cleaned up." I gave him an annoyed glance. "After that, I think I'll go get drunk."

"Consuming alcohol dulls your mind."

"All the more reason." I left before he could object.

§

"Missa Poole, suh?" Samuel caught me in the washroom.

"Yes, Samuel?"

Samuel glanced around nervously. "Ah wanted t' tell you 'bout that man, suh," he muttered.

I caught his anxiety at once, which evoked my own alarm. My jacket hung on one of the coat hooks; I shushed Samuel, herded him out into the hallway, and glanced toward my compartment. No reaction from Learnéd; he must have missed Samuel's indiscretion. "What about him, Samuel?"

"Last night, he left yo' compartment, and went into the baggage car. Then he came back, an' went up and down the whole train, lookin' everywhere. Ah followed him."

"What was he up to?"

"Ah don't know, suh. He told George—he the porter in the next car, suh—George asked him what he was doin', and he said he was a policeman, and George better keep his mouth shut." Samuel trembled at the memory. "An' he tol' me th' same thing later."

The poor man was thoroughly shaken. He would believe that story precisely because the police in this time dealt with blacks the same way.

"Lawd, suh, I don't want no trouble with the police!"

"Don't worry about that. He lied to you."

"He ain't no real policeman, suh?"

"No, he's not."

"Lawd, he scares me, suh!" Samuel glanced around again, visibly agitated. "That man got th' Devil in him! You can see it, the way he look at you."

Samuel was starting to panic. I needed to calm him down fast before he bolted. "You should be careful, but he's no devil. He's just not altogether right." I tapped my temple with one finger. "That's why I'm trying to keep him away from her. He's a wife beater; he hurt her before."

"Lawd! Is he dangerous, suh?"

"Not as long as you don't disturb him. Just keep a discreet distance, and you'll be all right."

"Yessah." Samuel was not happy.

"So what did he do?"

"Well, suh, like ah said, he goes in the baggage car, an' then he come back later, an' goes to the back of the train, lookin' here and lookin' there like he was searchin' fo' something. Then I see you and the lady go in her compartment. Then he come back, and goes back to yo' compartment."

That confirmed what I suspected: Learnéd was up to something. We missed colliding with him by sheer luck. "Did he look in her compartment?"

"No, suh, but he listen at the door fo' a moment."

That was a relief. At least Learnéd didn't know for certain that we tricked him and snuck out. "Well done, Samuel. You'd make a first rate secret agent." We missed seeing him altogether as we returned from the lounge.

Samuel grinned self consciously. "Thank yo', suh."

I gave Samuel's arm a friendly squeeze. "Keep your eyes open, and don't interfere in whatever he does. Everything will be all right."

"Yessah." Samuel was as pleased by my praise as he was worried about Learnéd. "She a fine lady, suh; a fine lady. Ah don't want t' see nothin' bad happen to her."

"You and me both."

§

A half-hearted wash made me feel half way human again, after which I wound up in the lounge car, sitting in a corner nursing a stiff drink and a headache. The room was fairly busy, with card games and conversations all around. The bartender was restocking his shelves while some men from the commissary building hustled a new keg of beer aboard. The weather was dismal: so much so that the lounge car's gas lights were lit, but the cold didn't keep some of the passengers from strolling the station grounds to work off their cabin fever.

The mood inside was somber, with more grumbling than real conversation, and the air was thick with cigar smoke. Parker sat in one of the overstuffed chairs, and we exchanged courteous nods when I passed by. The three ranchers were immersed in a poker game, while others stood or sat in small groups. Off in one corner, a young telegraph messenger took hasty notes as another group argued over some stock market matter.

I ignored them, and stared idly at the Sierras in the distance as I puzzled through the latest news. What was Learnéd up to? What was he searching the train for? And why go in the baggage car? Did I dare go to see what was in there? I was grateful for Samuel's warning; sleeping car porters were on duty twenty-four hours a day. Thankfully, Samuel sacrificed what brief naps he could snatch in the wee hours to bring me that report.

Right then, my life was in such turmoil that I didn't know what to do. For that matter, I hardly had the gumption to do anything. Eventually I decided I was hungry, and munched on bar peanuts and crackers rather than make the effort to go to the dining car.

About midday, there was an interruption. "Gentlemen, may I have your attention, please?" The subdued murmur subsided as they focussed on conductor Doggett at his favorite spot before the bar. "We have received word that we will probably be stuck here for another twenty-four hours due to conditions in the pass."

There was a chorus of groans and curses at that. Another day stuck here in the middle of nowhere aboard a crowded train was not welcome news.

Doggett seemed a bit put out at their lack of enthusiasm. "Please rest assured that we are receiving plenty of food and supplies, so the delay should cause no discomfort."

"Lousy way to run a railroad," someone grumbled.

"I've already missed my appointment," someone else said. "Can't they do better than this?"

"This bunch? Not likely."

I ignored their complaining, and went back to brooding over my own problems. This was not good. The longer we were stuck here, the greater the risk that Learnéd would get wise to us, or simply decide to act on his own. For that matter, I was living on borrowed time with her, and couldn't think of any way to get out of that.

However, as Doggett's announcement reminded me, that borrowed time was running out. I needed to make a decision on what to do about her, and our eventual departure was my last option point. The latest she—and Learnéd—would act is upon arrival in San Francisco, which couldn't be more than a day or two off. I had until then to come up with some bright idea to save my life and help her evade Learnéd and reach safety. Where that safety might be was beyond me.

"Mister Poole! I should like a word with you." It was Doggett again, coming on all huffy and righteous, which wasn't wise with my present frame of mind. He confronted me and shook a finger at my face. "Now see here, mister Poole! Your behavior is *quite* unacceptable! Unacceptable, sir! You must put a stop to it at once!"

I glowered at him as the chatter faded and the crowd focussed on our little drama. "What behavior are you referring to?" I demanded.

"I'm talking about your *assignations* with that...woman! I have received complaints from the other passengers about your nightly carryings on. And I have heard you, sir, night after night in her compartment. This is shameless! Shameless, sir!"

165

"Is it?" I was already in a foul mood, and if Doggett knew how close I was to taking my frustrations with Learnéd out on him, he'd probably wet himself.

"It is indeed, sir." Doggett was on a roll, obviously relishing the attention his display of righteousness brought him. "I *demand* that you cease this undignified behavior, and I *demand* that she stop inviting you to her compartment like a common harlot!"

"You do, eh?" I glanced over Doggett's shoulder, and gave him a grim smile. "You'll have to talk to her about that. Fortunate that she's standing right behind you."

Doggett spun around in panic: Arda was indeed standing behind him, having invaded this masculine holy-of-holies once again, and she was livid.

"Who are you to tell consenting adults what they can and ney can do in private?" she demanded as she bore down on him with eyes blazing.

Doggett retreated a step under her menace. "I..."

"Who are *you* to spread malicious gossip? Ney have you decency? Ney have you respect for women?"

Another step. "But, I..."

She was working up into a fine rage, which surprised and worried me. "And who are *you* to listen at doors to spy on lovers? Does this railroad tolerate this the sort of behavior from its employees?"

Doggett regained his composure enough to try to stand up to her, which was like standing up to a tornado. "Now see here..."

Bad mistake. She grabbed him by his lapels, lifted him bodily, and shook him like a terrier shaking a rat. *"And who do you call a common harlot?"*

"Arda, don't!" I yelled. She caught herself and set Doggett down again, but the damage was done. Parker was watching nearby, and his expression changed from amusement to astonishment.

"There ney iss *anything* common about me!" she shouted in Doggett's face. "*You* are an offensive worm who listens at doors and spreads gossip. If anyone should be ashamed, it iss *you*!"

"...I..."

She bore in, forcing him back against the bar, where the wide-eyed bartender hastily retreated. "You want me too, ney? It iss always the same with wormy little men like you. You ney can attract a woman, so you sneak around doors at night listening to what you ney can have!" If anything, Doggett turned even paler as a rumble arose from the onlookers. "You ney can have a woman, so you spread gossip and call uss harlots!" She grabbed his lapels again, but managed to restrain herself. "You ney deserve me! You ney deserve anything but contempt!"

"B-but I..." Doggett was sobbing in fear.

She yanked him forward until they were face to face, Doggett forced to stand on tiptoes. He unwittingly grabbed one of her breasts for support, then hastily dropped that hand to her hip, then frantically grabbed the bar. "I will invite *anyone* I please to my compartment, and we will do *whatever* we please in the privacy I paid for!" she snarled. "YOU ney will spread rumors and listen at doors, and you ney will annoy me and my friends again!" There was no threat to that; none was needed.

The room was dead silent after she stormed out until Parker took his cigar out of his mouth and muttered, "Whoa! Now that's a right little spitfire, ain't she?" Ed, one of the three cowpokes playing cards nearby, nodded. Doggett retreated in humiliation as soon as he thought it safe to leave the car.

It was only after I regained my composure that her reaction struck me as odd. She reacted like a lady from the 19th century would, if a lot more forcefully. But from what she told me, sex wasn't that important in her time. That was one more thing about her that didn't add up, not that I was surprised. Still, I couldn't help but wonder why Doggett's words were such a sore point for her, aside from his being an annoying little swine on general principle.

The murmur of conversation gradually built up again, and from the sidelong looks I received, I was sure the gossip mill was running full-tilt. I wondered if her display added to my masculine reputation, or whether I seemed more like her tame poodle than ever. More than that, I wondered if she was all right. As soon as it seemed prudent to do so, I headed for her compartment.

§

She didn't respond to my first tentative knock, but the sound of her crying came faintly to him from inside. "Arda?" I knocked harder. "It's me, Nate."

She opened the door after a bit. She was utterly woebegone, her shoulders sagged, and her face was puffy from crying. Her earlier rage was gone, leaving her wallowing in misery.

"Are you all right?"

"Please hold me, Nathaniel." She sagged into my arms, and started sobbing again, heartbroken.

"It's all right, Arda," I said gently as I rubbed her back to try and soothe her. "He's an offensive pimple, and you slapped him down every bit as hard as you did that cowboy."

She clung to me—tightly enough to threaten my ribs. "I am sorry, Nathaniel. I embarrassed you."

"No, you didn't," I gasped. I caressed her cheek, and when she lifted her head, I gave her a kiss. "Don't be upset. It was nothing."

"It iss, Nathaniel."

I managed to wiggle loose enough to breathe. "Why? Because of what that jackass said? Why be upset by him? You told me that sex isn't important where you come from, so why agonize over it?"

She hesitated, and looked into my eyes longingly. Then she tugged at my jacket, pulled it off, laid it carefully on the berth, and covered it with her oversized gladstone bag.

"You wanted to know about me," she said softly in a dead monotone. "I ney have told you since it iss too painful, but you have a right to know since you care about me." She clung to me for a moment, then turned away. After a couple of deep, shaky breaths, she said, "I...was bred to be a reward girl. I was an incentive for the Movement's managers who provide excellent performance. They made me take the Aphrodite so I could stimulate them to enjoy me."

"...you...were..."

She took a deep, shaky breath, and nodded. "I was a harlot, Nathaniel. I was bred to entertain the Loyal of the Movement." Her voice turned bitter. "Earn a high rating, and I am yours for two hours. Earn a higher rating, and I am yours for four hours. And so on."

"God..." I muttered in dismay.

"Hmph?" She looked at me curiously. "Oh."

"I am so sorry, Arda! I can't imagine how you could stand to have any man touch you after that!" I shouldn't have been surprised by then at the Movement's bestiality, but I was.

She sighed. "You ney understand Aphrodites, Nathaniel. I was insatiable. I always will be. I ney can stop myself." She turned her head away. "I know how your people think of harlots in this time. I will understand if you ney want me again."

I took her in my arms and held her close as I tried to get a handle on this newest revelation. It didn't surprise me in a way; it was perfectly consistent with the horrors of the Movement. She told me that sex was a privilege reserved for the elite, and I already knew about her relentless appetite: I should have connected the dots sooner.

I caressed her cheek tenderly with one finger. "It wasn't your fault, Arda. Don't feel ashamed."

"Thank you, Nathaniel," she murmured. "You ney are like the others. You ney use me. I am grateful for that."

I certainly couldn't blame her for her fate. She had no say in what they did to her before she was born. They didn't even allow her the will to resent their crimes. And obviously she couldn't be bound by the values of this society. Her world was a nightmare, and she was a victim of that evil. As I reflected on it, I realized that her past didn't matter. What mattered was her pain.

"You are so beautiful," I said to try to ease her sorrow. She eyed me uncertainly as I took her chin on one finger. "You are the most beautiful woman I have ever seen. Everything about you is flawless. It's uncanny."

She turned her face away. "I was made this way, Nathaniel. I was genetically engineered to be statistically perfect."

I cursed myself for stumbling over something I should have seen. There was no part of her, of her very existence, that wasn't touched by the Movement. I sighed, and hugged her close. "Still, you are truly beautiful for your own reasons. No one made you that way. No one can ever change that."

She clung to me, and sobbed.

After a while, I realized I was hungry, which reminded me that I missed breakfast, with a couple of drinks and some bar nuts for lunch. For that matter, Arda hadn't eaten in a couple of hours at least. That wouldn't do at all.

"Hang on a minute, Arda," I said as I guided her gently to the berth. She sat quietly, ignoring me as I stepped out and summoned the car's porter.

"Suh?"

"Please bring us something from the dining car." I gave the man a five dollar silver piece, enough for lunch and a generous tip.

"Yessah." He tipped his cap courteously. "Ah'll do that right away."

"And tell them it's for the lady who sits at the end table. They'll know what that means."

"Yessah."

Evidently they did. The porter brought back a tray heaped with baked trout, rice, peas, and hot rolls. Fish wasn't my favorite, but right then I was famished. I ignored my grumbling stomach and pressed her to eat.

"Here, Arda." I set a plate in her lap.

"I ney am hungry..."

"Arda, eat. You need this." I hugged her shoulders and offered her a roll. "It's for your own good."

She sat there for a bit trying to subdue her sniffles, then took the roll and ate mechanically, then tackled the fish.

"You ney are eating, Nathaniel?"

"I'm concerned about you." She paused and looked askance at me. "Well, yeah, I'll have some too."

I remained with her for several hours, comforting her and reassuring her that her past didn't matter. Eventually, we made love—genuine, passionate love—as the hour grew late. After a while I rolled off her, lay by her side, and took her in my arms. It was different this time; less frenzied, more a deep mutual exploration, a quest for mutual emotional release. For the first time since I met her, I felt not only physically drained, but emotionally as well. She cuddled close to me, sharing our body warmth against the chill draft off the window. Her breathing was deep and slow, and she was more relaxed than I had seen her in several days. Come to think of it, I hadn't felt this sense of deep emotional fulfillment with any woman for a long time.

"Thank you, Nathaniel," she murmured. "You make me feel good about myself."

I caressed her cheek, which brought on a tentative smile. "Please, call me Nate."

"But I like Nathaniel!" She giggled, and poked me playfully in my chest hard enough to knock the wind out of me. "It iss such a *big* name! We ney have names like that."

"Oh, there's nothing so special about it," I said cautiously. Learnéd was listening. "It's just a name."

"Such a heroic name. Na-than-i-el," she chanted, accenting each syllable. "Such a rich flavor! It feels good to say it."

I laughed in spite of myself. "You are full of surprises. I never know what to expect from you."

She sobered at that. "I am only human, Nathaniel, only who and what I am." She cuddled closer and murmured, "I will try ney to give you any unpleasant surprises, Nathaniel." She was aware of that black speck in my jacket's lapel after all.

She huddled in my arms, crying softly while I stroked her back and massaged her neck. She was so contradictory, with such a quicksilver personality, that I never knew quite what to make of her. She wasn't another cat-house chippie, or one of the loose, weak women who were drawn to powerful men. For all her faults, there was much about her that I admired...and much about her that I felt guilty for. That took some of the sting out of the thought that she may yet have to kill me.

Her tears subsided after a time, and she lay quietly, her breathing deep and slow, with an occasional sniffle. Finally she rolled over and picked up her watch. I caught a fleeting look at it: instead of hands, there were softly glowing digits that changed second by second. I couldn't read them, but I realized the hour was late. "I need to sleep now, Nathaniel," she murmured. "Please hold me." She gestured for silence, and carefully slipped out of the berth and started wrestling with her dress.

§

171

After our close run-in with Learnéd last night, we couldn't risk going to the lounge car again. Instead, we ducked into the restroom next to her compartment.

"Please help me, Nathaniel," she murmured softly as she clung to me. "I ney want to die any more than you do. Help me find a way to save uss both."

"I'll do anything for you, Arda. You know that."

"Yes," she whispered, and kissed me. "I am so sorry, Nathaniel. I am sorry for what I must do. I ney should have come here. I ney am good at this."

"If you were, you'd be no better than Learnéd." I hugged her and rubbed her back. "You're in a war, and no one is ever really prepared for that. War is a horrible affair; it brutalizes people, especially the innocent. All you can do is what you must, and pray that it will all mean something in the end."

"But...it iss wrong. You ney are at fault for what the Founder did. It ney iss right that you must die."

As worried about death as I was, I couldn't bear to see her agonizing over it. "Look...this world is a lot bigger than we are. Sometimes innocent people have to die, and it isn't right, but it happens. I don't want to die, Arda; I don't want you to die. I hope we can find some way out of this mess. But if it has to happen, if I have to die to stop the Movement, don't feel guilty. Don't hate yourself for it. The future is too important for our personal feelings."

She pulled away from me and stood in the middle of the room, her back to me, arms wrapped around her waist. "I sometimes wish I ney had broken," she said, bitterly. "At least I had my place, I had my duties. I ney was lost."

"You're free, Arda. That has to count for something."

"Free? Iss this free? Iss this worth so much pain?"

I took her in my arms again and tried to comfort her. On top of all her other problems, she had precious little self confidence, not that it could be expected in the Movement's world. Right then all her bold fronts couldn't shelter her from what she was, and what her existence cost her, and what she must do. Right then she needed me.

"We all pay a price for freedom, Arda. Yours was higher than most, but that makes freedom that much sweeter."

She leaned against my chest and stared at the wall for a time, lost in thought. "I hope you are right, Nathaniel," she said at last. "Sometimes, I ney can see it." Another painful silence. "At least I have you," she added at last. "At least you are here to help me face what I must do."

"Arda..." I hesitated, wondering if I should bring my suspicions up. "You're on a suicide mission, aren't you?"

She turned to me in surprise. "What?"

"If you change the future, you won't exist. Without the Movement, you won't be created."

She stared at me in confusion for a moment, then smiled. "You are clever, Nathaniel. Most people ney understand time travel at all." She wrapped her arms around my neck and kissed me. "Ney worry about me. When you...die...we will be trapped in the temporal causality loop together: I will be the cause, and you the effect. The loop will insulate me from the future. When it decays, I will be stranded here in this time, but I will be alive." She sighed, and kissed me again. "For all we know, we may be in that loop now."

That was a big relief, even if I didn't understand half of it. "I'm thankful for that, Arda. Are you sure?"

"Ney," she said, reluctantly. "This iss on the outer edge of theoretical science. We ney know for sure what will happen, but there iss every reason to believe that I will be cut off from the Movement and remain here in the new timeline." She hugged me, and buried her head in my shoulder. "But whatever happens, it iss worth the risk."

"Can't argue with that. What about Learnéd?"

She looked at me again. "If they ney are the cause of your death, they ney will be protected. They will cease to exist along with the Movement."

"Then you'll be safe, at least." I thought on that for a bit, then asked, "What about me? Will the loop protect me?"

She sagged in my arms, and turned her eyes away. "Ney. Your death iss the key."

"Whatever happens, the future is more important than my life." I rubbed her back with one hand, and gave her a little kiss. "If you have to do it, don't hesitate.. Ending the Movement is worth my life." Maybe she was right: maybe we were caught in one of those loops even then. It was hard to distinguish hallucination from reality, but it simply felt right.

"Thank you, Nathaniel." She kissed me. "Now, I really do need for you to hold me while we sleep."

*****

## "Day Nine"

I was curled up in my berth staring absently out the window and feeling sorry for myself when there was a sudden knock at the door. I rolled over, and Learnéd and I looked at each other in confusion. "Who can that be?" I grumbled as I clambered to my feet.

It was Parker, who greeted me with a big smile and a loud, "Well there you are, boy!" as he forced his way into the crowded compartment and thrust a hand at me. "Long time, no see. Saint Louie, wasn't it?" The look in his eye was decidedly out of synch with his hail-fellow-well-met bonhomie. "Three years if it's been a day, am I right?"

"Um...yes." I was stunned and alarmed by this unexpected intrusion. "It's...good to see you again, Ned."

"And who's your friend here?" He turned on Learnéd and stuck out a meaty paw. "Ned Parker, lawman from down Amarillo way. Pleased to meet you, mister, ah..."

"Learnéd," he said guardedly as he considered Parker's hand, but declined to take it.

Parker pretended not to notice. "Well, howdy there. You in the fight game mister Learnéd?" He came on like a stump politician, overwhelming us both with his bombast. "Always did enjoy a good bare knuckle bout, yes, sir!" He dug in his vest, and

175

produced cigars for both of us. "*Mano a mano*, no pretense about it, and the best man wins. Ain't nothing quite like it, wouldn't you say?" I realized he was studying Learnéd cautiously as he fingered the cigar in disgust. This big Texan was up to something, which was the last thing I needed.

Parker turned to me, not quite taking his eyes off Learnéd, who stared at him coldly. "So what you doing on this train, boy?"

"Um...I'm headed for San Francisco." Learnéd's icy look was giving me the creeps, even directed at Parker. "I have a fight scheduled."

"Do you now?" Parker's face split in a wide grin. "Well ain't that something? Hey, any chance you could get me a ringside seat? I'd sure love to see you in action again."

"Well, yeah, sure."

"This *is* good news, yes, sirree!" Parker clapped his hands together enthusiastically. "I heard you were on this train, so I thought I'd look you up for old times." He cast a calculating look at Learnéd, whose annoyed expression was as cold and hard as the Sierras. "Why don't you boys come on down to the lounge car for a drink and some old time palaver?"

I jumped in before Learnéd could object. "Sounds good, Ned. I sure could use a drink."

"Hot damn!" Parker gave me his rosiest smile yet. "And how about you, mister Learnéd? Care for a cold one? My tab."

"Ney," Learnéd said, bluntly.

"It's a free country," Parker said with a bit less cheer. "And that leaves just that much more for us, don't it, boy?"

"It does that, Ned." I headed for the door before Learnéd could find a reason to stop me. I seriously wanted a little chat with my 'ol' pal'. I managed to leave my jacket on the berth as we left.

§

"What the hell are you doing?" I demanded as soon as we were safely in the next car.

The glad-handing politician was gone, and in its place was a cold-eyed lawman. "I wanted to take a look at your bunkie." He gave me a stern eye. "He's that *hypothetical* copper you was talking about the other day, ain't he?"

176

"Um...yes," I muttered, too surprised to deny it.

"And I gather the woman is your *hypothetical* revolutionary?"

"...Yes."

"And that *hypothetical* situation you got caught up in didn't happen no years back, did it?"

"No."

"For that matter, it ain't so *hypothetical* at all, is it?"

"Um...no..." I had no idea how Parker got onto all of it, but there was no choice but to come clean. "It's complicated."

"I could see that." Parker studied me sternly for a moment, then, "I don't hold with revolutionaries, but that hombre..." His face turned tight and drawn. "I seen a lot of hard men in my time, but *damn* if he don't take the blue ribbon. He ain't entirely human, is he?"

"More than you know."

Parker drilled me with a hard look. "I got a nose for trouble, mister Poole, and I smell a rat. A big rat." We regarded each other in awkward silence. "Look here, son, you don't seem the type to get caught up in somethin' crooked. If you're stuck in the middle of something, now's the time to come clean. Maybe we can figure a way to keep you out of it."

"It's...not that simple, sir." My frustrations were getting the better of me under Parker's badgering. "It's not like you think."

"You in trouble, son?"

I felt cornered, my desperation rising to engulf me. "More than you can imagine," I mumbled.

"I got a good imagination, mister Poole."

"Not for this, sir." There was nothing I could do. Parker was on the scent and wouldn't let up, and there was every chance he would blunder into something and get us all killed. There was no choice but to bring him in and hope for the best. "This is beyond your worst nightmares."

Parker pondered that for a long moment. "Might be at that, if you're so shook up about it. Look here, son, if it ain't a matter of our law, then it's none of my business. But I'd hate to see you get in over your head in some bad deal. Maybe I can help...under the table, if it's not a matter of our law...and maybe even if it is."

That was more tempting than I could say. "How did you get onto this?"

"I was on the boardwalk there in Omaha when that feller came flying through the window. When I heard it was a woman that beat him half to death and pitched him like a horse shoe, I needed to find out more." Parker watched me to gauge my reaction, which told him a lot more than I might have realized.

"Later, I hear all sorts of odd things about her, like how she can put any four hungry men under the table. I seen her do it, too." More reaction; Parker nodded knowingly.

"Then I hear you're involved with her, and that some feller is holed up in your compartment, and that you have the porter watching him. Then there was how she picked that conductor up and shook him like a puppy." I cursed Doggett silently, which Parker also noted.

"Then there was our little *hypothetical* chat the other day; that really set me on the scent. And now I've met your mister Learnéd, and he gives me the willies. A big rat indeed, mister Poole."

"The biggest, sir."

"You caught up in someone's revolution, son?"

"Not that I want to be." Parker's stern look finally convinced me. We needed help, and he was perhaps the only man of this time who could do us some good. "Look, there's far more going on here than you realize. Keep this strictly to yourself, and avoid Learnéd at *all* cost. You can't imagine how dangerous he is. And if you really want to help...be in the lounge car tonight after it closes. All your questions will be answered, not that you'll believe a word of what you'll hear."

Parker eyed me doubtfully, then nodded.

§

I retreated to the lounge for a badly needed drink, but found precious little comfort there. "Beggin' yo pardon, suh," the bartender said when I ordered a beer. "Mah friend, Samuel, the porter in yo' car, he said to tell you if that feller in yo' compartment came in here."

That was bad. If Learnéd planted listening devices in this car, our ability to talk would be compromised.

"When was this?"

"Yesterday, suh. Not long after you left t' go see the lady."

"What did he do?"

"He was jus' here fo' a moment, suh. Ah think the cigar smoke bothered him, so he jus' took a look around an' left."

That was some relief, anyway, since it seemed unlikely Learnéd could have left a listening device unless he simply dropped it. That grim future copper was stroking my paranoia to the point where I hardly dared let my guard down anywhere at any time. Still, I wouldn't put anything past him... I noticed a mechanical carpet sweeper tucked in a corner behind the bar. That gave me an idea.

"I'd like you to do a little something for me." I took another of Learnéd's double eagles out of my pocket and laid it on the counter. The bartender's eyes bugged out at the sight of that glistening gold. "I want you to clean the carpet where he was standing, real thoroughly." I gestured at the rug sweeper. "And after that, wash down the tables and chairs everywhere he went. Scrub 'em thoroughly with hot water."

"Suh?"

Maybe I was being reckless to interfere with Learnéd planting his black specks everywhere, but was fed up with cowering before him, and if he was upping the stakes, then it was time for me to as well. I leaned over the counter and said in a conspiratorial hush, "It's important. He shouldn't be out in public in his condition."

"What?" The bartender was alarmed. "He got some kind-a sickness, suh?"

"It's not dangerous," I reassured him quickly. "If you wash your hands with soap and water afterward, you'll be all right. But we don't want to spread anything among the passengers, do we?"

"Lawd, no, suh!" The man was alarmed. "Maybe we should tell the conductor, suh. We can get him a doctor..."

"Look... It's my fault he's on this train." I nudged the gold coin forward a bit. "I don't want him to get into any trouble over this, so we'll keep this to ourselves and take a few sensible precautions. You follow me?"

"Suh?"

"It's nothing too serious." I slid the coin forward a bit more. The bartender couldn't keep his eyes off it, for all that he was alarmed. "It'll be all right. We just need to clean that area to be on the safe side, you know?"

"Well...all right, suh, ah'll do that fo' you," he said, doubtfully.

I nodded thanks to him, and slid the double eagle over the counter. "Just between you and me, right?"

The bartender slid the coin into his pocket. "Yessah."

"Good man. Now, set me up a whiskey, please." I needed it.

§

It was a couple hours, and more than a couple drinks later when I returned to the compartment. Learnéd sat in his chair as usual, and gave me a stern look when I came in. "You are drinking too much. It interferes with your duty."

"Like hell. It helps." I sagged onto the berth and stared out the window.

"You ney sleep properly, you consume alcohol, and you burn those things you inhale..."

"Cigars. You should try one. It'll make a man of you."

"You are a disgrace," Learnéd said, scornfully. "The Movement ney allows such self-destructive behavior."

I rolled over and glared at him. "Hey, I'm not even a citizen, remember? What do you care as long as you make your arrest?"

Learnéd fumed at me, and the look in his eyes gave me the creeps. "That iss true," he said at last, angrily. "You ney matter ass long ass you do what iss required. But you must take better care of yourself while you are still needed."

"Ah, t' hell with this," I grumbled as I clambered to my feet again. One thing I didn't need was another squabble with him.

"And where do you go now?" Learnéd demanded.

"To see her, as is my duty." I gave Learnéd a frustrated scowl. "The air is kind of thick in here."

"Ney forget your coat." Learnéd gestured at my jacket still laid on the berth. "It iss cold out there."

I hesitated as I wondered at this new development, then reluctantly took the jacket. "Thanks."

§

She seemed a bit surprised when I knocked on her door, but managed to cover it up, as usual. "You are here early, Nathaniel. Ney can you keep your hands off me?"

I didn't know what to tell her, especially as Learnéd was listening. His insistence about my jacket stroked my paranoia even more, since it could only mean he intended to ride tighter herd on us. I noticed the tension in her eyes, which made me cautious. "I'm feeling a bit lost," I said at last. "I was hoping we could spend some time together."

"That iss nice of you, Nathaniel. I enjoy your company." She drew me into the compartment, closed the door, and wrapped her arms around my shoulders. "We all have troubles, Nathaniel." She gave me a kiss and a quizzical look. "Perhaps we can help each other chase our troubles away, ney?"

I clung to her for a time, rocking her gently back and forth. That silent tenderness was what I needed right then, more than conversation or anything else. From the way she clung to me, she clearly needed it too. I could feel her tension as I rubbed her back, which didn't surprise me as she was under as much strain as I was. But after a while, I began to realize her tension wasn't fear. She was agitated, wound up, fighting to maintain self control. I took a deep breath, and caught the scent of her Aphrodite. She was in need, and trying not to show it.

"You ney look well, Nathaniel. Are you ill?"

I sighed. "No. I'm...weary, is all. It's been a hell of a trip." In spite of myself, I felt my own tension rising in response to her scent. I tamped that urge firmly down; this wasn't the time, and there were more immediate problems. Neither of us could afford the distraction.

"You poor darling." Her hands trembled. She kissed me gently, and wrinkled her nose. "You have been drinking. You are troubled."

"Yeah, I guess I am." Chief among my problems being that she still must kill me.

"And you ney are eating well. We should go to the dining car, and you must eat," she scolded me. "A big, strong man like you must need a lot of nourishment."

181

"Well...not like you do."

"Perhaps, but you ney can neglect yourself." I could tell that she was trying to take her mind off her need, but she was right, come to think of it, and her manner was far better than Learnéd's. She took my hand like a stern mother, and dragged me out the door.

§

Lunch was buffalo steaks again. Despite my worn state, my hunger surprised me, and I dug in with a will. She matched me bite for bite, both of us eating with grim mechanical intensity. The dining car was busy as always, but we ignored the crowd and the chatter of conversations. The tension grew between us as we ate in silence. She stared at her plate, afraid to meet my eyes, trembling slightly.

Finally, I reached across the table and took her hand. "Arda..."

She shook my hand off convulsively. "I am all right, Nathaniel."

"No, you aren't." I took her hand again and tried to draw it toward me, but wasn't strong enough to overcome her tension. "I'm worried about you."

She looked up at me. "You are kind, Nathaniel. Thank you. I am just...upset. You know how I get at times."

There was an awkward silence, then I said, "I wish there was some way I could make you feel better."

She gave me a fragile smile. "You have been a big help, Nathaniel." Our conversation lapsed, and we ate in silence. She poked half-heartedly at her meal, eating more from a sense of duty than any pleasure in it. "I must stay sane," she mumbled as she stared at her plate. "I will stay sane."

I watched her uncertainly as I sipped my coffee. As drawn and agitated as she was right then, I wasn't optimistic.

"I...must stay sane..." she muttered, over and over.

"Arda..."

"I am all right, Nathaniel."

There was nothing I could say, as much as I wanted to help her.

"I must stay sane..."

§

We returned to her compartment after lunch, and by then she was a nervous wreck. "Nathaniel?" She wrapped her arms around my shoulders as soon as the door closed, and looked longingly into my eyes. "I need you. Please take me."

"Arda..."

"Please, Nathaniel!" she pleaded. "I am in pain!"

"It's not right, Arda. I don't want to use you."

"I ney care," she said, sharply. Then, pleading, "I need you. Please help me." Her eyes were brimming, and she was trembling. My resolve crumbled at the sight of her agony, and it wasn't long before we were locked in a steamy embrace.

Honestly, my heart wasn't in it. I was too depressed by our problems and Learnéd's constant harassment, and I wasn't happy about how cold and physical our coupling was, but I did my best for her. She was relentless, even desperate; and when I gave up, she straddled me and plowed away endlessly as I lay there in a funk. I watched her for a while, bemused, as the time passed. From her expression, she wasn't enjoying this, but she was driven by her need. It confirmed what I suspected for a while: her urges must be overwhelming. They would have to be if she spent all day every day servicing the Loyal for hours on end. Truth is, if it weren't for her Aphrodite, I would have quit long since, if I even got started, and I felt guilty about the look in her eyes. She continued like a machine as the afternoon wore on into an early evening. Her desperation dismayed me, and I ignored my own growing discomfort if it would help her cope with the demons in her.

She stopped when I failed after several strenuous hours, and we looked at each other in uncomfortable silence. Her tears glittered in the faint moon light, which stroked my pangs of guilt even further. I gave her a reassuring smile, and caressed her cheek.

"Thank you, Nathaniel," she mumbled. She trembled slightly as she cuddled on my chest and I wrapped my arms around her. She was physically and emotionally drained, her breathing slow and deep.

"Are you all right, Arda?"

"Ney," she whispered hoarsely. "But I will manage."

I hugged her close, sharing their warmth against the chill in the room, and gently massaged her neck and scalp. We were both weary, and the bedding was soaked with sweat. More than anything, I pitied her; the Aphrodite in her was torture. Now that I had a chance to collect my wits, I wondered how intense her need could be. I had more sex with her on this trip than I normally did in a year...and it still wasn't enough to contain the demons in her. That must be part of why she deteriorated over these last few days. She must have some means of coping there in the future, and without it, she was coming unglued.

I felt bitter for her and the horrible existence the Movement inflicted on her, and it steeled my resolve that come hell or high water or whole legions of Learnéds, I would see the Movement crushed. Perhaps it would cost me my life, but it was well worth it. The last of my fear and doubt fell away as I lay there with her in my arms: I would see this through no matter the cost. And as my personal gift to her, I would see that she survived if at all possible. It lifted a terrible burden off my shoulders, and for the first time in days, I was at peace.

"I...must...stay sane," she whispered to herself.

"I'm sorry, Arda."

"Ney. I will be all right."

Other than that, neither of us spoke. Neither of us needed to.

Then I remembered our meeting with Parker, if he was still there as late as it was. If anyone could help us, it would be him, and I was more eager than ever to see him. "Do you want to talk about it, Arda?" I pointed at the door.

"Nathaniel?" She nodded, and gestured to me to be silent. "We should rest now. Hold me while I sleep, Nathaniel."

She crept silently off the berth and started wrestling with her dress. It took a lot more effort to get to my feet, but I managed.

§

The lounge car was dark and empty; even the rear brakeman was absent. Parker sat at one of the small tables, no more than a bulky shadow in the dark. That was a relief, as I was worried he might have given up on me. Maybe he could come up with a fresh outlook on this mess—figure a way out for both of us.

"Arda, here's someone who can help..." She let out a panicked squeak, and her weapon was out before I realized it. "It's all right!" I grabbed her arm and tried to push her away as Parker stared at her in surprise, but her muscles were rigid and iron hard. "Arda, it's Ned Parker! He's a friend." I said urgently. "He can help us."

"N-nathaniel..." She trembled on the edge of panic, her weapon shaking back and forth, its red light beam stitching a swathe on Parker's chest.

"Arda, he's a famous lawman...our law! Don't let your fear control you. He came here to help."

Parker considered the blunt muzzle two feet from his face, and the line of red light waving erratically back and forth in front of him, then nodded evenly to her. "Miss Arda. I'm pleased to meet you again," he said with remarkable aplomb. "Yes, sir, the rumors don't tell the half of it."

"He's here to help, Arda. Trust him."

She trembled, and her breathing was ragged, but she finally lowered her weapon, and slumped in one of the seats.

"Tell him everything, Arda." I was vastly relieved that she didn't kill our one friend in this world. "He has to understand all of it if he is to help us."

§

It took some effort to get her started, but once she did, Arda kept it brief and to the point, speaking in an emotionless monotone. It was still a good half-hour's effort to bring Parker up to speed while he sat and listened in stunned amazement.

"Science in my time iss a vast effort by the Movement probing the outer limits of knowledge," she came to at last. "One project stumbled onto a means of time travel. Naturally, the Movement kept that knowledge well hidden, but one of the technicians was Broken, and helped uss steal the prototype. That gave uss a way to fight the Movement, since we could hide in the past."

Parker spent the last half hour transfixed by her incredible tale. Now he leaned back in his chair and eyed her in disbelief. "Well, if this ain't the mommy and daddy of all stories!" he muttered at last. "And I thought I had this one figgered out."

185

"Every word iss true, Ned Parker."

He pondered her weapon, which lay on the table between us. "Yeah. It's too crazy not to be. Plus I wouldn't have believed anyone could draw as fast as you did. That's what these retros can do, eh?"

"Yes. That and more."

"And...you were made in a *factory?*"

"In a laboratory. We are artificially inseminated, genetically engineered for our roles, and conditioned to obedience."

"And you were..."

"A harlot," she answered, evenly. "They designed me to be attractive, and gave me an Aphrodite to make me inexhaustible." She was remarkably cool and collected compared to an hour ago.

"Good...God, woman, this is obscene! What they did to you was monstrous!"

She smiled, and took his hand. "You are kind, Ned Parker." Then she turned somber. "The Movement has reduced uss to numbers. They use uss and toss uss aside when they are through, and ney they care for the human cost. They ney even understand the concept. You see why we fight them."

"Damn!" Parker's face was livid with suppressed rage. "And you came here to change all that?"

"Yes." She glanced guiltily at me. "I have to kill Nathaniel to prevent the Founder from being born. I ney want to do it, but he ney can be allowed to breed."

"You were right, Nate," Parker said, angrily. "This is beyond anything I could have imagined. We have to help this poor woman." He drew his revolver and laid it on the table next to her weapon. "I'm with you all the way, little lady. You just tell me who to shoot."

Arda smiled at him wistfully, then picked up the revolver and bent the barrel like Learnéd did to my weapon earlier. Parker stared in amazement as she laid it in front of him again.

"Please understand, Ned Parker, you face an enemy unlike anything you have known. This weapon would be useless against him, and he will crush you and Nathaniel like insects if you get in his way."

186

"Good...God..." Parker managed at last as he stared incredulously at the ruined revolver. He sat there for a long moment, thoroughly shaken, then his gaze drifted to me. "Lord, Nate, you were right. I never would have..." He picked up the revolver and tugged on the barrel. "So...you did kill that man in Omaha?"

"I ney meant to," she said, defensively. "I panicked. People of this time are too fragile...I ney meant to kill him."

"This is the backside you spoke of, mister Parker. All that matters is destroying the Movement. For that, we need your help."

That snapped Parker out of his bemused state. "What chance do you have against them? Once you get to San Francisco, where can you go? From what you say, they'll hunt you down."

She sat and studied his face closely as she struggled with some difficult choice. I had no doubt as to what that decision was: whether to trust him, to trust both of us.

"There iss one other way," she said at last. "The resistance has established caches of supplies in remote areas at various times. One of those caches iss in the mountains east of SaFrisko. If I can elude Learnéd and reach it, I will be safe." That was a revelation and a vast relief, and I could see why she was reluctant to share it. It was her one hole card which Learnéd might not anticipate. "That has been my objective since I realized they were hunting me. The cache iss well defended. Once I am there, the Learnéd ney can get to me, and I can contact my people and call for help."

"How far is it from here, Arda?" I asked.

"I must leave the train when we reach the top of the pass. It ney iss far from there."

"Then our goal is to help you reach this cache. My plan to decoy Learnéd off your track is still our best bet."

"Nathaniel..." She took my hand. "He will hunt you down and destroy you! You ney know the wrath of the Pure Of Thought!"

"I must die to prevent a monstrous future," I said, evenly. "I have nothing to fear from them. I'll try to avoid them until you reach the cache and bring help. Then you can do it and be safe. If I can't, they'll spare you the anguish of killing me. I'm expendable. The future is what matters."

Parker nodded. "Like in the war."

"Right. Then it's settled. I'll decoy Learnéd. Mister Parker, I'll be obliged if you can see her to safety."

"You can count on that, son."

"Nathaniel... Perhaps..." She hesitated, then went on carefully. "There iss another way. Come with me. If we can reach the cache...you can join uss."

"Um?"

"Join the revolution. You are a good man, Nathaniel, despite your weakness. It will take time to train you, and build you up with 'retros', but you could be a great help to the resistance."

I was flabbergasted. "What good could I do?"

"You were a soldier in a horrible war. You are a professional fighter now. Your experience and outlook would make you formidable."

"God, that's tempting," Parker said.

"But what about my grandson? We still have to prevent that."

"If you come into time with me, you ney will be here to father the future," she pleaded with me. "*Please*, Nathaniel! It iss the way out that we both need!"

"But..." I struggled with my surprise at this unexpected turn. "...won't that change the future? Will it be there when we arrive?"

She hesitated, and her expression closed down as her bright hope was dashed. "I...ney know. We may arrive in the altered future, or we may remain with the future of the Movement. We might ney exist once the causality loop decays."

"You can't predict the outcome?"

She shook her head. "Ney. It takes huge computers to analyze so much data. This iss an unplanned change: there ney iss any way to predict the result. But whatever happens, we will be together."

I forced myself to give her a smile of reassurance I didn't feel. "That wouldn't be so bad, would it?"

She sighed, then turned her gaze away. "At least the Movement will be destroyed. Ass you said the other day, it iss worth our lives." She glanced at her wrist watch. "We must get back to my compartment. We ney can risk Learnéd prowling any longer."

Parker tugged at her sleeve as she stood. "I'll have a piece of that action too, miss Arda."

She smiled at him gratefully. "Ney, Ned Parker. You still have things to do here. This iss your time, ney the future. But thank you for offering. I know you would be a big help if it was possible."

She collected her weapon while I sat there in disbelief, trying to get a grip on her amazing offer. Parker took my sleeve as I stood to go. "You sure got yourself into a hell of a mess, mister Poole. I got to admit, you have style. We'll talk, tomorrow."

*****

# "Day Ten"

I skipped breakfast again the next morning, and took refuge in the lounge car where I could lose myself in the background chatter and try to sort out my mind. The place was busy with the after breakfast crowd relaxing over cards and gossip and a few copies of a pathetic local newspaper. Parker was nowhere to be seen, and I missed him. He was the tough lawman, far more accustomed than me to situations like this. There was a lot to think about, and I hardly knew where to begin.

The future I was responsible for was unspeakable, and I had to do something about it; that was a given. I certainly didn't want to die, but I was grimly prepared to accept that if it was the price of stopping the Founder and his madness. But her unexpected offer to go with her into that future left me floored. Truth was, I wanted to go with Arda. I wanted to help Arda and the resistance. I wanted Arda. I was ashamed of my part in what the Founder did, and wanted revenge for what she endured. The more I reflected on it, the more I came to admire the resistance. They did remarkably well to survive with what little they had, and even to strike back now and then against the might of the Movement.

But I couldn't see where following her would lead to, or what I would find when I got there, or what good I could do. Hell, from what she said, the mere act of leaving this time would take that future away, change everything around. What then? Would she cease to exist after the Movement vanished into limbo? Would I arrive in the altered future alone? Would being in transit through time when the change took place protect us somehow? Or would we simply disappear into whatever limbo the Movement was fated for? Would we wind up in one of those causality loops, doomed to relive this journey for all eternity? I sighed and shook my head in frustration. Whoever reduced such chaos to a hard science complete with working machinery must have been mad.

"Damn it," I muttered. "What's a man to do?"

I wondered if I was afraid; if I finally met a challenger I couldn't match. Learnéd was far more than a match by any rational standard, yet I was calmly prepared to go up against him and his

Movement despite the long odds.    It took a rare moment of introspection and a couple of beers to realize that I was afraid of the unknown.    I hardly understood the concept of time travel to begin with, much less deliberately changing the future.    It was all so complicated, so slippery.   I faced death before, and was ready to do so again if need be, but the formless, shifting shadow of that future unmanned me.

I toyed for a while with the idea of borrowing Arda's weapon and ambushing Learnéd.   It wouldn't solve anything in the long run, but it would take the immediate pressure off us, and it would feel so *damned* good.   That was mortally tempting: if she showed me how it worked, I could walk right into the compartment and sucker-punch him.    But then I starting having second thoughts about it.    I knew how fast his reflexes were: it would be too chancy, and if I failed, it would leave her helpless for his retaliation.

That notion passed, I stared out the window, lost in musing. For the life of me, I couldn't see what good I could do for the resistance, or what hope they had against the Movement.   Worse, and most damning, I couldn't even see the battlefield ahead.   As much as I wanted to go with Arda, that formless shadow daunted me.

My weary funk was interrupted at mid morning.   "Gentlemen, may I have your attention, please?"   It was Doggett at his usual station in front of the bar.   The subdued din faded as they focussed in him.   "We have received word that the line has been cleared.   As soon as they bring the last equipment down the hill, we will be getting under way again."

That brought an instant change to the glum atmosphere of the lounge.    The conversations became louder and more animated. Some hastily excused themselves and left to make last minute arrangements.    That news brought me face to face with my moment of truth, and right then I was too on edge to concentrate in all this noise and confusion.   I headed back to the compartment for my coat, and to give Learnéd an update so he wouldn't get antsy and do something unfortunate.

§

"Will miracles never cease?" he grumbled. "I am amazed this transport moves at all, with how poorly it iss run."

My annoyance got the better of me. "What? Don't they have snow storms in your time?"

Learnéd glared at me. "We predict such weather and plan for it. And we ney go over these mountains; we have a tunnel."

"Oh?" That caught my interest, being an old railroad man. "How long is it?"

Learnéd hesitated. "I ney know. It ney iss my concern. But it runs from here nearly to SaFrisko."

I was impressed. "Seventy-five miles or more, impressive." Learnéd gave me a smug look. "So how many died drilling it?"

That smug look vanished, replaced by a frown. "Labor expenditures ney are my concern, ney yours, either."

"Labor expenditures, huh? I guess that answers that one."

"Where are you going?" he demanded when I grabbed my coat.

"Out for a bit of exercise. I need to keep fit if I'm going to serve the Movement." I left before he realized I was making cynical fun of him. Perhaps the silence and the fresh air on the station grounds would clear my mind and help me put my thoughts in order.

§

The weather was raw and the wind stiffer than ever, with scudding clouds and a trace of snow. I paced up and down, ignoring the cold and the thin swirls of blown snow crossing the station grounds, fighting fatigue and frustration. Two men with a baggage cart were loading supplies into the diner, while the car toads went over the brake rigging one last time. The air was filled with the sharp smell of wood smoke and hot oil, made all the more vivid by the brisk air. I paused and took several deep breaths, savoring the sensations. It felt good to be alive.

A messenger boy brushed against me as he raced past, breaking my distracted haze. I sighed, and turned my attention back to pressing issues. Being the pivot point for human destiny was a crushing weight on my shoulders. I tried to imagine myself as part of a complex house of cards where one could safely be removed but another would bring disaster; but the concept was beyond me.

I was distracted by a figure walking across the grounds toward me. It was Parker. "Well, good day, mister Poole," he said when he arrived. "I trust you're feeling well today?"

I glanced around nervously, and gestured him to be silent. "I'm managing well enough, mister Parker. What-say we step in out of the chill?" Parker eyed me suspiciously, then followed me into the station.

§

"What's happening, son?" Parker asked once we were inside.

I gestured for silence again, shed my coat, then my jacket, and led Parker across the waiting room before I risked talking to him. "Learnéd put some kind of listening device on me. He could hear every word." I gestured to the coat laying on a bench across the room.

"That so?" Parker growled. "I sure don't take a shine to this mister Learnéd, I can tell you that. Seems to me that boy needs some hangin'."

"That and more, sir." I gestured to him to speak softly since the room was crowded.

"So, what you going t' do, Nate? About her?"

"God, I don't know." I ran my hand through my hair in nervous frustration. "I want to go with her, but what good could I do?"

"Son..." Parker took my elbow and gave me a comforting squeeze. "Either way, your life here is ended. You got nothing left to lose, so you might as well." He paused, and studied me closely for a moment. "You knew it last night, didn't you?"

"Yes, sir."

"And as for doin' some good, the one thing I've learned to fear more than anythin' is a man with nothing left to lose. You was in the war: you know what it's like when you go into battle, and you know your life is over. Anyone with sense would run, but you go on anyway. Courage don't come from bein' brave; it comes from knowin' you have a job to do, a big job, something more important than your life. It comes from knowin' folks are counting on you, and whether you live or die don't matter compared to their safety."

He was right, I knew. I felt that way many times during the war. It was an ugly feeling, but strangely uplifting.

"That sets a man free in the most terrible way," Parker went on, reflecting. "I recall when we was at Chattanooga, up there on the ridge. We watched your boys climb right up that slope, which by rights was impossible. We threw everything we had at them, and they *just kept coming.* God, I still can't believe it!"

"Yeah," I muttered. "I was there..."

§

*...Chattanooga: they cringed under the plunging artillery fire, staring up at the rows of rebel trenches three hundred feet above them on the top of a sheer rise. All he could remember was feeling empty right then; like nothing mattered any more. Nothing except that ridge, and those trenches, and all those cannon. They couldn't retreat: the Union Army was trapped, and the only way out was over that ridge. They couldn't retreat, and they couldn't stay where they were...*

*...They did something impossible that day: spontaneously, without anyone ordering it or thinking about it, the whole Corps surged forth in one common impulse, climbed that ridge, stormed that line, and drove the rebs off in utter rout. Divine Providence was their usual explanation, when any of them dared think of it...*

§

..."You was there, huh?" Parker shook his head in rueful admiration. "Damn, boy, you gave us a scare! I like to wet my pants, 'cept I was too busy running."

"I had the shakes for the rest of the day."

"You see? You never can tell about a man until he meets the elephant. Facing your fear, that's the test of us all."

I was silent for a moment as I brooded on the past. The memories still left me in a cold sweat, even years later. "You never can tell," I said at last.

Parker nodded. "You've been there, Nate. You met the elephant, an' looked him square in the eye. I can't speak for you, but I'd go with her. They have ridges to climb, too, and I get the feeling they're a mite short on talent for this kind of thing. With your experience, you could make a real difference."

194

"I don't suppose we ever know unless we try," I muttered to myself.

"You're a free man now, son: free like you could never be before, free to do what you think is right. That's better than playing the human sacrifice, however things work out." He gave me a wry grin. "And she's who you'll come marching home to."

"There is that," I said, sheepishly.

"And you know, I envy you, and not just because of her." Parker's tone turned hard. "There are some things a man can't ignore, even if they don't apply to him personally. If you're wonderin' about yourself, you might keep that in mind."

That was reassuring in a way. A man has to have purpose in his life, and right then my pending death meant I had no more purpose. Nothing to live for. Nothing left to lose. Now that I thought about it, I never really did have a purpose. My life was an aimless quest to find some meaning for existence. Now I had it. Now I was free to do what was right.

"But from what she told me, my leaving this time will change everything. I don't even know where I'll wind up, or what the world will be like." I turned to Parker in frustration. "How can I plan for the future when that future won't be there?"

Parker reflected on that for a bit. "You got me there, son. Arda and her people...they're messing with things that mankind ought not to. There's no way I can see to call it. All you can do is put your faith in the Good Lord, and do the best you can." He gave me a wry smile. "Remember, God watches over fools and children."

"Maybe so," I said at last. "At least I'll get my shot at Learnéd."

Parker's features hardened. "Yeah, well, I might take a crack at this mister Learnéd myself on general principle."

I took his arm in a cautioning gesture. "Don't. I'm not sure bullets would even harm him."

§

Parker headed back to the train, leaving me to recover my coat and return to pacing the station grounds. Despite Parker's words, I was still lost about what to do. I was grateful for his perspective, but I still wasn't convinced...

195

...No, admit it: I was afraid. Afraid of the unknown, afraid of enemies I couldn't hope to match, all at sea over a future I didn't understand, and which probably wouldn't be there when I arrived, anyway. "God, what a mess," I groaned, not caring if Learnéd heard or not. Maybe what I should do was close my eyes and charge that trench line, knowing I would die, giving up all hope, and pray that my fate would mean something. Like I did at Chattanooga...

The smell of roast chicken penetrated my thoughts. It was coming from the dining car.

§

Arda was already hard at work on a plate of roast chicken and dumplings when I arrived, and she greeted me with a wain smile. "How are you today, Nathaniel?"

"Managing, I guess." I sagged in the chair opposite, and gestured to the waiter.

"You look tired."

"I am. It's been a long trip, for both of us."

"It has," she mumbled.

I needed to talk with her in the worst way, to express my doubts and get her perspective. And I could see that she wanted to talk with me in turn, but the specter of Learnéd loomed over us both. We both needed comfort, but we couldn't do more than utter vague generalities at each other.

"Well, we'll be moving again shortly, and you should complete your journey soon. So cheer up. *Change,*" I emphasized the word, "is always good for the soul."

"Perhaps you are right, Nathaniel."

I wished silently that she would call me Nate, if only once. "Getting off this train will feel good, too."

She sighed, but didn't answer. The waiter returned just then with a steaming plate. I hadn't realized how famished I was, and dug in feverishly. It was some time before we could get back to the conversation.

"It pains me to see you like this." I tried to send encouragement to her with veiled hints. "I hope you can get beyond your problems, and that tomorrow will be better."

She sighed. "Truth, I ney think about tomorrow. Today iss enough of a burden to bear." She lowered her head. "Sometimes I am tired. Sometimes I wish I could find peace with myself." She was silent for a bit, then, "Sometimes, I ney care about life any more."

That was not good. She needed reinforcement more than I did. "Don't think like that, Arda. You are alive, you are gifted, there is so much about you that is beautiful and desirable."

She smiled. "You are a naughty man, Nathaniel.

"You make me think naughty thoughts." I wiped my fingers on a napkin, and took her hand. "Be strong; a better world will come for you some day."

"Some day?" The look in her eyes said she understood my meaning. "I hardly believe in some day any more, Nathaniel."

That wasn't promising either. She had precious little faith in their resistance, or in the success of their strategy. And she was weary of the fighting and the danger; weary of hiding and struggling; weary beyond endurance. I'd seen it before in the faces of my comrades in the 27th Illinois. I silently cursed Learnéd and his little black specks which kept me from comforting her in this moment.

"You are tired from this journey, Arda." I squeezed her hand for reassurance. "Once this trip is over and you rest up a bit, life will look good to you again."

"I suppose you are right." She gave me a forced smile. "We all have our mortal moments, ney?"

"Tomorrow is always new, always different. Every day is a chance to start over."

Her smile was more genuine. "You are a poet, Nathaniel."

Our conversation petered out, and we went back to chicken and dumplings, but enough was said, for now.

§

After dinner, I escorted her back to her compartment. "So, will I see you again this evening, Nathaniel?" she asked as I left her at her door. The stark look in her eyes said there was more to her invitation than her words let on.

"Yes, I'd like that."

"Good." She pulled me close, and gave me a kiss that peeled the paint off the bulkheads. "Get some rest, Nathaniel. We will be in San Francisco tomorrow afternoon. I plan to make this a *memorable* evening." She gave me a quick, nervous smile, and closed her door.

§

I felt an overwhelming need to avoid my future puppet master right then, so I headed back to the lounge car. The place was busy as the bored passengers mingled and gossiped. From how the room quieted when I came in, Arda and I must be high on the list of lively topics, not that I cared. All the seats were taken, so I ordered a beer, and settled for an out of the way corner of the bar. The bartender drew a cold one, added a cigar from the box behind the counter, and left me to nurse my troubles in brooding silence.

Parker was right: there was nothing left for me here, and I might do some good there. I owed the Movement for what they did to Arda, and I owed my multi-great grandson for creating that horror to begin with. Still—admit it—the future scared me. Maybe I had no real future at all. Hell, I couldn't even be sure the future had any future at all.

Honestly, I was at a loss for what to do. Maybe it would be easiest just to let Arda do her duty. It wouldn't hurt much, and I was well accustomed to pain. It was the one sure answer, and for all its shortcomings, it might be better than wandering up and down the ages on a wild goose chase...

A noisy argument distracted me. Those three ranchers were parked at a table playing cards. They'd held out on the Reno Sheriff to the extent of beer money, at least, and were spending it lavishly now. I couldn't tell if they were wagering on their game, but they argued and fussed as if they were. Or perhaps they just liked to argue.

The one named Frank clambered to his feet, wandered over to the bar, which was tricky navigating in his condition, and banged his beer mug on the counter. "Hey, boy, let's have another one."

The bartender hesitated. "Well...beggin' yo' pardon, suh, but you look a mite under de weather," he said, carefully. "Could I fix you some coffee?"

Frank was a mean drunk, with an ugly fire in his eye. I watched him cautiously, my left fist cocked down beside my waist, waiting for him to explode.

He looked about ready to. "You watch your place there, nigger!"

"Yessah." The bartender averted his eyes and poured another drink in tense silence, then stood dejected as Frank stumbled back to his friends. I slowly relaxed, and went back to leaning on the bar. Our eyes met, and I gave the bartender a small shake of my head in sympathy. Like most people in this time, I didn't care for blacks; didn't like to think about them. They represented too much pain for themselves, for the country, for their former masters. It was easier when they stayed in the background, which most of them instinctively did anyway.

"Can ah get you anythin' else, suh?" the bartender asked, softly.

I considered him somberly, then took another sip of beer. "You were freed during the war, weren't you?"

The bartender's face closed down with the wary look blacks showed the white world. "Yessah. Ah was a house boy in 'lanta fo' the Sherman soldiers came."

I took another sip as I reflected on that. "Atlanta, huh? I was there." I looked him in the eye. "I was with the 27th Illinois."

"Was you, suh?"

"Yep." I killed the last of my beer, set the mug on the bar, and watched as the bartender refilled it. "Yeah, I was there, all right." I drew on my cigar, took another sip of beer, and brooded as the bartender watched in silence. "Small world, ain't it?"

"It sho is, suh," the bartender whispered...

§

*...A small world. Atlanta. Their weary columns were met with a joyous flood of freed slaves, poor miserable creatures who greeted them with tears of joy and praise unto de Lawd fo' de comin' of de Sherman soldiers. They all felt ten feet tall that day, proud to be Americans, and proud to march with Uncle Billy Sherman as he scourged the South with torch and sword...*

§

199

...And here stood one of those miserable creatures; once property, bred for servitude, now a man.

"I was one of those Sherman soldiers," I said, solemnly. "I helped set you free."

The bartender was crying silently. "Well...ah thank yo' fo' that, suh." He wiped a tear from his cheek with the bar towel. "I sho do for that, suh."

I stared into my mug as the bartender tried to compose himself. I used to believe in all that—Emancipation, old Long Abe's dream of freedom from sea to shining sea. Somewhere along the way I forgot what it felt like to be praised as a liberator, what it felt like to struggle and fight and endure—and die—for something bigger than I could see. And there standing in front of me was at least one man whose life I made better; one example which said that all the bloodshed mattered. It made me feel all watery inside.

The bartender sniffed and went back to wiping the bar, lost in his own introspection.

And the struggle wasn't over. Arda's struggle: against hopeless odds, against an evil more monstrous than chattel slavery. An evil I caused; an evil my eighth time removed grandson unleashed on humanity. I read somewhere once that Abe Lincoln famously remarked about feeling the lash on another man's back. I finally understood what he meant. And I finally accepted that I must do something about it.

I finished my beer, tipped the bartender a quarter, and gave him a nod, man to man.

§

I paused at the door to the platform and wondered whether to head for the compartment, but decided I couldn't stomach Learnéd right then. In any case, I needed a breather, and it wouldn't hurt to size up the situation.

If anything, the weather was colder. The brisk air helped clear my head, and breathed new life into me. I stood for a long time staring sightlessly at the Sierras. For the first time in a long time my spirit was untroubled, my mind at peace. I was committed to what was probably a hopeless cause which would probably result in my death, but I was content for the first time in years.

The afternoon sun gleamed off the snowcapped Sierras, their radiant white silhouetted between the pale blue sky and the gray bulk of the mountains. It was ominous, foreboding, and beautiful. I drank in the sensation, all the sensations around me, knowing that I would soon be leaving this world forever. Whatever natural beauty might still exist in the future I couldn't say, but it wouldn't be the same as standing here, now. I would miss it.

A few hours before sunset, the snow plow inched into the yard at a walking pace, and was switched onto the wye to be turned around. The wrecking train followed, its huge steam crane trailing. Right behind that came a locomotive towing another locomotive. A short while later, another locomotive came in pulling six mangled box cars.

Shortly after that, the steam line was disconnected from the 'Overland', and two large locomotives took its place. Other locomotives were on the move, coming out of the roundhouse and coupling up to their trains with a flurry of whistles and clouds of steam. The station boys were busy running orders back and forth to all the trains stuck in the yard, while the stationmaster himself delivered orders to conductor Doggett. I boarded the train reluctantly, but my mind was made up at last.

§

"So, you return," Learnéd greeted me with his usual scowl. "I was wondering if you deserted."

"I was going to, but I missed your warmth and good cheer," I grumbled.

"And you are drinking." Learnéd fanned the air in disgust. "You are a sorry specimen, even for a citizen."

"Yep. And I'm your past, too." I eyed him bitterly. "My luck, you're probably my descendant."

"I ney am bred like cattle!" Learnéd was on his feet, hot with anger, and grabbed me by my jacket. "You offend me, *citizen*..." Then he hesitated, and seemed to go off into another of his trances, which gave me a chance to realize I was pushing my luck. Learnéd came back to the present, shoved me back onto the berth, and gave me an icy look. "You and I have ney in common," he growled. "Your insults mean ney to me."

"You got that right."

I slumped on the berth and stared at nothing in dejection while Learnéd glowered at me, and finally took his seat again. I was unspeakably weary from having to tiptoe around him, and from having to constantly suppress my own rage at the evil he represented. I wasn't used to being the weakling, of being afraid to snap back or fight back for fear of what could happen. I needed to for Arda's sake as well as my own, but the tension was wearing me down. That would end soon, and I hoped fervently that we would meet again in the future. But for now, I would bide my time while warming myself with thoughts of fitting justice. In the end, sensibly, I curled up in the berth and stared out the window. I hardly noticed or cared as the 'Overland' got under way.

*****

## "Day Ten: Afternoon, Evening"

The 'Overland' crawled out of Reno at a snail's pace despite having priority over all other trains. I lay brooding on my berth, absently watching the passing landscape in the dim afternoon light, and wondered what came next. Now that all was said and done, I was anxious to get on with it. I remembered moments like this during the war; waiting nervously for some battle or other to start, listening to the distant cannon fire and the crackle of musketry, and trying to suppress my fear.

*"You have nothing left to fear, nothing left to hope for,"* Parker's words came back to me. *"All you have is a job to do, a big job, something more important than your life, and whether you live or die don't matter."*

He was right, and I took comfort from that. For better or worse, I was committed to a mighty cause. That gave me a strange feeling of peace: I wanted some reason for my life for the longest time, and now I had one. I just wished we could *get on with it.*

I threw a quick sidelong glance at Learnéd sitting in his chair, arms folded as always. His forbidding frown and hard eyes gave me the willies. How much did he know? How much did he suspect? Would he remain sitting there long enough for Arda and me to make our escape?

And how soon would that come? Up ahead, the Sierras towered over us, spread from horizon to horizon in a forbidding ice covered wall of stone. The sight was intimidating, and I wondered idly what the Donner party must have thought when they stared up at those mountains. What was taking so long? We weren't going much faster than ten miles an hour.

Another glance at Learnéd; I couldn't help it. Learnéd stared back at me like a hawk. In the back of my mind, I recognized that as an intimidation tactic. Those cold, dark eyes were terrifying; what effect would they have on Arda's people, who were conditioned to obedience?

One of the locomotives gave a whistle signal, faint in the distance. It was shrill, yet melodic; a bugle call sounding the charge against the mountains. Our two locomotives surged ahead, their exhausts deeper and more urgent. It was a comforting sound; reassuring me that we had the latest and best of mankind's science to call upon.

Somewhere up there in that frozen hell, she would try to reach safety and I would go with her; leaving this world and everything I ever knew behind. As Parker said, I had nothing left to lose, but the unknown future loomed in the darkness ahead like the forbidding Sierras. At least when we marched south with Sherman, I knew we would be walking on familiar ground, and fighting human enemies who shot at us with simple Enfield muskets. The challenge then was understandable, if daunting; the danger we could comprehend; the fear we could cope with. Now I would face inhuman monsters supported by the Devil's own science, and the battlefield was the length and width of time itself. I felt awed and humbled to march in this campaign.

The train rounded a broad curve, and I saw another train right ahead of us. One mystery solved, anyway. It was the rotary snow plow; its steam powered fan munching through a steady diet of minor avalanches and snow drifts which it tossed to one side in white bursts as it carved a swathe wide enough for our train to follow. Three large locomotives pushed it, followed by the work cars and caboose. Right then they were making fair time for such a cumbersome piece of machinery, although they slowed occasionally when they hit heavier snow drifts. As I watched, the snow plow came to one deep cut packed by an avalanche. The three locomotives dug in, and the plow inched ahead, hurling a white geyser to one side, and clouds of black smoke and soot upward. Our car slammed back and forth as the locomotives slowed to keep from overrunning the plow train, causing the cars to bang together.

Learnéd came over and glanced out the window. "I ney am surprised by how poorly this iss done," he grumbled as he watched the plow in action. "The Movement iss far better organized than you are in these chaotic times."

I glanced at him in annoyance. "Just remember it was us who conquered the West and laid tracks over these mountains."

Learnéd snorted dismissively. "All you did was make a crude beginning. *We* built a perfect world on the ruins *you* left behind." He gave me a hard look. "We solved all the problems of the perfect society, *including* how to deal with heretics, and those who fail in their duty to the Movement."

I tried not to show any reaction to what was clearly a threat, and wondered what brought this latest display on.

He returned to his chair. "I have tolerated your insolent conduct because you serve the Movement, but we know you ney are properly conditioned. Ney let your misguided thoughts betray you. Failure ney iss acceptable, and willing disobedience iss dealt with harshly."

The plow trudged ahead relentlessly, half submerged and all but hidden by their combined exhausts. A whistle sounded faintly, and our two locomotives dug in, sending a shock wave down the train as the slack ran out. We were moving again. I watched in silence, worried if he realized we were plotting against him. Or was this another intimidation tactic to keep me in line as the moment of truth approached?

"This will be over soon," he said, with an icy look in his eyes. "Remember your duty to the Movement for a little while longer." The uneasy silence returned; I propped up on my berth by the window, Learnéd in his chair with arms folded, watching.

§

Night came early at this time of the year, and even earlier here in the shadow of the Sierras. The sun slipped behind the mountains well before dinner time, casting the land around us in shadow beneath a pale winter sky. A few wispy clouds drifted before the wind, colored in purples and oranges by the fading light, their edges painted in liquid gold. It was an awesome, majestic sight; something I never really appreciated before. Now that I was on the edge of losing that beauty forever, of leaving this mortal coil either head first or feet first, the spectacle was bittersweet.

Learnéd pondered me suspiciously as I made ready to meet with Arda in the dining car again. "I ney see how you find the strength for her."

"Don't knock it." I was feeling a bit above myself since, with luck, this would be the last time we'd speak. "You might want to give her a try. Do you some good, I'd say."

Learnéd frowned. "I ney consort with harlots."

"Too bad. You don't know what you're missing. Not that I care." I finished buttoning my jacket, and wondered briefly if I should risk taking my heavy coat. I would need that later, but taking it might alert him. All I could do was hope Arda's cache was near the right of way.

Learnéd caught the door, stopping me as I tried to leave. "Remember," he said sternly. "She iss a dangerous criminal. Ney let her hormones get to you, or you will start thinking with your glands. That could get you killed."

I managed to conceal the flush of fear that swept through me. "Yeah. Well, after tomorrow she'll be your problem, and I'll be glad to get rid of both of you." I pushed the door open against his grip. "I'll have some fond memories of her once this is over. You, I can't say the same."

"Remember to send food," was his last demand.

§

I was on my way through the next sleeper when I ran into conductor Doggett coming the other way. Doggett frowned, and continued in stone-faced silence, having lost enough run-ins with us that he probably wished the trip was done and he was rid of us.

"Mister Doggett, when will we reach the top of the pass?" I asked him when we met.

Doggett looked at me curiously, then dug out his timepiece and studied it. "I would think about midnight." He conspicuously omitted the usual 'sir'.

"Thank you," I mumbled as he went on his way. Midnight. That was a long way off.

§

She was at her usual table, picking a plate of lamb chops and fried potatoes. "Good evening, Nathaniel," she greeted me with a nervous smile. "I hope you are feeling well. We shall be busy this evening."

"Yes, fine, thank you," I muttered as I took my seat.

The waiters were hard at work, but they were used to giving her priority service, so it wasn't long before I dug in with a hunger that was one part fear and one part anticipation. She continued to pick at her plate half-heartedly.

"Are you all right, Arda?" I gestured at her half finished plate. "You aren't eating."

She sighed. "I ney am hungry. There iss too much on my mind. I know I should eat." She picked up her fork and forced herself to dig into the fried potatoes.

"Everything will work out, Arda."

She gave me a wain smile. "I hope so." She busied herself with her utensils. "I have enjoyed your company, Nathaniel," she said between bites. "You have been very kind to me, and made this journey so much more bearable."

The tension between us was acute; the unspoken reality behind her words haunted us. As we sat eating in painful silence, I wondered idly what would happen when we made the journey into time. From what she'd said, we wouldn't even reach the future; we'd be stuck in one of those loops, reliving this journey endlessly. That brought to mind Learnéd's question from when we first met. I could picture it in my mind: the two of us together, dining on roast chicken and buffalo steaks by day, fornicating like mad minks by night, riding a ghost train across endless plains to eternity. Would we become a folk legend, I wondered? A ghost story maybe? Fanciful perhaps, but with this time travel, who could say? At least, however it turned out, we would be together. Perhaps being stranded in her compartment forever wouldn't be so bad after all.

A troubling thought crossed my mind: would Learnéd be trapped there with us? At least we could tell him to go to hell, assuming he was, although he'd probably kill us both in one of his rages. Not that I was eager to die, but we would have the satisfaction of seeing the look on his face when he realized the Movement he was created to serve no longer existed.

Of course she didn't know as yet that I intended to go with her. She was still faced with the decision of whether to kill me or not. I could tell that she was dying to talk about it, about so many things, but Learnéd boxed us in so tightly that we were almost mute. That damned black speck in my lapel was only one visible symptom of the greater fear he instilled in us. Right then I felt smothered; I could appreciate how she must feel, coming from a world where fear was the state politic.

"I'm sure you will find what you're looking for when *we* get to San Francisco," I hinted to her. "I'm looking forward to seeing it once we arrive."

She gave me another hint of a smile. "That will be nice." Perhaps she knew I would go with her; or at least she hoped I would.

I was relieved to have that choice nailed down; it left me strangely at peace. I had a load of grief to deliver to my multi-bastard-grandson, and I intended to hunt Learnéd down and settle some scores. Oddly, I felt free like I hadn't for a long time, and that gave me some small glimmer of hope. Honestly, I had no idea what I could have done otherwise. I knew I would brood over that question for years to come.

All we could do now was avoid Learnéd until we reached the top of the pass and got off this train. I was under no delusions about the challenges ahead. The first part would be the worst:

sitting here helplessly, praying that Learnéd wouldn't make his move until it was time to leave. At least, after we left the train, we could run. I dug my watch out and checked the time. Hours to go.

§

By time we reached Truckee, California, I was a nervous wreck. Both trains stopped for water; a long process which did my mood no good. They slogged away relentlessly for over two hours to get this far, which used up the supply in their tenders in a hurry. As I watched impatiently, the snow plow and its three locomotives drew up under the water tower one at a time for a much needed drink. It was brutal work for the train crews in the fading twilight as they carefully positioned each tender and hammered away the caked ice on the water tower's spout. Then it was the 'Overland's turn to refill their two locomotives. The whole thing took nearly an hour and a half while the crews endured bitter cold and treacherous ice as they struggled with the heavy water column. Other than that water tower and another small station, Truckee wasn't much to write home about. But it was the last outpost of civilization until we crossed the pass. The snowfall was still mild at this altitude. Further up was where the plow's three locomotives would have their work cut out for them, if they didn't have to resort to blasting fallen rocks and trees with gunpowder.

§

Time crawled by on hands and knees while we ate in tense silence. I was so preoccupied with worry that I hardly realized what I was eating. She poked at her plate unenthusiastically, if relentlessly. I was bemused once again by how she could pack it away; those retros demanded a stiff price. But there were greater worries right then. Aside from brief non-committal exchanges, the silence was palpable.

The dining car was filling up, and the noise level crept upward. The crowd was in a festive mood, having escaped from Reno and anticipating their arrival in San Francisco tomorrow. I hardly noticed in my preoccupation.

"Are you all right, Arda?" I asked for the umpteenth time. I was taking a chance on alerting Learnéd, but from the strained look on her face and her sagging posture, I wondered if she would last.

209

She glanced nervously at me.  "Yes," she mumbled.  "Be patient with me, Nathaniel."

We were well into the mountains by then.  The train was working its way up a steep grade along the edge of a narrow valley. To our left was a pine covered slope, with rock outcroppings that came within inches of the window.  To the right, the ground fell sharply away, with the tops of tall pines at eye level in the faint moonlight.  I could just make out the track running along the other side of the gorge, no more than a few hundred feet away and considerably higher than we were at the moment.  There was a long way to go.

She stirred again, picked up her fork, and started poking at her nearly empty plate.  "Iss there anything more eat Nathaniel?"

I was stuffed, but I was worried about her appetite.  She was only on her second plate, and dinner time was waning.  I gestured to the waiter.  "What do you have left in the kitchen?"

The man thought for a bit.  "Well, suh, we have some potatoes left, an' some green beans, an' ah think maybe a bit of lamb. Should ah fetch some fo' you, suh?"

"Yes, please.  A large plate for the lady."

"And bread, too," she added.

The car lurched and swayed as we rounded a curve sharp enough to lean us over even at this low speed.  The screech of steel on steel set my teeth on edge as the car changed course.  We reached the end of the gorge, and the train was reversing course to continue its relentless climb up the opposite slope.  We came out of the curve after what seemed like forever, and now the moon was on the other side.  The train crawled up grade along the far side of the valley, the locomotives pounding away for all they were worth, their booming exhaust echoing off the rocks around us.

"Here you go, ma'am."  The waiter set a fresh plate before her.

The food was a bit dry, but there was still plenty of it.  I poked at mine to see if I could stuff any more down my throat, while she went back to eating listlessly.

The train plunged into another tunnel, then turned along a ridge heading west again.

§

We were up in the high country, and out from the lea of the mountains. The snow pile was in earnest here, and the train slowed to an unsteady crawl as the rotary ahead of us struggled to clear a path. Much of the track from here over the pass had been covered with snow sheds; long wooden covers intended to keep winter at bay. While the snow sheds worked, it was like going through a continuous tunnel. The locomotives strained on the heavy grades, and trains traveled through a choking cloud of smoke and soot which made each trip a nightmare. Worse, train crews were blinded by the dense fog; signals were overlooked, and collisions were common. That was before the modern steam plows came along. Since then, the road started tearing the sheds away wherever possible, but there were still long stretches of them.

The dining car was sealed fairly tight, but there was still a thin fog of wood smoke which stung the eyes and made some people wheeze. We emerged from another stretch of snow shed, and as the view cleared, I saw a breathtaking winter panorama glowing faintly in the twilight. The train was crawling along a narrow ledge blasted into the side of a sheer mountain, and we were several hundred feet above ground level—if one could call the ground hereabouts 'level'. The rock face was inches from our left windows, while the tops of pine trees drifted past the other side.

"It iss beautiful ney with all the ruins," Arda whispered.

"Nature as it was meant to be." The train rounded a curve, and I spotted a flat area in the distance. "There. Donner Lake."

"We lost so much," she said, sadly. The mystic mood was banished, and I went back to worrying and waiting.

§

I finally gave up on dinner, annoyed by how slowly the minutes were passing, and sat nursing my coffee as I kept a wary eye on the room. The crowd was thinner, and those remaining were mostly into dessert. The waiters were clearing away the last dishes, and a few card games were starting up.

I noticed that she was fiddling with another of her futuristic gadgets. I worried that it might be a weapon before I saw a small lighted panel with some sort of diagram on it. She pondered it for another moment, then slipped it back into her pouch.

Finally the tension of sitting there got to me. "Arda, we need to take a break."

She looked me, then nodded. It took some effort to get to my feet after sitting so long. I offered her my hand and helped her up. As she rose, a movement at the far end of the car caught my eye; it was Learnéd, talking with the steward. "Oh, Jesus," I muttered as he looked in our direction. She glanced at me curiously and started to turn, but I covered that by grabbing her around her waist and pulling her to me. "It's him," I whispered as I nuzzled her neck and she looked at me in confusion. "We have to get out of here. Stay calm."

She let out a gasp, and I felt her stiffen in fear. Then her survival instinct and her training as a pleasure girl kicked in. "Nathaniel!" she giggled. "You *are* the naughty one!" The genuine terror in her eyes was all that gave her away as she threw her arms around my shoulders and turned her back on Learnéd. "What will people say about uss?"

I managed a quick peek; Learnéd was watching in the distance, as was the steward and most of the passengers. At least it seemed unlikely he would try anything here with so many witnesses.

"They'll say the worst, I'm sure." I managed somehow to keep my voice even.

"Then we might ass well give them something to talk about, ass they will do so anyway, ney?"

"That sounds like a plan." I nuzzled her neck, keeping a wary eye on Learnéd.

"Perhaps we should find some privacy," she said with an amorous laugh. "Before we shock these good people." She tucked her arm in mine, and half dragged me past the kitchen toward the rear door.

§

We went to ground behind the door of the next car. I peered anxiously around the corner of the window to see if Learnéd was following, while she leaned against the wall behind me, weapon held by her side in a death grip, trembling. Time seemed to stop as I waited, but there was nothing but the squeal of the wheels on the rails and the pounding of my heart.

212

"N-Nathaniel..."

"Sssshhh!" I gestured for silence. "I don't see him." I had no idea what to do if he did appear. She was in no shape to use her weapon; perhaps I could snatch it from her and kill Learnéd myself, if I got lucky. That thought warmed me.

It seemed like forever before I decided he returned to the compartment. "I think he's gone," I said, softly.

By then, Arda was so shaky that she could hardly walk. I steadied her as we made our way the short distance to her compartment. When we finally reached that illusion of safety, she broke down and cried, clinging to my shoulders.

\*\*\*\*\*

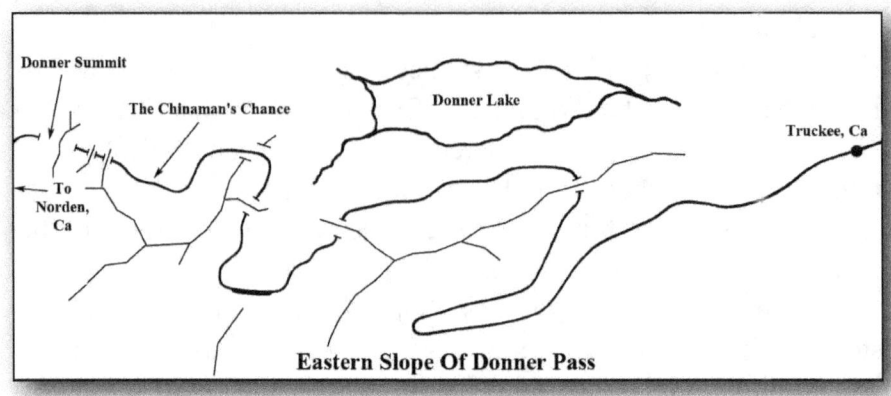

Eastern Slope Of Donner Pass

## "Day Ten: Night"

It was another half an hour before Arda recovered her composure enough to return to the dining car. Dinner was long past by then, with only a few lingerers over desert and cards, and we were able to reclaim her table by the kitchen. She sat with her back against the wall, nervously watching the far entry in case Learnéd came in again. She was wain and drawn, and her lovely face was creased with tension. I bundled my jacket and sat on it, since there were urgent things to talk about. Learnéd might get suspicious and come looking, but that was a chance we had to take.

"It'll be all right, Arda," I murmured. I took her hand to comfort her. "We'll reach the summit before you know it. We need to be careful until then, but there's no reason to panic."

"I...am sorry, Nathaniel," she whispered. "I am so afraid of them...I ney could help it."

"You did great. They conditioned you to be afraid, but you can overcome it. You broke conditioning, remember?" The depth of her terror worried me; she may have broken her conditioning, but she hadn't escaped it entirely.

She sighed, and nodded. I noticed that her other hand was down below the table. Curious, I leaned forward and looked over and saw that she held her weapon in her lap, her hand rigid with tension. "Arda, you need to put that thing away," I said, evenly. She stared at me with wide, fearful eyes, her face tight and drawn.

Her other hand trembled slightly in mine. "Arda, we don't want a gunfight in here. If Learnéd comes back, we'll fool him like we did last time." I was worried that she might panic at anything, and start shooting. I suspected those strange weapons packed a wallop.

She hesitated for a long moment, then nodded reluctantly, and slipped the weapon back in her pouch. "He...was probably here to order food," she murmured. She didn't sound convinced of that.

I realized to my dismay that I forgot to send food to the compartment. I cursed myself for that; my preoccupation almost brought on the disaster we were fearing. "You're right, Arda. He seems to stick close to home most of the time."

"They...are...creatures of habit." She lapsed into nervous silence, and stared at the table, taking refuge in their misperceptions. Self-denial was one of her many weaknesses. Or perhaps the Movement was such a nightmare to them that she couldn't look at Learnéd objectively. That was one more thing to worry about. He was fairly predictable; the same could not be said for her. Right then, I was praying that she would hold together until it was time to go.

She closed her eyes, and her head sagged. "I must stay sane," she whispered. "I must stay sane. I must stay sane..."

§

The cars slammed together as the locomotive exhaust became a muffled roar, which snapped me out of a distracted haze. We must have hit a patch of ice, causing one of the locomotives to lose traction. She gasped, and reached for her pouch. "It's all right, Arda." I squeezed her other hand reassuringly. "It's nothing." She hesitated, trembling, then her hand slipped back to her lap.

The train was on a broad curve, so I craned my neck and saw the problem through the window. The lead locomotive had lost its footing, its drivers spinning madly, rimmed with fire, as a cascade of sparks flew up the stack. The hogger shut off, which stopped the slipping, then cautiously opened up again. It took a delicate touch on the throttle to coax the best out of their mechanical beasts without losing traction. The second locomotive slipped, then dug in again. Slowly at first, then more surely, they gained speed, and closed on the plow train ahead of us in the gloom.

She was fiddling with that small box again. She shook her head sadly, and slipped it back into her pouch without offering any explanation. I didn't ask for one.

We went back to waiting.

§

Time crawled by on hands and knees as the tension wound higher and higher. My stomach ached and my nerves were frazzled, and despite the tension, I was half dead with fatigue. I realized vaguely that I had been up for more than sixteen hours after precious little sleep. Thinking was an effort.

"Will you be needin' anythin' mo, suh?" The waiter's question yanked me out of a half-doze with a spasmodic twitch. It took a moment to recover my wits.

"Ah...coffee, please. Extra strong."

"Yessah." The waiter withdrew.

I stared at nothing, and wondered absently what to do if Learnéd came back. My fighter's instincts gnawed at the problem, trying to find a way to take an inhumanly strong opponent down hard and fast. There must be some vulnerable spots. Even if he was iron hard, he could feel pain. Maybe a kick where it counted would be the best move; or maybe go for his eyes. It was all in vain. Learnéd would trample us without breaking into a sweat.

There was a faint whistle in the distance. I dug my pocket watch out and studied it for the who-knows-how-manyth time. The minutes seemed to drag by like hours, the hours like centuries. I silently cursed in frustration as I put it away again.

Diner was done, and the room emptying. A few groups relaxed at the tables, drinking coffee, and playing *Vingt et un* in preference to the crowded, smokey lounge car. The waiters loitered at their stations, and the scullery boy was polishing silverware.

"It won't be much longer, Arda."

She sat with her head down, eyes closed, nervous and withdrawn. The tension was palpable, and she was starting to crumble under it. She nodded faintly. We long since quit pretending to be part of the after dinner socializing.

"I must stay sane," she muttered. "I must stay sane..."

§

*...he was standing amid the smoldering ruins of a vast city. All around him were the mangled corpses of soldiers and civilians. Some were individuals: male and female, tall and short, lean and fat, young and old. Others...the others were identical...copies of Learnéd...hundreds, thousands of them. They all died savagely; the civilians' faces contorted in terror, the soldiers' grim with fatalism, the Learnéds with no expressions at all...*

*...In the distance, amid the ruins, there rose a vast temple, like a great cathedral made all of shimmering glass...but distorted...monstrous...inhuman...cursed with an unholy beauty which summoned the damned to their fates...*

*...A shadow fell across the area like a dark cloud. He turned and looked up...it was Learnéd...the Founder...John Brown...himself...all rolled into one, towering above the ruins...*

*..."Blasphemer" His voice rolled like thunder. "This iss your doing. You made Me. You made the Movement. You are me, and this iss what you wrought in your madness. Ney have you shame?"...*

*...He felt shame, shame for what he had done, and wept as his soul was drawn slowly out of him by the demented gaze above. Without willing it, he turned and ran toward the distant temple...*

*..."Fool, do you think you can change fate?" His voice rolled. "The future iss ass it iss, ney more, ney less. It iss ass it was meant to be."...*

*..."Never!" He ran harder, swerving through the ruins and stumbling over corpses.*

*...She was standing in front of him...towering over him like the Founder. "Ney run, Nathaniel," her voice rolled. "It iss useless."...*

*..."I'm trying to help you! To save you!" he cried...*

*..."Pathetic little man," she said, sadly. "Ney even a citizen. The future iss ass it iss, Nathaniel: ney more, ney less. It iss ass it was meant to be. You ney can change what will be."...*

*...He ran desperately, heart pounding and lungs burning...he must reach the temple...it was his only hope of salvation...he wept in fear and shame...he had nothing to live for, nothing to hope for...*

*..."You are foolish, Nathaniel," she said.*

*"Run little man," the thunder of His voice came from her lips as she beckoned to him. "You ney have the strength...you ney can even drill a tunnel from here to SaFrisko."...*

*..."I must make it!" he cried as her cloying scent flooded his senses. "I must save you!"...*

*..."You are noble, Nathaniel, but it iss hopeless," she said with her seductive, sultry voice. "You made the Founder, and He made the Movement, and the Movement made me. You ney can save me, for I am you."...*

*..."No! I - I must..." He faltered as her scent broke down his will. "I must reach the temple!"...*

*..."Ney struggle against fate, Nathaniel. The future iss ass it iss, ney more, ney less."...*

*..."I..." He stumbled to a halt as his need rose in him, burning, uncontrollable. She was standing in front of him in the temple doorway, naked, her skin glistening with sweat. She raised her arms, beckoning him to his doom.*

*..."Come to me, Nathaniel"...*

§

"...Nathaniel?" Arda was shaking my arm. "Wake up."

"I beg your pardon, sir, madam," the steward said politely as he gestured toward the door. "We are closing the diner for the night."

I was surprised to see that the room was empty, and the gas lamps were being extinguished. I must have drifted off for a while. "Ah...yes, thank you." I handed over one of Learnéd's double eagles to settle our tab. The waiters were scrubbing the tables and sweeping the floors, while the sounds from the kitchen told a similar story.

"Well, Nathaniel," she said somberly as she slipped her arm around mine. "Shall we adjourn to my compartment?"

§

I paused on the open platform between cars, and took a look around to get oriented. The night sky was amazingly clear, with a half moon casting eerie silver highlights on the pine trees as the train crawled past. We were well up into the mountains now; the train winding back and forth as the track followed a narrow ledge blasted out of the rugged landscape. There was a haunting and foreboding beauty to it, accented by the thunder of our locomotives up ahead, and the scent of pine and wood smoke, not that I was pleased by the sight.

I grabbed the hand rail and looked ahead. The plow train was perhaps a half mile ahead of us, their collective headlights illuminating the white plume thrown up by the rotary. The snow pile was in earnest now, and they were fighting a bitter headwind coming over the pass.

I pulled my jacket tighter against the chill, and studied the sky. It was clear for now, but the first signs of a storm were gathering in the west. The pale light faded as the moon was covered by scudding clouds, and the icy wind picked up. This clear weather wasn't going to hold for long.

§

She pulled me into her compartment by my lapel before I could say anything, glanced down the corridor, then closed the door with a swift gesture for silence. "Well, Nathaniel, are you ready for more?" she said in her sexy come-hither voice as she pulled my jacket off and threw it on the berth. She was tense, agitated, her face grim and withdrawn.

"I...don't want to risk being thrown through the window," I mumbled.

She chuckled, humorlessly. "You are wise, Nathaniel." It struck me once again what a consummate actress she was; part of her conditioning as a service girl, no doubt.

The recording device was on the berth next to where she threw my jacket. She gave me a quick hug, then picked it up and activated it.

"Touch me, Nathaniel," the box commanded as she laid it gently by my jacket.

"Um..." my voice replied hesitantly.

219

"That iss a good boy, Nathaniel," the box said. She gestured urgently for silence, then eased the door open just a crack, her weapon at the ready. I wondered what she was doing. If my timing was correct, there were another couple of hours before we would reach the summit; why she was starting her deception now?

"Do you like what you see?" the box crooned.

"Yes," the box answered itself.

She gestured silently, and slipped into the hall.

"Ooooh! Yessss," the box moaned as I followed.

§

"Well, Nathaniel, the time has come," she told me once we were in the hall. "I am leaving now."

"What? Are we there already?"

She nodded, and held up the little box she fiddled with earlier. "This iss an inertial navigator. We should reach the top of the pass in about fifteen minutes."

"Finally!" My relief was heartfelt, as was my thankfulness that she had another of her little futuristic miracles. We would have missed our mark otherwise. "I don't know how much longer we could fool him."

"Yes," she said, somberly. "We are near the cache. With luck, I can lose him long enough to reach safety." She drew close and gave me a long, sentimental kiss. "You have been so kind, Nathaniel. Thank you, for everything. I...hope...if the Learnéd catch you...that you can kill some of them..." She was fighting back her tears. "...and you will die bravely...a-and without pain..."

"I'm going with you, Arda."

She studied my face in silence, then nodded in obvious relief. "Thank you, Nathaniel."

She gave me another hurried kiss, then carefully reentered her compartment and riffled through her oversized bag. "Touch me, Nathaniel," the box sighed as she stuffed a couple hard rolls and some cheese in my pockets. Then she produced her little sensor box and ran it over my jacket until she found the listening device again. She fished a pair of scissors out of her bag, carefully cut away the patch of material it was embedded in, and left it on the berth next to her talking box.

"Ohhh, yesss..." the box groaned.

She eyed me standing there in confusion, then tore the cover off the berth and wrapped it around my shoulders, then closed the door quietly as we left.

"All right, Nathaniel," she said, somberly. "We go."

§

We waited at the door until the train emerged from another tunnel before risking the icy platforms between cars. Even so, we were still blinded by the billowing smoke from the locomotives. The train was crawling along a cliff face, fighting a heavy grade. The smoke was trapped under the heavy wooden snow shed built over the track to protect against avalanches. The wind shifted, forcing most of the smoke out through the open side of the snow shed so we could at least see the next car.

"You ready?" I called to her as I considered the open gap between cars anxiously.

"Yes."

I took a deep breath of fresh, biting cold air, choked on the lingering fumes, and jumped across to the next car. She followed nimbly. The next sleeper offered a brief respite from the cold, but then we faced the next set of platforms leading to the lounge car. Arda stepped nimbly across, then caught me as I slipped, and lifted me bodily onto my feet.

"Thanks," I muttered.

"Be careful, Nathaniel. I ney want to lose you."

§

Beauregard Doggett was off on his rounds when we arrived in the lounge car. The rear brakeman sat in one of the plush chairs at the rear of the car, idly watching the snow through the windows. He stood and stretched as we came in, but ignored us. Parker was waiting for us near the head of the car. He wore a new revolver, and his shiny tin star was prominently pinned to his coat. "Nate, miss Arda." He nodded to us solemnly. "I figured you'd make some move tonight." The rumbling and squeaking of the car as it rocked along covered our low voices.

"We are leaving, Ned Parker," she said. "We are near the cache, which iss our one chance to reach safety."

Parker eyed us doubtfully. "In shirt sleeves? It's Godawful cold out there."

"We ney have a choice," she said, simply. She was cool and focussed. "The time has come, so we must do our best. We will be all right."

"How can I help? Should I try to stop him?"

"Ney, Ned Parker." She laid a cautioning hand on his arm. "You are helpless against him."

Parker shook his head sadly. "I'd still come with you, if I could. I just hope you know what you're doing." He considered her for a moment, then peeled off his jacket and offered it, but she shook her head, so he wrapped it around my shoulders instead. It was big enough to go over my jacket and the blanket with room to spare. "Good luck to both of you."

The brakeman stood at the rear door, bored with his monotonous routine of waiting for a whistle signal to head out and protect the rear of the train with his lantern. His gaze was lost in the swirling snow that fled behind us, and he looked at us in surprise when we came to the rear door. Parker gave him a hard glare, and the man flinched. "Raw night," he muttered, and walked away.

"You two take care," Parker said wistfully. "Miss Arda, it's been an experience meeting you. I don't think this old world will be the same without you around."

"Thank you, Ned Parker." She kissed his cheek. "For everything."

Parker offered his hand. "And Nate, damn, but I envy you, boy. You give 'em a few licks for me, okay?"

I took his hand and nodded to him in turn. "Thanks, mister Parker. I'll do that."

"Call me Ned, son."

Parker held the door against the gale whipping around the back of the train, then forced it shut behind us as the brakeman watched in amazement. Parker gave him another hard look. "You didn't see anything."

The man nodded.

§

It was raw cold on the exposed rear platform, and the shrill, snow-laden wind whipped at us. I gasped, and pulled the blanket tighter around myself, not that it helped much. The locomotives were straining up ahead, their exhausts a full-throated rumble that reminded me of the cannon fire we faced at Chattanooga. For all their effort, the train was slowed to a crawl by the steep grade. I risked a quick peek ahead, but couldn't see more than half the length of the lounge car in the swirling snow and smoke. The locomotives thundered somewhere in the gloom, their wheels squealed on the icy rails, their mechanical parts hammered. The sound echoed from the hills around us as an earthquake rumble.

I clung to the handrail, disoriented by the dark and the rocking motion of the car. "Where are we?" I yelled.

"Near the top of the pass," she yelled back. "There are three tunnels ahead. We get off after we pass through the third one."

I looked around nervously. To our left, faintly illuminated by the two red marker lanterns on the rear of the car, was a sheer wall of blasted rock with barely enough room for the train to crawl past. To the right was—nothing. I couldn't resist the urge to lean over the edge of the platform and look down. Visibility wasn't more than twenty feet, but what I could see was a sheer drop into the swirling darkness.

Up ahead in the gloom, the lead locomotive blew its whistle briefly. "Careful!" She yanked me back just as the car plunged into the first tunnel.

"God!" I gasped as the choking cloud of smoke overwhelmed us. The locomotives were working flat out, pouring out burning clouds of soot and ash that filled the tunnel in an instant. I buried my face in my sleeve and tried not to pass out from the fume. We came out of the first tunnel almost at once, but I was too blinded by smoke to notice.

"Soon, Nathaniel," she said.

There was barely enough time to catch my breath before the whistle blew again, and we plunged into the second tunnel. Once again the foul exhaust engulfed us, painfully hot where we were chilled a moment before. I gasped and choked from the fumes, and instinctively clung to Arda.

Thankfully, both tunnels were short; we emerged from the second almost before I realized it. The locomotives struggled on the slippery rails, their speed reduced to a fast walk despite the shower of soot and cinders they blasted to the darkened sky. The cars banged together as the locomotives fought to keep the train moving. What must have been an uncomfortable ride for those inside was hell here on this open platform.

"You all right?" I managed to gasp.

"Yes. We are almost there, Nathaniel."

The locomotive blew its whistle again, and we plunged into the third tunnel before I could say anything more, or even take a proper breath. The train surged ahead as the locomotives found dry rail, the shock all but tumbling me over the railing. I forced my eyes shut and clung to Arda, trying desperately to breathe. This tunnel was a lot longer than the other two. The air was hot and foul, burning my throat and lungs. I gasped, fighting to contain my panic and fight off unconsciousness as we rolled on through the stygian gloom for what seemed an eternity.

The shock of the icy headwind jolted me and helped clear my head when we emerged from the third tunnel. I gasped for air, trying to fight off my dizziness as I clung to the handrail.

"There, up ahead." She pointed up the right of way, as the train moved into a broad curve, to a dim light obscured by blowing snow. "That iss the check point."

I strained my eyes to get some idea of where we were. The lights of the snow plow extra were faint in the distance ahead, little more than a red glow amid the snowfall. A small building of crude boards sat by the track, half buried in snow. It was nothing more than a telegraph station; no one in their right mind would get off a train here.

The first locomotive lost its footing again, its drivers spinning madly as a shower of sparks flew up from its smoke stack. The cars rattled and banged together as the train slowed.

"Get ready, Nathaniel." Her voice was low and tense.

"I must be mad," I grumbled. I was about to jump off a moving train in the dead of night into an early season blizzard at the top of Donner Pass.

The snow was thinning a bit. The locomotives dug into the grade, and began to accelerate again. The track was level here at the crest, which was the only reason the train hadn't stalled. There was no sign of life aside from the light showing through the telegraph station windows. The telegraph operator had the good sense to stick close to his stove unless there were orders to give to a passing train. A shrill gust of wind brought new snow and a bitter blast of cold that made me cringe.

"All right, Nathaniel. Now!" Without another word, she stepped off the platform into the night. I followed before I could lose my nerve.

*****

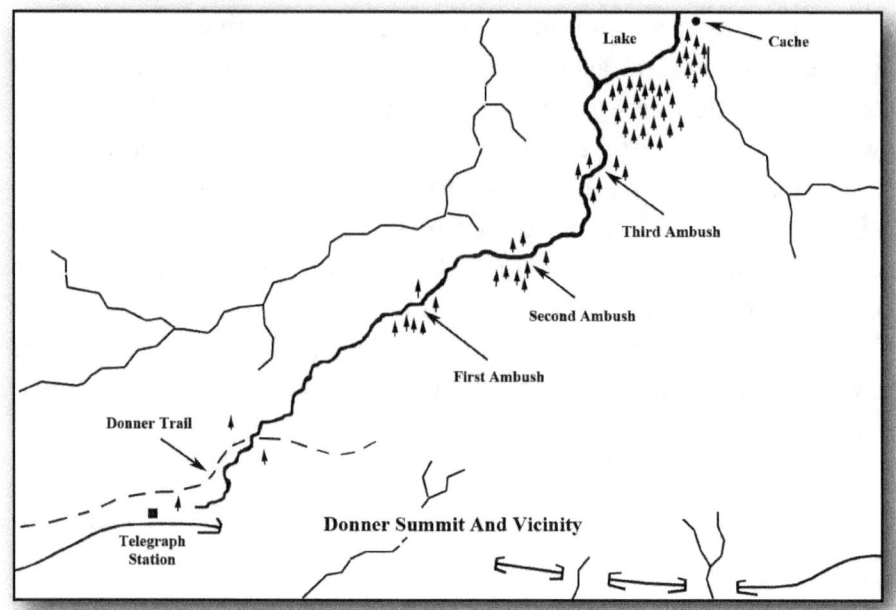

Donner Summit And Vicinity

## "Day Eleven: Morning"

I lay in the snow at the base of a low embankment with the wind knocked out of me by my fall while the train crawled slowly ahead. She knelt beside me, her strange pistol at the ready, wire tense, searching the darkness. The last car faded into the distance until all I could see were the two red lanterns on its rear platform. The train accelerated on the downgrade, the locomotives' exhaust muffled by the snow, and soon even the red lights vanished in the gloom.

"We're in it now," I muttered as the rumble of the train faded into silence.

"Quiet!" she hissed. She was searching the night, looking slowly back and forth, following her eyes with that strange weapon. The darkness was all but absolute. The telegraph station a hundred yards away was invisible except for the faint light on its train order semaphore. I wondered vaguely if she could see anything in this stygian gloom, then remembered that she could see body heat. Learnéd would be easy to spot in this frozen hell.

After what seemed like forever, she relaxed a bit. "Well, Nathaniel, I think we eluded him."

"Wonderful." I struggled to my feet, and tried to knock the caked snow off my trousers without much success. "All right, how far is it to this cache of yours?"

"About twenty kilometers." She gestured northward into the night, at a shallow down angle, while she continued searching. "That way."

"Twenty kilometers?" That didn't sound good. I assumed the cache was nearby or she wouldn't have left the train without overcoats. "How many miles is that?"

"Miles?" She sounded doubtful. "I ney know. It iss some way distant."

"Great. Now we need to worry about freezing to death."

"Oh. You ney have our endurance, do you?" she said, quietly. That was just what I needed to hear; she lead us into this frozen hell without stopping to think that I didn't have her supernatural strength. I should have known better.

"Dammit, I won't last an hour in this!"

"I am sorry, Nathaniel." She considered me for a moment, then pocketed her weapon, pulled something out of her pouch, and after fussing with it, handed me a large pill. "Here, this will help."

I fingered it suspiciously. "What is it?"

"It iss part of a standard survival kit. It accelerates your metabolism. Suck on it ass it dissolves. It will make your body produce enough heat to keep you going for a while, but it drains your reserves, so we have to hurry."

I fingered the large pill doubtfully. It was a hard, featureless lump in my palm, all but invisible in the faint twilight. For that matter, I could hardly see my hand, and she was but a vague shadow outlined against the white background. I wasn't thrilled with the idea of taking some mystery pill from the future after all she told me about their retros, but I didn't have much of a choice. I shivered in the cold, and my teeth chattered as I struggled with my apprehension. As much as I was loath to trust it, if this didn't work, I didn't have a hope. I glanced at her unhappily, and envied her retro-enhanced strength. She stood in two feet of snow, eyes roaming the blackness, apparently comfortable in a dress and light jacket as the wind tore at her hair.

"Damn it," I grumbled, and popped it into my mouth. It was hard, like a piece of rock candy with an odd orange flavor. I pulled the blanket tighter, with Parker's jacket over that. It was large on me, which helped. "I must be insane." I cringed under another icy blast. The only sign of human presence was the telegraph station vaguely visible in the blowing snow. I was mortally tempted to take shelter there until morning. We could come up with some excuse for the operator.

"Come, Nathaniel. We must hurry." She turned and headed back along the track toward the tunnel. I never felt so lost as I turned my back on the only shelter for miles around and trudged after her.

We were in a shallow trench dug by the rotary snow plow, and had to make our way along the track for a short distance before we found a low spot in the lea of the tunnel entrance where we could clamber out. After thrashing through four feet of packed snow, we found ourselves on open ground. The shrill wind piled the snow in drifts, so once we were out in the open, we found relatively easy passages. It was still slow going.

I shivered and looked around in dismay as I sucked absently on the orange lozenge. The night was abysmal. My eyes were adjusting to the dark, but there wasn't much to see beyond the vague shadows of large rocks and the occasional stunted bitter pine. I glanced at the sky: the half moon was masked by the scudding clouds, blotting out what little light there was. I prayed fervently that she knew what she was doing. I couldn't even be sure which way we were going in this gloomy maze.

The ground sloped down from the right of way for about fifty yards before we hit a gully which turned out to be a frozen creek bed. "This iss the landmark," she said. "We must follow this to the lake."

"Thank heaven for that! I can't see a damned thing."

The ground was more open on the far side, so I searched for a way across. The ice made ominous cracking sounds when I gingerly tried it. The creek was five feet wide with shallow banks, but we had to grope for several yards downstream before we found a spot where we could cross.

There was a narrow trace on the other side, visible only because it was fairly level and free of rocks. I finally figured out what it was when I spotted a row of piled stones along one side. It was a rude wagon trail, with markers of stones cleared from the road set every fifty yards or so. It apparently was unused this time of year. There were no wagon ruts, no hoof marks, not even animal tracks; no sign of life other than our own footprints, but there was only one thing it could be.

"The Donner trail," I muttered.

She paused to look around her. "Hmph! So it iss." She made her way back to me. "Are the legends about this place true?"

"Yeah. It happened, all right." *Just* what I needed to be reminded of.

She gave me a kiss on the cheek. "We will be safe, Nathaniel." She headed down slope, holding my hand to keep me from losing her as I sucked on the lozenge and wondered how long I would last. The trail helped for a short distance, anyway.

The snow came, and fell steadily, although it wasn't bad, considering. At least it was still early in the season, for which I was wearily grateful. There were week-long storms up here during the high winter which dumped up to ten feet of snow at a time. As is, it was several feet deep, which made each yard gained a minor miracle. My feet were numb, my hands hurt from the bitter cold, my lungs ached, and I trembled so hard that I could barely keep moving at a staggering walk. I was still on my feet, but the thin air and the cold were already telling. My heart pounded, and I felt strangely agitated. But when I thought about it, I didn't feel the cold so much as I was aware of it. And somehow, despite my many pains, I had the strength to plod ahead, wading through snow up to my waist at times. It must be that pill of hers, I realized vaguely. Whatever it was, it was remarkable. I should have been dead by then.

§

The storm faded sometime before dawn, and the first pale morning light found us trudging through a forest of scraggly pines. The snow cover was thinner here in the shelter of the trees, so we made better time.

"How much further?" I asked at one point.

She studied the ground ahead of us. "We have come perhaps five kilometers. The cache is by that lake." She pointed to a flat snow field wedged between two mountains about eight or nine miles ahead. "There iss a cave overlooking the lake. Once we reach it, we will be safe."

"What about food? Shelter? We can't last like this for long."

"The cache iss equipped with an environmental system, and there are survival suits and ample field rations. Once we activate the force fields. It will take the Learnéd more power than they have to break in." She considered me closely. "How are you feeling, Nathaniel?"

"I'm alive, which surprises the hell out of me," I grumbled. Then, "I'm famished."

"It iss the pill, it iss burning up your fat reserves." I finished the lozenge some time ago, but its effects still kept me moving. "Eat some of the food I gave you."

I dug a hard roll out of one pocket and attacked it ravenously as we walked. It didn't last long—I ate like a starved wolf—but I felt a bit stronger by time I was finished.

"You should have enough to keep you going for now," she said as I attacked a second roll. "We will have plenty of hot food when we reach the cache."

"One hopes." I didn't have much body fat on me to begin with, another thing to worry about. I caught a faint movement in the distance; a snowshoe rabbit, the first sign of life we'd seen. I cursed silently, and wished I still had my Colt. Right then I was hungry enough to eat that poor creature raw.

"How long until Learnéd shows up?" I asked after a bit.

She pondered as we walked. "That ney iss easy to say. It depends on how long that recording fools him. At best, he will be after uss by now; perhaps sooner." She turned and gave me a predatory smile. "But we can keep ahead of him until we reach the cache, and we will be ready for him when he gets there. Just think, Nathaniel. With luck, we may kill another Learnéd."

"I wouldn't mind that at all," I muttered.

§

We trudged on; one exhausting, mind numbing step after another as the morning passed. The day was clear and bright, but bitterly cold, with a stiff wind coming over the pass from the west. Aside from a rare bird and one fox, there was no sign of life. Nature had the good sense to hunker down in this kind of weather, which was more than we could say.

The silence was oppressive, and soon the barriers between us started to evaporate. This was our first chance to really talk without Learnéd eavesdropping, and as we walked side by side I made the most of it. She, in turn, soon loosened up and started telling me about the future and...at long last...about herself.

"Reward girls ney serve for long before we are used up. The physical strain..." She stared at nothing as we trudged along, reflecting bitterly on her past. "Thankfully, the Aphrodite helped me when I needed it. When I Broke after four years, I seduced one of my assignments to help me escape. That was three years ago— my time. I have been with the resistance for two years now."

That reminded me of something I hadn't wondered about until then. "How old are you?"

She glanced at me. "Seventeen years."

I paused in confusion. "Seventeen? Then you were..."

She nodded. "I was ten when they put me to work. Reward girls are genetically engineered to mature early. It saves the Movement time and money."

I cursed in bitter rage. Pressing young girls into prostitution happened in this time, but it was something decent people didn't like to think about. Now that I did, I could see that the things which appalled me the most about the Movement had their roots in this time. This 19th Century wasn't so civilized after all, when one took a hard look at it.

"Ney be angry, Nathaniel," she said. "It ney helps to agonize over it now."

"I'm not mad at you. It's...all our fault; here, in this time...all the evils of the Movement..."

She gave me a kiss. "Ney be angry. Your time ney could know." She took my arm and tugged gently, getting me moving again, then fell in beside me. We walked silently for a while.

"What did you do?" I asked finally. "After you escaped?"

"I..." She glanced at me solemnly, then turned away. "I was a fugitive. We Broken, the few who evade the Pure Of Thought, must fend for ourselves ass best we can in the ruins around the Temples." She sighed and shook her head in sorrow. "Sometimes, when we need food, we sneak back into the Temples to raid the feeding centers and storerooms." She was silent for a time. "That iss dangerous. The Pure Of Thought know it iss our vulnerable spot; they set ambushes for uss."

We trudged on for a while, both wrapped in grim silence.

"There are those who ney are broken...administrators and supervisors...my former assignments," she went on at last. "They provided me food. I...followed my needs. I ney could stop myself. Women like me are popular, Nathaniel, especially when we ney are rationed or supervised."

I could imagine the treatment she must have endured in her helpless desperation, and fought to suppress my fury; not at her, but at the Movement and its sanctimonious piety; another evil inherited from this time. "It's all right, Arda," I murmured.

She sighed, and we trudged along in silence for a way. "I saw many men," she said at last. "But they ney were enough. Always, ney enough." She clung to my arm for comfort. "I ney will be free of the Aphrodite, ever. At least you understand; ney many men do."

"Don't they have an antidote?"

She shook her head. "They ney bothered to develop them. Citizens are disposed of when no longer needed. Those who have adverse reactions to retros are, too."

We trudged on as I fumed at the Movement.

§

A faint whistle reverberated off the mountains, drawing my attention. A freight train was climbing the pass in the distance behind us: twin pillars of smoke crawling upgrade with a string of dull red, black and yellow freight cars following. There was a spurt of steam from the lead engine, and some time later, the faint sound reached us. I forced myself to shrug it off, turn my back, and go on.

We followed the creek down a long plateau that paralleled a ridge line. The ridge towered to our left, its pristine white broken by dark clumps of pine, all silhouetted against the beautiful pale blue sky. To our right, the ground crossed a low rise, then sloped away into the broad, winding valley that the train came up. That bare, flat area in the distance was probably Donner Lake, bordered by the faint smudge of another train climbing the pass. Despite my exhaustion and the bitter cold, I saw the beauty of it. There was majesty in these mountains. It was places like this where nature proclaimed itself, where it defied puny men and their contrivances. It was places like this that reminded men that we were not the masters of this world, and it would not yield without a struggle. It let me see myself in perspective, which humbled and inspired me.

§

Our conversation picked up again after a time.

"Yarl, he iss our leader, will want to know all about you." She glanced at me. "You two are much alike. He iss uncommonly strong-willed for our time. He led the effort to steal the time machine, and came up with our strategy."

"Sounds like someone to know."

"He turned a loose band of fugitives into our resistance."

"He was the one who recruited you?"

"Yes."

One of the men she...knew. "Are you...in love with him?"

She gave an exasperated snort. "Nathaniel, I am madly in love with any man who iss riding me." There was another uncomfortable silence, then, "I am sorry, Nathaniel. I ney want to hurt you. He iss nothing to me, any more than the others."

That hurt, despite already knowing about it. "Any more than me?"

She gave me a solemn look. "You are different, Nathaniel. You care about me. I am grateful for that." She rubbed her cheek against mine for reassurance, then went on. I followed, swearing in silent rage. I wanted a crack at my misbegotten great-to-the-eighth grandson in the worst way. If I got the chance, I would personally castrate the bastard.

§

We were silent for a while as we slogged through the snow, each bitterly reflecting on our own thoughts. I was occupied trying to work through the end of my former life and the unknown future ahead. She showed me the truth about my preconceptions which I wouldn't have understood otherwise, and I needed to rethink everything.

She was a conundrum. Despite her past, despite her strange ways and unnatural powers, despite the fact that she came to this time to kill me, I wanted her. I would have to accept her past, to put my masculine sense of possession, of betrayal behind me. Normally, I would never consider any harlot—even a reformed harlot—as a serious prospect. But she was different. Her past wasn't her fault; harlots usually don't enter that line by choice, and the Movement even took the ability to choose from her. She was a victim, and tarring her with the righteous morality of this time was wrong.

She was tough and independent, bright and quirky, alone and vulnerable. That appealed to me in an odd way. She was a challenge; one that didn't involve fists or guns; a challenge to the better side of me which was buried and all but forgotten all these years.

I would have to learn not to be possessive, not to be jealous when she sought the release she had to have. Perhaps I could; I was reacting with the morality of the 19th century, and I could see now that this time was no more than a precursor to hers. That brought another disturbing matter, another paradox, to mind. She was a few paces ahead of me, and I struggled to overtake her.

"There's something I don't understand about all this," I called to her. "...this time travel..." I was struggling to express concepts I vaguely comprehended. "...I mean, this loop you mentioned..."

"A temporal causality loop?" She eyed me curiously.

"Yeah. You said the plan was to kill me to change the future. My leaving with you wasn't part of the plan. What will happen? Where will we wind up?"

She gave me a wistful look. "You are good, Nathaniel. Most people of this time ney understand time travel at all."

"I'm not sure I do, either."

234

"I ney know what will happen, Nathaniel." She turned and walked beside me again. "You are correct; that would be an unplanned change. There ney iss any way to tell what the effect will be. A loop caused by your death would cancel out due to hysteresis. I can only guess, but I think your leaving this time will have the same effect."

A best guess: by an emotionally unstable half-wit driven near-mad by the retros which made her at all functional. God must have been laughing at me. "What then? Didn't your people have some idea of what would happen?"

"Ney. Our computing power was ney sufficient for so huge a projection." We walked on in silence for a bit before she added, "All we could project was that your death iss the key factor, but beyond that, we ney could say. Anything could happen."

"But what about us? Will we be together?"

She paused. "I ney know. We may return to the new future, or we may be caught in a causality loop for ever." She hugged me uneasily. "But whatever happens, we are linked. I am the cause, you are the effect. We will be together."

"That's good enough for me."

She watched curiously and a bit apprehensively as I took her in my arms and looked into her icy blue eyes, eyes filled with pain and longing. Then, gently, I kissed her.

"Nathaniel..."

"I love you, Arda." I was a bit surprised that I said it under the circumstances, but not that I meant it. "Whatever happens, I don't want to lose you."

She was silent for a long moment, then sagged against my chest. "I...ney can be faithful to you, Nathaniel. I ney will be free of the Aphrodite, ever. It ney matters in our time, but you come from a different world."

I hugged her close. "First we survive. We work that out later."

"But we ney can be sure we will still exist once the time line iss changed," she said, plaintively.

"We'll work that out later, too."

She looked at me, her eyes brimming. "Thank you, Nathaniel," she whispered at last.

Yes, I could do it; I could accept her challenge, assuming we came through this alive, together, unchanged by their tampering with time. That decision relieved me in a way. It was strange: she had to come into her distant past to find love; and I only found it in this waif from the distant future.

"Damn, I hope we succeed in this. Parker said it yesterday; some things are so evil that they can't be ignored."

"He iss a good man," she said, wistfully. "It iss a shame we ney could take him." She took my arm and walked close by my side. "But we have you, and we will change the future together."

"Assuming we get there."

She nodded grimly. "Assuming we get there."

We trudged on, each preoccupied with their own thoughts. Despite my weariness, I was happy that one question was resolved between us.

"Nathaniel?" She hesitated, then turned to me. "Are there many men like you in this time?"

That caught me off guard. "Um...in what way?"

"Men who ney are afraid. Men who know how to fight. Men who are willing to stand up for a just cause."

"Why, yes, thousands of them. Millions, I daresay."

"Do you...think any of them would support the resistance?" she asked, carefully. "Would any of them help fight the Movement?"

That thought took me aback. "Yes, I'm sure there are." I caught where she was going, and the idea thrilled me. "We would have to select them carefully, choose ones who are honorable men, and are willing to risk their lives for justice."

"Men like Ned Parker."

"Yeah." The idea churned in my mind like a fever, making my heart race and my breath shaky. "We'd have to approach them carefully—face it, this future of yours takes getting used to—but if we explain it right, we might get a few. More than a few."

"Especially if we recruit from all time." Her eyes glowed with excitement. "The Second World War would give uss many prospects."

"By God, you may be onto something, Arda!" Then her last statement caught me. "World war?"

"There have been six of them that we know of."

"Why am I not surprised?" I grumbled.

"There were plenty of men killed, men we could recover. That way, taking them would ney affect the time line." She was getting excited. "Nathaniel, we have it! We can defeat the Movement ney by changing time!" She threw herself into my arms and hugged me enthusiastically, evoking a grunt of pain.

My hope grew as I thought about it. She was right; we could match the armies of the Movement by recruiting skilled soldiers from throughout history. Take a few here and a few there, and by time you added up all mankind's wars, it would run to quite a number. And if they all arrived at the same moment...they could overwhelm the Movement in a swift coup. Our cause wasn't hopeless after all. We could be together!

"But...what about me leaving this time? What about the changed future? We still can't be sure we'll reach your time."

Her face fell, and she stared at me in pensive silence. The sight of her drained of hope tore at my heart. Then her eyes lit up again. "We ney will leave! We will stay at the cache. There iss food, and power, and it iss well defended. We can communicate with the resistance to help them plan the coup. Nathaniel, we can do it!"

We hugged in heartfelt relief, both of us weeping tears of joy at our deliverance.

"We ney can go back," she said at last after she got her sniffles under control. "We will be stranded here, but we will be together." She gave me a kiss that should have melted the snow around us. "Yarl must hear this! Come, Nathaniel!" She turned and plowed ahead with renewed enthusiasm, and for once I was able to keep pace with her.

§

It was early afternoon of a short and dismal day when we reached a scrub pine woodland about half way to the frozen lake. I paused with a weary sigh as my strength gave out, and leaned against a small tree as she halted, then came back. I was ravenous again; her pill was a wonder, but it carried a price. I dug a piece of cheese out of my pocket and wolfed it down, then scanned the trees ahead uneasily. "How far is it to the cache?"

"We have come about ten kilometers. It iss some way ahead yet..." Her eyes grew wide with alarm, she grabbed my jacket and yanked me savagely to the ground as the tree next to us exploded.

"What the hell...?"

By time I recovered from my surprise, she was crouched behind a large rock with her weapon out, and was scanning the high ground behind us. "Verdamme," she muttered at last, and glanced at me nervously. "We ney fooled him, Nathaniel."

*****

## "Day Eleven: Afternoon"

I rolled over and scrabbled on elbows and knees to the rock where Arda was hiding. *"What was that?"*

She glanced at me anxiously, and gestured with her pistol. "One of these."

"Good...Lord!  That thing would make great artillery!"  I suspected all along that their weapons were potent, but this firepower was stunning.  That tree was shredded and scattered across the landscape.  She trembled as she peeked gingerly over the rock for a few seconds at a time, trying to spot Learnéd.  I scrunched up and peeked cautiously around the side.  "Where is he? Do you see him?"

"Y-yes.  There iss a heat source up there on the ridge...hidden in the trees.  It iss him."

I couldn't see anything but high, rocky ground to our flank and rear; excellent sniper's country.  With this clear, bright sunshine we would stand out against the blank snow like sore thumbs.  There was no sign of Learnéd, and I envied her heat sensitive vision. "What is he doing?"

"Hiding.  Observing uss."  She looked at me in near panic. "What can we do, Nathaniel?"

That tremor in her voice wasn't good.  She was the revolutionary, and if she was at a loss, I doubted if I could do much.  "Can you hit him from here?"

"I-if he makes a mistake and shows himself."  She was so shaky that it seemed doubtful.  "But the range iss long.  It takes a lot of power for each shot, and I ney have a spare power core."

239

A small pine tree to our left exploded, showering us with grit and burning splinters. There was no warning, no sound of a gun shot; just a sudden thunderbolt from nowhere. "Dammit!" I desperately wished I still had my Colt, not that it would do much good. "Isn't that a bit much for a hand weapon?"

"The Movement lives by intimidation, Nathaniel."

I leaned back against the rock and wondered what to do. This was no place to make a stand, especially against a long range attack of that power. "We need to get to the cache and yell for help."

"How?" She slumped down next to me, trembling and sobbing. "He iss up there where he can see uss clearly."

I realized something vital: for all her abilities and knowledge, she was not a soldier. She was a frightened young woman, trapped in a frozen hell, and hunted by her worst nightmare. If we were going to get out of this, I would have to be strong for her. I took her hand and tried to comfort her.

"We'll do this skirmisher fashion. You go first. I'll use your weapon to cover you, then I move past you while you cover me. We'll leapfrog back step by step until we're out of range."

She shook her head. "These weapons are biokeyed, Nathaniel. You ney can fire it."

I cursed in frustration, reminded of her words about being victims of our own technology. We would have to depend on her steadiness, which seemed doubtful. "We go anyway and hope for the best. You first. You'll catch him by surprise." She stared at me, trembling, fear plain in her eyes. "It'll be all right," I said softly. "You can do this."

"Can we, Nathaniel?"

"Hey, I'm the expert here; trust me. This is no worse than we faced at Chickamauga Creek." No need to mention what our losses were. I gave her an insincere smile and squeezed her hand for reassurance, then studied the ground ahead of us. "See? Over that way. Hit that little low spot, then dive behind that rock. It's thirty feet, hardly anything, and that way will give you the best cover." A patch of snow to our right erupted, dousing us with grit and damp steam. "You can do it, Arda."

"All right," she said uncertainly, and gathered herself for the dash.

"Go!"

She sprang forward with an anguished sob, plowed through the snow as fast as possible, and tumbled behind the rock; safe. And Learnéd was alert to what we were doing. I sized up the situation as my pulse rose and my limbs trembled—like so many times during the war. Learnéd would be ready for me, and he had a clear shot. *'Best do it now,'* I decided, before I could think about it. I jumped to my feet...changed course on split second instinct, and sprawled to the left around her rock as the spot where she went earlier erupted.

"Nathaniel!"

"I'm all right!" I scrunched up behind the rock, nursing a cut on my forehead where I hit a branch. The cold no longer bothered me, and I was too hyper to notice the icy wind. "Now you. Aim for that small stand of trees." It was a long way to go, a good fifty feet or more, but the ground fell away there, offering shelter behind some pine saplings. "Don't run. Throw yourself head first."

"Nathaniel!" She was sobbing.

"NOW, Arda!"

She let out an inarticulate whimper and sprang to her feet, slipping and scrambling through the snow, and tumbled headlong over the lip of the ravine just as the saplings above her head were sheered off.

Then it was my turn, and this time there was only one direction I could run. This was suicide, but what choice did I have? I took a deep breath, sprang to my feet, and ran for dear life. It went on forever. Time seemed to slow down as I slogged through a nightmarish world remote and dreamlike and as thick as glue. My lungs burned as I slipped and slithered and trudged through hip deep snow. The ravine was miles away. Somewhere in the back of my mind, I knew Learnéd should have fired. I could feel that little red dot centered in my back. I should be dead, blown to bloody tatters by now. I trudged on and on, lungs burning and limbs flailing as the ravine grew closer and closer. Why was I still alive? Did Learnéd miss? My fragile hold on life would last no more than a few seconds. I cringed unconsciously, waiting for a thunderbolt that didn't come as I crept forward ever so slowly. Then suddenly I was standing on the lip of the ravine. Without thinking, I threw myself across and landed on the ground below with a sickening thud.

§

I lay there for a moment with the wind knocked out of me by my fall, and stared up at the bright blue sky above, amazed that I was still alive. I made it. I was shaken by the ordeal and battered from the fall, but I was alive. I stared up at the sky and the wall of rock towering over me, too distracted to do anything but marvel at my luck. That ravine was actually a cliff a good ten feet high. I was amazed that I hadn't broken my neck.

The sound of sobbing penetrated my mind. She was huddled at the base of the cliff, clutching one arm and crying like a lost child. There were scratches on her face, and her lip was bloody from bashing against the rocks. "Arda?" I rolled to my knees and scrabbled over to her. "Are you hurt?"

She shook her head spasmodically, too terrified to speak or even look at me. I checked her over quickly; her arm was scraped and her dress torn, but she'd been lucky too.

"Nnnaathaaniellll!" she wailed, and buried her face in my shoulder. I let out a grunt of pain and tried to wrestle myself loose before she collapsed my ribs. It took all my strength to fight her off, then to steady her as she trembled.

"Get hold of yourself, Arda!" I grabbed her shoulders and shook her. "Arda! You're panicking. Don't let your Smarts rattle you; that's what he wants."

"H-he will k-kill uss!"

"Think, Arda!" I shook her again as she sobbed. "You can do this. Don't let fear rule you."

She clung to me frantically for the next few minutes as both of us fought for self control. Her sobbing ceased, and her panicky gasps steadied into deep, rapid breathing, although she still trembled. "You are right, Nathaniel," she said at last. "I panicked." She looked at me with solemn, tear filled eyes. "I will be all right now, thanks to you."

"Okay, this cliff will give us cover, but we have to move."

We gained about three hundred yards at a drunken stagger before Learnéd struck again, claiming another pine tree. We went to ground behind a fallen log, and peered anxiously through the trees. Learnéd was barely visible at the top of the cliff, searching the ground carefully. As we watched, he took careful aim, and an explosion erupted somewhere off to our right.

"He sure has plenty of ammunition," I grumbled. "He'll level the whole damned forest if he keeps this up."

"They carry more weapons than that one, too," she said.

Learnéd hesitated, then fired again. Something squealed and thrashed briefly off to our left. It was a bear, or what was left of one. The sight was sickening, even at a distance. "Can't he see us?" I whispered.

"Ney. We are too far away for his heat vision."

"Too cold, too." I was starting to feel the chill again. "Well as long as he's up there, we have a few minutes. Do you have any more of those pills?"

"Yes." She dug into her pouch and came up with another. In the daylight, it was bilious orange, like a piece of rock candy. "But it iss too early to take another one. If you use them too fast, they start to consume muscle mass ass well as body fat."

"We can't afford the luxury of playing it safe." I popped it in my mouth without hesitation. "What about you?" I asked as she put the little case back in her pouch.

"I will manage, Nathaniel. You need these to keep up with me and my retros." She watched me closely. "Are you all right? You ney look well."

"Actually...I'm not." I rubbed my forehead and sighed in fatigue. "I feel a bit woozy."

"You need to eat. If you ney eat, the pills will drain you fast enough to make you sick."

"Ah...right." I dug a hunk of cheese out of one pocket, and wolfed it down in three bites. It helped a little. "All right, I'll manage, but we need to keep moving. Let's use this chance to gain on him. The trees will give us cover, and it will take him time to climb down that cliff."

We went back to leapfrogging. It took nearly an hour of scrambling from tree to rock before we moved out of range. Learnéd stayed on his cliff top vantage point, firing at random, sometimes near, sometimes far. At one point, Arda saw him trying to climb down the cliff, and fired at long range to force him to cover. That produced a flurry of return fire which drove us on. Once over her panic, she held up well during the ordeal, and by time we were out of range, she was calm and deliberate again.

"Okay," I said as I studied the ground behind us. Learnéd was nowhere in sight. "Now we run like rabbits for the cache. We can stay ahead of him all the way."

That was wishful thinking. The snow was hip deep.

§

We finally reached the end of the scrub pine forest, and headed down a long, shallow valley. The snow pack thinned out, blown into drifts against the rocks by the bitter wind. We were able to make better time, but it was still knee deep and slow going. Worse, the sky was beginning to cloud over, and the wind was picking up. I glanced at the sky uneasily; a storm was coming in. There was no telling how long it would take, but I guessed that another blizzard would hit the area by dark. I was ravenous again, and dug one of the hard rolls out of my pocket and munched it as we trudged along. It helped a little, but there were only a couple left. At the rate I was consuming them, I would run out long before we reached the cache. After that, I faced a race against time before my strength gave out.

It wasn't long before we came on the frozen creek again. Ahead, another four or five miles away, that creek flowed into a broad lake backed up against mountain peaks rising on all sides.

"There iss our objective." She pointed to the lake ahead. "We go down to the lake, and along the shore. It iss not much farther."

"Good. I don't like the look of that sky..." I caught movement out of the corner of one eye. "Look, there." Off to our left, up the grade, a figure in a brown coat was zipping along among the trees at at an amazing speed.

"He has a thrust pack," she said, fatalistically. "With skis and thrust packs, they can easily outmaneuver and outrun uss."

I looked closer, and saw that he wore a bulky object held to the small of his back by a heavy belt. It was pushing him along on skis far faster than we could trudge through deep snow. I cursed myself again: Learnéd's trip to the baggage car should have alerted me. If I'd followed up on my suspicion, I might have found that gear, and we could have changed our plan. Too late now for anything but regrets. "We are in trouble," I said. "Can you pick him off?"

"Ney. He iss out of range."

The figure paused to look us over, then scooted on ahead, weaving expertly through the rocks and trees.

She watched him go, then turned to me with renewed fear in her eyes. "I was mistaken. His gestalt iss here."

"Are you sure he's not the one from the train?" I asked as I watched the retreating figure.

"Ney unless he thought to bring snow equipment on the off chance he might need it. They ney intended to wait for me in SaFrisko. I thought they would link up and move against me there, but they came ahead to meet uss. And they came equipped to search this country."

I decided not to mention the baggage car. "But why come here? What are they up to?"

She considered for a moment as we watched the figure vanish into the trees ahead. "They must know of the cache. That iss the only reason they would strike here. They are moving to pin uss between them to keep uss from escaping."

"You have a spy in your midst?"

"More likely they captured one of uss and processed him." She shuddered, and gave me a bleak look. "Any secret can be extracted if the subject iss expendable."

"They tortured some poor devil," I muttered, bleakly.

"Their methods ney are so crude." she said in a tight voice. "The...right retros will reduce any mind to compliant mush. They can extract anything the subject ever knew, every thought from the crèche on. There ney iss much left, after."

One more ugly detail from an ugly future. "How did they wind up out here in the middle of nowhere?"

245

She searched the hills carefully for the second Learnéd, but he disappeared in the distance. "He summoned them. There iss a town a bit further down the track where the trains stop to uncouple the helper engines. They must have planned to board there and take me by surprise." She shuddered, and clutched herself. "They intend to process me, then take out the cache. Thankfully we left the train when we did. It threw them off our trail temporarily."

I brooded on that, and began to understand how difficult it was to fight a team of telepaths. "Can they find the cache without following us?"

"That ney iss likely. They are will hidden."

"Then we double back! Get back up to the railroad and make a run for it. We can come back later."

She shook her head. "They would ney leave uss an escape route. The one behind uss iss their beater, driving uss forward like game. The one we saw on the ridge will observe and keep uss from escaping into these mountains."

I cursed in frustration; only now, when it was called to my attention, did I realize that Learnéd's shooting was awfully poor. "You knew, didn't you?"

"I suspected." She held up her weapon. Her hands were blue and shaking from the cold. "These have sophisticated fire control systems. They hit anything within range, every time. I hoped he was alone, and we could outrun him," she added, defensively."

"Damn," I grumbled. "With those cannons, they can get us in a cross fire and pick us off, no problem."

"Ney. They want the cache. They will drive uss to it. The real danger will come when we reach the lake."

"Is it that important to them?"

"A cache iss built around a temporal node—an artificial focus point in time. That iss how we travel back and forth; it provides uss a beacon to home in on. If they destroy it, it will isolate most of this century. That iss one of their best strategies, and it has been very effective. They are dividing uss, pinning uss in time, blocking uss in faster than we can build new temporal nodes."

Then I thought of something. "Why don't you use your time machine to escape?"

"I ney have it, Nathaniel. It iss very large, and sends us to where we want to go. We have to contact them and provide coordinates."

"Well? Why don't you?"

"I have to reach the cache first. There was a call point in SaFrisko, but that iss probably gone now. The emergency beacon in the cache iss our only way to contact them."

I sighed. So we're chasing our tails, huh?"

"In four dimensions, Nathaniel." She considered the landscape ahead of us, then headed on down the creek. I followed without another word. There was no other choice. I was hungry again.

§

Mid day wore on into afternoon as we trudged along, keeping a wary eye for any of the Learnéds. The clouds were thicker, blocking the feeble sunlight, which made the cold all the worse. My hands and face were numb, and I couldn't feel my feet. I was still moving, but I was running out of steam fast. Worse, I ate the last of the food by mid day, and was starving. Her energy pills were amazing, but they demanded a price. I finally stopped and leaned against a pine tree, too weary for the moment to go on. My lungs burned, and my legs ached from plowing through deep snow.

"It's no good," I told her when she doubled back to me. "I don't have your strength. I can't keep up. Leave me, get to the cache and call for help. I can take care of myself."

"Ney, Nathaniel," she said sternly. "We stay together, ney matter the risk."

"You came here to kill me, remember? I'm expendable. Maybe I can draw them off, stall them while you get clear."

She smiled; a bold front. "You are noble and brave, Nathaniel, but I can take care of myself too. I ney need rescuing."

"You're being irrational, Arda. Control your emotions and do what you know must be done."

She dug in her pouch and produced two more of those energy pills. "It ney iss wise to use these now, but we have ney choice. It will give you strength, but without food, you will deteriorate rapidly." She hesitated, then handed one to me. "You should last long enough to reach the cache, but we have no time to lose."

I must have been more depleted than I thought, for as soon as I started sucking on one, I felt a surge of strength accompanied by severe muscle cramps. It wasn't much, but it was better than nothing.

She tucked the other pill into my trouser pocket. "This iss the last of them. Save it for emergencies, Nathaniel."

She turned and went on. I followed wearily, feeling a bit stronger, but still staggering from fatigue and the cold. If this wasn't an emergency, I'd hate to see one. As we trudged along, I heard her muttering over and over, "I must stay sane, I must stay sane, I must stay sane..."

§

The creek wound along the valley floor, and eventually passed through another small copse of pine trees. The land was a bit more rugged here, and I fell behind her as I struggled along by hanging onto the trees. "Dammit, when is this going to end?" I muttered to myself. I still found the strength to keep moving from somewhere, but I felt strangely hollow, and every step was a monument of labor. She paused just ahead at the far side of a small clearing and turned to me...

"Nathaniel! Look out!" I ducked instinctively as the tree I was passing exploded; then recovered and leapt, half tossed by the explosion, half sprawled head first as I flew across the open space. It seemed to take forever, lost in some unreal time and space like I felt during the rout at Chickamauga Creek, before I landed next to her where she hid behind another rock.

"There are three of them!" she wailed, and pointed to where the latest attacker was hiding among the trees on the ridge overlooking us.

"Are you sure?"

"Yes. The one behind uss ney could get this far without my seeing him." She was shaken, her features contorted in terror.

"That was damned close!"

"They are trying to kill you!"

"I thought they were trailing us."

"Trailing me. They ney need you."

"Life is cheap with these bastards," I grumbled.

"You are a threat. They will kill you to get at me."

"Yeah, they would." It made sense: eliminate me now, and she would be so rattled that they could box her in at leisure. I peeked carefully around my rock, but could see nothing. I crawled around to the other side of the rock and studied the open country ahead. There was no sign of the second Learnéd. At least there was only one to contend with. "We have to get past that one up there before the other one overtakes us."

"How?"

That stumped me. A large rock to our left exploded, showering us with fragments. He was trying to drive us out into the open. "Dammit!" I sized up the terrain again. We couldn't retreat over that open country as long as the third Learnéd was up on there on the hill. "We have to kill him." She looked at me blankly. "If I draw him out, can you pick him off?"

"Me?" she squeaked in near panic. "N-nathaniel, I ney..." She cowered behind her rock, tears flowing down her cheeks. "I ney killed anyone before! I ney can do it!"

I cursed in frustration. She had become more and more erratic over the last few days, and she was finally falling apart under stress. Why couldn't she have held together for a few more hours?

"Yes, you can, Arda!" I grabbed her shoulders and shook her to snap her out of her panic. "It's easy, too easy." She started crying uncontrollably. "Arda! *Listen* to me. It's simple. You take position where you can see him, but you're still under cover. When I draw him out, you pick him off."

She clung to me, threatening my rib cage. "I-I ney can!"

I was starting to share her desperation. She had our only weapon, and she was falling apart rapidly. "Yes, you can, Arda. You have to." I wrestled her around until we were face to face. "Arda, you have to do this. Think! Don't let your emotions run away with you, not now."

Another pine tree exploded nearby. She whimpered, and collapsed into my arms. "Neyyy!" she moaned.

I tried to lift her head, but her shoulders and neck were too stiff, so I was forced to roll her on her side next to the rock so I could face her. "Arda, you need to get hold of yourself," I said, evenly. "You can do it. You said your weapon never misses." She fought back her tears, but trembled in misery and fear. "Use your mind, Arda. Don't let your emotions get the better of you. Think! You can control your fear if you try." I picked the weapon up, and pressed it into her hand. "All you need do is stay low and pick him off when I draw him out." I smiled to reassure her, and gave her a little kiss on her forehead. That seemed to calm her a bit, although she was still trembling. "Can you do it, Arda?"

"P-perhaps. But my power cell iss very low."

I gave her a smile I didn't feel. "We have a saying in this time: 'Fortune favors the bold'."

"Does Fortune have another power cell?" she whimpered. "I only have one or two shots left."

I scanned the wooded ridge nervously. Learnéd was out there, somewhere, focussing in on me. "Then we make every shot count," I said at last. "It's all we have." Another rock exploded to our right. Learnéd was still trying to flush us from our hole.

I thought furiously while she burrowed into the undergrowth and took position, anxiously scanning the forest with her pistol at the ready. I could hear her muttering faintly, "...I must stay sane. I must stay sane..." A small pine tree exploded to our right, and she cringed, but held her place.

"Here I go, Arda," I called, then sprang to my feet and made a mad dash for another rock. Somehow I managed a quick glance to my left as Learnéd rose to a half crouch and drew on me...

...Her weapon made a shrill buzzing sound. The third Learnéd exploded.

"Nathaniel! I got him!" She was on her feet, laughing hysterically, as excited as a small child at Christmas. "I did it! I got him!"

"Good work, Arda! That's the spirit."

Her face was flushed, and she was dancing in agitation. "Hurry, Nathaniel! We must go!" She grabbed my arm, and half dragged me along the creek. "Losing one of their gestalt will stun the others for a few seconds."

*****

# "Day Eleven: Afternoon"

We headed down the valley as fast as we could, recklessly burning energy as we thrashed through the deep snow. We couldn't keep that up for long, and our panicked strength gradually failed us. We slowed to a steady crawl, and finally had to stop for breath. I leaned against a tree, hands on my knees, blowing hard. I was shaking with fatigue, to my dismay, and she was showing signs of exhaustion as well.

"I don't think I can make it, Arda," I said at last. "Those pills knocked the stuffing out of me."

"You are a long way from finished, Nathaniel." She tugged at my arm, trying to get me moving. "Even with the pills, your body can only convert fat so fast, so you will need frequent rest, but you can still do it."

I found that hard to believe just then. Aside from the physical demands of our trek, the raw cold was sapping me, and my stomach was an aching void. Right then, I would have given my soul for a steak dinner—hell—for a loaf of bread.

I took her in my arms. "Look, I'm slowing you down. Leave me. Run for it." I hugged her, and took her by her shoulders, meeting her earnestly eye to eye. "Get to the cache and call for help. If I make it, all fine and good, but what matters is you."

She looked at me solemnly. "I ney will leave you for them."

"I'm only a toy for your pleasure, which was a hell of an experience, I can tell you." I caressed her cheek with one finger. "I'm expendable. You aren't. You need to get back to tell them about your recruiting idea."

"Ney, Nathaniel." She hesitated for a long moment. "You are a man I can respect. You ney are a toy to me. You helped protect me from the Learnéd at great risk to your life. You came with me when I needed you. I ney will leave you now." She gave me a rather forced impish grin. "And I have come to appreciate your...personal qualities."

There was an awkward silence as we stood there gasping for breath. "Is there any hope for us, Arda?" I asked at last. I should have kept my fears to myself, but I was too lost by all this.

"I ney know, Nathaniel," she said, softly; and the fear and longing in her eyes tore at my soul. "I ney promised you anything except exile and death, and a chance to fight for a cause you can believe in."

I chuckled mirthlessly. "Well, you certainly delivered on that." Her hurt look pained me. "At least we're together. I wouldn't have missed this for anything." I paused to work a cramp out of my belly. "And...to answer your question, being stuck in your compartment for eternity wouldn't be bad at all."

"Thank you, Nathaniel." She kissed my cheek tenderly. "And I promise ney to throw you through the window, ever."

We held each other for a moment's comfort, then I turned and checked the ground behind us. Learnéd was nowhere in sight, but he was out there. I still felt weak, but our brief pause let me recover some of my strength. "We better go."

We headed down the valley, making the best time we could. As we trudged along, I heard her muttering, "I must stay sane, I must stay sane, I *must* stay sane..."

§

We moved on, one weary step after another down the creek toward the distant lake. I reeled from hunger and cold, and hardly knew or cared where we were any more. All I could do was to focus on putting one foot in front of another, in front of another, in front of another, just like we did in those miserable forced marches during the war. The wind tore at us, and there was a brief snow shower, an ominous warning of the storm yet to come. I managed a look at the sky: it was not promising.

We reached another rocky area after a while, and took advantage of the cover to catch our breath. "I'll be so damn glad when this is over," I grumbled. "I hope this cache of yours is warm."

"It iss. And I will be happy too." She turned to me after studying the landscape ahead of us. "But can we reach it? They have uss boxed in, and there ney iss any other place to go."

"There are only two now," I said, sternly. She needed the reinforcement, like any young recruit. "So we're back to where we were before. We only have to elude the the one ahead of us."

"Can we?"

"Hey, trust your native guide..."

"Nathaniel!" Arda dove for cover as the snow by her side exploded. I found myself behind a large rock without knowing how I got there. The shot must have come from a stand of pines directly above our path. I shook off my dismay and scrambled across the open space to where she cowered behind another rock, narrowly avoiding another thunderbolt from above.

"Damn it! Where did he come from?" We were safe from Learnéd's fire for the moment in a jumble of rocks and scraggly trees, but we couldn't hide here forever, and our only avenue of retreat was covered by fire from the slope above. "He has us pinned down."

"Four of them!" She sobbed in despair. "It iss hopeless."

"Only three now," I reassured her. "Remember?"

"They hunt uss, Nathaniel," she whimpered. "They ney care about the cache now. Ney can harm the Pure Of Thought and live to tell of it." She was crumbling even faster than before.

"So what's new?"

"I am sorry, Nathaniel. I have lead you to your doom."

"Get hold of yourself!" I snapped. "We're not done yet."

She looked at me incredulously. "They can outrun uss, and they have far more firepower. What more can we do?"

"We can fight! We can keep trying! They haven't won until they kill us."

"You must ney let them take me prisoner." She pleaded with me with stricken eyes. "P-promise me, Nathaniel!"

"Arda..."

"They will process me! Nathaniel, promise this for me!"

I yielded to her terror. "I promise. But we're not finished yet. We have to keep trying."

She shuddered. "What good can it do?"

"We had a saying when I was in the Army: when we advance, we're fighting for our country; when we retreat, we're fighting for ourselves. It's time we quit worrying about the future and start fighting for ourselves!"

*"But how?"*

My mind raced feverishly as I tried to figure a way out of this. "You...said killing that one stunned them?"

"Y-yes."

"Would it make them angry? Reckless?"

"Y-yes. It would also destabilize them. They depend on their gestalt to combat the effects of so many Smarts."

"Good. Then they won't see what we're doing." I gathered myself reluctantly, and selected a small pine tree a few paces to the left. "Get ready," I said to her. "I'm going to draw his fire so you can pick him off."

"Nathaniel..."

"Arda," I said, sternly. "Just like before."

She trembled in near panic, but nodded spasmodically, and took station behind her rock with her weapon at the ready. I took a deep, nervous breath, then steeled myself and leapt across to the next tree. No reaction from the Learnéd. I glanced back and saw Arda crouched behind the boulder, peeking carefully through the pine foliage. She seemed steady enough—no worse than I was, anyway, and she had the raw recruits' advantage of a fortified position, while I was advancing empty-handed against an enemy armed with field artillery.

Best get it done. I gathered myself carefully, resisting the urge to peek around the tree, then sprang up and dove ten feet to a nearby rock outcropping. "Where are you, you bastard?" I muttered as I peered carefully at the trees above. This was probably the last thing they expected. Hopefully it would confuse him, cause him to make a mistake. If so, it hadn't happened yet.

Another look at Arda, then I selected a large tree to my right, and lunged again. Nothing. What was his game? I risked a quick look around to see if he was maneuvering in turn, or if one of the others was sneaking up on our flanks. Nothing.

My next lunge took me to a tumbled rock at the base of the slope. Still nothing. I risked a quick peek at the stand of pines, but got no sight of him. This wasn't working. Learnéd must see what I was up to, and realized we were trying to trap him. All he needed to do was hunker down until the other two showed up, and it would be all over. I had to do something, but what?

There was another rock a good thirty feet to my right.  That was a long way to go at this range, but it would put me in position to start working my way up the slope.  That wide open gap would make me a tempting target; I would have to chance it and hope that in his unstable condition the urge for revenge would overcome cold reason.  This was no time to be timid: I jumped to my feet and ran headlong.  That rock exploded as I sprawled behind it, showering me with hot fragments that stung like birdshot...

Arda's weapon buzzed.  There was a muffled, wet-sounding *THUD!* followed by several sharp *CRACKs!* from up the hill.

"Two of them, by God!"  I was ecstatic as I rushed to comfort her.  "They aren't superhuman after all, are they?"

"Nathaniel," she said in a small voice.  "My power cell iss empty."

That wasn't good.  I thought about it, then asked, "Can you use the power in his weapon?"

"Yes."

"I'll get it."

I clambered up the slope reluctantly, sure I wouldn't like what I found.  It was worse than I expected.  For all the horrors I witnessed in the Civil War, the sight sickened me.  What remained wasn't a body so much as scorched tatters, and the smell...

I fought down my queasiness, and searched the area.  Learnéd's skis and thruster were there, but the weapon was a fuzed mass embedded in his remains.  Her shot must have hit his weapon and set off its power charge, which incinerated him.  There was the tattered remains of a heavy belt which must have held small gear, but any spare power cores he carried must have cooked off.  There was nothing but fused bits embedded in scorched flesh.  I turned away and dragged the skis and thruster down to Arda, reminding myself all the while that it was no more than Learnéd deserved.

"No luck on the weapon, but I found these.  Can we use them?"

She fiddled with the thruster, then her shoulders sagged.  "Ney.  It iss biokeyed to the Learnéds."

I cursed fervently in frustration, then took her in my arms.  "We'll just have to hope we get lucky.  How much further is it to the cache?"

She studied the land ahead. The creek meandered through a rocky woodland before emptying into the lake—plenty of cover for us, and for the remaining Learnéds. "It iss about two kilometers more. We travel along the edge of the lake to that peak." She pointed out a sheer bluff looming over the lake beyond the woods ahead. "The cache iss in a cave at its base."

"A mile or a bit more, hmm?" I studied the ground carefully. "Thank Heaven for that."

She looked at me anxiously. "But there iss another Learnéd ahead of us."

"I don't see him. Do you?"

"Ney."

"Um...are you sure he's still there? Could they maybe decide to cut their losses?"

"Ney." She shook her head emphatically. "They are programmed to be fearless, and to react violently to any danger. They have lost two already, and they ney know my weapon iss exhausted. They will be cautious now, but they ney will give up the hunt ass long ass one of them iss alive."

"So he's playing cat and mouse, huh?" I worried over that, but there wasn't any choice except to go on. The Learnéd trailing us was invisible in the undergrowth, but he was there, and the one ahead of us had plenty of time to choose his ambush. We were about to be caught between the anvil and the hammer. Our one chance was to get past the anvil before the hammer could strike.

"I hope this is all worth it," I grumbled. "If we reach your cache, we'll need help to defend it. How many of your people will come to help us?"

"Perhaps two, maybe three."

"Two or three? Is that all? Can't your people do any better if this is so important?"

She glanced at me crossly. "We will be lucky to get that many. We do the best we can for our numbers."

That brought up something I never thought to ask. "How many of you are there?"

She hesitated. "Twenty-two, all told," she said, carefully.

"T...twenty-two? Is that all?"

She turned defensive.  "We are the largest and most successful revolutionary group ever formed against the Movement."

"Twenty-two?  That's not very reassuring!"

"Well it iss all we have," she snapped.

I bit back a cutting remark.  Considering what she told me about the Movement's mind control, I shouldn't be surprised.  It was my own fool fault for not asking before.  "Let's get this over with."  I turned and fought my way among the rocks toward the distant shore.

§

We pressed on, moving cautiously from tree to tree, separated by a dozen yards, advancing like skirmishers.  The snow was relatively light under the forest canopy, but the tangled undergrowth slowed us up.  I was eventually forced to follow a faint game trail that seemed headed for the lake.  Arda struggled through the tangle on my left, making poor time for all her strength.  I used my modest advantage to scout ahead, leaving her free to focus on keeping up.

I tried to pace myself, to conserve my strength for one last crisis when we reached the lake.  Despite that, my legs were aching again, so I paused for the umpteenth time to catch my breath, and turned to watch Arda as she trudged through the undergrowth.  She glanced at me, and I gave her a wave for encouragement.  She nodded, and plowed on.

My gaze drifted back along the trail.  I couldn't see more than a hundred yards or so in this tangle, and Learnéd could be a lot closer and still remain hidden.  He was pacing us no doubt, waiting for us to reach his opposite number ahead.  He would have acted by now if he was going to, so we faced no immediate threat.  But that wouldn't last much longer.  The forest around us was eerily silent, save for the faint crunch of Arda's footsteps, my raspy breathing, and the whisper of the chill wind.  This place gave me the creeps.

My strength was coming back, and Arda was abreast of me, so I turned and headed down the game trail.  It wouldn't take much longer.

§

We finally reached the lake in the mid afternoon, and crept along it for a short way until we reached an imposing bluff that formed the lake's eastern shore. We went to ground in some tangled undergrowth about a hundred yards from the shore, and looked anxiously for Learnéd. I was weary from our long hike, and Arda showed her fatigue as she knelt beside me. My legs were stiff, and I absently massaged a painful cramp in my right calf as I knelt on one knee. The cold was starting to bother me again. I thought fleetingly about taking that last energy pill, but it would take too long to go to work. We had to do this before the Learnéd behind us caught up.

"This iss where we are in the most danger, Nathaniel," she said. "This iss where they will strike."

I figured that out already. "We're still ahead of the one trailing us. That leaves just one in our way. He can only cover one route, so the question is, which way do we go?"

The rocky outcrop overlooking the lake was about three hundred yards ahead. There was a narrow shelf, thick with second growth pine and underbrush, between the shore and the piled loose rock at the base of the cliff. There was a narrow track, likely a game trail, along the cliff base. We couldn't go that way; it was too obvious. The other two choices were to go down the middle through the woods, or to the left along the shore. Each had its advantages, and each its weaknesses. Each gave us cover to evade Learnéd, and each gave him plenty of opportunities to ambush us. No matter how we sliced it, it wasn't good. I desperately wished for my Colt. For that matter, I would give anything for another power core for her weapon, or even one more shot. Not bringing spares was poor planning on her part, not that it did any good to blame her now.

Even if the Learnéds didn't know where the cache was, this was a choke point they couldn't overlook. Plus if Arda was right, they weren't interested in the cache any more. Whether they intended to kill me and process her, or simply kill us both, this was the coffin corner; this was where it would happen. From the look of things, the Learnéd had all the odds in their favor. Our survival depended mainly on outguessing them.

"Where are you, you bastard?" I muttered as I studied the barren landscape with paranoid attention. My wind was up, and I was trembling with anticipation. We were walking into a trap, plain as day, but there was nothing else to do. There was no sign of the Learnéd.

"Do you see him?" I whispered.

"Ney," she whispered back. She was crouched next to me, huddled close by my side, searching the woods too.

My attention centered the game trail again. It was *so* obvious; would Learnéd think we wouldn't risk it? Maybe we should take the obvious way, and hope Learnéd would figure otherwise. Just how clever was Learnéd, for all his retros? How wood-crafty was he? How clever is too clever?

"Can he see us with his heat vision?"

"Ney well in this brush unless he gets close, since we are so cold."

I watched the overcast sky for a moment. The light was poor, and that storm was getting closer. One good thing: if we reached the cache and locked the Learnéds out, they would be at the mercy of the approaching blizzard. I wouldn't mind that at all.

I pondered the scene again. Decision time. The game trail was out: scrambling along the base of the cliff on piles of loose rock would take forever, and there would be no retreat if he cornered us. I thought fleetingly about the woods, but the undergrowth was thick, and it would be slow going, and Learnéd could be anywhere in that tangle. Our best bet was the shore line.

"If we stick to the underbrush along the shore, maybe we can avoid him," I whispered to her. That wasn't a good choice, not that there were any. At least the fading light made us harder to see. The shallow bank would give us some cover, and the open lake on our left would prevent Learnéd from sneaking up from that way. Yeah, the shore was our only hope.

Mind made up, I turned to Arda. "All right, look: I'll go first. If he's waiting there, I'll flush him out." I held up a hand to silence her half-voiced protest. "If we do run into him, I'll do my best to hold him off. You run for the cache and get help. Don't worry about me, I can take care of myself."

"Nathaniel..."

"Arda, listen to me," I said, sternly. "Take it from an old campaigner; our goal is a fighting retreat. You have to get word of your recruiting plan to your people. That's all that matters."

"They will kill you!"

"No, they won't. I'll tell them who I am; they won't dare harm me once they know the score."

She blinked in surprise, and looked at me solemnly.

"No matter what, if Learnéd shows his ugly mug, you high-tail it for the cache. Alert your people, and get help. It's our only chance."

She was terrified, huddled by my side, watching me with wide, anxious eyes, but she managed to nod silently.

"Be strong, Arda." I caressed her cheek and gave her a little smile of encouragement. "We're almost there. Only a bit further, and we'll be safe." I gave her a little kiss for reassurance. "You with me?"

"Always, Nathaniel."

§

I studied the undergrowth in the faint light while I gathered my strength and nerve, then crept carefully along a line of underbrush to an open space a good fifty feet wide. It took a lot of nerve, but I finally scuttled across the opening and plowed into some more brush. I watched for the next several minutes, searching the woods ahead for any sign of activity. Right then, I fervently wished I had her heat vision; that could make a difference in this close, dim light.

Nothing. I scuttled another fifty feet, using several small trees as cover, and went to ground behind a rock. No sign of Learnéd. At last, I turned to check on Arda. She was just visible in the underbrush a hundred feet away. I gestured to her, and she scrambled after me, taking cover in the brush I just vacated.

I scuttled another fifty feet to a large tree... There was a sound to my right...I went to ground in near panic. It was a squirrel. I lay there for several minutes cursing silently and trying to calm my nerves, then crept the rest of the way to the tree. There was still no sign of Learnéd. So far, so good.

Another scrambling run and I reached the shore. After another look around, I gingerly tried the ice. It held under my weight; that was one big worry taken care of. Another wary look around: nothing. I turned and gestured her forward, then crept along the shore while she scrambled after me.

The silence was eerie. All I could hear was the pounding of my heart and my rasping breath, and the faint crunch of snow under my shoes. The silence was almost supernatural. I felt every pebble underfoot, every twig I brushed against. I heard the faint creaking of the ice and the blowing wind. I paused: nothing. *'Where are you?'* I thought.

The lake shore was a shallow bank about two feet high, with underbrush and trees hanging out over it so that I was repeatedly forced out onto the ice. I moved forward cautiously, peering around each bush as I came to it, then inching along to the next bit of cover. There was no sign of Learnéd, and that was getting on my nerves. Better an enemy I could confront openly, no matter how much I was outclassed. I glanced back, and saw Arda hugging the bushes about a hundred feet behind. She seemed frightened, but in control. Good.

I glanced across the lake; no sign of life, and those storm clouds were getting closer. The wind was picking up, muffling the faint crunch of the snow. Two hundred yards to go. I took a deep breath and pushed on, treading carefully on the slick ice, searching the underbrush.

I finally came to an overhanging tree, and paused to size up the terrain ahead. The cliff towered against the clouds not more than a hundred yards away. If we could reach *that* rock, it was a straight shot across the shelf to the base of the cliff. A hundred and fifty yards or less...

"Naaaathanielllll!" Her scream jolted me like a shot. I spun around searching for her in confusion, then ran back to help her. She was up on the bank, wrestling with the Learnéd, who for all her strength was more than she could handle. I cursed myself for not seeing it: Learnéd anticipated our move. He figured that I would tell her to run, and positioned himself in some undergrowth above the shore where he could grab her after I passed.

261

Without thinking, I jumped up on the bank as Learnéd shoved her off her feet and reached for his weapon. His back was turned for an instant, so I waded in and threw a savage right to the kidney with everything I could muster. It was like hitting a brick wall. Learnéd gasped, recoiled, then turned and backhanded me, sending me flying down the embankment and onto the ice.

*****

# "Day Eleven: Afternoon"

I lay stunned where I fell for a long time, staring up at the sky through a gray haze, too dazed to understand what happened. My breathing was labored, and the world spun slowly around my head. Gradually I regained focus, and with it the pain came. And the cold. And my exhaustion. It took a while, but I finally got it together enough to move. I struggled to roll over, which brought on a wave of nausea. I lay back and breathed deeply to clear my head. The bitter cold shocked me, revived me, forced the nausea back, and I lay there for a time trying to remember what happened.

Some disturbing thought nagged at me from a distance. Something was wrong, but I wasn't sure what. My mind was too cloudy to make sense of it, but the sensation wouldn't go away. After a bit, I struggled to sit up, and sat staring at the patch of ice in front of me. My thoughts were labored, and I was seeing double. The nausea returned, and I vomited. I vaguely realized that I had a concussion. I heaved again, got nothing, and sat rocking back and forth, trying to make sense of it all.

I hurt everywhere, but the worst seemed to be in my jaw. I tried to feel the side of my face, but when I moved my left arm, there was a shooting pain in my shoulder. I gingerly probed with my other hand, and found that I had a broken collarbone. That wasn't all. My hand came away bloody when I touched my face, and more ginger examination revealed that I was bleeding from a massive abrasion on my left cheek. More pain and blood told me I lost several teeth, although my jaw wasn't broken, for a miracle.

Then I remembered where I was, and what happened. That snapped me out of it, and I looked around vaguely. Learnéd stood on the embankment some hundred feet away with his weapon trained on Arda, who lay sprawled at his feet sobbing hysterically. I realized without really understanding that she needed me. That goaded me to action, and I struggled to my knees, which took some doing since I was still dizzy and disoriented by Learnéd's hammer blow. My left leg was wobbly and numb below the knee, so I had a leg injury too. After a few seconds rest, I struggled to my feet, which took some doing, but my leg functioned. Learnéd and I stood looking at each other for a moment, then I cautiously limped across the ice, scrambled up the embankment, and half-knelt-half-collapsed to my knees by Arda.

"Arda? I'm here." She was completely broken, sobbing like a lost child. "Arda...it's Nate. I'm here, sweetheart." She sat up and buried her head in my chest, and her trembling arms hugging me so hard that I had trouble breathing. "It's all right, Arda. Don't be afraid."

"N-nathaniel..." she murmured, then broke down crying again. I hugged her close and rocked her gently back and forth, trying futilely to comfort her. She was shattered by the mere sight of Learnéd. Her nightmares were all too real, and one of them stood over us, weapon in hand, ready to pronounce Judgement.

I turned to him. "So now what?"

He gave me an angry glare. "Now we wait for my counterpart to arrive, then we dispense Justice."

"Justice? Not likely." I turned my attention back to her. "Arda? I'm here for you, love."

"N-nathaniel..."

A short time later, I heard a faint humming, and the other Learnéd came down on his skis. Now that I could see two of them together, they really were duplicates. It was hard to credit: I'd seen identical twins before, but these two were uncanny. Every feature, every gesture, every hair was the same, one to the other. They weren't human; they were two...things...stamped out in a factory.

"So, which one are you?" I demanded of the new arrival. "Are you the one from the train?"

"Ney," the newcomer said, angrily. "He iss dead, thanks to you and your harlot."

"Good. He got what he deserved." I looked him in the eye in a last futile gesture of defiance. "You may be the law in your hellish future, but your kind aren't welcome here."

"We ney asked..." the second said, contemptuously.

"...Ney we need your approval," the fourth one added.

I ignored them, and went back to comforting her. "Don't be afraid, Arda. You can control your fear. Don't give them the satisfaction of breaking you."

"I-I'm sorry, Nathaniel."

"Well, we gave it our best, and it just wasn't good enough. Win some, lose some, you know?" I gently caressed the spreading bruise on her cheek. "Be strong, Arda."

"You...are strong for me, Nathaniel," she gasped.

Arda and I were both dead; that was plain. The only question was how it would be handled. Would they kill me out of hand to further break her spirit before going to work on her? Would they even bother if they had those hideous retros to work with? The many times when I faced death in battle or later, I felt fear, or regret, or despair: now I felt cold, savage hatred; the murderous rage of a cornered beast determined to avenge himself on his tormentors. As I knelt before our executioners, I swore to myself that I would save her—somehow—and punish them—somehow. As I knelt before them simmering in rage, Parker's words came back to me from some lost time and space:

*'...you have nothing left to fear, nothing left to hope for. That sets a man free in the most terrible way...'*

He was right. My life didn't matter: what mattered was saving Arda from those horrible retros, and punishing the Founder and his Movement. I was liberated; liberated to do what must be done.

The second Learnéd dug into his backpack and produced a small black case, while the other one kept us covered. At the sight of it, Arda whimpered and buried her face in my shoulder. The cold, sadistic gleam in their eyes made their intentions plain: they would process her right before my eyes; make me watch as they reduced her to a vegetable and raped the secrets of the rebellion out of her mind. What would they do then? Kill her? They weren't that human. They'd probably leave her out here, lost, insane, and helpless, to freeze to death.

*'...you have nothing left to fear, nothing left to hope for. That sets a man free in the most terrible way...'*

I couldn't—wouldn't—allow that to happen.

The second Learnéd opened the case and extracted a small, shiny cylinder. The sight of it filled me with revulsion. There are some things better left undisturbed, some inventions left uncreated. Those retros were the Devil's work if ever there was such. What especially galled me was that my descendant was the one responsible for that nightmare future, and for the two inhuman monsters standing over us. After all I went through during the war, after all the struggles of this great nation to achieve a new pinnacle of liberty and justice...only to see it collapse into a horrible world of the living dead. I felt betrayed. Arda should have killed me when she had the chance.

Learnéd pulled the end off the cylinder, revealing a slender needle. I instinctively turned her away, and she looked up. At the sight of the needle, she whimpered again, and buried her face in my chest. If I was going to spare her, I needed to act fast. But what could I do? I was helpless against the two of them, even without their weapons. As badly hurt as I was, I couldn't do more than annoy them.

I glanced fleetingly at the cliff towering nearby. Another hundred yards, a hundred and fifty at the most, and we would have been safe. I desperately wanted her to run for the cache. I couldn't hold both of them for more than a few seconds, but at least she would have a chance. But she was too shaken, too demoralized, too paralyzed with fear to even try.

The fourth Learnéd must have anticipated me, and shifted to one side to cover us from the flank. I thought about snapping her neck: I had strong hands and one good arm still, but my brief confrontation with the fourth Learnéd showed how resilient they were. I felt the muscles in her neck and shoulder with my good hand; they were like iron. The retros she needed to fight them made her too tough for me to intervene now when she needed a final friend.

Then I remembered something: something she told me about earlier, something which set this whole chain of events in motion to begin with. There *was* a chance to save her; a way I *could* be her final friend and bring vengeance upon my misbegotten grandson.

*'...you have nothing left to fear, nothing left to hope for. That sets a man free in the most terrible way...'*

I had nothing left to live for, but I was about to die, and my death might as well mean something. Yes, that was the answer—my way to spare Arda this final horror, and thwart the Movement once and for all.

I struggled to my feet, then helped Arda up, holding her against my chest with my good arm. I nuzzled her cheek, and gave her a final kiss, then gently eased her to one side. I truly was liberated as I faced the Learnéds. "Well, I suppose you two are proud of yourselves," I said with all the scorn I could muster.

The fourth Learnéd eyed me coldly. "It ney is a question of pride..."

"...We are the will of the Movement," the second went on.

"Hmm, yeah, I can see why you wouldn't be proud of that." I gave her a little smile of reassurance before I stepped away from her and confronted them. "We're proud. We killed two of you, and if she hadn't run out of ammunition, we'd have done for all four of you as you so richly deserve!"

The second one paused. "She will pay for her sins, ass will you!"

"You are a fool after all," the fourth sneered. "You had the chance to do your duty to the Movement, but you betrayed uss. Tell uss, before Judgment, why you turned against the future?"

"Because she has a soul, and you don't. That should be simple enough, although I doubt if you can understand it." They wavered for a moment between confusion and anger. "She was right about you," I went on, scornfully. "She said you were too mentally lock-stepped, too rigid to think on your feet like we do."

"We are the Learnéd!" the second shouted. "We are the elite of the Pure Of Thought!"

"Elite?" I snorted in contempt. "If you are, that doesn't say much for your Movement, does it?"

I glanced at Arda, who looked deep into my eyes, hers calm and aware at last. She nodded to me, then stepped to one side, watching as the verbal sparring match went on.

267

"Two of you dead, killed by a mere slip of a girl," I crowed. "Two *elite*, taken down by a common pleasure girl, a whore, a mere *citizen*, a broken one at that!" I shook my head and laughed. "I bet that'll read *real* impressive on your report, won't it? Or do you plan to cover this up so your masters don't see what bunglers you are?"

"We ney keep anything from the Movement!" the fourth snapped.

"Really? And did you tell them about the other one that was killed last year?" The way they reacted told me my guess was right. "And now two more, by one hapless young girl." I shook my head in mock dismay. "I sure wouldn't think much of it, if I was your boss."

"You ney are our boss!..." the second yelled.

"...We are the Loyal of the Movement!" the fourth said.

I considered the two carefully, thinking fast. There were differences between them after all: the second one seemed more excitable than his counterpart. I played to him, going on as if they hadn't spoken. "So tell me, what will they do with you, now that the bodies are piling up? Will they brew up more of you...more proven failures? Or will they write you off? If I was your boss, I'd give you your walking papers, toss you out on your ugly faces, and leave you to rot in the ruins with the rest of the Broken."

"We are valued servants of the Movement!" the second yelled.

"Really? You sure don't look like it, considering how we played you on the train, and ran you a merry chase since. That speaks loads for the superiority of *real* human beings, doesn't it? Our only misfortune is that she ran out of ammunition, or we'd have collected your scalps too."

"You are ney important!..." the second howled.

"...You are defeated!" the fourth yelled. They were both agitated now.

"True enough, I'll grant you that. You win some, you lose some. It happens." I gave them a heartfelt contemptuous sneer. "But I'll tell you something; people in this time think highly of freedom, and we're not afraid to die for a noble cause. Look at our Civil War, you'll see."

"Your people ney matter!..."

"...You ney even are citizens!"

"Thankfully. And don't be so sure about that not mattering," I said to the second. "I wagered and I lost, fair and square. But her idea of recruiting soldiers from this time is a stroke of genius."

The two of them froze, and eyed her in confusion. They weren't accustomed to mere citizens giving them back-talk, and they were at a loss. I had them! "Imagine it: an unlimited supply of hardened combat veterans, each one despising your priceless Movement, and each one willing to do something about it."

"That ney iss possible!..." the second sputtered.

"...The disruptions to the timeline would be terrible!" the fourth protested.

"Yeah, that would make a mess, wouldn't it?" I paused and gave her an appreciative glance and a comforting smile, then confronted the second again. "Even better. We don't care; it's not our future being destroyed. We don't want it, anyway. Good riddance, says me."

"Heretic!" the second screamed. He was trembling in rage.

"Yeah, I sure am, aren't I?" I carefully avoided looking at their weapons. As powerful as those weapons were, it wouldn't hurt much. It couldn't. "And you know what? I'm proud of that, too. I sure wish I could see the look on the Founder's face when it all comes apart. I just hope they catch that damned-fool crackpot alive, and string him up from the nearest tree like he so richly deserves!"

"HERETIC!" they screamed in unison. They must have been hanging onto sanity by their fingernails.

"Don't you love it? That murdering, inhuman psychopath will finally get what he deserves—*justice for all his crimes!*"

Arda's mission would be complete, and the future would be saved. Too bad we couldn't be together, but my memories of our brief time together comforted me.

"Yep, Ol' Billy Sherman's boys will liven things up right quick up there in the future." I forced out a chuckle. "You know, I'll bet Bobby Lee's Virginians—that's General Lee, *sir*, to you—would love a piece of this one, too."

269

"We ney fear your people!" The second was so agitated that he dropped his little black case and almost fumbled his weapon as he pulled it out.

"You should. Sherman's bummers and Lee's Virginians together on the same team?" I let out an appreciative whistle. "Man, oh, man, what a fight that'll be!"

"Y-you a-are heretics!" the fourth yelled. "Impure!"

"U-u-unc-clean," the second babbled. Their eyes were glazed, and they were drooling, shaking in supreme agitation. They must be linked to their gestalt, and their conditioned rage was overwhelming them all. In the back of my mind, I was surprised they lasted this long, but they wouldn't last much longer.

"Things will soon be jumping up there in the future, *citizen*. Shame I won't be there to see it. It's the end for your miserable Movement—and you!"

"Thank you, Nathaniel," she said as the second Learnéd raised his weapon.

I steeled himself for the thunderbolt, forced myself not to flinch or close my eyes... The weapon buzzed; she let out a shuddering scream as her left leg was vaporized to the hip. She collapsed on me as I tried to catch her, dragging me to the ground.

"ARDA!" They shot the wrong one! "Arda! No!"

She looked up at me, trembling, her eyes glazed with agony. "N-nate..." I held her by my one good arm, her head in my lap, and tried helplessly to comfort her as she died.

"S-so much for your...brilliant plan," one of the Learnéds snarled. "The Movement iss eternal!"

"Justice iss swift and certain!" the other yelled.

"You filthy, murdering swine!" I lost it, staggered to my feet in blind rage, and rushed the fourth Learnéd, who met me head on and shoved me back effortlessly. I stumbled over her remaining leg and landed beside her, breathing hard and glaring at them with fathomless hatred.

"Ass for you," the fourth said as they trained their weapons on me, "You meddled where you ney were wanted..."

"...interfered when you should have helped..."

"...and now you will receive Justice, too!"

"She was right about you," I snarled. "You were too stupid to see me coming."

"You ney matter..." the fourth sneered. They were both agitated, but under control again.

"...We have beaten you..." the second added.

"...the Movement has prevailed once again..."

"...Justice iss done."

"Justice! Like hell! I saved her from your Justice!" I struggled to my knees, ignoring the pain in my rage. "You won't torture her to death now, you filth!"

Both Learnéds hesitated, looked uncertainly at each other, and then at her corpse laying between them.

"That's right!" I yelled with all the venomous hate as I could muster. "You were too smart for your own good, and I made a couple of fine monkeys out of you both. Now you won't get her cache, *or* the rebellion, or *her!* So who won now? You two can go to hell, *citizens!*"

They turned on me with eyes blazing, incensed that I tricked their prize right out of their hands. "You have passed Judgement on yourself..." the fourth said, angrily.

"...You had the chance to do right..." the second went on.

"...but you betrayed the Movement, sided with the heretics..."

"...seduced by that harlot, ney doubt..."

"...helped her kill two of uss..."

"...TWO OF USS!..." they screamed in unison.

"...And you helped her escape Justice..." the second said.

"...betrayed your duty once again..."

"...you are a heretic..."

"...irredeemable..."

"...for which you shall die..."

"...ass iss only proper," the fourth concluded.

For a fleeting instant, I thought about revealing who I was. It would save my own life, and would be the ultimate revenge against these two monsters. They wouldn't dare harm me, and I would make certain I never fathered if I had to have myself castrated. But they would no doubt force my destiny on me somehow, and without her, I had no reason to live anyway.

I resisted the urge to turn and face my executioners as the fourth Learnéd moved to one side and they coolly leveled their weapons. Instead, I turned to Arda, laying dead by my side. Perhaps it was my imagination, but she seemed at peace. She was a tragic figure sprawled there in trampled snow tinged with her life blood. No more of the arrogant temptress or she-beast or the coquette; all that remained was her, a hapless waif battered by life. So much had been done to her, so many had used her, so many hurts, but now it was over. Her face was calm, eyes closed, at peace. I felt a small sense of satisfaction at that. I kept my promise to her, even if unwittingly. I uttered a prayer for her soul, and wondered if God still existed in her time. I wanted so much to...

*****

# "Day Eleven: Twilight"

...I was standing in two feet of snow, buffeted by a bitter wind. The shock of it stunned me and took my breath away.

"What in Heaven's name..." I looked around in surprise, and saw that I was standing on the shore of a frozen lake beneath a row of jagged hills covered with scrub pine. "How did I get here?" For the life of me, I had no idea where I was, or what I was doing here.

The icy wind cut me like knives, and I realized I was dressed in ordinary street clothes. My only protection was a jacket several sizes too large for me, with a blanket beneath. If it weren't for them, the bitter cold would have struck me down in an instant.

I frantically searched the area, a harsh landscape of rocks and pine trees huddled along a narrow shore under an imposing cliff. Everywhere I looked, the land was covered with a thick layer of snow. Where was this place? How did I get here? I last thing I remembered was sitting in the dining car of the 'Overland', waiting for the train to depart, contemplating the roast chicken. What happened between there and here—wherever 'here' was—was a blur.

As I tried to make sense of it, a vague impression came to me of jumping off the train in the middle of the night. Then I realized where I was: in Donner Pass, in the winter. The Donner party came to mind, and my heart beat faster as a wave of fear swept through me. I was in a desperate fix.

The wind whipped at me, its icy fingers tugging at my clothes. I pulled the jacket tighter, and noticed a tin badge pinned to the lapel. "What the hell is this?" I muttered as I examined it in dismay. It was a Texas Ranger's badge, which made this all the more ominous. "What happened to me? What am I doing here?"

Strange thoughts stirred in my mind...vague impressions of a beautiful, imperious woman...and a desperate flight...and a gun battle... I looked around nervously, but the scared rocks and toppled pine trees in those memories were gone as if they never were. "This can't be happening," I groaned. "Am I mad?"

A faint whistle sounded in the distance, echoing faintly off the rocks around me.

"No, this can't be," I whimpered as images and memories—fleeting, too outlandish to understand—came to my mind. One particular memory stopped me in dismay. "A...temporal...causality...loop," I muttered, not sure where I heard the phrase and vague on what it meant. I puzzled over it, wrestling with concepts beyond my understanding. It was a bizarre, alien notion: all I could grasp was a vague impression that I...died...and my death triggered some sort of...rift...as if everything leading up to this point had been...knotted...bundled up and tossed aside...as too painful for the Universe to endure. It made me frantic just thinking about it.

Another whistle sounded faint in the distance, rolling off the mountains around me.

More vague memories, mere impressions, came drifting up. I looked around again, nervously. My two—was it two?—attackers were gone, even their footprints erased. I looked down, expecting to see her mangled body...but the snow was undisturbed. For that matter, I was uninjured himself, despite my memories.

"This...just can't be happening," I muttered.

All I could be sure of was that I was standing in two feet of snow at the top of Donner Pass having vivid hallucinations. What, how, *why* eluded me. The rest—memories and sensations too vague to grasp—could mean anything. Was I insane? Was this a dream? Was I punch drunk from too many bouts? Or—and I couldn't dismiss the notion, no matter how disturbing it was—did something monumental really happen which I had only vague impressions of now? What?

The wind picked up, cutting me like a thousand knives. The sight of that sky was alarming. Foul weather was headed this way. I was weak and numb from the cold, my hands and feet were frozen, and I was staggering with fatigue. I had to find shelter quickly. I searched the area again, but saw nowhere to hide.

The whistle sounded once more, distracting me at last. I searched the distance, and saw a freight train climbing slowly toward the crest of the pass. I could just make out a small shack, likely a telegraph station, right beyond the entrance to a tunnel. I must have walked a dozen miles after leaving the train. That distant shanty was the only shelter for miles around. If I could reach it, I could hole up there and try to figure out what happened while waiting for another train. *If* I could get there; that was a long way to go. The sky was darkening, and the wind was picking up. My chances of making it weren't good.

The whistle echoed off the cliffs. It began to snow lightly, and the wind was bitter. There was a blizzard coming on; it would be here by dark. I drew the blanket and coat around me and tried to fight off my trembling. I stamped my feet to get some feeling back into them. The day was waning, and that sky was ugly. It was a long way back to the railroad.

Another memory arose, crystal clear in my mind: the sight of *her* laying naked on a sleeper berth in the soft moonlight. Her features were obscured by shadow, and I didn't even remember her name. I felt a deep sense of loss, and moreover, of guilt. There was some dark, terrible guilt surrounding her, some burden upon my soul, but I couldn't recall why. I knew that image would haunt me for the rest of my life.

We must have fled the train together, pursued by someone...or something. It was an act of suicidal desperation, and it ended here in blood. I looked at the spot where she lay in my memory, haunted by things I couldn't comprehend. *'There's nothing more I can do,'* I thought. I didn't understand why, but whatever happened here seemed right. I preyed that whoever she was, whatever happened, the rift I supposedly caused spared her, somehow.

I distant whistle came again, breaking my distraction. I had to get moving. I put my hands in my pockets...and felt something. It was a large orange piece of rock candy. It seemed familiar somehow. I puzzled over it for a moment, trying to understand why it seemed so important. But this was not the time; I had to get moving. At least the sugar would give me some strength. I popped the candy in my mouth, hunched against the bitter wind, and headed up the valley toward the telegraph station.

*****

# "Epilogue"

"...and that's the Gospel truth, Tom."

Tom sat there for a long time after I finished, stunned by what I told him. Our eyes met, and there was a sick hollowness in his, like during the war, in men who had seen too much to endure any more. He believed me. "Good Lord almighty," he muttered at last.

"Am I mad, Tom?"

He studied my face with a stricken look as he pondered that. "You...never were one for lying or making up tall stories, Nate. But if it did, why didn't any of the others say anything?"

"I don't know, Tom. This time travel thing...maybe they don't remember...maybe I was caught in one of those loops..."

"It's utterly fantastic." He shook his head in dismay. "Time travel? Revolution? And those inhuman medicines..."

"I know it's hard to believe..."

Just then, Sister Grace came in with fresh bandages and my evening bowl of soup. "Well, have you had a pleasant chat? It's getting late, so you'll have to come back tomorrow."

"Ah...yes," Tom muttered. "How is he doing?"

"He's mending well enough, and I expect he'll be out of here in a few more weeks." She set the tray on the bed and shook her finger at me. "And you remember, Nate Poole, that the Good Lord has shown you a new direction. You need to set aside your evil past, and work toward a better tomorrow."

"You will take good care of him, won't you?" Tom asked.

"Of *course*," she snapped. "Now *if* you will excuse me, I have work to do. The weather's turning down, so you'll want to be getting on home."

Tom glanced at the window, and nodded absently. It was snowing. He stood up and gathered his winter things. "You take care of yourself, Nate. And when you get out of here, look me up and I'll see what I can do to help you."

"You haven't answered my question, Tom."

He hesitated. Someone called from down the corridor, and Sister Grace bustled out to help with another patient, leaving us alone with that question.

"I have to know, Tom. Am I mad?"

"God, Nate," he whispered. "I don't know." We looked at each other in silence, each of us afraid of the answer. "I hate to say it," he said at last, "but I hope you are."

§

Later, after the hospital quieted for the night, I stared at the ceiling and wondered if I agreed with Tom. It was incredible, impossible, too horrid to be real. I had to be mad...but how did I survive in that icy hell? Why was I so wasted and thin, like I'd starved for weeks? That orange candy... The wind shrieked and rattled the window. It couldn't have happened. I pulled the cover tighter and tried to fight off the memories. I had to be mad.

The boy came through on his rounds to stoke up the fire. The subdued light flickered on the ceiling like a live thing. The world turned hazy as I sank into a Laudanum stupor, and the flickering light reminded me of moving shapes...people...Learnéd... Doggett...Jim...*her*. Each time I thought of her, I felt hollow inside, like I lost someone. She must have been dear to me for uss to be ass intimate ass my memories showed. And I couldn't remember her name.

The snow was really coming down. I hoped the telegraph operator in his shack up there in Donner Pass was all right. The gusty wind rattled the window and moaned like a damned soul. I pulled the covers tighter to try to ward off the memory of that wind, and brooded as I watched the flickering fire.

The tragedy of it all was that her mission failed: I was still alive, and despite all I had lost, I was still a man. The memory came again, crystal clear, of *her* laying naked on a sleeper berth in the soft moonlight, her features hidden by shadow. Her womanly scent came to mind, stirring me in spite of myself. Maybe my surviving was God's will, but I couldn't see how, unless God has turned against us. That image will haunt me for the rest of my life.

The Laudanum began to tell...and I sank into a dim half-sleep...ass the wind howled...the memories...what was her name? Her name...

## The End

# "Addendum"

## Common Railroad Terms

Bend the iron  set a turnout to route a train onto another track.

Big hole  emergency air brakes come on.

Big hook  heavy duty steam powered mobile crane.

Brakeman  crewman who handles turnouts, car brakes, etc.

Car toad  rolling stock repairman.

Fireman (boy)  crewman who keeps up steam in the boiler.

Gandy dancer  track laborer.

Hogger  engineer.

In the hole  go onto a side track to let another train pass.

Roundhouse  circular locomotive shop built around a turntable.

Semaphore  trackside control signal with a movable signal arm.

Snow shed  continuous wooden cover built over the track to protect trains from avalanches.

Train order  written movement orders sent by telegraph and given to train crews at wayside stations.

Turnout  a special track section which can be set to send a train in either of two directions.

Wye  a three-sided track formation for turning equipment around.

Yard bull  railroad police.

Yard goat  small switching engine used in railroad yards.

*****

# A Brief Note From The Author

Thank you for reading this novel.  This one was a challenge to write, and I hope it was a good read for you.  I would love to hear from you, my readers, to let me know how I am doing as an author.  Every bit of input helps me to make my next effort a better product for your enjoyment.

All my best,

Bob Boyd

You can learn more about me, and keep up to date on my efforts through our Blog:

**Facebook.com/The Written Wyrd**

# Titles from The Written Wyrd
## 2021-22

**The Diplomacy Trilogy** - Science fiction humor.
First contact from the aliens' perspective in a trio of lurid tell-all memoirs written by a team of alien diplomats sent to earth to open an embassy.

**The MacKenna Trilogy** - Science fiction military drama.
He was earth's greatest soldier; they needed his skills once more, but they didn't realize how wrong bringing him back from the dead was.

**Nature's Way** - Environmental disaster / apocalyptic horror.
This is the last day of our last stand against Nature out for revenge!

**Trial** - Science fiction political thriller.
The aliens demand justice for their murdered ambassador while right wing extremists plot revolution; which is the greater threat?

**Overland** - Period science fiction drama / romance.
He was trapped between a beautiful genetically enhanced revolutionary from the distant future and the inhuman monster sent to destroy her. Can he survive caught up in their titanic battle?

**Playing God** - Apocalyptic horror.
Brenda discovers she is the Dream Girl of a mad scientist capable of altering the past. Can she find a way to undo the disaster he wrought and prevent a nuclear holocaust?

**The Big Snow** - Environmental disaster / adventure.
A passenger train is wrecked at the top of Donner Pass in the worst storms in recorded history. Can the railroaders get the passengers to safety?

(continued)

## Young Adult Demi-Novels:

**Diplomacy's Children** - humor / adventure.
A young alien space fleet recruit faces his greatest challenge in a self-centered, foul-tempered human youngling he is ordered to keep in check.

**Star Flight** - adventure.
She was an outcast, cursed with supernatural powers. She was offered a reprieve, a chance to start over, but could she survive the challenge?

## Short Story Anthologies:

**Deus Ex Machina** - Humorous fantasy collection.
From bungling wizards to moronic barbarians to redneck elves, here are the old tales of epic adventure as we would love to see them told - just once.

**Ghoulish Good Fun** - Macabre collection.
Reality is a cruel practical joke. Laugh along with it if you dare!

*****

Available in print and Kindle from Amazon,
and in PDF and ePub downloads from Smashwords.
Visit our web site for details.

**http://www.the-written-wyrd.org**